ABOUT THE AUTHOR

Well where do I begin?

To start off with, I'm a 54 year old gay guy living in England, UK and I live with my soul mate, a very special man indeed.

In the past I have only ever read other guys works but one day I decided that for once I would like to direct the plot. So what appeared to be a quick bash out on the keyboard for a couple of pages story proved to be the beginnings of an interesting new hobby.

I hope that you will enjoy reading my stories as much as I do writing them!

Other titles available:

A Biker's Tale – Part 1 (The Initiation of Danny Challetts)
A Biker's Tale – Part 2 (Running with the Pack)
A Chance Encounter
Army Bad Lads
Austin Mannuelo: The Confession of a Male Escort
Becoming a Model Patient
Diary of a Prison Officer – Part 1
Diary of a Prison Officer – Part 2
Diary of a Prison Officer – Part 3
Doing Time
Erotic Short Stories
Lost Innocence
Second Time Around
Shooting Stars
Summer Camp
The Calling
The Kidnapping of Ryan Millshank
The Naked Waiter

ISBN: 9798363720604
Imprint: Independently published

DIARY OF A PRISON OFFICER – PARTS 1, 2 & 3

All characters contained within are entirely fictional; any similarity to any real or fictional person living or deceased is totally unintentional. Do not read this story if you do not enjoy reading about consensual sexual activities of an exhibitionist nature. Otherwise read on......

SUNDAY 10TH JANUARY

Dear diary, this feels very strange indeed! I haven't written a diary entry since I was fifteen; when filled with angst against the world in general and in particular that I was unable to lose my virginity no matter how hard I tried. I would fill page after page with my rantings. So here I am now some thirty years later making another go of it.... why? I hear you ask. Long story, let's just say that after spending twenty years in the army and a failed marriage behind me I think it's time to get my head together and climb out of the doldrums I have been wallowing in for the last eighteen months and this seems as good a place as any to start. So thank you diary, although you say nothing back to me you are going to help me put my thoughts down on paper and let me see the world as it really is, for a change.

MONDAY 11TH JANUARY

I have decided the first part of my recovery plan is getting myself a job. Yes I know, financially, I don't need to work full time thanks to my army pension and divorce settlement but a man needs to feel fulfilled and bouncing around these four walls and going down the pub is doing me no good at all. So I went down to the newsagent this morning and picked up last week's local paper to see what jobs were available that might be suitable for me and of interest. Initially I couldn't see anything at all, but then over a second cup of coffee it caught my eye. There tucked away in the corner was the strangest sounding advert I have ever seen, naturally it piqued my interest and I couldn't resist giving the number a call. This is what the advert said, what do you make of it?

"Are you fit and of sound mind? Do you believe in tough love? Do you agree that everyone deserves a second chance but if they refuse to reform they should be punished? Are you available to start immediately? If so, why not start a new career with the prison service. Give us a call on 0800 012 3456 and ask for an application pack"

When I called the number I got an automated message asking me to leave my name, address and to list five attributes I consider the most important to me. Mmm, this was unexpected – five attributes, did they mean mental, vocational, physical or all of them? So I hung up, left it a few minutes before calling back and this is the message I left for them.

"Hi my name is Samuel Telby and my address is Flat 135, Berghouse Court, London, EC1V 4XA. My five most important attributes are: Fairness, Loyalty, Fitness, Open-mindedness and Stamina. I would be very grateful if you would send me the application pack as the job advertised sounds very interesting and I would like to learn more about it. Thank you."

There, that's it all done, on to the next job application; well it will be next week as there aren't any other jobs that are any good. By for now diary, it's the end of a mentally exhausting day and I'm just about beat, so it's shower and bed for me. Night night.

THURSDAY 14TH JANUARY

The application pack has arrived through the post. All I can say, it seems the ideal job for me. I'm just worried it's going to be too good to be true. I spent most of this morning reading and rereading the information booklet and job specification, then this afternoon I took my time and completed the application form with great care. I then raced down to my local post office to return it by recorded delivery.

In brief, this is what it's all about:

HMP Ollerton is a failing prison and is in urgent need of modernisation and change in focus. The prison service is seeking a complete change of staff under the guidance of the new Prison Governor Liam Havers. He requires from his staff total trust and loyalty, ability to withstand the pressures associated with policing dangerous and difficult male prisoners, willingness to undergo professional and on the job training. In return a generous salary and benefits package is provided for the right candidates.

So diary, what do you reckon? Too good to be true? All I hope is that it is genuine because it's right up my street and something I can sink my teeth into. At last I will have a job that I can utilise all my discipline and combat experience to a positive effect. I will just have to keep my fingers crossed and hope to hear from them.

FRIDAY 22ND JANUARY

Dear diary, major peed off that's how I'm feeling right now. Still no news about this prison job but at least there's been another job in the paper which may be promising, a Physical Education Officer at the local college. Only trouble is its part time, three days per week though with reasonable salary. I decided to go out tonight and hitch up with my long time friends Tom and Mike down at the Kings Head. I've known Tom since I was a kid and I met Mike through my ex-wife, we remained friends even after our divorce. I chatted about the two jobs and discussed the merits of each with them. It wasn't a great surprise for me when they gave the thumbs down for the prison job but it was a big thumbs up for the college job. Their logic being that working in a college with nubile young females would be vastly preferable to working with pent up volatile male prisoners. I could see their point, when thinking with your dick, but thinking long term from the vocational perspective it would not be as satisfying. Tom changed the conversation slightly by bringing up the subject of his eldest son, Aaron, now 23 years old (crikey I remember taking a telephone call from Tom, proud as punch when Chrissie gave birth to him at home). Last week he'd told Tom, out of the blue, that he and his girlfriend were going to get married as she'd fallen pregnant and he wanted to do the decent thing. Naturally they were both shocked but pleased that he was doing the decent thing and now the wedding organising machinery had kicked into action. Aaron has been busy planning for his stag do and asked Tom to join him, mainly so that he could act as the responsible one to make sure everything ran smoothly and didn't get too extreme. For Tom this is a double edged sword, yes it's a sensible idea but he's going to feel like a granddad surrounded by Aaron and his young friends. As he was recounting this to us Mike and I reached the same conclusion simultaneously and announced in unison, to our amusement, why don't we join you and keep the old codger company? He was relieved with this idea and I have a sneaky feeling that he was hoping we would say that. He didn't have precise details about the date or the venue but would give us a call once he had any more info. Over the next couple of pints we took a trip down memory lane, recounting all the escapades we had got up to..... It was a laugh but god, how old do I feel now thinking about the years that have flown by! After parting company with the guys I called into the local chippy and treated myself to a large back of chips and a battered sausage, I was starving.

SUNDAY 24TH JANUARY

Tom called; he says the wedding is going to be Saturday 6th March   at 2.30pm at the St. Edmunds Church on Station Road. The stag do is going to be on Saturday 27th February starting at 8.00pm and going on till late. It will start off with a sit down meal at the local Indian restaurant before moving onto the Sundown Nightclub where a function room is going to be hired and a female double act are going to entertain the some fifty guests (I didn't dare ask what the entertainment theme would be!). It sounded really good and I told him so, yes, he agreed Aaron has certainly swung into action now, it's a shame he left it so late to tell us as it leaves little time to arrange things what with the baby due to be born at the beginning of April, never mind, life is never neat is it Sam he asked? Aah, that explains the closeness of the wedding date. We chatted for a bit longer before arranging to meet down at the Kings Head again next Friday, timetables permitting.

TUESDAY 2ND FEBRUARY

Dear diary, I'm as happy as a sand boy and the postman is once again on my Christmas card list. It finally arrived in this morning's post, an official looking envelope marked "HMP Services", with fingers shaking I carefully opened the envelope to reveal a single sheet of paper with three lines of writing on it and this is what it said:

"Dear Mr Telby,

We have received your application and can confirm that an interview has been arranged for you on Monday 8th February   at 9.00am. Please bring with you your passport, driving *licence and two proofs of address. You will be required to undergo a physical fitness test and medical examination so shorts should be brought with you.*

We look forward to meeting.

Yours sincerely,
PG Liam Havers"

I literally danced for joy around my living room, I picked up the telephone to spread the good news but then remembered the reaction I had received previously and in any case I didn't want to jinx my chances of getting this job, so I put the phone down again with a rueful smile. Shit! I thought to myself, what am I going to wear to the interview? All my suits have definitely seen better days and my shorts are a little worn. Tomorrow I will go into town and buy myself a new suit and sports shorts – and a pair of shoes that aren't scuffed to hell......

WEDNESDAY 3RD FEBRUARY

I didn't know clothes shopping could be so tiring. I've spent nearly all day going from department store to department store, bespoke tailors to bespoke tailors searching out the ideal suit at a reasonable price for me. Finally I made up my mind which one I liked the best and bought it, and then it was on to the shoes, then the shorts. It was all so expensive! Hopefully it will all be in a good cause if it helps swing the job for me, plus it's been a long time since I devoted a whole day to retail therapy and paying attention to my appearance.

Looking in the mirror, I can see the tell tell signs of a forty five year old man; the ever deepening wrinkles around the eyes and across the forehead, the white hairs flecking my close cropped beard and showing up in ever increasing numbers on my head. My green eyes still twinkle but have that worldly air about them which only comes from a lifetime of experiences, some good some bad. I don't think I've ever been described as handsome but I must be fairly pleasing to the eye because I've had my fair share of lovers (and wife) none of whom have ever called me ugly, but for me my best attribute must be my body. Ever since being in the army I have had a well toned body, not overly muscular but defined enough to draw glances when I wear just my shorts while jogging round the park or in the swimming pool. I'd be lying if I said I didn't enjoy the attention but I'm not so egotistical to believe that I'm the best thing since sliced bread and the ground that I walk on should be worshipped!

On Friday I shall go and get my hair clipped short again which will make me look the part for a prison officer (not jumping the gun here am I?)

THURSDAY 4TH FEBRUARY

Dear Diary, nothing much to tell you to be honest, have been loafing around as usual. Gave the flat a spring clean, it's a task I've been conveniently overlooking for too long and boy did it need it! Four bags of rubbish, three dirty dusters and half a can of polish later and the place was looking good as new. This has helped motivate me to get back into the fitness regime of jogging in the evening and going swimming in the morning starting from tomorrow..... but first a pint while Eastenders is on. After all I will want to be as fit as I look.

SUNDAY 7TH FEBRUARY

Oh boy, am I like a cat on a hot tin roof! I have sorted out my outfit for tomorrow twice so far, ironed everything and polished my shoes and now I am pacing around like a caged lion. I would go out for a change of scenery but it's raining heavily and I've already been out for my jog round the park. I've been very good I have done my daily run every day since Thursday and been swimming twice. I have even cut out the beer, how dedicated is that? It's going to be a long day tomorrow so I'm going to have an early night and try to get some sleep, over and out.

MONDAY 8TH FEBRUARY

Oh diary where do I begin? I know I said yesterday that today was going to be a long day, I just didn't know just how long it was going to be and what I was going to be put through. I'm glad I didn't know in advance otherwise I think I might have changed my mind there and then. Sorry, I'm jumping the gun and racing ahead. I will start again at the beginning.....

6.30am

My alarm clock buzzes, my brain wakes slowly but my body jumps to attention. I'm sitting upright by the time my eyes are fully open. Something doesn't feel quite right. It takes a minute to register, I'm naked, and my T-Shirt I wear to bed is lying crumpled on the floor. I must have been hot in the night. Shrugging my shoulders I pick it up, fold it and place it on my pillow for later. I saunter to the shower, wash and have a shave before drying myself and going to the kitchen (still naked) to make myself some breakfast. Two coffees and a bowl of muesli later I feel human at last, checking the clock I see it's time to get ready. So I get dressed and spend the next half hour perfecting my attire and appearance. Last job of the morning is to pack my bag with the necessary documents and the all important shorts.

8.30am

Having studied the London A-Z I'd planned my route carefully but I had forgotten just how slow and irritating the rush hour traffic can be, nevertheless with nerves still intact and not too hot under the collar I arrived at the imposing front gates of HMP Ollerton Northern entrance. As I stopped the car at the barriers an armed guard walked up to my car indicating that I should wind down the window and produce identification. Trying to disguise my nervousness I handed him my letter from the Liam Havers, he quickly scanned the contents, looked me straight in the eye and said "Welcome on board Mr Telby" with a quirky grin. I replied that I was only at the initial interview stage and that his congratulations were a little premature. "Sure" was his only response before walking back to his station and pressing the release button allowing the barrier to rise and let me inside the prison car park. There were few parking spaces available considering its size but eventually I found a spot and pulled in. Finding the main entrance was a doddle, the prison walls were over thirty feet high and with only one small door the choices were limited. I went to bang on the door when I noticed a push button the right, duh! Who would have heard me knocking anyway? Pressing the button firmly I just hoped it was ringing somewhere because I couldn't hear anything. Almost immediately I heard a whirring noise, turning my head in its direction I saw a CCTV camera pointing at me. I showed my letter to the camera which seemed to do the job as the door clicked open after a short delay and silently opened. Stepping inside I was greeted by the sight of a plain reception room with a large table facing me, with a sheet of paper upon it, a chair adjacent to the table with an empty box on the seat, in one corner was another metal door, in another corner was a large scanning device (just like you get in the airports) and the ever present CCTV camera watching me. Walking over to the table I could see that the sheet of paper was actually a set of instructions which read as follows:

"All job applicants are to read and follow the instructions exactly. Failure to do so will constitute a refusal and jeopardise your application. There is a purpose to each requirement, do not question them; they are also a test of your trust in your potential employer and the establishment.

1. *Step up to the CCTV camera and announce your name, address and purpose for being here.*
2. *Return to the table, empty the contents of your pockets and place them on the table. If you have a bag, empty its contents also onto the table.*
3. *Remove all of your clothing until naked, fold them neatly and place them on the chair in the box provided. They will be returned to you after your interview.*
4. *Walk over to the CCTV camera, reconfirm your name before holding your arms out to horizontally from your sides turn slowly until facing away from the camera.*
5. *Spread your feet until they are two feet apart, place your hands on your buttocks and bend at the waist as far as is comfortable. Pull your cheeks apart.*
6. *When you hear a buzzer, stand up and walk slowly through the scanner before returning to the table.*
7. *You are permitted to wear the shorts you have brought with you but no other article of clothing is permitted. Personal possessions are not to be brought with you.*
8. *When you have completed these tasks knock on the door and you will be escorted to the interview room."*

I think it's fair to say that I was surprised by the instructions and I read them twice over to make sure that my eyes weren't deceiving me, but no, they were there in black and white. Whatever my personal thoughts on the matter were irrelevant and if I wanted to progress with my application compliance was necessary. So I walked over to the camera proceeded to give my name and address and a short speech about my aspirations of becoming a prison officer and how pleased I was to be given this opportunity.

Then returning to the table I emptied all of my pockets and the bag I had with me placing the items neatly on the table. Then with my back to the camera I removed my shoes placing them in the empty box; then my socks, rolling them up and putting them in my shoes; unbuckled my trousers then carefully stepped out of them before folding them and placing on top of the shoes; my jacket followed, then my tie and shirt leaving me standing in my pants. With a momentary pause I quickly pulled them down, added them to my other clothes, then turned round and walked back to the camera. Feeling a little foolish I restated my name before lifting my arms up and doing a slow pirouette so that I was facing away from the camera. Spreading my legs I dropped my arms and reached behind me lightly holding my cheeks. Bending over at the waist I felt my face flush, I'm not sure if it was from the position or the embarrassment of doing a moony to whoever was behind the camera. When I pulled my cheeks apart I felt cold air blow over my anus making it quiver and to my surprise my cock filled a little in response. I seemed to hold that position for an eternity as the camera zoomed in and out judging by the sound of the whirring noise behind me. Finally the buzzer sounded and I released my cheeks, stood upright stretching my back as I did so. As casually as possible I sauntered over to the scanner, stepped through it and quickly returned to the table where I retrieved my shorts. I was relieved to feel the material slide up my legs and the waistband fit snugly against my flesh. The one fly in the ointment was due to my semi-flaccid cock being of a decent size it flopped around quite noticeably within my shorts as I strode up to the door and knocked three times.

The door opened to reveal a uniformed prison officer, in his fifties who introduced himself as Archie after shaking my hand. He asked me to follow him (not much choice there!) down a long corridor, this judging by the signs on the doors lining the corridor was the administrative part of the prison, at the very end was a door signed "Interviews" and it was through this door I was shown. The door closed behind me, in front of me was a long table behind which sat three men, again in their fifties all in prison uniform reading their paperwork. At the sound of my entrance they slowly lifted their eyes and smiled in unison.

"Ah, Mr Telby, it's good to see you" said the man in the middle. "Let me introduce myself and my colleagues. I am Liam Havers, the prison governor and the gentleman to my right is my twin brother Max, and to my left, my youngest brother Adrian."

My surprise must have been evident on my face because all three burst out laughing and Liam started to speak again.

"An unusual situation I know, but it is all above board I can assure you. My brothers and I have been involved with the prison services all our lives and when the opportunity arose to reform this failing prison it was one we couldn't resist. We have mortgaged ourselves up to the hilt to purchase this prison from the Government, it is the first venture of its kind and they are monitoring our progress closely. We will receive generous funding if we can restore law and order within these walls, reduce the rate of reoffending when the prisoners are released and eliminate the physical abuse between the prisoners. How this is achieved is our business. Unfortunately many of the existing prison staff are as corrupt as the prisoners and will be replaced as quickly as possible. We are adopting a fast track employment system so providing you pass this interview, the medical and the physical fitness tests today we will be looking to start your training and employment with us on Monday 1st March   . There are twenty prison officer positions to be filled and thirty applicants we will be interviewing today and throughout this week, so I don't need to point out that competition is fierce and the slightest mistake on your part will affect your prospects."

I gulped silently to myself, I didn't realise how sought after this job was, mind you the wages and benefits were generous so I shouldn't have been that surprised especially with the recent downturn in the economy etc. Doing my best to retain a confident manner I agreed that the position must be very attractive to a lot of people who want to do this type of job.

"Indeed." Liam replied. "We are however looking for a certain type of person with the right experience, capabilities as well as attitude. This we saw in your application a great deal, however when it came to the first of the practical tests this morning we were a little disappointed in how you responded. We are looking for a 100% pass rate at this stage yet you only managed to score 85%. Would you like to know where you lost those percentage points and if you wish to, how they can be regained so that you pass that test?"

With genuine confusion in my voice I said "I am really sorry to hear that, I thought I had followed the instructions closely and did everything required of me. Yes I would very much like to know where I went wrong so that I can correct this situation as I want this job and don't want any avoidable issues to stand in the way."

"Excellent response! You're correct in that you followed the instructions, yet we felt there was some reluctance on your part. This was demonstrated by the way you turned your back to the camera when undressing; you hesitated before pulling down your underpants and rushed to put your shorts on. We must have confidence when giving you instructions that you will follow them to the letter and you will not question them. Unfortunately with the type of prisoners we have in here, the slightest chink in our armour will enable them to break through and risk the success of our endeavour. I am going to ask you to remove your shorts, fold them neatly, hand them to me and then sit back down in your seat. Please do so now."

Knowing what was at stake, I didn't hesitate for a second. I stood straight up, pulled my shorts down, stepped out of them before folding them neatly and placing them in Liam's outstretched hands. I then sat back down in my seat, trying to act as normal as possible in the circumstances and ignoring the fact that my cock was now semi-hard and I was the only naked person in the room!

It was very surreal, the rest of the interview carried on as if there hadn't been an interruption, the questions were what I expected and I had little difficulty answering them. Then there was a knock on the door and a young Asian man walked in, from his uniform he was obviously an inmate, pushing a tea trolley. As he walked past me he did a double take at the sight of my naked body, but said nothing, merely bowing slightly as he left the room. I had little time to react, probably just as well considering how quickly I had dropped points in my first test. Just as the conversation was drawing to a close and I had finished my cup of coffee, Liam pushed a hidden button and a couple of minutes later there was a knock on the door.

"Come in!" was all the Liam said.

In walked two men, one in a white coat, the other dressed as a physiotherapist. I guessed my next two tests were about to begin. The guy in the white coat was introduced as Richard (the prison doctor) and James (sports coach). Liam smiled warmly at me, informing me that I had not only had I passed the interview but I had also regained the lost points from the first test. He then went on to say that I would first have a medical assessment with Richard, followed by the fitness test with James then a final short after exercise check-up again with Richard. If all tests were successfully passed then I would be invited back into the office for the return of my clothing and signing of the contract. Standing up I walked over to the table and shook all three interviewer's hands before turning to follow Richard and James out of the room.

"Mr Telby, have you forgotten something?" Liam called after me with a chuckle.

I turned round at the sound of his voice looking in his direction I saw him pointing to my shorts still folded neatly on the table in front of him.

"No Sir, I didn't forget about them. I simply assumed that you would tell me when I could have them back and didn't give them another thought. Is it okay to put them back on again?"

"Mr Telby, you are growing in my estimation and I think you will be a valuable asset to the team. With that 'can do' attitude you will go far. Yes you may don your shorts again."

Slightly embarrassed to have five pairs of eyes focused on me I was more than happy to pull my shorts up, and thanking them once again followed Richard to the medical centre. As I followed him up the stairs I guessed he must be in his late 60's or early 70's, presumably this job was to top up his pension. Richard made small talk as we entered his office/consulting room.

As I sat in the chair opposite him I felt more at home having had more medical check-ups than I care to remember while in the army and had a pretty good idea on what would follow. Sure enough Richard pulled out a three page document from his drawer and started filling in the standard information i.e. name, address, family medical history & personal medical history. Then he took my blood pressure, general stats, weight, lung capacity and temperature. Still sitting in his chair but leaning forward he asked me to stand in front of him and to remove my shorts. I followed his request and naked once again I calmly watched him gently roll my balls feeling for any unexpected lumps before turning his attention to my cock. He pulled the foreskin back and examined it closely for any abnormalities, so close in fact that I could feel his breath on my sensitive head. It pulsed and expanded in response until it was fully erect at just over eight inches long. Richard seemed very pleased with this result and commented on its healthy appearance and functionality. Not knowing quite how to respond I simply said that I had no complaints with it, he laughed and said he didn't think I would or anyone else would for that matter! He turned in his chair; opening a drawer he retrieved a pair of latex gloves and a tube of KY. Uh oh, I know what they're for I thought to myself.

"Please turn round, bend over at the waist and pull your cheeks apart." Richard said in a neutral voice.

As I pulled my cheeks apart I heard the snapping of the gloves being put on and then felt the cold gel being applied to my anus. His finger felt large to me and my ring tightened in response as it smeared the gel around my ring.
"Relax please otherwise you will experience some discomfort."

I did my best to relax, taking deep breaths as I felt pressure being applied. Eventually the finger pushed in up to the first knuckle.

"Mr Telby, you really must learn to relax. From your tightness I can tell you are not used to having objects inserted up your anus, I am not going to hurt you, now please try harder."

"Yes Sir, you are quite correct I am not used to having things up my arse! My wife used to try to push a finger up me but I didn't like it. I am trying to relax honestly but this position is uncomfortable for me."

"Mmm, let me think." Richard said deep in thought gently pulling his knuckle out. "Okay, hop up onto the couch, lie on your back and pull your knees up to your chest."

Open to any suggestions to move this situation on, I did as I was bid. To be honest it was a new position to me but somewhat reminiscent of the missionary position! I said as much to Richard who smiled in response but said nothing, instead he picked up the tube of KY and stepped up to my exposed anus and slowly squirted a liberal amount onto my hole. It momentarily clenched at the cold jolt but slowly opened again as the gel warmed up. Richard looked down at me and started to ask me about my life in the army and seemed genuinely interested in the answers I gave. I give him credit for his distraction method worked a treat, I barely registered his finger's entry into me until I felt his knuckles brush my crack and his finger tip was pushing against my prostate sending throbbing pulses into my cock. I looked up at Richard and grinned saying

"Well doctor you seemed to have reached the spot!"

"Indeed I have, well done. You have a perfectly healthy prostate and rectum. I often find this position is successful for those tighter than average rings, and yours has got to be about the tightest I have come across for many a year."

"Really, I am surprised." I replied quite genuinely. "I would have thought most of the men in this prison would be in the same position as me."

"Oh you'd be surprised."

With that he withdrew his finger, wiped it clean on a tissue and announced that the medical was over until the post fitness test. As I pulled on my shorts again I saw the figure of James standing in the doorway casually watching me or rather my crutch as it bobbed around behind the fabric as I stood up again. Richard told James that he would join us in the gymnasium shortly to carry out the tests. James nodded an acknowledgement.

"Are you ready Mr. Telby?" James asked. "If so, we'll start your fitness assessment in the gymnasium downstairs, please follow me."

Not waiting for a reply he marched briskly along the corridor, down the stairs and back along the main corridor, almost to the main entrance then through a side door into what had to be the best equipped gymnasium I had seen in a long time, it even had three frosted glass shower cubicles at the far end. For the next hour I used every piece of equipment with James watching intently and writing endless notes on my progress. By the time I had completed the last test I was hot and exhausted, sweat was pouring down my face and pleased to be taking a breather.

I heard the door open behind me, looking round I saw Richard walk in carrying a small bag and clipboard. Walking over to me he placed his bag down on the floor and took out a small thermometer and a stethoscope.

"Mr. Telby would you please lower your shorts down to your knees and bend over at the waist, as you did in my office and spread your cheeks please. I am about to take your temperature."

Doing as I was instructed I avoided looking at James for I could feel his eyes on my body and did my best to not react when I felt the rectal thermometer push up inside me.

"Okay, if you would stand up again, clench your cheeks to hold the thermometer in please and I will measure your heartbeat now."

I felt the cold metal stethoscope explore my chest and back all the time hearing approving grunts and the scratch of pen on paper. Then the gentle pressure of a hand pushing me over, as I bent over I felt the thermometer being pulled out.

"Well Mr Telby I am pleased to be able to confirm that for a man of your age you are perfectly fit and healthy and I will have great pleasure in recommending your employment here. Please pull up your shorts and we will return to the Governor's office."

As I did so, James came over and shook my hand congratulating me on passing the fitness and medical tests and expressed how much he was looking forward to working with me in the future. I smiled politely and thought I bet you do!

I followed Richard back to the office in silence, thinking how much I would like to have used the shower facilities had I been given the chance as I no longer smelt as fresh as I did before I entered the gymnasium. Shrugging my shoulders, it was pointless worrying about it, I had already passed the interview and tests and it was now just a matter of signing on the dotted line and getting my clothes and possessions back. Richard opened the door for me and ushered me inside, waiting for me were my three interviewers, this time though they were standing casually chatting by the coffee table at the far end of the room near the main window. On the coffee table sat the box containing my clothes and personal possessions. They turned as one on my entrance and walked over, each one shaking my hand and congratulating me on successfully passing all tests put to me. Liam led me to the desk upon which lay my new contract and indicated that I should sit down and read it carefully before signing it, in the meantime I gratefully accepted the cup of coffee Max held out towards me. Half an hour later I had signed the contract, arranged to start my training on the 1st March and finally wearing my suit again. I'm not sure if it was my imagination but I am sure that Adrian did his best to slow me down and divert my attention as I was dressing as if to prolong the exposure of my flesh to their gazes. Oh well, no business of mine, it didn't bother me in the slightest.

11.30am
Back in my car now, trying to stop myself from grinning like a Cheshire cat, I reviewed the last three hours. What a strange experience it had been but if I am being honest with myself I had found it slightly erotic. I had the distinct feeling that my experiences were only just beginning with that place. Hey ho! That's as may be but reality was soon kicking in, my stomach was growling I needed something to eat and fast!

12.00 Noon – 7.00pm
Quick visit to Burger King for a Whopper Meal and then it was time to continue with my clothes shopping, I would need more than one shirt, tie, trousers and jacket in my wardrobe. I finally got home just before 7.00pm, if I bumped into one more shopper I would scream!

Well diary that was my day, slightly unusual I think you will agree...... I can't wait for the 1st March to arrive.

FRIDAY 12TH FEBRUARY

Met up with Tom and Mike for our weekly drink in the Kings Head, they found it hilarious listening to my interview ordeals. Naturally I left out the bit about finding it a little bit erotic; I simply don't think they would have understood. As far as they were concerned a man's arse was a one way street and only a woman should take pleasure in the sight of a man's body. Having said that, I too was of that frame of mind for many years, all through my army service and my marriage I maintained the insecure all-macho stance of a he-man. However since I left all the mind-numbing crap behind me I have become more relaxed in myself, don't get me wrong I'm not gay or anything like that, never had sex with a man or wanted to. I'm just happy to be me with nothing to prove. Sorry diary for getting all heavy with you, but who else is going to listen to me? Ah well, the lads are good for me. They stop me from moping and keep my feet on the ground; in return I make them laugh with my antics and out of the norm way of thinking.

FRIDAY 26TH FEBRUARY

Dear diary, sorry I haven't written anything for the last two weeks. I have picked you up every evening only to put you back down again simply because nothing out of the ordinary has happened. I feel very much in limbo; everything is ready for my new job on Monday but before then is the stag do I am going on tomorrow evening. At the time it seemed like a good idea but now it's almost here I am reluctant to go, it's easier to be a couch potato – which is precisely why I am going to go, I refuse to let laziness win over being sociable. Apart from anything it would be letting my mates down, which for me is a big no no.

SUNDAY 28th FEBRUARY

Oh boy, what a night we had last night! There was absolutely no way I was in a fit state to write an entry when I got home late last night/early this morning, I was totally wrecked. I woke up this morning with a thumping headache! As I sipped my coffee this morning with the curtains firmly drawn I tried to remember the events of the previous evening. I am ashamed to say this is what I remember of it.

7.30pm
Met up with Mike and Tom at Mike's house before catching a taxi over to the restaurant.

8.00pm
Inside the restaurant it was chaotic with the waiters struggling to cope with the demands of a thirty strong group. Us oldies were given pride of place next to Aaron on the big table on the condition that at the nightclub we would take a back seat to let the youngsters do their thing. Oldies indeed! But watching Aaron and his friends it really did make me feel nostalgic for the days when I was his age. Ah well, can't turn the clock back, just got to get on with life while you still have it!

10.00pm
Our group has consumed vast quantities of food and Indian beer (some of us are already a little merry); it's time to waddle over to the Sundown Nightclub where the other

twenty stag guests are waiting for us. The manager greets Mike, explains the house rules, he then leads us up to the top floor and through controlled access double doors. Inside is a large dance floor, a dedicated bar and at the other end of the room a large stage with boxes of props adjacent to it. Two barmaids and a barman stand behind the bar waiting to serve us with a ready smile. The next hour is spent getting everyone served with drinks and getting the party started.

11.00pm
With a great fanfare the female double act make their entrance and receive a great number of appreciative wolf whistles in response. They were in their late twenties/early thirties and dressed in tight fitting leather cat suits with buttons running from the neckline down to the crutch, very attractive and immaculately manicured. They introduced themselves as Zara and Ingrid and were from Russia, which drew further wolf whistles! The youngsters surged towards the stage area leaving Mike, Tom and I behind at the bar making ourselves comfortable on the bar stools.

To my surprise the girls were brilliant at winding up the lads to fever pitch with a mixture of songs, jokes and smutty innuendos. For over an hour the energy levels in the room rose and fell as directed by the girls, all the time the drinks were flowing and the lads were slowly getting drunk.

Mid-Night
The girls announced that it was now time for a little competition; they wanted four volunteers with the winner getting a £50 voucher off their next visit to the nightclub. There was no shortage of volunteers after the prize was announced with at least twenty guys energetically waving their hands in the air trying to be picked. Naturally as the stag groom, Aaron was picked along with three other handsome young men. From the back of the room Mike called out encouraging words of advice to his son. We clapped enthusiastically as the four men climbed up on stage and now stood a little nervously in a line aware that everyone in the room was watching them.

"Right guys" Zara announced as she walked up and down the line of men. "This is what we're going to do. We're going to blindfold you, then, each of you is to strip down to your boxers. Don't look so alarmed, we will be sparing your modesty by erecting the shoulder high black plastic curtain you see to your right before you strip so only we can see you, none of the audience will be able see anything. Okay?"

The four of them looked at each other distinctly nervous but with their friends in the audience egging them on they finally nodded to one another and agreed to the game. Ingrid jumped off the stage and fetched four blindfolds from the prop box, climbed back up and then proceeded to blindfold each of the contestants. Zara then followed behind making sure that they could see nothing through the blindfolds, then, spaced them out ensuring they had room to move without bumping into each other and gauging the others progress. When all were done Ingrid reached for the curtain rail on which the black plastic curtain appeared to rest and pulled it along the stage in front of the competitors. However the black plastic curtain was actually only a foot wide, the remainder of it was totally clear, providing the audience with a perfect view as if the curtain wasn't there at all! Ingrid turned to the audience and made an exaggerated "ssshhh" sign with her finger on her lips. To reassure the guys she asked them to reach out and touch the curtain and confirm that they were hidden from view, which they did and said they were happy with it. Then turning to the audience she asked us if we could see the four guys, understanding what was expected from us we all shouted a loud "No!"

"Now then, what we want you to do is to remove each item of clothing and hang them on the curtain rail in front of you, take your time, we don't want any accidents with you tripping over now do we? Okay guys? Let's do it!"

As if by magic the music in the room changed to the strippers tune, making everyone chuckle including the contestants. We began to clap in time to the music and this spurred on Aaron to make the first move by undoing the buttons on his shirt and slipping his arms out of the sleeves before draping it over the rail in front of him. Then he pulled the T-shirt off over his head revealing his well developed torso with a smattering of dark hair, despite myself I found my eyes drawn to him and I felt my gaze drop to his waist line where I could just see the waistband of his pants peeking above his jeans. Movement to his left caught my eye, Jason, his best man was catching up, he had removed his T-shirt and was in the process of unbuckling his belt. He let his chinos drop to the floor revealing a pair of hairy muscular legs before stepping out of them and throwing them onto the rail. Lee and Simon, the other two contestants were a little slower having chosen to take off their shoes and socks, then their jeans. I had to start supping my beer to disguise the fact that my mouth was getting dry and had to discreetly adjust my crutch. I was mentally wrestling with myself, these were guys I knew and yet I was getting aroused by this drunken stag do competition. Within a couple of minutes just as the music reached a crescendo all four guys were standing in just their underpants or boxer shorts. Unknown to them Ingrid had been silently collecting up their clothes and placing them in a neat pile on the bar next to Mike for him to look after.

"So who wants the £50 voucher? Raise your hands now if you still want in, it's your free choice, if you want out take a step back and sit down on the floor." Zara said to the guys.

With only slight hesitation all four hands rose into the air to the delight of the audience and to my surprise Mike was one of the loudest with his whistling and handclapping.

"Okay guys let's do it! The first guy to remove his underpants, throw them into the crowd and wank himself off to orgasm will win the £50 voucher, the guy who comes second will win a £30 voucher, the guy who comes third will win a £10 voucher and the guy who comes last will get a box of tissues to clean up the stage!"

The room went silent for a minute before the crowd started to wolf whistle and cheer loudly. Ingrid started the music again; I was too intent on watching the action to even notice what was being played. I think Aaron was initially too stunned to react however he soon realised that he was trapped by his own enthusiasm so with a shrug of his shoulders he announced

"You're on – come on guys, let's show them what we're made of!"

With that he grabbed the waistband of his pants, pushed them down and quickly stepped out of them before raising them over his head and threw them into the crowd. A cheer went up with enthusiastic clapping. He started to play with his balls and cock quickly arousing it to a decent erection of six inches. Not far behind him Jason threw his boxer shorts into the crowd, there was silence for a second before an even louder cheer went up. Jason's cock was already standing erect and it had to be the biggest cock I had even seen. No word of a lie but it had to be at least ten inches long and very wide, any wonder he always has a crowd of girls in attendance! He was busy whacking his cock off as if there was no tomorrow. Lee and Simon in unison threw their pants as far as they could but this only served to slow them and their cocks were only semi hard before Jason started to shudder and rock before with a guttural grunt he spewed jet after jet of jism into the air before landing with a distinct splat on the stage and curtain. There was an audible intake of breath round the room which turned into a roar of approval. Aaron started to pant and grimace, then he went rigid and spewed sunk all over his hands and the floor. Claps and cheers met this spectacle. Simon started to panic realising that two guys had already beat him and his cock started to soften as his concentration lapsed. Lee, bless him, always the quiet one (except apparently when orgasming) cried out and howled as his spunk became airborne much to the amusement of the audience and his fellow competitors.

With a loud clap of her hands Zara announced that the game was over, Simon was to stop beating his meat and that the competitors could now remove their blindfolds. Well, their expressions were comical to say the least! It went from relief to have the blindfolds off and being able to see, then came the realisation that the curtain was not black but see-through and they could see the audience, then finally it dawned on them that the audience had been able to see everything from start to finish. To give them their due they did recover from the shock remarkably well, initially they flushed red with embarrassment and their hands flew to cover their crotch. I thought Aaron was going to lose his temper but at the sight of his dad, Mike, giving him a standing ovation he lost his embarrassment and his hands dropped to his sides. Deciding to go with the flow was the best course of action; he started to chuckle himself, then turned towards Jason and shook his hand to congratulate him on winning the competition, all the time trying not to stare at the pendulous cock facing him. He then shook the hand of Lee before clapping Simon on the shoulder in commiseration. Ingrid signalled to the guys that they were to join her by the microphone where she handed the £50 voucher to Jason, the £30 voucher to Aaron, the £10 voucher to Lee and the box of tissues to Simon, which he took with a grimace before kneeling down and carefully wiped up each pool of cold jism. When he rejoined the group Ingrid and Zara thanked them for being such good sports and for having gone with the spirit of the game, was there anything they wanted to say. Aaron, sharp as ever asked Ingrid who had thought of this game because this certainly hadn't been on the planned itinerary. Laughing she said it was the bright idea of your father, he said that you were cocky enough to go through with it and he was right! Fair enough he replied but it's his 50th birthday on June 12th   and it will be payback time -

dad you've been warned! Mike, by now very drunk roared with laughter and told him to bring it on.

Shortly afterwards the four guys were allowed to leave the stage and retrieve their clothing. To my surprise they seemed in no hurry to do so as their mates surrounded them and much raucous male bonding ensued.

2pm
Feeling distinctly drunk I leave the club along with the others, all fully clothed now and catch a taxi home before falling fully dressed onto my bed and slipping into oblivion.....

MONDAY 1ST MARCH

Dear diary, the big day finally dawned, the first day of my new job. Daunting would be a very good word to describe it but at the same time it was exciting. I arrived at the staff car park a little early as I already had experience of the traffic levels, this time when I entered through the controlled access door and into the reception room things were a little different. This time there was a prison guard sitting behind the desk, checking the new recruits in off his list and ushering them down the corridor to the fitting room where we were kitted out with two sets of uniforms, one to wear now and the other for spare. From there we waited in what we would call the classroom sited adjacent to the gymnasium until all twenty new recruits had arrived. Liam entered without warning closely followed by Max and Adrian, as a group we went to stand up but with a relaxed gesture Liam indicated that we were to remain seated. Liam informed us that Max would be responsible for training us initially and then Adrian would take over when it came to going "live" on the shop floor, as it were. Any questions or problems should be directed to them in the first instance, with that he and Adrian withdrew leaving us under the care of Max.

The rest of the morning up until lunchtime was pretty mundane, making sure that all personnel records were correct and up to date, then came the usual breaking the ice exercise where we all had to stand up and introduce ourselves, give a little speech about our backgrounds along with likes and dislikes. The guys seemed by and large a likable bunch and I think we will bond pretty well over the coming weeks and months.

Lunch was a buffet style affair served to us in the classroom by a couple of inmates dressed in catering attire. One looked familiar to me, perhaps he was the same guy who brought the tea trolley in during my interview, whatever the reason he took no notice of me. I was simply another face in the crowd.

The afternoon was more interesting, we were given a more in depth explanation for the mass recruitment and the direction in which the prison was heading. In the long term they wanted HMP Ollerton to become a flagship of excellence for prisons in the UK and lead the way in reforming other failing prisons. Before that could happen there was a lot of work to do and was summarised as follows:

1. Eliminate prisoner violence
2. Eliminate prisoner intimidation
3. Eliminate prisoner drug abuse
4. Eliminate prisoner sexual abuse
5. Eliminate smuggling into/out of the prison
6. Reduce rates of reoffending by at least 50%

This will be initially be addressed by monitoring every prisoner and room in the prison, at present workmen are installing damage proof CCTV monitors into each cell and room within the prison and the outside areas. Once completed implementation of the new prison rules would start following 24 hour surveillance of all areas including cells.

Someone in the class mentioned that it sounded draconian. Adrian laughed in response, saying that it may indeed but as mentioned during the interviews the new management believes in tough love and sorting out the criminals once and for all by whatever method works successfully. Sounds fair enough to me. By the end of the afternoon my head was reeling from all the facts and information that had been imparted and I was glad when it was time to leave.

So that diary was my first day at work, my brain aches and all I want to do is fall into bed and sleep like the dead, so night night until tomorrow.

FRIDAY 5TH MARCH

Sorry diary, a bit late I know but I simply haven't had the energy to maintain my diary for the last couple of days. Not only have I been mentally exhausted every day but I have also been physically tired too. Each day at work followed a set routine:

09:00 – 10:00hrs	Fitness class in Gymnasium
10:30 – 13:00hrs	Prison Theory & Practice – Classroom
13:00 – 14:00hrs	Lunch
14:00 – 17:00hrs	People Management - Classroom

I never realised how much was involved with prison work and the responsibilities that came with being a prison officer. By the end of next week we will have trained enough to be introduced to the prison and the inmates and get down to the real work – what a scary thought now that I know the realities of prison life! One consolation is that my body is becoming more toned and even fitter, not only that but I am regaining my confidence in dealing with people again which I had lost somewhat since my divorce. Something inside me is looking forward to the conflict management, perhaps because it seems akin to being in the army again, who knows, time will tell.

FRIDAY 12TH MARCH

Same excuse again! Busy week but what an eye opener! Yesterday we completed our training course and today we went on a walk about the prison and its grounds led by

Max and Adrian. Each of the six wings were being modernised and made more secure (or should that read more manageable for us staff?) and all of the CCTV installation had been completed much to the disgruntlement of the inmates! Needless to say that there was a lot of jeering and catcalling from the gang members and leaders but the average inmate was either wary or respectful which was the reaction we were seeking. Outside were the kitchen gardens, recreational green (used for cricket, football or rugby depending on the season), the small prison farm where pigs and chickens were kept, and finally the multi-faith chapel which had fallen into disrepair. It was in this last building which held the biggest surprise for us. It had been converted into a small cinema but one in which would be used for correction treatment of inmates who had broken the rules. I asked for an explanation, but was told to be patient as all would be revealed. At one end of the room was a huge white viewing screen facing twenty five rows of chairs capable of seating up to five hundred inmates at any one time. Then at the back of the room behind the last row of chairs was a door marked "Staff Only" with a controlled access keypad. Adrian tapped in the pass code and ushered us through the doorway, the sight that met us was astonishing. It was a cross between a gymnasium, shower area and torture chamber. In one area there was a leather sling, a large wooden St. Andrews cross and a vaulting box. Each device had hand cuffs attached at each corner. In another area was what looked like a dentist chair along with an operating table, again with restraints attached to each arm. In the shower area there were two handcuffs hanging from the tiled wall above which a single shower head could be seen. What puzzled me was a second hose which came out of the pipe feeding the shower, it had a rounded end with holes (looked rather like a pepper pot!) and hung redundant on a hook next to the shower head. There was also a commode (toilet seat fitted within a chair) made from clear plastic suspended over a clear plastic tank with water inside. From the ceiling over each device was a CCTV camera standing safely away from the wet area near the entrance was a handheld video camera and stand. On the other side of the entrance was a large wardrobe sized metal cabinet securely locked, inside which we were told were implements to be used in the correction treatment. With the tour of the correction room over we were led outside and back to the main dining hall for the inmates from where a lot of hammering noise was emanating. Inside two of the maintenance crew were attaching a large notice on the wall in clear view of all diners, this is what it announced.

"With effect from Monday 15th March   the following rules will be implemented:

1. **Possession of weapons, drugs and contraband of any kind will be strictly prohibited.**
2. **Violence or abuse of any kind will be strictly prohibited.**
3. **Smuggling of weapons, drugs and contraband in or out of the prison will be strictly prohibited.**

The first infringement will result in temporary (48hrs) loss of all personal possessions.
A second infringement will result in permanent loss of all personal possessions.
A third infringement will result in public correction in the chapel.

Any further infringements will result in public and prolonged correction.

If you have any questions regarding the above rules please speak to a member of staff."

Then underneath in bold red writing was another announcement.

"There will be an amnesty for weapons, drugs and contraband on Monday 15th March from 00:01hrs to 23:59hrs inclusive. Any prohibited items found after the amnesty period will result in due punishments described as above."

Adrian warned us that Monday will be busy but the rest of the week will be busier as the rules will have to be implemented as the toughest inmates will seek to resist and break them. We have been warned to make sure that we're thoroughly rested this weekend ready for next weekend.

SATURDAY 13TH MARCH

Time out with the boys tonight, met up with Mike and Tom and had a real laugh at the Kings Head supping a few pints and enjoying their down to earth sense of humour. I kept my tales of my job pretty lightweight with no mention of the new rules made. Tom was slowly coming round to the idea of me working for the "establishment" but Mike still needed convincing and thought I would have been better off working for the college. Ah well, time will tell and all that.

MONDAY 15TH MARCH

First day of the new regime and the amnesty produced a flurry activity from the small time crooks and regular guys who were sensible enough to understand that the writing was on the wall for their activities. By the end of evening some two hundred weapons had been surrendered and several kilos of drugs. I expressed my admiration on how successful the amnesty had been to my supervisor, Pete. He snorted and laughed saying that he thought less than half of the gear had been handed in, so tomorrow will be long and tiring as there will be some tough nuts to crack.

TUESDAY 16TH MARCH

Dear diary, Pete was sooo right! During our morning briefing the first of the gang leaders were to be targeted. His gang name is "Flick" on account of his favourite weapon being a flick knife cunningly disguised within a toothbrush, his real name is more mundane – Charlie Smith. His reputation was of being fearless and the first to wade in if a fight broke out, although he wasn't the tallest or heaviest built of guys he was strong and knew it. He was being targeted to send a strong message to the rest of the gangsters.

So after the briefing six of us donned riot gear and armed with stun guns we marched into A-Wing and climbed the stairs onto the first floor and headed for cell 59 where Flick was housed. The normally noisy wing fell silent as the inmates realised something was happening and stopped to watch the proceedings. Arriving at the cell, the door was flung open catching Flick by surprise; he was sprawled out on his bunk reading a glossy girlie magazine. The look of shock rapidly changed to the customary aggressive expression and demanded to know what was going on. He was told that he and his room was being searched for prohibited items. Laughing in response he said that we would find nothing; his mirth was short lived because unknown to him using the CCTV installed in his room we had watched him secreting his stash of weapons and contraband. Within a couple of minutes we found the first of his knives, his face fell as he realised the game was up. We radioed back to the control room that we required a belongings box ASAP (this is a large plastic box on wheels which can be secured with a padlock and chain used to store confiscated items). Five minutes later the box arrived and we continued searching the room, as each article was examined it was placed into the box with prohibited items being placed into a separate bag. As bit by bit his cell emptied of his personal possessions Flick became agitated protesting at the treatment he was receiving. He was told in no uncertain terms what the new rules were and as he'd broken them he was facing the confiscation of all his possessions for 48 hours, he'd get them back if he was a good boy.

He smiled quirkily and said "Sure. I think I can do good."

Within ten minutes his cell was empty and the box was brimming full of his clothing and personal bits and bobs, the only items left was his bedding and the clothes he stood in. Now we turned our attention to Flick, telling him to remove the clothes he was wearing. Backing away from us he made for the doorway in a bid to escape, without success as Pete blocked his route and drew his stun gun.

"Now son, you can do it the easy way and do as you're told or you can do it the hard way. We will stun you, then strip you and you'll wake up aching all over. Either way you're going to be naked for the next 48 hours." Pete told him as he cocked the trigger of the gun.

Gulping audibly Flick thought for a second or two before pulling his prison issue sweatshirt over his head and handed it to me, quickly followed by his T-shirt revealing his smooth chest covered in green and red dragon tattoos with their tails trailing down his muscular biceps. Despite myself I could not help but admire his physique and thought he really was quite attractive in a bad-boy way. Catching my eye he grinned impishly before slipping his hands inside the waistband of his jogging bottoms and pushing them down to his ankles. As he stepped out of them he straightened up revealing the fact that he had been going commando and his decent sized cock bobbed at half mast indicating that he wasn't too bothered by this turn of events. Last to go were his socks which he threw in the direction of the box announcing that he had complied with our request so, were we happy now?

Pete nodded indicating that he was satisfied with the outcome and turned on his heels pushing the now padlocked box in front of him. As we filed out of the cell Flick followed us asking what he was supposed to do now and what about the box. Being the last one out I turned round, trying to keep my eyes on his face I replied

"You need to carry on with your normal routine, your prison job is to be carried out and meal times attended etc. Your box will be returned to him in 48 hours time."

"That's easy for you to say, it's not you who's naked!"

"True enough, but rules are rules and you broke them. Make sure you don't break them again otherwise you'll be in this state again and next time it will be permanent. Besides, I don't think you'll be the only one in this predicament by the end of today." I smiled as I walked out onto the landing.

Flick followed me clearly wanting to continue the conversation, momentarily forgetting himself until he realised he had the attention of the entire wing. Frowning he looked around before yelling out

"What are you lot staring at? Never seen a man's knob before? Get a life!"

I chuckled at this latest outburst all the way down the stairs and caught up with my colleagues before leaving the A-Wing and making our way over to B-Wing. Word gets round fast in our prison; the inmates on B-Wing were waiting for us including our next target, Tyler Abegundi. Flick had been our warm up in preparation of this man; Tyler would need more careful handling. He didn't bother with weapons or drugs to rule this wing, he didn't need to; he was a mountain of a man, tall and very muscular with huge fists which could break bones with ease. He was normally placid but when riled he went ballistic and his sadistic nature became evident. Self-confident as ever he casually leaned against his cell's door frame clearly in view of the wing as if holding court.

"Gentlemen." his voice boomed along the landing towards us "You won't find any prohibited items in my cell; you're wasting your time. So don't think of pulling that stunt you did on Flick with me."

"Come on Tyler, don't play dumb with us." Pete retorted with equal confidence "You know your activities have been closely monitored by us. Rule 2 - Prohibition of Violence & Abuse was broken this morning when you threatened to break the jaw of your new cell mate in the wash room because he hadn't yet agreed to spread his legs and let you shove your donkey dick up his arse. As this is your first offence under the new rules you will forfeit all of your personal possessions for the 48 hours."

"I don't think so and you can't make me!" was the gruff reply.

Peter walked up to Tyler and spoke quietly in his ear indicating that he had a proposition for him if he co-operated with us. This change of tactics clearly surprised him because Tyler's eyebrows rose momentarily before nodding his head in the direction of his cell and walked inside.

"So what are you guys offering me in exchange for my kit? It had better be good or I am going get real mad with you" he said, glowering down at us as if to emphasise his point.

"Relax will you." Pete replied in a calming tone. "What we have in mind you will definitely enjoy. You will no doubt be aware of the new rules and the penalties that will be imposed. We will need volunteers to assist in administering punishment for persistent offenders and you are the perfect candidate what with your physical attributes."

"What do you mean by attributes?"

"Firstly you're built like a brick shit-house so no one messes with you, we don't want any resistance from the inmate being punished and your reputation will be an advantage. Secondly you must have the biggest dick in this prison which when on show will put the fear of god up most inmates reducing repeat offending."

"So what's in it for me?"

"Basically you get to shove your dick or anything else you care to use up the arse of any repeat offender that is due to be publicly corrected. If I'm not mistaken you have to go to great lengths to persuade guys to let you shaft them, this way you get your way without having to break any rules and as often as corrections are required. So are you interested or not?"

"If this is for real then count me in, it's an effing nightmare trying to get my rocks off in this place. What do you want me to do then to make it look a genuine bust?" Tyler was all business now and even seemed keen to go with the sweetener offered to him, it clearly appealed to his desire for power over other inmates.

"For a start, we'll handcuff you, stand you outside on the landing while we strip your cell and pack the box up. You can curse at us if you want, we'll ignore it. Then I'll get my stun gun out and threaten you to comply when your handcuffs are removed. It would be better to strip on the landing so that all can witness your reluctance to comply."

"Well what are we waiting for? Cuff me and let's get the show on the road, my balls are getting heavy and I need an arse to break real soon."

Without further delay I brought his hands behind his back and handcuffed them before pushing him out of the cell onto the landing where the inmates were still avidly watching the proceedings betting on the outcome. As his cell was stripped and his belongings packed into the box I stood guard over Tyler as he cursed and swore at us acting his part really well. A few minutes later the job was completed and Peter joined us with stun gun drawn instructing me to release the handcuffs. He then told Tyler to remove his clothing voluntarily or be stunned and we'd strip him while he's out cold. Still acting in character Tyler snarled at us but started to undress as instructed. He crouched down and removed his trainers and socks, handing them to me before standing up and pulled his sweatshirt over his head revealing his heavily developed chest and arms. His black skin gleamed like polished obsidian in the prison lighting with just the odd curly hair dotted over his chest. Without pausing he took hold of the waist band of his jogging bottoms and pushed them down past his equally developed thighs and calves. Stepping out of them he stood tall and proud in just his boxer shorts, pausing to see if we were satisfied. Peter nodded to the shorts and indicated that they were to come off too. Sighing loudly Tyler pulled his boxers down slowly and stepped out of them. He was deliberately drawing attention to his cock which although was flaccid, hung down his leg some seven inches long and three fingers wide. No wonder no one wanted to accommodate it! His balls were equally magnificent like black polished billiard balls. Apart from a few discreet quiet whistles there was no reaction from the rest of the wing, whether it was due to being in awe or because of Tyler's fearsome reputation I didn't know nor particularly care. We informed that in 48 hours his box would be returned to him before leaving the wing to carry on to C-Wing, then D-Wing, E-Wing and finally F-Wing.

All in all it was very draining having to mentally battle with naturally reluctant inmates to persuade them to part with all of their possessions and clothes. In fairness to them, there was only one inmate we had to actually use a stun gun on, the rest saw sense and complied with our demands.

The final job of the day before heading home was to place an amnesty box on each wing with an additional warning that from tomorrow everybody's room will be searched. Today was a gentle warning; tomorrow the rules will be enforced more rigorously!

WEDNESDAY 17TH MARCH

Day three of the new rules and if anything it was harder than yesterday, not so much mentally as physically. Due to time constraints we were working in twos with fifteen minutes allowed per cell. This meant that we had little time to chat with the inmate concerned other than to tell them what was expected of them and the consequences if they did not comply. Following yesterday's events everybody knew the score and each amnesty box had been pretty well filled up with weapons and drugs. As a result most cells proved to be clean of prohibited items and on each wing there was on average maybe only five or six inmates who had be stripped of their clothes and possessions, they had been foolhardy enough to believe that we wouldn't carry out our threats.

At lunchtime we finally sat down in the prison canteen which we share with the inmates. I was surprised how well the naked inmates were integrating with the clothed ones. I had half expected them to remain hidden in their cells waiting out their 48 hour punishment but I was wrong in my assumption. The ring leaders had gained some kudos by flaunting their nakedness, by showing that they had lost everything at the hands of the management yet carried on as if nothing had happened just added to their reputation. As to the other inmates it very much depended on their standing beforehand, but in general the lower ranks stayed where they were and subjected to the expected light hearted ribbing you get between men. I was just finishing my desert and chatting to George, a prison officer who had started at the same time as me, when I felt a tap on my shoulder. Turning reflexively I was faced with a black cock which all but slapped me on the nose, I recognised it instantly, it was Tyler's. Semi-erect it was now about nine inches long but still three fingers wide. Despite myself I couldn't help but notice that his cockhead was black as well, the only other black guy I had seen naked had a pink cockhead, I made the mistake of voicing this observation. He had clearly been planning to bump into me and this simply added to his amusement and he chuckled as he sat down opposite me.

"Well boss, you don't know that much about us black guys do you? I suppose you've only ever stuck to your nice white boys, eh?"

"No Tyler, I never had sex with either black or white guys. I am actually straight; I have been all my life."

"Yeah right, I've seen how you've been watching me when you think no one's looking and I'm not the only one who thinks like me."

"Really and who else is of the same opinion?"

"Well, Flick for a start and Dinesh from D-Wing thinks so too. We think it's cool to have gay prison officer, it's not often we get to have one."

"I've already told you I'm not gay. Why do you think I am and what difference would it make?"

"Apart from the way you look at us, it is the way you interact with us and the genuine interest you show in our well being. If you were totally straight you wouldn't give a shit about us. When you were outside my cell yesterday and as I removed my shorts you just couldn't take your eyes off my body could you? I'm not imagining it but I'm sure I saw you unconsciously lick your lips and adjust your trousers. Am I right? As to the difference it would make, perhaps none, who knows. It's just nice when a guy can be honest about himself, mutual respect can grow as a result, even friendship?"

"Like I said before I've never had sex with a man before but you're right lately I have been finding the male body strangely fascinating despite myself. I didn't realise that I had been making it so obvious, I apologise, it is unprofessional of me and it won't happen again. I do hope that we have mutual respect, it's part of my job to engage with inmates and help where I can."

"Okay Sir, I get you, well if there's anything I can do to help you out you just let me know." Tyler said with a wink as he stood up and joined the other inmates making their way out to the kitchen gardens for the afternoon shift.

I looked at George and asked him what that was all about.

"Dunno Sam, but just looking at his member makes my eyes water. How anyone man or woman could accommodate that thing is beyond me!" he remarked grimacing.

The afternoon bell rang indicating that lunch was over. The rest of my day was spent doing paperwork and supervising the art class.

THURSDAY 18TH MARCH

Dear diary, much of today has been spent returning the confiscated possessions back to the gang leaders, or should I say they had been instructed to collect them from the governor's office. If I was of a suspicious mind I would think that my sexuality was being tested to the extreme. I'm not making much sense am I? Perhaps as always it's best that I start at the beginning. Then you can see for yourself if my suspicions are correct or not.

When I clocked in this morning there was a note in my pigeon hole that I was to report to the governor's office first thing. I knocked on the door and Liam's distinctive voice invited me in, I had a sense of déjà vu because Liam, Max and Adrian sat behind the long desk as they had at my interview. In the far corner of the room I spotted the six locked boxes containing the gang leaders' possessions. I sat down on a chair to one side as indicated by Liam before I was told that they wanted me to act as an assistant to the doctor and be a witness to the proceedings. Fair enough I thought; it would be a change from the routine so I said that I would be happy to oblige in whatever capacity required. This seemed to be the correct response and as three men smiled, Liam picked up his phone and spoke briefly into it before making small talk with me for a couple of minutes until Richard (the prison doctor) walked in wearing his familiar white coat and carrying a small leather bag I had often seem him with.

At 9:00am on the dot there was a knock on the door and in walked Flick, he hesitated briefly at the sight of the five of us but carried on walking until he stood in front of the desk facing Liam as instructed, with his hands clasped behind his back displaying the tattooed dragon's tails curling down his arm. Liam informed him that his possessions were to be returned to him but before this there were some missing details on his medical records which needed completing and this was the ideal time to collect the information. Flick nodded his understanding, I couldn't help but notice that he clenched his buttocks repeatedly as he nodded and I wondered if he was more nervous than he was letting on.

"Okay, Flick" Liam started apparently reading from a record sheet. "Outside the prison environment would you describe yourself as normally being gay, straight or bisexual."

"Straight"

"Have you ever had sex with a man?"

"Yes, but only within the prison. You know how frustrating it can get inside."

"Was it anal or oral sex, were you passive or active?"

"Oral, I was sucked off."

"Okay, final question for now. When was the last time you ejaculated?"

"Yesterday evening, I gave myself a hand job in the showers."

"Thank you, if you don't mind the doctor is now just going to carry out a few physical checks to verify your answers."

"Be my guest, I've got nothing to hide."

Richard took this as his cue, slipped on a pair of latex gloves and asked Flick to face him. He gently cupped Flick's balls in his hands and appeared to weigh them. He agreed that they seemed reasonably light in keeping with being emptied yesterday. He then asked Flick to face towards the desk and rest his elbows on it, thereby bending over at the waist and exposing his anus for examination. It also gave me a perfect view of it. Even to my untrained eye it looked small and tight, virgin territory a small voice said in my head. Richard retrieved a tube of KY from his bag and liberally lubricated his finger and Frick's anus. At this latest development Flick looked over his shoulder frowning but said nothing. I pulled my chair forward until I was within touching distance of his anus so that I could get a good view of the impending penetration. Richard nodded approvingly before saying

"Good thinking Sam, I want you to see exactly what I am doing because I shall require your assistance in a minute. Is that okay?"

"Sure." I said nodding, not taking my eyes off the small puckered pink hole before me.

By now Flick had stopped looking over his shoulder, instead he was looking straight ahead of him and as Richard's finger tip started to push against the tight entrance he bowed his head to disguise the discomfort or embarrassment he was experiencing. After a couple of minutes it was becoming apparent that Richard would be unable to enter further than the first knuckle without causing Flick pain. It was then I had an idea, or rather a memory floated to the surface.

"Richard" I said tapping him on the elbow. "Why don't you try the technique you used on me during my medical assessment? It worked for me, so I can't see why it won't work for young Flick here."

"Excellent idea!" he replied, gently pulling his finger out of the tight hole. "Flick, would you please stand up and turn around. No, really there's no need to cover your erection, we're all professionals here and we've seen it all before many times. That's better, please relax, it will make things a lot easier for you. Okay, now step backwards until you are sitting on the table. Okay, now lean backwards until you are lying on your back, bring your knees up to your chest and wrap your arms behind your knees. That's excellent, thank you."

Oh my god! I was now beginning to see what attracted men to other men..... and what Richard had seen the day he examined me. Flick's anus was being forced to relax due the position he had assumed and at the same time was more visible to all in the room. Flick was doing his best to retain his dignity as all five of us were now standing round him peering down at his hole.

Richard wasted no time in applying further lubrication to the hole and using the same distraction techniques on Flick that he had with me. He spent about ten minutes discussing with him his opinions of the new rules, at the end of which his whole finger was buried up to the hilt and gently stroking his prostrate which was bringing gentle groans from Flick. Adrian pointed out to the group that Flick was now sporting an erection which brought a chuckle from everyone except Flick.

"Oh man did you have to say that?! It's bad enough that I have a finger up my arse but I am sporting a boner too!"

Liam appeared to consider this for a minute before announcing

"That's a fair comment actually. Okay, here's what I propose. Flick, you can let go of your legs. Max, you take hold of his left leg and Adrian you take his right. That's it, hold them up and slightly apart that way Flick will be more comfortable and you see that his cock has now been released. Now Sam, what I want you to do is to slip on a pair of gloves and lubricate your index finger. That's right, now slowly insert it into the anus taking the same care that Richard took. When your finger is fully inserted I want you to feel around until you can feel his prostate."

Saying nothing in response I did as I was instructed. It was the first time I had ever stuck a finger up a bum (including my own), it was very different to a vagina and in this case a lot tighter. I finally understood why the anus was called a ring; it was smooth just like the inside of my old wedding ring but a lot softer and warmer. It was so erotic feeling around knowing that my finger was the inside a living breathing person who by the sound of it was beginning to enjoy the sensations I was arousing.

"Now Flick." Liam continued "You have two options now. Would you like Sam to withdraw his finger and you will now be free to collect your belongings or would you like some relief for your aching cock?"

"Sir, I really need to shoot a load." Flick's reply was rather hoarse. "I don't think I can hold off much longer!"

"Sam, I want you to explore your boundaries and take a step beyond them. Firstly, keep your finger inside Flick, then with your spare hand I want you to take hold of Flick's cock and wank it off to orgasm. I know this is a new experience for you but think of the relief you will be bringing to our inmate."

Keeping my mind as blank as possible, not really taking in the enormity of it all, I did as I was told. Within a couple of minutes I felt his cock throbbing in one hand and his anus clenching round my index finger of the other hand, and then he shot load after load of jism all over his chest and stomach. As his cock subsided and started to shrink I gently pulled my finger out just as Richard came over a wad of tissues to wipe ourselves clean.

Max and Adrian released their hold of his ankles and Flick was allowed to stand up again, which he did with a sheepish grin saying "Thanks guys, I think!"

"No thank *you*." Liam replied. "You have complied with all that has been asked of you. We can now confirm that your records are fully up to date. Please collect your belongings from your box, you are now free to get dressed. We trust that we won't need to see you in this office again under these circumstances will we?"

"No Sir." and with that Flick went to collect his belongings and it was almost comical watching him scurrying over to the box with his name on it and rifling through it for his clothes. In less than thirty seconds he was dressed and making his exit. I was sorry to see his naked body clothed again. Liam must have read my mind as he laughed and assured me that it won't be the last time we see him in this predicament, well that was his feeling at least. It was 9.55am and we just had a couple of minutes to touch base and for me to be told that the next session would be run in exactly the same way.

Sure enough at 10.00am just as we had sat back in our chairs there was a knock on the door and in walked the massive frame of Tyler. Liam's preamble was word perfect and I took the opportunity to study the muscled frame of Tyler's back and legs. Evidently he was calmer than Flick because his massive hands hung relaxed down by his sides and his cheeks never clenched once.

Then the questions and answer session started.

"Okay, Tyler" Liam said, again reading from the record sheet. "Outside the prison environment would you describe yourself as normally being gay, straight or bisexual."

"Straight"

"Have you ever had sex with a man?"

"Yes, but only when there's been no pussy to shag."

"Was it anal or oral sex, were you passive or active?"

"Both oral and anal, I was sucked off and I did the fucking, the only way man."

“Okay, final question for now. When was the last time you ejaculated?”

“Last weekend, just before I got busted by you guys. My balls are nearly blue they’re so full!”

“Thank you, if you don’t mind the doctor is now just going to carry out a few physical checks to verify your answers.”

“Uh huh? Go ahead, doesn’t bother me none.”

By now Richard had a fresh pair of gloves on and asked Tyler to face him. He gently cupped Tyler’s balls in his hands and announced that they did appear to be very full and heavy. He then asked Tyler to turn around, bend over at the waist and with his hands pull his cheeks apart. Without hesitating the black guy turned round, bent over and expertly parted his cheeks for our inspection. I crouched down and inspected it closely with Richard by my side. We both agreed that it looked as tight and virginal as Flick’s had.

“Damn right it is, nothing larger than a finger has ever been up there or ever will!” came the gruff response.

However unlike Flick, Tyler seemed to have little difficulty in accommodating Richard’s finger nor mine when it slid in after Richard’s had exited. I felt around until I found his prostate and started to massage it from the inside, this seemed to go down well with the patient because he clamped down on my finger before standing upright and taking a step forward leaving my finger behind. As I looked to Liam for guidance at this apparent defiance Tyler spun on his heels and faced me with hands on hips. In front of me standing erect was his humungous ebony cock, it had to be at least twelve inches long but still three fingers wide as it had been when flaccid. The foreskin had naturally pulled back revealing the equally black cockhead smooth and shiny under the bright office lighting.

“I think this is what you’ve been looking for, isn’t it. Now be a good boy and give my cock a good sucking.” Tyler said with a lustful gloating expression on his face.

I was in a quandary, the straight part of me was repulsed at the very thought of it yet, the new developing side just wanted to grab hold of it and lick it like it was the last lollipop in the world. I looked over at Liam hoping he would have an answer to my predicament; sadly it was not to be when he replied.

“Sam, it’s entirely up to you. No one is forcing you one way or other. The only comment I would make is that by offering relief to Flick you got to know him a bit better, he respects you more which can only be a good thing and he will be a lot calmer now having shot his load. I dare say that will be true for Tyler.”

"Oh man, if you could just do this for me then I would be the best behaved inmate on my wing, just a perfect pussy cat." Tyler confirmed as sincerely as he possibly could.

With a silent groan inside I nodded my agreement and indicated that he should step up to me. As the knob bounced in front of my mouth I could smell the faint aroma of the man, not strongly but just a little, clearly he had recently showered. For a moment I wondered if he had been expecting some action but then dismissed the very idea as being absurd and turned my attention to the task at hand. Tyler took a half step towards me, placed one hand on the back of my head and with the other hand guided his cock towards my lips. My mouth opened instinctively and waited for the inevitable, I didn't have long to wait. With a subtle thrust of his hips, the cock was in and completely filling my mouth, it kept on sliding in until it hit the back of my mouth making me gag reflexively. The head withdrew slightly before hitting the back again; once more I gagged to a loud tut above me.

Max knelt down beside me and in a quiet voice instructed me to breathe in gently through my nose as the cock entered, to completely relax my throat and breathe out as the cock withdrew. He also told Tyler to be patient as I this was the first blow job I had ever given. We tried again with me following Max's guidance, this time although I gagged slightly I was able to swallow more of his cock and after a few more thrusts was able to get about six inches of the cock in my mouth and down my throat. In the background I could hear words of encouragement. This spurred me on; I took hold of his hips and pulled him closer towards me. As a reward for my eagerness . upped the tempo and really started to fuck my face, with considerable concentration I was able to time my breathing to his thrusts and before I knew it my nose was brushing his pubes and his cock was buried fully within me. All of a sudden he started to shudder and growl, his cock pulsed (I guess he was shooting his load down into my stomach). Slowly it subsided and he pulled it out much smaller and covered in saliva and jism. It certainly came out easier than it went in! I gave a loud belch, which caused a round of laughter, licked my lips and in a rather a hoarse voice asked for a drink of water to wash the spunk down. Richard helped me to my feet and led me to my chair while I got my breath back under control, then hand me and Tyler a tissue each to wipe ourselves clean.

Liam glanced at Tyler who was busy wiping his now flaccid cock clean and said

"Tyler, I never thought I would say this but thank you for helping to educate Sam here. You have done all that was asked of you and you have shown a side of you rarely seen by us prison staff. Please collect your belongings from your box, you are now free to get dressed. We can now confirm that your records are fully up to date."

Tyler didn't seem in a hurry to get dressed, he walked over to box, unlocked it, retrieved a pair of shorts, holding them casually in his hands he turned towards us and said

"Pete mentioned something about my services being required to administer punishment to prisoners, was he being genuine or was he just using that as a ploy to get me to go along with the punishment?"

Liam looked at him thoughtfully for a moment, while Tyler pulled his shorts up and retrieved a T-shirt, before carefully replying.

"No Pete was telling you the truth about requiring volunteers, we're currently drawing up a shortlist of possible candidates and yes you are one of the candidates being considered."

"Seriously? That's brilliant, I've done nothing but think about it for the last two days and I think I would be perfect for it, don't you Sam? When will I know if I've been successful?"

"That very much depends on you to be honest, we will be assessing everyone over the next few weeks and your behaviour will be scrutinised meticulously, one foot wrong and you will not be considered further. We have to be absolutely sure of your commitment and that you will not abuse your position of power over the inmates."

"Okay okay, serious stuff then. Count me in though, I promise I will be as good as gold. What can I do to convince you of my sincerity?"

"Well, for a start, once you are a volunteer punisher your services can be called upon at any time, day or night and it is important that you provide a highly visible deterrent. All volunteers will be permanently naked except for a red beret (like the military police). So if you want to make a real start with your training and show us your commitment then I suggest you remove all your clothing from the box, you may keep your other possessions, surrender them to us now and remove your shorts and T-shirt you have just put on."

Tyler was cornered, if he refused to do so then his voluntary career was over before it began, however he thought quickly on his feet.

With a simple "Right you are then." He took off his T-shirt and stepped out of his shorts, once again revealing his magnificent cock, placed them on the table and proceeded to remove the rest of his clothes from the box. Within five minutes we had a pile of clothes on the table and one aroused Tyler wheeling his box out of the room. Liam called after him that we would be in contact with him. I asked Liam what the plans were, he replied that he had no plans but it seemed like a good idea at the time! He was sure that he would think of something soon.....

There was a knock on the door, it was 11.00am already! As we drank our second cup of coffee of the morning Eduardo from C-Wing walked in, as naked as the other two men had been. He was a handsome young man, slim and no older than twenty three. He was in prison for drugs offences and it was these that had been found in his cell resulting in him being stripped of his possessions. He had a certain juvenile cockiness which was endearing rather than annoying as can often be the case.

As he stood facing Liam listening to the preamble I studied the young man's figure. His jet black hair was cut short and his skin had the typical Mediterranean olive complexion except for his cheeks which were a glowing white, I guess from wearing Speedos when out sunbathing. His legs were hairy as were his arms but his back was quite smooth.

"Okay, Eduardo" Liam asked. "Outside the prison environment would you describe yourself as normally being gay, straight or bisexual."

"Bisexual"

"Have you ever had sex with a man?"

"Yes both inside and outside of the prison. I enjoy it, I like girls but I also like guys."

"Was it anal or oral sex, were you passive or active?"

"Both and I am versatile."

"Okay, final question for now. When was the last time you ejaculated?"

"This morning, I was fucked by my cell mate and I came without touching my cock."

"Thank you, if you don't mind the doctor is now just going to carry out a few physical checks to verify your answers."

"I have told you the truth, I have nothing to hide."

As this was the third time we had carried out this scenario I knew what was expected so while Richard proceeded to weigh Eduardo's balls I slipped on a pair of latex gloves and started to lubricate them with the KY. Eduardo's cock rapidly expanded and became erect, from the corner of my eye I could see that he was watching me getting prepared; clearly the anticipated procedure was turning him on. I asked him to turn around, bend over supporting himself on his elbows and to spread his legs wide.

He smiled and said "Si, Senor" before doing as he was told. I squeezed a little of the KY onto his anus and carefully smeared it around his ring before gently inserting the tip of my finger as I had with the other two guys. I could feel the difference immediately, with Flick and Tyler there had been a lot of resistance and they had clamped down on my finger every time my finger moved inside them, however with Eduardo my finger slid in easily right up to the hilt. It was only then that he clenched momentarily, gave a little wiggle of his hips and looked over his shoulder at me with a smile on his face.

Richard stood beside me and quietly spoke into my ear suggesting that I try to insert another finger or two to assess how anally experienced Eduardo actually was. I withdrew my finger and applied more KY to my fingers before placing two of them at his entrance and smoothly pushed them inside until I could go no further and then pulled them out again. As Eduardo had shown no reaction I decided to try a third finger, as I inserted the three fingers I detected more resistance and as I sank in up to the third knuckles he started to clench down hard on my fingers and his body language made it clear he had reached his limits. In response I withdrew my fingers and wiped them clean on some tissue offered to me by Richard, who asked me what my conclusion would be to this exercise. I thought carefully for a moment before replying.

"Well, I would say that this young man is certainly comfortable with having objects inserted up his rectum and judging from the dilation he is more that capable of accepting most cocks up him."

Richard nodded sagely and agreed with me, he then invited Eduardo to stand up as the inspection was over. As Eduardo stood up and stretched his back and arms, Max whispered in Liam's ear who nodded and then turned to Adrian who also nodded thoughtfully after a couple of seconds. Max looked over to Eduardo and said

"You have done all that has been asked of you and we confirm that your records are fully up to date. You are now free to get dressed and can collect your belongings from your box; however we are curious about the statement you made about being able to ejaculate without touching your cock. We wonder if this is an empty boast."

Eduardo gave a nervous laugh and assured us that what he had said was the truth and if required he would demonstrate this fact to us. Max nodded and said that they would like to see this trick. Eduardo simply smiled in response then looked at me and said that he would like me to help him.

"Help you? In what way?" I asked, clearly naive despite me being a man of the world as my mates call me.

"Si, I would like you to fuck me. I will lie on my back on the floor and you will insert your cock up my arse and fuck me until I cum."

He left me in no doubt that he was serious, again I looked over to Liam who smiled and nodded encouragement. Mmm this was really pushing my boundaries; I had never fucked a bloke before. I've had anal intercourse with a woman and it was okay, at the end of the day a man's hole can't be much different to a girl's can it? So feeling just a little self conscious I removed my uniform, placed it neatly folded on my chair, I didn't look up until I was standing stark naked and playing with my cock to wake it up again. Richard walked over to me and with a wink squeezed a generous amount of KY onto his fingers before taking my cock in his hand and lubricated it from base to head. Well that did the trick! My cock was rock hard within a few seconds and I was ready to go! By now Eduardo was laying on his back with a chair cushion under his hips, with his arms wrapped round his knees exposing his anus to me which was still glistening from its previous lubrication and was just slightly open. It was the sight of this that drew my eye and all I could think about was sliding my cock into it and shooting my pent up load deep into him. Wasting no time I knelt down and then placed one hand on his thigh, with the other I guided my cock to his waiting hole. Then when my head has gently pushing against the ring I removed my hand from my cock and held onto his other thigh. In one smooth thrust I fully entered him and buried myself up to the hilt causing a groan of pleasure to escape from his lips. Giving him a moment to adjust to the impalement I looked down at his cock and it was throbbing with a life of its own, then slowly I thrust in and out gradually building up the tempo trying to reach further and further inside, only stopping when my balls slapped up against his cheeks. He let go of his legs and let his arms flop onto the floor, I moved my hands to his ankles and spread his legs wide so the others could have a clear view of his cock. On and on I banged his butt, it felt so good, never had I fucked a guy's arse before nor one so much younger than myself! Eduardo was constantly groaning and slowly he started to writhe around, then arching his back and a thrash of his head he yelled out as his cock suddenly spewed out jets of jism all over his face and chest. His anus clamped rhythmically down on me which tipped me over the edge and I shot my load too deep into his bowels before collapsing on top of him, smearing his jism all over my chest.

For several minutes we simply lay there catching our breaths, as I raised myself up Eduardo caught me by surprise by kissing me hard on the lips. My face must have been a picture because he chuckled as so did everyone else in the room. Once more Richard did the honours by offering us tissues to clean ourselves up with, as I wiped myself off I could not help but wonder what else could happen today, little did I know! As I put my clothes on again lost in my own thoughts I didn't hear Eduardo come up behind me on his way to his box, he whispered in my ear making me jump.

"Senor, any time you would like to fuck me again just let me know, your cock is very big and I love it!"

"Uh thanks, I'll bear that in mind."

"Please do."

Then without further ado he trotted over to his box, opened it and quickly got dressed before pushing it out of the door with a cheery wave to everyone in general. There was about ten minutes spare before the next inmate was due so Liam took the opportunity to quiz me on the last session and had I enjoyed fucking Eduardo. I gave my honest feedback and yes I had enjoyed myself.

"So, would you still describe yourself as being straight or bisexual now?" Liam asked with a raised eyebrow.

"I guess, if I'm being honest I'm swinging more to being bisexual if this morning's experiences are anything to go by" I replied, before continuing with "Why? Does it make any difference?"

"No, it makes no difference at all. I was curious that's all."

It was now 12 Noon and right on time there was a knock on the door and in walked Dinesh, the other inmate who thinks that I am gay (I was beginning to wonder what he knew that I didn't). I think it would be fair to say that his is striking rather than handsome in the classical sense, not only in his looks but also in his demeanour. Authoritive would be a good way to describe him. I would put him in his early forties, of Indian origin, dark skin with a full head of hair cut fashionably short and a close cropped beard, again trimmed in a fashionable style. His body was hairy but he clearly kept it neatly trimmed, he was heavy set without being overweight, toned without being overdeveloped. He carried himself well; with confidence as if being naked was the most natural thing in the world. Perhaps this isn't surprising considering the fact that he was a master fraudster!

As before, while he stood before Liam with his arms crossed before him, I took my time to study him and wondered if I would get to fuck him like I had Eduardo.

"Okay Dinesh" Liam said having done his speech "Outside the prison environment would you describe yourself as normally being gay, straight or bisexual."

"Gay"

"Have you ever had sex with a man?"

"Yes, of course I am gay."

"Was it anal or oral sex, were you passive or active?"

"Both oral and anal, I have done everything you can think of and have enjoyed it all."

"Okay, final question for now. When was the last time you ejaculated?"

"Yesterday, I fucked and sucked off one of the guys on my wing."

"Thank you, if you don't mind the doctor is now just going to carry out a few physical checks to verify your answers."

"Be my guest, I have no reason to lie to you."

Richard and I worked smoothly as a team, he weighed Dinesh's balls concluding that they had indeed been emptied recently, while I donned on a new pair of latex gloves and retrieved the KY. By the time I was ready Richard had instructed Dinesh to bend over the desk and spread his legs for our inspection. He was more than happy to oblige and even helped us by resting his chest on the desk and using his hands to spread his cheeks. I could tell that his hole had seen action because as with Eduardo it wasn't clamped shut tight, if anything it was slightly more open which I found curious.

I liberally applied the KY to his anus, which quivered in response and my fingers. I gently pushed my index finger inside and met no resistance, so I withdrew it and inserted a second finger, again I met no resistance. It was time to lube up a third finger, I was expecting the same resistance that I had with Eduardo but no, the three fingers slid in easily. With the three buried fully inside Dinesh I asked him if he was okay, he replied that he was and that there was plenty of room for more. I glanced and Richard who raised an eyebrow and encouraged me to continue, so withdrawing once again I applied some more lube and started to insert four fingers, again they slid inside quite easily. I now had the attention of the whole room; Max, Liam and Adrian along with Richard were now standing round me to get a good view of the proceedings. Richard told me to leave my fingers inside Dinesh and to tuck my thumb in behind them making a cone before pushing my hand further inside. I carefully followed his instructions and was surprised to find my hand sinking inside up to the widest part of my hand, where at last resistance was met. Dinesh was breathing heavily and now supporting himself on his elbows, looking over his shoulder he told me to keep going because he could take it and started to push backwards against me. I kept up the gentle pressure from my end and slowly the resistance from his ring gave way and my hand slid in smoothly up to my wrist bringing a sigh from him and the guys standing next to me. For a while his ring clamped tightly against my wrist, once it had relaxed I gently pulled my hand out with a quiet slurp and the hole slowly closed behind me. Dinesh stood up and turned to face us; I was a little disappointed to find that his cock was flaccid rather than being stiff like the other guys had been after I had explored their arse.

"Welcome to the noble art of fisting Sam, I think you're a natural, well done." Liam said patting me on the shoulder.

"I would agree with you there" Dinesh agreed. "Will that be all Sir, or can I help you with anything else? Like return the favour perhaps?"

"Er, no, that will be all for now but thank you for the offer!" I managed to reply, my cheeks had clenched so hard I was getting cramp in them.

Liam intervened and thanked Dinesh for being so amenable, his medical records were now complete and that he was free to collect his belongings from the box and get dressed. Dinesh nodded in response before striding over to his box and quickly got dressed. He repeated the invitation to me with a wink and then left the room with his possessions before I could respond.

Still puzzled by the state of Dinesh's cock I asked Richard for an explanation, if there was one.

"Sam, it's simple physiology really. Dinesh was concentrating so much on relaxing his anus that his arousal levels were suppressed. You will find that in a more relaxed situation and prolonged activity that his arousal levels would have risen again and it is common for recipients to orgasm spontaneously as Eduardo did earlier on this morning."

"You're absolutely correct Richard. I have witnessed this and indeed experienced it on several occasions." Liam added.

I was stunned by this latest comment and could only look at him in surprise. Ignoring my expression Liam announced that it was now 1pm and time for lunch, we had one hour before the next inmate was due. As we made our way down to the dining hall small talk was made and continued until we sat down in the private area for senior staff. We sat in silence eating our food before Liam started talking business. He asked Richard for his opinion on this morning's proceedings and whether or not I would be able to assume his role for future sessions. Richard gave his feedback on the morning and to my relief gave me a big thumbs up. However I had a couple of issues to raise.

"Future sessions? You mean that there will be more of these? I thought this was a one off!" I said in all seriousness.

"Good God no, this is simply the first one, we will be carrying out cell searches randomly for the foreseeable future in a bid to eliminate the prohibited activities. We predict that these type sessions will be repeated on a weekly basis and with training this is something you and Adrian will be able to do without the need for Max, Richard and myself to be present. As you can appreciate this is time consuming and we simply can't spare the manpower, plus we need to explore the processes for the next level of punishment."

"The next level?"

"Yes, the public corrections but this is a little further down the road, we haven't even reached the stage of repeat offenders yet but that will come soon, probably within the next month when we have a new batch of inmates. The new ones always try to push the boundaries." Liam announced with confidence. "This afternoon I want you to assume Richard's role, he will be there simply to advise you if necessary. You know what's required so I don't think it will be too much of a problem and you have shown a great deal of competence, a willingness to learn new skills and expand your experiences beyond your comfort zones."

"Thank you. I will do my best this afternoon."

By now lunch time was nearly over so we made our way back to the governor's office and prepared ourselves for the last two sessions of the day.

At 2pm there was a knock on the door and in walked Jarek from E-Wing, I could tell immediately that he was of Eastern European origin, Polish in fact, just by his colouring. He was of average build and height with light brown hair and pale skin. As he stood with his back to me listening to Liam's speech I couldn't help but look at his white cheeks, clearly they had never seen the light of day. Unlike the four guys before him he didn't appear comfortable with his nakedness judging by the way he kept his genitals covered by his hands despite Liam's invitation to relax.

Then Liam started to ask the same questions he'd used this morning.

"Okay, Jarek, outside the prison environment would you describe yourself as normally being gay, straight or bisexual."

"Straight"

"Have you ever had sex with a man?"

"Never, it is disgusting and against God's rules."

"How have you felt about being naked for the last 48 hours?"

"Very uncomfortable, it is degrading having others stare at your body all the time."

"Do you think the punishment will deter you from offending again while in prison?"

"Definitely, I cannot tolerate being like this again."

"Okay, final question for now. When was the last time you ejaculated?"

"With all due respect that is none of your business; however I have to admit I had a wet dream a few days ago."

"Thank you, if you don't mind Sam is now just going to carry out a few physical checks to verify your answers."

"What do you mean physical checks?"

It was at this point I stood next to Jarek and explained what I would be doing. He frowned and was clearly unhappy with this, however he did place his hands behind his back when I asked him to and made no comment when I gently cupped his balls to weigh them. I decided they did feel heavy and wrote this down against his records indicating that he hadn't ejaculated for several days. But when I asked him to turn round and bend over this was a step too far for him and he point blank refused to despite my assurances that it wouldn't hurt. In the end I had to get assertive and pointed out that if he failed to comply with my request he would not be permitted access to his possessions until he did so, in other words he would remain naked until then. His jaws were clenched tightly as were his fists but slowly he turned round and bent over at the waist. I slipped on a pair of latex gloves, lubricated the index finger of my right hand and with my left hand spread his cheeks. Even with my untrained eye I could tell his hole was virginal, it was so tight and clearly clenched that I had to tell him to relax several times. When that didn't work I resorted to teasing it gently before pushing my finger tip just inside. He reared up in response and clamped down hard on me pushing me out, it actually hurt my finger! I stood up and announced that the test was now over, as far as I could tell nothing had ever been up there.

His relief was immense and when Liam invited him to collect his belongings he ran over to the box and scrambled into his clothes, muttering in Polish all the time, before quickly disappearing out the door.

Liam asked me how I thought it had gone; I concluded that it had been good experience for me to show how different the reactions can be to what is asked of the inmates, he nodded in agreement. With that it was time for the final inmate of the afternoon, Tony from F-Wing.

When Tony knocked on the door and walked in I was sure I was going to have the same difficulty with him as I had had with Jarek. I would say that he was probably an ex-Hells Angel in that he had tattoos all over his arms and neck, still wore his hair in a ponytail despite being in his fifties and had numerous piercings all over his body. He had a decent body except for the beer gut which he wore with pride and had a reputation for being handy with his fists.

In his defence his manner was easy going and appeared completely comfortable with his nakedness; standing quite casually listening to Liam doing his speech, then came the questions to which I listened with interest to see what the answers would be.

"Okay Tony" Liam said. "Outside the prison environment would you describe yourself as normally being gay, straight or bisexual."

"Straight"

"Have you ever had sex with a man?"

"Yes, inside here only, not much choice is there?"

"Was it anal or oral sex, were you passive or active?"

"Both oral and anal, I have fucked a few guys and been sucked off too but that's my limit."

"Okay, final question for now. When was the last time you ejaculated?"

"This morning, I received a blow job in my cell."

"Thank you, if you don't mind Sam is now just going to carry out a few physical checks to verify your answers."

"Whatever, it's all the same to me."

Gaining confidence, this time I decided to be seated and had already slipped on a new pair of gloves before I asked Tony to stand in front of me while I weighed his balls. Although they were large in size I gauged that they were quite light confirming his statement that they had been emptied this morning. With this new confidence I asked him to turn round, bend over and support himself by holding onto his knees which he did with no hesitation. This presented me with a hairy crack and an anus which looked to me like anything but virginal! I applied a generous amount of KY to his hole and deftly inserted my index finger up his rectum bringing a little sigh of contentment from Tony. Withdrawing it I inserted two fingers again with relative ease, I was beginning to wonder if I had another Dinesh on my hands, but I needn't have worried because Tony was unable to accommodate three fingers. This led me to the conclusion that Tony was actually taking it up the arse despite his assertion to the opposite. I wrote these thoughts down on his report by made no comment to Tony himself.

I decided that I had finished testing him so invited him to stand up and clean himself off using the tissues on the side. As he did so he swung round revealing an erect cock of average length but with a comparatively large head, anyone on the receiving end of that would certainly feel it I thought to myself. He must have read my mind because he invited me to sample it any time I like as I was just the type of guy he liked to fuck with, I thanked him for his offer but declined it as tactfully as I could. He smiled and shrugged his shoulders then asked if he could have his possessions back now. As with the other five inmates Liam thanked him for cooperating with us, that his records were now up to date and yes, he could collect his belongings and get dressed.

Ten minutes later I was sat round the table with the other four for a thirty minute discussion on my progress this afternoon. At the end of the meeting I agreed to give running the post-punishment sessions a go as I was confident of my abilities to handle the punished inmates.

And that diary was the end of my long and tiring day at work! Driving home I mulled over the day's events and my reaction to the different situations I had come across. By the time I got home I hadn't reached a conclusion other than to take each day as it comes and make sure that I don't get pressurised into doing things I don't feel comfortable doing.

FRIDAY 19TH MARCH

Dear diary, compared to yesterday work was uneventful, business as usual you might say. Everyone apart from Tyler was dressed as before and you would have been forgiven for thinking nothing had changed, and yet it had. There was a degree of calmness about the place and there was a little more respect for the staff, at least on the surface and just as importantly there was less bickering between inmates. As I walked back to my car at the end of the shift, I was both glad the week was over but at the same time I was looking forward to the next week too! Went down the King's Head and met up with Mike and Tom for our usual get together. It was great to let my hair down and talk about things other than law and order, the only trouble I had was as the beers flowed it got increasingly harder to keep my mouth from spilling the beans over the unorthodox events in the governor's office.

I think it would be fair to say that today was another eventful day at the office, so to speak. It was visiting day and one that will go down in history as the first real test of the new regime and I am relieved to say we pulled it off to great effect. The inmates concerned have been left in no doubt that the management mean what they say and that the rules will be implemented.

The day started off as usual with a briefing meeting for the day ahead, after that we did the rounds on the wings before getting ready for visiting period. As the inmates filed in and greeted their visitors waiting for them I took my position at one end of the room along with three other prison officers spaced around the room. Our role was to provide a visible deterrent to any obvious misdemeanours, but it was the hidden CCTV and microphones which would be used to detect any rule breaking. Our CCTV control room would feed back through our ear pieces if any inmate was to be detained after the visiting session.

For an hour I stood there carefully watching the inmates but for the life of me I could not spot any wrongdoing, however as the visitors filed out of the room my earpiece crackled into life and informed me that Jarek, Sayeed and Gus were to be detained. Jarek indeed! It was only yesterday he had declared that he had learnt his lesson, clearly not. I'm going to enjoy this I thought to myself. As was prison policy we had to have two officers per inmate for our own protection and also to prevent possible claims of abuse etc. George and I selected Jarek (at my suggestion) and as he made to rise from his seat I walked over to him and placed a hand on his shoulder and said.

"Not so fast Jarek, we need to have a word with you."

"Oh shit guys, what now? Why do you keep hassling me?"

"You were observed on CCTV receiving a small packet from your visitor and slipping it down the front of your trousers. As you are well aware this is against prison rules and you are required to surrender it immediately." I replied in the most authoritive voice I could muster.

"I haven't done anything wrong and I don't have to prove anything. This is typical, you're just targeting me because I'm Polish and think I will take your crap." Jarek said getting agitated.

"Come on Jarek, you can do this the easy way or the hard way, which one do you want?"

"Just fuck off and leave me alone! I'm going back to my cell; now get your hands off me." He growled and stood up shaking my hand off his shoulder and marched off.

We couldn't let him get away with this unacceptable behaviour and rebelliousness, so in unison we ran after him, caught up with him and pinned him to the wall, with his back to us. Before he could react we had his hands behind his back and quickly handcuffed, then turned him around facing us.

"So it's the hard way then." George said sternly before continuing "You do realise that you have just broken another rule which is refusing to comply with a request made of you by a prison officer. By my calculations that is the third infringement since the new rules came in, so not only will you be permanently losing all your personal possessions you will also be the very first recipient of the public correction in the chapel. I hope that you are proud of yourself."

Wisely Jarek said nothing but I could tell from his expression that he was majorly pissed off by this announcement, in fact he must have been boiling inside because he suddenly blurted out

"You are corrupt and perverted you pigs. I thought this country was fair and lawful but it's not, it's disgusting and you make me sick!" Having got this out of his system he stood there glowering as if to dare us to take the next step. We had no option but to continue and show that we meant business. With a nod from George I knelt down in front of Jarek and undid his belt and pulled it free from his jeans, then undid the button and unzipped the flies before pulling them down to his ankles. There was no sign of the packet seen on the CCTV.

"I told you there was nothing there."

"I haven't finished yet" I replied, at the same time I slipped my fingers into the waistband of his pants and slowly pulled them down, again to his ankles. His tackle swung uncomfortably close to my face as I looked inside the pants, still there was no sign of the package and said as much to George.

"Don't be fooled Sam" he replied. "I bet you'll find them clenched between his cheeks."

Determined to keep up a professional appearance I nodded my understanding and so with my right hand I reached up between his thighs and felt between his clenched cheeks. I told him to relax, deciding the game was up he did so and I then found the small packet I had been seeking. Examining them I suspected they were illegal drugs and passed them to George for safekeeping.

"Right then Jarek, you know what comes next don't you? We're going to have to strip you here and then go and clear out your cell. This evening you will be taken to the chapel for your public correction, do you understand?"

"Yes."

I then set about removing his shoes and socks before asking him to step out of his pants and trousers, leaving him just wearing his T-Shirt. Unlocking his handcuffs we removed his T-Shirt before putting the handcuffs on again and leading him out of the visitor's room. In the corridor waiting for us stood Dave and Mick guarding a naked Sayeed, who like Jarek appeared very unhappy with his situation. He stood between the two officers covering his genitals as best he could. It really was a shame because he was a good example of a man in his prime, muscular with no trace of middle aged fat appearing, youthful but had lost all trace of any adolescent gawkiness. Seeing Jarek naked with his hands tied behind his back must have surprised him as his hands dropped to his sides momentarily, letting me have a good view of his sizable packet nestling beneath a black bush of pubic hair. His skin was an even light mahogany all over indicating that he perhaps being naked wasn't all that unusual for him, only his cock and balls differed being slightly darker in colour. He spotted me studying his body and his face flushed red with discomfort, however I was more interested in the fact that his cock swelled and bobbed in reaction.

The sound of doors opening broke my reverie, looking over my shoulder I saw Tim and Steve escorting the naked figure of Gus, in appearance he looked very similar to Jarek but darker in colouration but that's where the similarity ended. Where Jarek was moody, close minded and aggressive, Gus was cheerful, broad minded and cocky. Jarek was uncomfortable being naked but Gus seemed to be in his element, revelling in his new found freedom and his erection was testament to his enjoyment of being naked in public. Returning my attention to the job in hand I led Jarek back to his cell and with George's help we removed Jarek's belongings and took them back to the stores department where they'd be distributed out amongst inmates who may be lacking certain items. As we removed his handcuffs he went to say something and then thought better of it, smiling in acknowledgement I told him we'd be back for him at 8pm.

Before then there was a lot of work to be done, afternoon rounds of cell checks, paperwork and then monitoring the evening mealtime in the dining hall. There was a buzz about the place; word had got around about the three guys getting caught. They were now subject to the ribbing that had happened last week especially as this was no longer a novelty. In the dining hall was a large poster advertising the first public correction in the chapel at 8pm, there were 500 seats available on a first come first served basis, there seemed to be a continuous crowd around this poster, clearly this was going to be a popular event.

At 7.45pm I collected Jarek from his cell, he was very quiet as I handcuffed him once more with hands behind his back. He had also lost a lot of his aggressiveness, hopefully this was a sign of things to come. He shivered slightly as he stepped outside of the prison wing and into the evening air, which I had to admit was slightly chilly. I encouraged him on and within a couple of minutes we arrived at the chapel's main entrance. Not giving him time to react I pushed him inside and directed him to the front of the room where Liam was already standing on the podium and giving a speech to the expectant audience (all seats had been taken and there were even guys standing at the back and in the side aisles!). As we stood there with all eyes focused on Jarek, Liam explained that once we had gone through to the correction room then the video cameras would be switched on and the audience would be able to watch the action going on live care of the huge viewing screen. Liam invited the inmates to make themselves comfortable and enjoy the viewing, with that he stepped down and handed over to Max who would be supervising the audience.

The three of us walked down the central aisle, with Jarek doing his best to ignore the comments and sniggers coming from several guys, when we got to the door Liam tapped in the pin number and we stepped inside. On the other side of the door was a little hive of industry. Richard and James (the sports coach) were busy prepping the equipment and Adrian was standing in front of the metal cabinet which had been locked the last time I had been in the room. This time the doors were open and I could see several shelves chocked full of dildos and butt plugs of various shapes and sizes along with cans of Crisco and bottles of J-Lube. Liam left us and headed for the mobile video camera, turned it on and swung it round so that we were being recorded. Richard by now was in the shower area and indicated that we were to join him, so taking Jarek by the arm I pointed him in that direction and walked him forward with one hand on his arm.

When he was positioned in front of the shower I unfastened his handcuffs and then quickly fastened him to the handcuffs either side of the shower head. Jarek looked at us suspiciously but said nothing. James by this time had stripped down to his usual T-shirt and shorts, commenting that he was likely to get wet in the next few minutes and retrieved the shower head from its stand on the wall before turning the shower on and adjusting the temperature until it was pleasantly hot. Without saying a word he turned aimed the jet of water on to Jarek and continued until he was wet all over, then handing me the showerhead he soaped him up all over. Still Jarek said nothing, simply closed his eyes wishing it was all over, that is until James soaped up his genitals and arse crack when he started to growl menacingly but James simply ignored him. In fact this seemed to appeal to his playful side because he took extra care with his cock and balls, positively massaging them until he was fully erect, then her turned his attention to the crack and really took his time with it before moving lower and soaping up his legs and feet. Once he was finished he asked me to hand him the showerhead, thoughtfully he took great care to ensure that all the soap was off from every nook and cranny. Once he was satisfied he kicked at the insides of Jarek's ankles forcing him to spread them wider and wider until he could go no further. Richard came over with a can of Crisco, opening it he took a small chunk and warmed it in his fingers before kneeling down between Jarek's outspread legs and applied it to his crack. Alarm spread across Jarek's face but he was powerless to do anything except hang his head in shame as he felt Richard's finger slide up inside him greasing his ring and rectum. Richard spent several minutes warming up the ring in an attempt to relax it, making encouraging comments all the time to Jarek. This seemed to work as finally two fingers made a very snug entrance to the previously virginal hole. James in the meantime had placed the showerhead back in position and taken the douching tube (I had since been informed about this tool and its use) from the holder and was adjusting the flow and temperature to body heat. He then joined Richard and gently inserted the tube's nozzle deep into Jarek rectum, in response Jarek groaned and arched his back at both the sensation of being penetrated by the metal tubing and the feeling of warm water flowing up into his guts. Richard asked me to quickly fetch a bucket from the cabinet which I did immediately and handed it over to him without saying a word because I was too busy watching Jarek's stomach distend with all the water inside him. Finally when James was satisfied that there was enough water inside he withdrew the nozzle and told Jarek to release the water into the bucket underneath him. Needing no second telling a jet of water mixed with faeces shot out into the bucket and continued for what seemed ages, finally it slowed to a trickle and a relieved sigh from Jarek. If he thought his ordeal was over, he was very much mistaken as James immediately reinserted the nozzle and water once more flowed up inside him before withdrawing it to allow the mixed effluent to escape into the bucket. This cycle was repeated another three times until the water ran clear.

Releasing his handcuffs an exhausted Jarek was relieved to be escorted over to the massage table and once he was comfortable and lying face down he was handcuffed securely by the wrists and ankles. The table had two comfort holes in it, one for the face and the other for the genitals, from my vantage point I could see his bollocks and cock swinging freely. James took another chunk of Crisco and applied it to Jarek's crack, rubbing it in until it softened and then began to massage the anal ring. He continuously inserted a finger, swirled it around before withdrawing it and then reinserted it again. For over ten minutes his did this until he was able to insert two fingers simultaneously with ease, all the time Jarek was groaning and his cock was getting harder and harder. I nearly forgot to mention that Liam had been filming all of this action panning the camera around to catch all of our reactions along with Jareks before zooming in again on the anus receiving the attention and occasionally underneath the table. Richard wandered over to the metal cabinet and retrieved an assortment of different sized dildos ranging from normal cock size up to the ten inch variety! He meticulously greased up each one with plenty of Crisco and arranged them in ascending size deliberately in view of Jarek, now that's what I call sadistic.....

James picked up the smallest dildo first and with relative ease pushed the head inside, pausing a moment to allow for adjustment to the intrusion and then smoothly pushed the whole length inside so that the dildos balls were pushing against his crack. He fucked the hole for a few strokes before fully inserting it again and resting his whole weight on it. After a couple of minutes continuous pressure James pulled the dildo out and threw it into the now empty bucket before picking up the next sized dildo from the floor. He asked me to step over and pull Jarek's cheeks apart, at the sound of his voice Jarek looked over his shoulder at us with an unreadable expression. He glanced at the camera now pointing at him before burying his face into the hole again, no doubt wishing the punishment was over! As I leant over the table and pulled his cheeks apart I could see that his anus was beginning to loosen up and opened a little. I have to admit that I was beginning to feel aroused by this situation and more than once the thought of sinking my cock into his arse sprang to mind before being dismissed again. James expertly inserted the slightly bigger dildo and repeated the process all over again. When this dildo (large cock sized) was removed I took another peek at the anus, the hole remained open for several seconds before it twitched and closed up again.

Whilst this had been going on Richard had been busy adjusting the "dentist" chair, he had attached two metal leg supports complete with leather straps. Once he was satisfied he nodded to James and together they released Jarek from the massage table before escorting him over to the chair. Once he was comfortable they handcuffed his wrists to the chair's arm and secured straps round his chest. They then tilted the chair backwards until he was lying horizontal and then lifted his legs onto the leg supports and strapped them securely into position. The lower part of the chair was folded backwards resulting in Jarek's bum hanging over the edge and with the leg supports tilting outwards his crack was parted exposing his anus to everyone who cared to look. James wasted no time in fetching the unused dildos and expertly slid the next one deep into the waiting hole bringing yet another groan from Jarek before fucking him energetically with it. I could not help but notice that through all of this Jarek's erection had not subsided one little bit and was now beginning to leak pre-cum. After half an hour James had worked up to the largest sized dildo, some ten inches in length but still not as big as Tyler's monster cock. When the final dildo slipped out, Jarek's hole was so relaxed and loose that it failed to close up for several minutes, this fact was not missed by Liam who filmed the slow closure in its entirety.

Richard announced that the punishment session was over and that Jarek's anal ring had now been stretched sufficiently to withstand the pounding it would get should Jarek break any more rules. This made Jarek look up in alarm making James laugh and say that they could have stretched him a whole lot more (excuse the pun) than they had so far. James and I undid all the restraints and helped Jarek to his feet, who was stiff in more ways than one. Looking down at his own cock he asked Liam if he could beat himself off, Liam nodded and Jarek started to wank himself off. I couldn't resist the urge any longer, so kneeling down behind him I slowly pushed two fingers up into his rectum and felt around for his prostate. Having found it I massaged it firmly and constantly until he started to orgasm. I didn't need to look up to tell this because I felt his anal ring contract and grip onto my fingers, his cheeks clenched and he started to shake before spewing his jism in thick ropes all over the floor. When he released my fingers from his tight grip I gently removed them and wiped the grease off on a spare sheet of tissue.

James guided Jarek back to the shower area, told him to wash himself off and to hurry up as he had an audience to address in five minutes. Jarek said nothing except give him a weary, resigned and horrified look all rolled into one but did as he was told. Liam continued to film him all the while including as he towelled himself dry and then followed him outside into the main part of the church where his audience were waiting for him.

As Liam reached the podium he turned the camera off and indicated Jarek was to join him and face the audience, who initially clapped and wolf whistled but then slowly fell silent. Liam then did a post-punishment speech warning them that any one of them potentially faced being in the same situation if they continued breaking the rules. Jarek was only one step away from the ultimate penalty of being locked in the stocks and available for 'use' by anyone who wanted to use his services. I think Jarek was too stunned by this latest announcement to react; he simply looked down at his feet avoiding the gazes of the front row of the audience.

Finally it was all over and my shift was done. Back at home I sat in my armchair with a can of beer in my hand and reviewed today's events and my reactions to it. I careered from being disgusted with everything to being turned on by it all, the only thing for certain was that by the end of it I had a throbbing hard on which wouldn't go down and as I adjusted my crutch I spontaneously exploded and made a wet sticky mess in my boxer shorts!

FRIDAY 26TH MARCH

Dear diary, another great day at work and another step closer to accepting that man to man action is as hot as man to woman action. Not only that I got to play being doctor today, no wonder Richard came out of retirement to work at the prison!

After the usual prison rounds and opening up the cells Adrian and I set up camp in Richard's surgery. Adrian decided that he would ask the questions and write down our findings while I would do all the physical work (as I had last time). Personally this was fine by me.

At 10.00am our first visitor arrived, Gus knocked on the door and walked inside confident as ever. Adrian started with a preamble and then started asking the prepared questions:

"Okay Gus, outside the prison environment would you describe yourself as normally being gay, straight or bisexual."

"Bisexual"

"Have you ever had sex with a man?"

"Yes, of course many times."

"Was it anal or oral sex, were you passive or active?"

"Both oral and anal, I have done loads of things including what Jarek had done last night."

"Okay, final question, when was the last time you ejaculated?"

"Last night, Tyler fucked me senseless."

"Thank you, if you don't mind Sam is now just going to carry out a few physical checks to verify your answers."

"Ah, I've been looking forward to this bit" and grinned broadly at me.

I raised an eyebrow but tried my best to keep my face composed when I asked him to step up to me where I was sitting in Richard's chair. Cocky now he stood in front of me, half erect, with his hands on his hips. I ignored his dick and cupped his balls trying to weigh them which was getting tricky as they were tightening as a result of his erection. Finally I decided that they were rather light and told Adrian so. Next I told him to bend over the couch and spread his legs while I put on a pair of latex gloves and fetched the KY. He was just so cocky I could slap his arse! It was round and very pert (for a guy) and as I lubricated his hole my cock sprang to attention and I wanted so badly to fuck him there and then. He easily accommodated three of my fingers and as I went to insert the fourth, he looked over his shoulder and said.

"Not so fast Sir, I need my hole warmed up by that big cock of yours first, then I will be able to take more than four fingers if you know what I mean."

Indeed I did! So with permission from Adrian I dropped my trousers and then my boxers before slipping my rampant hard on up his arse. As this was now my second time fucking a guy I felt more confident and set about giving him a fuck that he wouldn't forget in a hurry. I was banging away and he was loving it, he backed on to me as much as he could and met my every thrust. By the time I shuddered and shot my load of jism deep into his rectum I could tell that his hole was getting very loose indeed. Pulling out I wiped my cock clean and told Gus to climb up onto the couch on all fours and to face away from me. His ass lips looked slightly reddened and very moist from all the lube and my jism, reaching out with three fingers they disappeared inside his hole with ease. I pulled back and inserted four, I felt a faint quiver of resistance but then pushed them up to the hilt before pulling back again leaving a slowly closing hole behind. I tucked my thumb in behind my fingers to form a cone and pushed in until the widest part of my hand met some resistance and his hole actually felt like a ring. I asked Gus if he wanted more, he nodded his head and braced himself for what was to come. I told him to relax before applying a steady pressure which did the trick and before I knew it my hand slid inside completely up to the wrist with his ring gently clamping down. The feeling of his warm silken flesh enveloping my hand was mind blowing! I kept my fist motionless to give him time to adjust to the intrusion; while I did I recalled that Gus confessed to having been fucked by Tyler last night. If he was able to take the whole of that monster cock, no wonder he was able to accommodate my fist and then I had an idea. Again asking him if he was okay, which he replied that he was; I slowly started to push my fist in further inside inch by inch until I reached the second sphincter separating his rectum from his bowels. Unlike his anus this inner ring was tighter and would need loosening up carefully if I was to go any further.

So I spent the next half an hour massaging the ring and gradually increasing the number of fingers that I could insert from one, to two, then three and finally four. Gus was panting and sweating, his upper torso was flushed but at no time did he ask me to stop. So at long last I was ready to tuck my thumb behind the fingers and telling Gus to brace himself I started the final push. The resistance was great but slowly ever so slowly it gave way and with a growling groan from Gus the ring gave way and my fist slid past it and into his bowels. I carried on pushing and again my hand inched its way up inside Gus, by now three quarters of my forearm had disappeared. We must have forgotten that time was passing, Adrian was transfixed by the spectacle unfolding before him; so much so that he hadn't noticed that it was now 11.00am and time for the next inmate to arrive, until that is there was a knock on the door. All three of us instantly froze and held our breaths.

The door slowly opened and in walked Sayeed, the expression on his face was priceless. He had been looking down as he came in and looked behind him as he closed the door. Then he turned round and saw my arm buried deep inside Gus and Adrian looking on in awe. His mouth dropped open and he flushed a bright red clearly embarrassed by what he saw. Adrian looked away and back to his paperwork. I half turned and smiled and putting as much calmness into my voice as I could, I asked him to take a seat and we would be with him in a minute. He stammered an okay and sat down on the chair indicated. I did however notice that again his cock was slowly swelling between his outspread thighs.

Gus was getting restless so taking the hint I gently pulled my arm back, his anus gripped my arm almost lovingly as it exited. Again there was resistance from the inner ring but with patience it released my hand and the rest of my exit was a lot easier. My hand finally reappeared with a wet sloppy squelch, poor Gus collapsed in a heap with a quiet groan and a hole that still hadn't closed properly. Using a handful of tissues I gently wiped his cheeks, crack and hole clean, the tickling sensation produced by the paper caused his ring to clamp shut tight again. I then wiped my forearm clean and removed my soiled gloves. Anyone walking in now would never guess what had just happened.

When Gus had recovered he climbed off the couch and stood facing us with hands clasped behind his back as cocky now as when he had first walked into the room. Conscious of the over running of the session Adrian wasted no time in telling Gus that he was free to collect his box of possessions and get dressed again. I watched him step into his clothes and as his pert little bum disappear into his pants and then jeans I still could not believe I had been so far up inside him, part of me was wishing I could still be there or at least for a replay. Who knows one day perhaps.....

As Gus shut the door behind him we turned our attention to Sayeed who by now was getting a little restless, any sign of arousal had disappeared with his cock hanging flaccidly over his balls between his legs. As I donned another pair of latex gloves Adrian asked him the routine questions.

"Sorry to have kept you waiting Sayeed, hope you didn't find the show too shocking."

"Umm, it's not something I've ever seen before or thought humanly possible. I do hope that you're not going to try anything like that on me!"

"It's not on our agenda but we would seriously consider your request should you change your mind" Adrian replied with a chuckle.

"Definitely not!" came Sayeed's emphatic reply.

"Okay Sayeed back to the task at hand, I have some routine questions to ask you. Outside the prison environment would you describe yourself as normally being gay, straight or bisexual."

"Straight"

"Have you ever had sex with a man?"

"Only On the odd occasion. When my needs have been too great to be resisted any longer."

"Was it anal or oral sex, were you passive or active?"

"Oral several times, my cell mate gave me a blow job each time. Anal only once, in the showers late one night, a guy there begged me to fuck him, so I did."

"Okay, final question, when was the last time you ejaculated?"

"Last week in my cell, I gave myself a hand job."

"Thank you, if you don't mind Sam is now just going to carry out a few physical checks to verify your answers."

"None of your funny business now, I've told you the truth to your very personal questions, so why do you need to do these tests?"

I beckoned him over to where I sat and informed him that these tests were to complete his medical records and for no other purpose, no other inmate has refused so far nor has anything been done against their wishes. Sayeed still seemed a little reluctant but chose to say nothing before walking over to me and standing in front of me with his hands crossed in front of him with a frown on his face as he looked down at me. I reached out and gently cupped his balls which in my mind felt heavy and possibly a little tender from the way he responded to my manipulation of them.

"I get the distinct impression Sayeed that you are suffering from a term we call Blue Balls i.e. too much semen stored in your balls caused by lack of release resulting in aching and soreness. Am I correct?"

"Yes Sir, they are indeed tender."

"I would recommend that you release it as soon as possible but first I need to complete the final test. Please turn round, bend over at the waist and grasp your knees." I said in the most doctor-like voice I could muster.

"Is this absolutely necessary?"

"Yes."

"Well, I suppose so but I have a proposition to offer you."

"Go on, what do you have in mind?"

"I really don't want you anywhere near my back door. However I will let you do what you want on condition that when you have finished I can do what I want to do?"

"Mmm. What do you think Adrian?" I asked looking in his direction.

He simply shrugged his shoulders before saying "We need to complete the tests so why not? I can't see what harm it will do and it will get Sayeed's co-operation."

"Okay, you have yourself a deal" I said returning to face Sayeed "now please turn round and bend over."

Smiling gently to himself he did as he was told, as he grabbed his knees he clenched and released his cheeks a couple of times before relaxing and giving me a clear view of his hairy crack. I located his anus nestling amongst the black hairs, it was pinkly glistening and really quite appealing in its obvious tightness. I unintentionally licked my lips before I applied a large glob of KY to the hole and smeared it round with my index finger before applying a little pressure and pushing inside up to the first knuckle. It was tight, but not as tight as Jarek's had been. So I left the finger there for a couple of seconds for the ring to adjust to the intrusion before pushing in a little further. After further massaging and applying pressure I managed to fully insert my deep inside him bringing a stifled groan from his lips.

All the time I was feeling around inside seeking his prostrate he was clamping down hard on my finger, I had to tell him to relax otherwise he would chop my finger off! Finally I found it and was satisfied that it was normal so I slowly withdrew my finger and wiped it clean. I told Sayeed that he could stand up the test was over, I was satisfied with the results, they agreed with his statement.

"Of course they do, I was telling you the truth, I am an honourable man and never lie. Now we had a deal, are you going to be as honourable as me Sir?" Sayeed said looking at me with a new found confidence.

I must admit I was a little taken aback by his statement and simply replied "Of course, we had a deal, you've kept your end of the bargain so why wouldn't I? Now what was it you had in mind?"

"First of all I want you to remove your clothes and then kneel down in front of me."

I didn't need to ask what he had in mind having been in a similar position before! I glanced over at Adrian who simply raised his eyebrows and gave a quirky smile in encouragement. There was nothing for it but to keep the promise so looking Sayeed back in the eye I slowly and confidently stripped off my uniform placing each item on my chair neatly folded. First the jacket, then the shirt, next my shoes and socks, then my trousers leaving just my boxers shorts to go; then with a faint smile on my face I pushed them down and stepped out of them and placed them with the rest of my clothes. Now fully naked I knelt down in front of him as instructed and looked up at him for the next instruction.

He didn't say a word; he simply held his erect cock in his left hand and guided my head with his right hand until my lips met his cockhead. The first thing I noticed was the smell; he certainly wasn't as fresh as Tyler had been. I guess he hadn't washed since the previous evening as it had a distinctly prawn-like smell but thankfully there was no sign of any smegma, I would have heaved my guts up if there had been! Instinctively I opened my lips and licked them with my tongue to wet them, just in time as his cock was shoved inside. I felt both hands grip my head; unlike Tyler he showed no consideration for me, as he thrust his cock straight to the back of my mouth and down my throat. I gagged reflexively but just managed to stop myself from being sick and then concentrated on breathing in time with his thrusts. I expected him to keep going until he shot his load but he obviously had other plans as he abruptly pulled his cock out of my mouth and told me to stand up.

Confused I did as I was told and asked "What's wrong?"

"Nothing is wrong." He replied very seriously, then, he cracked a smile and chuckled "You're doing very well, much better than I anticipated actually. But it's time to take it to the next stage and it's going to be even better. Have you been fucked before?"

My face blanched and I stammered "N-n-no. Is this really necessary?"

"Excellent!" He replied "A virgin hole! Just what I like! Yes it is necessary, this way you'll know the joy of having my cock from both ends. What could be nicer?"

A lot of things I thought to myself but wisely kept these thoughts to myself.

"Walk over to the couch, bend over and spread your legs wide."

I did as I was told and prayed to god that it wouldn't hurt as much I imagined it might. Just as I was thinking this I felt two hands grasp my cheeks and pull them firmly apart allowing cool air to waft down my crack; then before I could react a hot wet tongue made contact with my anus. It surprised me to say the least then I felt the tongue lap all round my hole and flicked in and out coating it lavishly with saliva, despite myself I moaned in reaction to the pleasurable sensations I was experiencing and began to back onto the tongue. This seemed to go on forever but was probably only a couple of minutes in reality and then it was gone. In its place was something much bigger, much,

much, bigger in fact it felt enormous! Looking over my shoulder in alarm I saw Sayeed carefully guiding his erect cock between my cheeks and pushing against my back door. From the glistening appearance of the cock I guessed that he had lubricated the whole length of it. Seeing me watching Sayeed smiled and told me to relax, the more I relaxed the less it would hurt and the more I would enjoy it. Unable to think of anything worthwhile to say in response I looked away and closed my eyes to concentrate on relaxing as best as I could. The pressure was gradually building and eventually my ring stretched and gave way and allowing his cockhead to slide in. Aargh! I cried out at the intrusion, it felt enormous as my ring clamped shut around his shaft; all I wanted to do was get it out straight away. I tried to pull away but Sayeed had taken hold of my hips and leant all his weight on me effectively pinning me down and preventing me from moving. He remained motionless for a couple of minutes and slowly the pain subsided as I became accustomed to its presence, then I felt it move further up inside me and continue until I felt his thighs pushing against my outspread legs and his balls gently slap against mine. I had never felt so full inside and despite myself it began to feel strangely good.

Then the fucking started in earnest! Pain erupted through me again but quickly died down as it had come, in its place was an intense sensation, impossible to describe, with each thrust my cock pulsed and expanded until it was rock hard. Harder and harder, quicker and quicker he banged into me, until I could bear it no longer and with a load groan my cock exploded shooting jism out trapped between my stomach and the plastic couch cover. Sayeed was oblivious to all of this for he kept hammering away until he started to shudder and then with a growl he convulsed and shot his load deep inside me before collapsing on top of me. I could feel his hairy chest scratch my back and his hot panting breath on the nape of my neck. After a few minutes I felt him shift his weight and then push himself up, in doing so his shrunken juice covered cock slid out of my sloppy hole and I felt strangely empty.

"Thank you Sir, if you don't mind me saying you have one hot hole, it's a shame you're not a poof coz I could shag you every day and for me being a straight guy that is a big thing."

Standing up myself I gingerly touched my aching hole and said "Uh, thanks I think. That is everything now isn't it?"

"Yes Sir."

"Good. Well, in that case you're free to collect your belongings and return to your cell." Adrian informed him.

Having cleaned myself and the couch up I got dressed and watched Sayeed leave the room with a distinctly smug expression on his face.

Adrian turned towards me and said "That went rather well didn't it?"

"I wouldn't say it went quite as I expected! But I have had worse days I must admit."

That dear diary was the last of the excitement for that day, thankfully. The rest of the day was business as usual although I did walk rather stiffly for the rest of the day, can't think why can you? Oh and I found out that what goes up must come down. Yup, when I got home I found that my shorts had been soiled from all the spunk that had leaked out, yuk!

Needless to say that later that night down at the Kings Head with Mike and Tom I forgot to mention my sexual exploits, I really don't think they would have understood.....

MONDAY 29TH MARCH

After a quiet weekend spent catching up with household chores, food shopping and then spending quality time watching Sky Sports and several cans of beer it was back to work.

As soon as I walked on to E-Wing I could tell something was up, many inmates seemed agitated and others withdrawn. I asked Mick (fellow prison officer) what was going on as we did our rounds checking the cells and inmates. He said that late last night things had kicked off between Jarek and Vince, a newcomer to the ward. Vince was a nasty bit of work and had taken an instant dislike to Jarek. He started shouting xenophobic insults across the wing and then went on to shout homophobic insults based on what he had been told by other inmates who had witnessed Jarek's punishment in the chapel. Jarek naturally took exception to this and waded in with his fists to put Vince in his place, which he did to great effect. The two men had fought like wild animals and by the time Jarek had beaten Vince into submission the wing had been trashed and most inmates had run for cover, except for a few that had been egging them on. The prison staff arrived just as Jarek was dealing his last punch to Vince's very bloody head, who then crumpled into an unconscious heap. Jarek was immediately overpowered and frogmarched into solitary confinement and checked over by the medical staff. Satisfied that he was okay they left him alone and turned their attention to Vince who was still unconscious. He was carried to the hospital wing where he was kept under close supervision until he regained consciousness and early this morning was fit enough to be returned to his cell. Jarek was still in solitary confinement waiting for his visit from the Governor.

I didn't see Jarek until later that afternoon; he was looking a little worse for wear with bruises beginning to appear all over his face and naked body. He carried himself with pride and confidence because he had won the fight and was still top dog on the wing regardless of the price he would no doubt have to pay for the fight.

And there was indeed a price to pay, which came as no surprise for anyone least of all Jarek. Liam walked onto the wing late in the afternoon and announced that Jarek will be punished on Wednesday 31st March   in the stocks sited at the entrance to the wash area for two hours between 20:00hrs and 22:00hrs. There was little reaction to this announcement on the surface, but underneath there was a quiet buzz and word would no doubt get round very fast.

When he had finished talking to the inmates Liam spoke to Mick and myself asking us if we would volunteer to oversee the punishment and maintain order with overtime being paid. We confirmed we would, for myself I was more than a little curious to see what would be involved during the punishment.

TUESDAY 30TH MARCH

After the morning round I was called to the wash area where Mick and Dave were already waiting for me. We had the delightful task of erecting the heavy wooden stocks, which took us the rest of the morning to do simply because of the weight of the components and the lack of instructions! When it was finally complete boy did it look imposing, I sure wouldn't want to be incarcerated in it for it had all the appearance of a medieval instrument of torture. Physically it was situated in the centre of the entrance hall of the wash area so you could hardly miss it but it was easy to walk round when not in use, apparently it was going to be sited there permanently as a constant reminder to the inmates of the ultimate punishment. It had two sturdy legs at either end of a horizontal bar, on top of which sat another bar attached by a huge hinge at one end and secured by a padlock at the other. In the middle of the bar was a hole cut approximately six inches in diameter and either side was another hole about three inches in diameter. These were where the neck and wrists of the inmate would be secured to prevent their escape. Set in the floor about three feet behind the stocks were metal rings where the inmate's ankles could be secured further reducing their range of movement. I was getting quite turned on by the thought of Jarek being placed in the stocks and several times I had to adjust my trousers discreetly as a result.

On the wash area notice board we put up a large A3 poster announcing the first ever punishment by stocks tomorrow evening at 20:00hrs with Jarek being the first participant. Inmates will be able to participate in whatever activity they wish but physical injury will not be permitted under any circumstances.

Within an hour word had gone round the whole prison and there was a constant stream of inmates to read the notice board and examine the wooden stocks. The whole prison was buzzing with excitement, except that is for Jarek who managed to combine a look of being major pissed off, total resignation and a determination to maintain control of his wing. Oh, and as for Vince, he was keeping a very low profile. He knew that he was responsible for Jarek's coming punishment and was worried what the payback would be afterwards. Not only that he had a problem of his own; while he had been unconscious in the hospital wing his punishment for starting the fight had been meted out. He had had his clothes removed leaving only the sheets to cover his modesty. Unknown to him he had also had his cell stripped of all belongings as was now the routine, no one took much notice any more except for the inmate involved. When Vince had recovered from his beating he was escorted back to his cell amidst vocal protests about his lack of clothing which did not go down well with the other inmates. They told him to grow up, he had been man enough to start a fight so he should be a man enough to take the punishment; at least he wouldn't be in the stocks tomorrow night. He seemed to realise that he was on dodgy ground so kept his head down for the rest of the day doing his best to avoid Jarek.

WEDNESDAY 31ST MARCH

Dear Diary, today I completed the first month of my employment at HMP Ollerton and it has been just as eventful as the rest of the month. It has given me much to think about. When I first applied for the job I thought it would be a good move for me, that I would enjoy the change in my career and hopefully the job itself. That thought has proved to be a total underestimation. I now know that I have found my vocation in life, I find myself acting as a father figure for many of the inmates; sharing their up and downs, providing a firm but fair and approachable point of contact for many inmates who know they can talk to me about anything on their minds. I also suspect that my activities in the post-punishment tests have been relayed amongst them adding to the impression that I am a decent guy willing to give and receive.

But what has hit me the hardest has been the seismic shaking of my previously rock solid heterosexuality. I knew man to man sex went on but it had never occurred to me that I would ever participate in it let alone enjoy it! Now if anyone asked me how I would describe my sexuality I would have to hand on heart call myself bisexual because as things stand at this moment in time I would have a hard time saying which gender I prefer, the jury is very much out. Men and women are different having their own flavour, if you'll excuse the expression! Anyway, I am digressing; today's events have sealed the fate of my heterosexuality.

I will skip the bit about my day shift, it was very much business as usual and I don't want to bore you by repeating what I've already described before. So straight to this evening's events, it really started at 19:00hrs when I escorted Jarek from his cell, again he was very quiet and subdued so I did my best to lift his spirits by giving him positive affirmations and a couple of light hearted jokes. The best I could draw from him was a quirky smile and he withdrew into himself once we walked into the entrance hall of the wash area and he saw the stocks. Mick had removed the padlock and the top stock bar; he had then attached a set of hand cuffs to each of the metal rings ready for Jarek's incarceration.

I guided Jarek to the rings in the floor and attached the cuffs to his ankles, then got him to lean forward putting his neck and wrists on to the half-circle grooves on bottom bar. Mick then swung the top bar over and then gently down onto the bottom bar ensuring that Jarek's flesh wasn't nipped in the process. When he was satisfied that all was okay Mick attached the padlock locking the bars into position. Jarek was now bent over at the waist, not the most dignified of positions but then it wasn't supposed to have been. We then called Richard to let him know that we were ready for him. Ten minutes later Richard came down pulling what looked like a very large vacuum cleaner, I asked him what it was. He informed me that it was a portable colonic irrigator designed for when a shower system can't be used.

Not needing to explain further Richard got on with the job in hand, starting by reaching into his pocket and taking out a small tub of Crisco and smearing a load of it along Jarek's crack and pushing a wad into his anus with two fingers and spreading it all around inside his rectum and anal ring. In response to this intrusion Jarek shifted his weight around but was unable to avoid the roaming fingers and his greasing up. After a minute he gave up and accepted his fate. Once Richard was satisfied that Jarek was thoroughly greased up he turned his attention to the metal douching tube attached to the end of the machine's flexible hose (this actually had two pipes inside). When the tube was greased he deftly inserted it into Jarek's anus, just a little bit, maybe an inch or two. He told me to turn the motor on, which started whirring, then the pipe flexed and water started to pour into Jarek's rectum. It continued for a couple of minutes before stopping and reversing the flow allowing the faeces and water to exit through the other pipe. Richard then pushed the tube in further and the process started all over again. This cycle was repeated until some eighteen inches of pipe had been pushed up inside and Richard was satisfied that Jarek had been thoroughly cleaned out. Richard then withdrew the piping and re-greased Jarek's crack and arse. He then packed up the machine and wished us good luck because it was going to be a busy evening for us; the timing of this punishment had been deliberate as these two hours were the peak time for the use of the washing facilities so the greatest number of inmates would be going past.

At about 19:50 the first inmate entered the entrance hall seemingly oblivious to the announcement that had been made on Monday because he was caught by surprise by the stocks and explanatory poster. He stopped beside us and asked for an explanation, by the end of it I was not convinced by his naivety because he asked all the right questions but his attention seemed very much focused on Jarek's body. Either way he sauntered off into the wash area for his shower. For the next twenty minutes inmates filed through, some made a point of greeting Jarek with others simply looked either at the posted or at Jarek without comment. It wasn't 20:30 that the pace picked up with the first inmate showing interest in using Jarek's services, it was Eduardo who having thrown me a wink walked round to the front of the stocks and told Jarek to open his mouth. True to form Jarek began to protest until he was reminded about the poster, with a loud sigh he closed his eyes and opened his mouth. Eduardo wasted no time in slipping his cock into the waiting mouth, egged on no doubt by the gathering crowd; his action seemed to break the dam of their reservation. Within a minute or two another inmate had slipped his cock into Jarek's arse and was pumping away with great vigour (again I suspect putting on a performance for the crowd). I couldn't help but feel sorry for Jarek, I know he was being punished for a good reason but his humiliation was total, no longer was his pride intact. Eduardo and Bert (the one doing the fucking) seemed to be working in tandem plunging in and out at the same time. For nearly five minutes they continued until Eduardo started to shudder and then ejaculated down the throat, shortly followed by Bert. Again in unison they pulled out their still dripping cocks and went back to the wash area to clean up. Their positions were immediately filled by the next waiting participant who set about relieving their own needs with gusto.

I suppose this continued for the next half an hour until the imposing figure of Tyler made his entrance. His booming voice stilled the others into silence when he announced that it was his turn to partake of Jarek's love tunnel, the guys stepped aside including the inmate who was already inside Jarek! Tyler was clearly turned on by the whole scene for his enormous cock was rock hard and standing upright. Standing behind Jarek he pulled his cheeks apart and from where I was standing I could see that his hole was getting very loose and sloppy from all the fucking it had received and jism was slowly dripping from his slightly puffy lips. Satisfied with what he saw Tyler aimed his cock at the hole and in one smooth thrust expertly inserted it halfway in. Jarek groaned in reaction and tried without success (because Tyler was holding him securely by the hips) to move away in an attempt to avoid the impalement. Then adjusting his position slightly Tyler continued to slowly push until his cock was fully buried up to the hilt. Remaining stationery for a moment he allowed Jarek to get accustomed to him before he started the fucking in earnest, slowly at first but gathering momentum all the time until he was really hammering away. On and on he went, Jarek was moaning in time to the thrusts, whether it was from pleasure or pain was impossible to tell but it didn't matter he was getting fucked and that was that. With a loud cry Tyler bucked and shuddered before collapsing on top of Jarek having shot load after load of jism deep inside him. When he pulled out there was a squelchy plop and an audible gasp from the audience as the hole recently vacated seemed unable to close up, I could see deep inside him and now I understood the term "tunnel of love".

If I had thought that was horny what followed blew my mind! Following Tyler was Gus, as cocky as ever; he knelt down, facing towards us, between Jarek's legs and took his semi-flaccid cock in his mouth and started to give him an expert blow job. Then quite casually he reached up with one hand exploring along his crack until his fingers found the sloppy hole, finding their target they honed in on it. The finger tips disappeared straight away and then up to the second knuckle with ease. Four fingers were now fully inserted up to the palm and Gus used them to fuck Jarek in time to the blowjob. Almost imperceptibly he started to tuck his thumb in behind the fingers (I knew what was coming next) without missing a stroke. Any resistance from Jarek's ring was disappearing fast and before we knew it Gus had inserted his whole hand and was gently fist fucking the hole. Abruptly a muffled cry (due to a cock already being in his mouth) came from Jarek and Gus enthusiastically swallowed the whole load of jism, except for a small trickle from the side of his lips. When Gus had finished sucking him dry and the cock had shrivelled to its normal state he gently withdrew his fist and took his time massaging and stroking the stretched anal ring until it had almost closed up again. Standing up he bowed to the stunned audience before slapping Jarek's arse and disappearing into the wash area.

There was just half an hour left of his punishment period and the tempo slowed considerably, Jarek gave a further four blow jobs and received one more fisting – from me! I just couldn't resist it. Liam's words about me being a natural fister were echoing in my ears. As my hand slipped inside his rectum, I savoured the resistance giving way and the smooth slide into the enveloping silky warmth. I gave him a firm but steady fisting to loosen him up, then, a thought occurred to me which I brought to life immediately. Stepping up close using my free hand I guided my cock in beside my wrist and as it slid in I held it in my hand before fucking him until I orgasmed. After I had withdrawn and cleaned myself up it was time to release Jarek from the stocks and let him wash himself off in the showers. He walked away very stiffly in a slight daze, after all two hours is a long time to be bent over in the stocks especially when getting stuffed from both ends! Mick and I were still clearing up when he returned from the showers looking a lot fresher than before but he was unable to meet our gaze and quickly disappeared back to his cell.

Finally my shift was over and I was able to make my way home to a readymade meal care of my microwave and a cold can of beer from the fridge in front of the TV. Thinking back over the last month's events all I can think of is how much I have enjoyed and learned from the journey I have been on. I can't help but wonder what next month will bring!

THURSDAY 1ST APRIL

A new month has begun and the Easter holidays lay ahead of me, a whole four days of freedom from the usual routine of work. On the one hand I'm lucky because I'm one of the few Prison Officers who has been granted the whole weekend off (favouritism I have heard muttered by some), on the other hand having four days off with nothing planned seems a waste of time when I could be earning double time. But as they say all work and no play makes Sam a dull guy so I will just have to find something to occupy my time, starting with housework and ironing tonight so I don't have that chore hanging over me for the rest of the weekend!

FRIDAY 2ND APRIL

Well diary, I have had a more interesting day today than I thought I would, or perhaps curious would be a better term.

This morning first thing I jumped into the car and paid a visit to the local supermarket and stocked up with some groceries, I don't know if I'm being paranoid but I am sure that I caught more than one person giving me the eye up. It got to the point that I stopped and checked my reflection out in the shop window. No, everything seemed in order, just my usual jeans, trainers and tight fitting muscle top. Okay, I know that my physique has improved since I started at the prison but I didn't think it was that much improved! The other thing which has occurred to me is that perhaps I am developing what I have heard called 'gaydar', that is being able to sense when another guy is interested in you.

When I was bent over one of the freezers trying to decide which pizza to have tonight, something made me look up and straight into the eyes of a cute looking shop worker, he must have been all of eighteen with big blue eyes and a thick mop of blonde hair. He flushed bright red having been caught in the act of staring at me and gave me a weak smile in an attempt to cover up his embarrassment. I winked in response and gave him a broad grin before looking back at the pizzas on offer. When I had made my choice and looked up again, the young lad had disappeared. Feeling a little disappointed I silently chided myself because he was far too young for me – I was old enough to be his father!

Then as I was queuing up at the checkouts, I was lost in idle thought when something caught my eye and as I looked over to the next till a guy, perhaps in his thirties gave me a sly smile before quickly looking away as his wife looked up from what she was doing and spoke to him. I was so surprised I failed to respond and stood there in a daze, until a loud cough behind me brought me back to reality and I started to unpack my shopping onto the conveyor belt. Finally the checkout girl was all touchy feely and overly friendly. Enough was enough! I had to get out of there quick before anything else happened.....

Back home, having unpacked and made myself some lunch I felt bored and lonely. Refusing to give into this self-defeating frame of mind I decided it was time for some company, and I knew just the place for it – the leisure centre. It's always guaranteed to be busy; I could get some exercise and was bound to bump into someone I know. Which is exactly what happened and led to an interesting meeting with Jason (Aaron's best friend, who went to the stag do).

I paid the entrance fee and made my way to the male changing rooms as normal, found the locker I had been allocated and followed the routine I always do. Call me OCD if you like but I have always done it since being in the army. I opened the locker; then removed my trainers and socks before stuffing the socks into the trainers and then into the locker; off came my jeans to be folded neatly and placed on top of the trainers; next my muscle top and finally my boxer shorts, again both were neatly folded and placed into the locker. Standing there comfortably naked I retrieved my towel and swimming trunks, placed them on the bench, then put my sports bag into the locker, spun the combination lock and turned back towards the bench. As I reached for my trunks I heard my name called and looked over in the direction of the voice. Walking briskly towards me was Jason with a Cheshire cat smile on his face; reaching me he dumped his bag on the bench, gave me a great big bear hug and a hearty slap on the back, seemingly oblivious to my state of undress.
I coughed loudly to draw his attention to the situation as a couple of guys were beginning to stare and I was feeling distinctly uncomfortable.

"Sorry Sam!" Jason chuckled stepping back, "I didn't mean to embarrass you but I am just so pleased to see you. I've been meaning to catch up with you ever since Aaron's stag do but I've lost your mobile number and felt a little awkward asking the other guys for it again."

As I listened to him I donned my swimming trunks and slung my towel over my shoulder before replying "I didn't know you had my number in the first place, not that I mind you having it, I'll give it to you now if you wish."

"Oh that would be great! Let me just get a pen out of my bag and I'll make a note of it" he replied doing exactly that.

Closing my eyes to aid concentration I gave him my mobile number and got him to repeat it back to me for accuracy, only then did I ask him what he was doing here.

"I have been putting so much weight on recently that Aaron and his dad has started to pull my leg about me getting fat and no longer being a babe magnet. They suggested that I follow your example by getting out and exercising more, which is why I am here. I thought I would start off gently by doing some swimming, gain a bit of confidence and see if there's anyone who can give me some guidance on doing things the right way. That's why I'm glad to have bumped into you. You're exactly the right guy for the job, that is, if you don't mind....."

"Well, I'm flattered naturally, that you feel I'm the man for the job" I replied, a little surprised by what I had just heard "but I must warn you that I'm only an amateur and not qualified as a sports physiotherapist. I can tell you what's worked for me and what hasn't; then the rest will be up to you. Anyway, you don't look overweight to me."

"Oh I am, believe me" Jason retorted with a frown. "You'll see in a moment."

Without further ado he removed his Jacket, slung it on the bench and then started to remove his jumper.

"Before you go any further Jason, have you located your locker yet?" I asked with an amused smile.

"Oh shit, no I haven't! Thanks Sam. See I know I'm going to be in good hands..... Now where is it? Ah there it is. That's handy; it's only a couple away from yours."

Having opened the locker Jason threw in his jacket and jumper before his shoes, socks and jeans joined them. He paused momentarily standing in just his T-shirt and pants, then apparently having summoned up the courage he removed his shirt, threw it in the locker before slowly peeling down his pants and stepping out of them. As he stood up straight again his huge cock swung pendulously from side to side above his hairy balls.

I could not help myself but to whistle appreciatively and mutter "You sure are a big boy!"

"I know, this is exactly what I meant" Jason responded prodding and poking at his developing beer belly.

I chuckled before saying "Okay your stomach could do with a little toning up but that wasn't what I was referring too...."

By now Jason had put on his Speedos but his ample package was still very evident for all to see (should they wish to look), he glanced over to me with a strange expression on his face before it lifted to be replaced by a smile and a slightly camp "All the girls say that!"

In a more serious tone he asked me to have a look at him and let him know what parts of his body I thought he needed to pay attention to and then did a slow pirouette with his arms lifted slightly. I deliberately took in every part of his body; his muscled hairy legs, slightly prominent beer belly, his hairy chest and arms were decently proportioned, his bum was masculine in it's squareness as was his jaw line. He wasn't classically handsome but all the same was very pleasing to the eye and was sporting a trendy haircut and razor thin goatee and beard. I was slightly envious of the fact that he could sport that style of beard due to the blackness of his hair whereas my hair had always been too pale a brown to carry off such styling, made all the worse by the increasingly common white hairs.

"All in all" I announced "you're not in bad shape, you've just got to lose that tummy of yours. Cutting out the beers and junk food along with some decent exercise should sort out in no time. Now shall we go for a swim before we get done for loitering?"

We spent the next hour in the main pool alternating between serious length swimming and getting our wind back breaks treading water and making small talk. By the end of the hour we were both exhausted and glad to stand for a few minutes under the invigorating hot showers. While we were towelling ourselves dry and dressing once more we talked more about the exercises he should be doing on his own.

"Well, what are you doing tomorrow for exercise?" Jason asked casually.

"Oh, I shall probably do a couple of laps of gently jogging around the park, but that will be all. Why? Would you care to join me?" I replied just as casually.

"Would you mind? I haven't done any jogging for years. Well not since school at least."

"Of course I don't mind. You know where I live, just call round, say 10.30am and I'll break you in gently, so to speak" I said with a smile.

"You're on! See you tomorrow then." Jason said clapping me on the shoulder and headed for the car park.

I went in the opposite direction having walked to the leisure centre from home. Well, I only live a mile and a half from there; it seems crazy to drive that short distance to a place you're trying to get fit in! Twenty minutes later and I was back home again with my mind focused on locating all of the men's fitness magazines and books I had stashed around the flat and never quite got round to reading. If I am going to be a fitness coach I must at least sound like I know what I am talking about!

So my Friday night has not resulted in me being down the pub as usual talking to Tom and Mike in the Kings Head over a pint or two of beer, instead I have had my face stuck in umpteen magazines and books formulating a fitness routine for Jason.

SATURDAY 3RD APRIL

Woke this morning bright and early with the sun streaming in through a chink in my curtains, lay there listening for a few minutes to the cheeping of a couple of sparrows on my bedroom window ledge before passing traffic drowned them out. Oh the joys of living in central London I thought to myself, one day I hope to be able to move out into the suburbs and away from the traffic and pollution. In the meantime I am enjoying the facilities and convenience that living here offers, who knows one day....

Having got up early I had time to enjoy a leisurely breakfast and pop down to the newsagents to fetch the daily newspaper. I was still reading it when there was a ring on the doorbell, leaving the paper open where it lay (to make it look more casual) I answered the door to a bright eyed and bushy tailed Jason, wearing jogging bottoms and sweatshirt, clearly raring to go.

"Come in, come in young man" I greeted him with a smile.

"Morning Sam, I hope I'm not too early."

"No you're right on time, I'm actually running a little behind time, so please make yourself comfortable while I just get my running gear on" I said as I wandered into my bedroom and retrieved a pair of shorts and a muscle top from my chest of drawers. I quickly shucked my tracksuit bottoms and T-shirt, throwing them on the bed and was in the middle of putting the muscle top on over my head when I heard Jason's voice close behind me asking if he could use the toilet before we go for our run.

Not turning round I said "Sure, of course you can. It's the door straight in front of you."

"Thanks." He replied.

Strange I thought; I'm sure he's been here before so he should know where the toilet is. Shrugging my shoulders I thought no more of it. I quickly pulled on my shorts and was tying up the laces of my running shoes when Jason returned. Without further ado we made our way out of the block of flats and over to the park where our run would start in earnest.

Poor old (or rather that should be 'young') Jason, he was clearly out of shape and by the second lap of the park he was flagging. I looked over at him, he was red faced, sweat was pouring down his face and his gelled crest was distinctly wilted, his shirt looked like it had been in a wet T-shirt contest. Finally the ordeal was over for him as we reached the park gates and I told him he could stop and take a breather. His expression was a picture, there he was totally exhausted and here was I nearly twice his age scarcely panting.

"Let's go home Jason, you've earned a rest, how about you have a hot shower when we get back to sooth your tired muscles before we look at some exercises you can do before next weekend." I said as briskly as possible.

Jason didn't have the energy to say anything; he simply nodded, stood up straight and tried to match my pace as we made our way back to the flats.

In the bathroom I showed him how to operate the shower, where the soap, towels etc were kept and left him in peace while I laid out the light lunch I had prepared earlier on the kitchen table. I was just pouring the fruit juices out when I heard the noise of gently padding feet behind me, turning round I saw the naked frame of Jason walking in with just a towel wrapped round his waist, his lunchbox was making a distinctive bulge at the front.

"Does that feel better?" I asked, doing my best to keep my eyes off his crotch.

"Yes thanks, I almost feel ready to go again!"

"No I don't think so, one run per day is quite sufficient that is unless you wish to injure yourself. I thought we would have a light lunch and then I will show you those exercises before you leave." I said as I handed him a glass of apple juice.

"Sure, sounds good to me" he replied, making himself comfortable at the table and quickly started tucking into the salad and French bread.

When we'd eaten sufficiently I ran through the sit ups, press ups, squats and stretching exercises demonstrating each one to him. As I was showing him each one I got the distinct feeling his mind was elsewhere and asked him if this was the case. A little embarrassed he admitted he was a little distracted but wouldn't divulge any further information so I didn't press him as it was none of my business.

"Okay, let's see how much you have taken on board what I have said. Please join me down on the floor and I want you to do some press ups." I said in the best coach voice I could muster.

"I know how to do that." He responded.

"You might think you do but I want to be sure that you are doing it correctly."

With a sigh he laid down on the floor, feet towards me, head away and started to do a couple of press ups.

"No you're doing it wrong" I admonished him. "Your feet should be a foot apart to give yourself greater stability and place less strain on your wrists. Try it again please."

He did as requested and started once again, this time I had a good view between his legs and could see his balls swinging gently with each movement. I could just make out his cockhead hanging just below his balls. My cock twitched a little at the sight.

"Okay, that's fine. Now let's see you do some sit ups. I will hold your feet to provide you with stability, say do five for me."

Not saying anything, he simply sat in front of me with his feet flat on the floor; knees bent and then lay back on the floor with his hands behind his head. If I thought the previous view was good, then this one was fantastic! Jason's towel had slipped under gravity down from his knees to around his waist fully exposing his cock, balls and arse crack. I couldn't help but lick my lips in response. As he carried out the sit ups he kept his eyes focused on the wall behind my head, only when did he complete all five sit ups did he look down and realised that his towel had slipped exposing his assets.

"Sorry Sam, I didn't mean to give you an eyeful! It's my fault I should have got properly dressed and not been lazy by keeping just this towel on. I hope I didn't offend you in any way." He said as he quickly stood up and rearranged the towel to cover himself once more.

"Hell no!" I replied "I've seen it all before, both in the army and more recently in the prison service. Nakedness has never bothered me, don't give it another thought. I often walk round here naked when I'm alone, though not so often when I'm in company!"

"Cool! It's just that some people are bit stuffy when it comes to men's bits, for example my girlfriend. How she hates the sight of my bits on display except when we're having sex, says they're disgusting. Me, I can't see what's wrong with them personally."

"No, I can't say that they look wrong in anyway. Certainly nothing to be ashamed of, and if I remember correctly you didn't seem too averse to taking your kit off during the stag do!" I remarked with a chuckle.

"True. But it's amazing what a little bit of alcohol in your system can do for your courage! I hope you don't mind Sam but I really must be going now. It's nearly 2pm and I said I'd meet Kirsty at 2.30pm, if I'm not careful I'm going to be late and she doesn't like to be kept waiting."

"That's fine with me. I think to be honest we're just about done; I can see that you know what you're doing. Run along and get dressed, I don't want you to get into trouble on my part. Regarding ongoing training, how about we go swimming on Sundays and do jogging on Mondays and Thursdays. How does that sound?" I asked. "That way you get a couple of days rest in between each activity."

"You're the fitness boss. I'll do whatever you recommend." Jason replied as he hurriedly put on his rather damp and sweaty running gear.

"Next time we go running it might be worth bringing a change of clothing; that way you won't have to put on those rank sweaty clothes afterwards." I suggested.

"Good idea, I should have thought about that. Right oh, will do, I'll see you on Monday then? Will it be okay if I bring Aaron with me next time? It's just that he said if everything went well he would like to join us."

"Sure, more the merrier" I replied and shut the front door behind him.

MONDAY 5TH APRIL

Dear diary, sorry about not writing an entry yesterday but nothing happened. Literally! It pissed down with rain all day, spent most of the day lounging around on the internet and watching old movies on the TV. Waste of a day, I guess but I enjoyed it in a way.....

Back to today, went for our planned jog round the park with Jason and Aaron. This time Jason was more prepared, they both had a change of clothing and like me they wore shorts and muscle vests for coolness. To be frank neither were particularly fit and this time they were exhausted after one lap, so we had a five minute break slowly walking before picking up the pace again. The dynamics with the three of us was different and I felt more like a father out with his two sons; slightly distanced as the two guys are such close mates.

Back at my flat we took it in turns to have showers. Jason went first, then Aaron and finally me. Jason, as ever took the lead by returning from the shower wearing just his towel as he had on Saturday. Aaron looked slightly surprised and looked at me in askance.

"It's fine by me, as I've already told Jason I run a relaxed house here so wear what you please or not as the case may be. Just do whatever you feel comfortable with" I said.

"You're cooler than dad you know." Aaron called out on the way to the bathroom.

"Really? I always thought Tom was a laid back guy." I said to Jason who by now was sprawled out in my arm chair.

He must be comfortable in my presence I thought to myself because the position he has assumed leaves him totally open to view and he must know this. While the towel was still wrapped round his waist, one leg was draped over an arm and the other was lying straight ahead. His balls hung low almost touching the seat with his cock draped over one thigh held in place by the towel.

"He is, except when it comes to matters of the human body or sex, then he gets all prudish big time" he replied.

"Oh ok." Was all I said as I distracted myself with preparing lunch and drinks.

By the time I had finished laying up the table Aaron had returned wearing a towel wrapped tightly round his waist and walked over to the window commenting on the views I have from the flat.

"As you're back now, I'm just going to have my shower. I'll be back in five."

Nearer ten minutes later I walked back into the room feeling refreshed and a lot more fragrant! Deciding to be one of the lads I also wore just a towel, after all I have to live up to the rules I had set out.

Sitting round the table, lunch was a relaxed affair, the main topic of conversation being Aaron's wedding, honeymoon and how they had been getting since their baby had been born two weeks earlier than expected. I wondered if Aaron's keenness for the keep fit was to get some 'me time' away from mum and baby. I kept this thought firmly to myself.

Two hours later I had my flat back to myself having arranged to meet them on Thursday evening for the next jogging session. I spent the rest of the day trying to get the image of Jason sprawled out in my chair out of my mind, it was a task I found very difficult!

TUESDAY 6TH APRIL

First day back on the shop floor, so to speak, and it was all systems go from beginning to end. As ever we did hand over first catching up on events over the bank holiday weekend. It seems that on the whole the prison was quiet with the inmates being calmer; it might just be something to do with the fact that a large number of them had shot their loads either inside Jarek or over the shower floor. The only person who hadn't calmed down was Jarek, after spending most of Friday and Saturday inside his cell he had finally surfaced and kept asking when I was back on duty.

Despite being offered assistance by the other prison officers he wouldn't talk to them, insisting that he only wanted to talk to me. Flattering I'm sure, but I was a little apprehensive about what a previously angry young man wanted to say to me who's just been publicly fucked and fisted for two hours. Well he would just have to wait until the prison wing rounds had been completed.

Finally mid-morning I walked onto E-Wing with George and we went from cell to cell checking in on the inmates, I didn't see any sign of Jarek until I walked into his cell. He was lying sprawled out on his bed, naked obviously because this was now his permanent state of affairs, reading a girly magazine. He was surprised by our sudden arrival and looked distinctly uncomfortable.

"Come on Jarek, look lively" George boomed out "you know you have to stand to attention when your room is being checked."

"Er, do I have to Sir?" Jarek responded, flushed with embarrassment.

"Yes" was our simple answer.

Reluctantly he closed his magazine, climbed off his bed and stood up straight. The reason for his reluctance was obvious; he had a hard on which he was doing his best to cover up with his hands. Being the considerate people we are we chose to ignore this fact and proceeded to inspect his room. Once we were finished I turned to Jarek and asked him what he wanted to talk to me about.

"It's embarrassing Sir, is there anywhere I can talk to you in private?" Jarek asked.

"What's wrong with talking here?" I responded.

"Well, I need your advice and I want to show you something of a personal nature. You've been straight talking with me and I will trust what you say."

"Okay, let me finish the morning rounds, I'll then be back and we can talk in private in one of the interview rooms."

"Thanks Sir"

With that George and I resumed our rounds which we completed without further incident. Before I collected Jarek I cleared it with Max to make sure that it was okay to use one of the medical interview rooms. His response was positive and appeared pleased that I had gained the confidence of a previously troublesome inmate, I was free to use any room that Richard wasn't planning to use.

With the formalities over with I went over to E-Wing and escorted Jarek back to the main building and into one of the spare interview rooms. My impression of him was although he was still clearly a force to be reckoned with judging by the other inmates' reactions, the angry fire burning in his eyes I had seen previously had gone. In its place was a concerned expression and just possibly a little bit of maturity.

Closing the door behind me I gestured for him to sit on the examination couch while I pulled up a chair and sat down opposite him assuming as relaxed a posture as possible.

"Right Jarek, how can I help you?"

Jarek made no immediate reply. He sat on the edge of the couch, legs slightly spread with his hands gripping his knees and feet gently swinging backwards and forwards. He studied his feet intently for a minute or two before looking up at me.

"I've been doing a lot of thinking over the last few days, okay since my night in the stocks, and I have some questions I want answers to but I don't know where to look for them or who to ask."

"Well" I answered slowly. "How about asking me any question you might have. If I have the answer I will be honest with you, if not then I will investigate and come back to you. How does that sound?"

"Okay, I guess. The first question I have is; my girlfriend, Marita, has a visiting order and wants to see me but how can I let her see me like this? She will want to know why I'm naked while the other inmates are clothed. What am I supposed to tell her and how far do I go with the explanation?"

"I think you will find that when members of the public visit you will be provided with suitable clothing. In fact I am sure management have bought in specially designed boiler suits for inmates who have been permanently prohibited from having personal possessions. That way she'll be none the wiser and you won't have to tell her anything, unless you want to that is." I advised him.

"In what way are they special?"

"They are all in one and don't have any pockets into which items can be smuggled, if you catch my drift."

"Yeah yeah" Jarek sighed. "My next question is, after my night in the stocks, is that quits? When do I get my clothes back?"

"That's an easy question Jarek. You won't be getting your clothing back until the end of your prison sentence. You know from the rules. You lost the right to have clothing after your second infringement; you went on to commit two other infringements resulting in the stocks. The only time you will have any clothing will be for visitors."

"Mmm, shit. I thought that might be the answer." Jarek said scowling.

"How have you adjusted to being naked?" I asked, trying to get him to open up and express his inner feelings.

"At first I hated it, found it degrading and felt that everyone was laughing at me. It made me feel very angry and I wanted to fight anyone who reacted in any way to my nakedness. It is only during this weekend I have come to realise that it is only myself I have to blame for my predicament. I was given enough warnings and I chose to ignore them in my pride and bravado. Having been in the stocks and endured what I had to endure, my nakedness seems less significant now and something I am beginning to accept. To be honest I have other things on my mind."

"What things are those?" I asked becoming curious as to what those might be.

"During Thursday and Friday last week my arse and throat were very painful, I didn't want to eat or use the toilet it was that bad."

"Did you notice any bleeding?" I was now getting concerned.

"Not that I saw, if I had I would have called for the doctor straight away I can tell you. But by Saturday things were getting back to normal and Sunday everything was fine except for one thing."

"And what is that?"

"My turds are now like horse dollops and I'm sure my arsehole is bigger than it was before. I want you to check it for me to make sure that it is still in working order. I know I got fucked up the arse that night and I know some of the guys are pretty big but I've never heard of a guy's arse stretching so much just from being fucked!"

Well I had to smile to myself, he didn't have a clue that he had been fisted at all, no wonder he was surprised by the looseness of his hole!

"Regarding the size of your turds, it's probably a side effect of the stretching your rectum and anus recently experienced. As long as there's no bleeding when you go to the toilet then I wouldn't worry about it, you may find that they will shrink in size as your hole tightens up again. Have you tried pelvic floor exercises?" I asked trying to maintain a serious and concerned demeanour.

"I don't even know what they are" he replied, "nor do I know if my hole's working properly. Will you check it out for me please?"

"If that's what you want, then sure. Okay, let's do it. If you would please climb up on the couch, get on all fours with your head resting on your hands. While you do that I will get prepared."

"Yes Sir" was all he said in response.

Turning round I opened desk drawer and retrieved a box of latex gloves and a small can of Crisco. Slipping on a pair of gloves I opened the can of Crisco and turned back towards the couch to find that Jarek had obeyed my instructions and assumed the required position.

"Okay Jarek, I would like you to help me here. Please reach behind you and using both hands pull your cheeks apart, you may need to spread your legs a little to stabilise your position. It will make it easier for me to assess your hole."

Jarek made no comment but did as he was asked. It was a sight to behold, he arse cheeks glowed white under the harsh lighting. His balls swung freely and like his crack were virtually hairless. His cock was flaccid and diminutive in size; clearly he wasn't finding the situation erotic. I stepped up to the couch and took a closer look at his anus.

It didn't take an expert to see that it had seen a lot of action! The hole was fully closed but the puckered skin was distinctly pink and enlarged.

I took a small glob of Crisco and smeared it all round the rim, already I could feel that the muscle tone was laxer than would normally be expected.

"Please try and relax, I'm about to assess your anus's elasticity. I will be as gentle as I can, let me know if it gets painful or uncomfortable." I said as I started to insert my index finger, up to the first knuckle to start off with.

Getting no response from Jarek or resistance from his ring I slowly and gently inserted the whole finger until it could go no further.

"How does that feel? Any discomfort?" I asked.

"Fine, no discomfort at all" came the calm reply.

I withdrew my finger and then introduced a second finger and inserted both fully with virtually no resistance; however I did notice he shifted his weight a little. Again I asked the same question and got the same answer, so I withdrew the two fingers and introduced a third having applied some more Crisco to his slightly open hole. As I pushed the three fingers in up to the hilt I saw him shift around again, not saying anything with my free hand I felt between his legs and found that his balls had tightened and his cock was now a raging hard on! Deciding he was enjoying it so far I took it to the next level. Again I withdrew the three fingers and started to introduce the fourth.

As a method of distraction I said "I am very impressed with you Jarek, your whole attitude turnaround is remarkable considering what you were like when we had our first encounter in the Governor's office." All the time I was slowly pushing the fingers in deeper and deeper.

"What do you mean?" Came a slightly breathless reply.

"Well, for a start you were very unhappy with the thought of another man simply touching you let alone having anything as intrusive as this done. Today you seem very relaxed and are taking it in your stride. What's brought about this change in you?"

By now all four fingers were in as far they could go, I let them rest there for a minute so he could adjust to the intrusion.

"I dunno really. As you say at the beginning I found the very idea repulsive and against everything I have ever been taught. But having spoken to other guys and experienced things I didn't think possible my viewpoint has slowly shifted. What has surprised me the most is that some on the experiences are pleasurable, even this one I guess. Does this make me gay? Because I still fancy and miss Marita like crazy."

I withdrew the fingers and noted that the hole was slow to close; I smeared some more Crisco round the hole and plenty on the whole of my fist up to the wrist. In for a penny, in for a pound I thought to myself. I coned my fingers and thumb then gently started to push them inside. Again to keep up the distraction I hesitated as the fingers started to enter his hole before replying.

"I'm glad you're finding this pleasurable and I am close to letting you know the findings of my assessment. No, I don't think it makes you gay at all, simply more in tune with your body. I think it's important that you keep Marita close to your heart because you will need her when you are released. Now, tell me, are you feeling any discomfort?"

By now my hand was in up to the widest part of the hand, I stopped pushing while I awaited his answer and again to allow for its accommodation.

"Umm, only a little, a bit like near the end of my time in the stocks. It doesn't hurt, I just feel full. Yeah that's it, like when you're bursting for a dump. I think I'm about to shoot my load any time soon. How many fingers have you got inside? I've lost count while we've been talking."

As he asked this question, his ring gave up its slight resistance and the whole of my hand slid smoothly inside until it was buried up to the wrist.

"Aaaaaargh! I'm cumming! Eeeeeergh!"

Jarek's cock shot three large globs of spunk over the couch, all the time his ring spasmed and gripped my wrist tightly. His body shook several times and then he slumped forward until he was lying flat on the couch. As my wrist was still being firmly gripped I had no choice but to go with him, finally the anal spasming eased off and so did his grip. Pulling my hand out slowly it exited with a quiet plop leaving a ruined hole behind. I unpeeled the gloves and threw them into the bin and wiped my wrists clean of a little bit Crisco and juice, then sat back down in the chair to wait for Jarek to come round from his dazed state.

After a minute or two he lifted his head and looked at me with slightly glazed eyes.

"Jeez, I haven't experienced an orgasm like that since the night in the stocks! Sorry about the mess Sir. Have you come to a conclusion about my hole and exactly how many fingers did you have up me? Was it two or three?"

"Hey, don't worry about making a mess" I replied "the couch cover can be washed later. I'm glad you enjoyed the experience, like I said before it's a real turn around as far as I'm concerned. In answer to your question, yes I have the results of my assessment and what can be done about it. As to how many fingers I used, it was more than three; in fact I was able to insert the whole hand."

"What do you mean your whole hand? That's not possible! Are you really saying that you've been able to fist me? I've seen it done in a couple of blue movies but I always thought it was fake. Tell me you are kidding me, right?" Jarek fired at me all animated now.

"No I'm being completely serious. By the description you gave me towards the end of the assessment I strongly suspect that you were fisted during your time in the stocks, which is why your arse was so sore afterwards. Clearly no permanent damage has been done although there are obvious side effects which may be a good thing or not depending on your view point. There are a couple of exercises to tighten your anal ring if you wish or you can leave it as it is to allow easier entry in the future."

"I'm sorry Sir, but I really don't believe what you're saying is possible. It would surely have hurt me if you had; all I felt just now was a little discomfort but nothing more, then an incredible fullness before I orgasmed."

"Okay. I hear what you say but I have been honest with you. I'm going to ask you to do something, will you trust me? If you do as I say then you will have your proof."

"Yes Sir, of course I trust you."

"Right, get up on your knees facing away from me and put one of your hands behind your back." I instructed him.

Once he was in position I took hold of his hand and covered it liberally with Crisco, then brought his hand down to his crack, he had to twist slightly to do this but not very much.

"Next I want you to concentrate solely on the sensations received from your fingers, keep your anus relaxed at all times."

"Okay." Was all he said.

I coned his fingers for him and guided them towards his open hole and pushed them in until his first knuckles had disappeared.

"Now keep pushing your fingers in until you meet any resistance."

Looking at his hand I doubted if there would be any resistance as his hand was smaller than mine, sure enough, in less than a minute his hand had disappeared from sight up his rectum. He looked over his shoulder with a startled expression on his face, I noticed with a grin his other hand was at the front and was making jerking movements.

Within a few minutes his body was jerking and crying out he orgasmed for a second time. Once he had finished he pulled his hand out of his backside leaving a hole very slow to close. Grabbing a large wad of tissues I helped him clean himself all over until he was gleaming clean once more. His expression was hard to define; partly of satiation and partly of amazement.

"I believe you Sir, I apologise for having doubted you. Fuck, I can't believe how good that feels! I don't suppose there's any chance I could try it out on you is there?"

"In a word no, for several reasons; firstly, it wouldn't be ethical on a professional front. You came to me asking for advice and guidance, which I have given as your prison officer. To go along with your suggestion would cross the professional boundary and potentially cause both of us problems by blurring the basis of our relationship. Secondly, on a personal front, and this is to remain just between the two of us. I've only ever been fucked up the arse once and that was in the line of duty, so to speak." I replied a little gruffly.

"Sorry Sir, I didn't mean to speak out of turn, you don't have to give me an explanation after all I'm the inmate and you're the officer." Jarek said suddenly all petulant.

"Look there's no need to be like that. Personally I like you, but I think it's best to keep things simple and I am just being honest with you as I have always been throughout our interactions. Right back to business, now you know the reason for your hole's condition did you want to tighten it up or leave it be?" I asked.

"I think I'll leave it be for the time being if you don't mind, I can see that there may be some advantages to being able to accommodate large objects, at least I won't have to fear advances from any of the larger endowed prisoners!" he said with a chuckle before adding "Oh, and by the way it doesn't change how I feel about Marita you know."

"Of course not, now if that's everything I think it's time we got you back to your cell before they think you've done a runner."

With that I escorted him back to E-Wing and went for lunch, I was famished as well as parched (too much dribbling I think!). After lunch I submitted my report to Max detailing what had been said, what happened and the results before resuming my normal duties for the afternoon which passed without incident.

WEDNESDAY 7TH APRIL

Dear diary, another interesting day at the office and one that has given me much to think about! This morning I turned up for work as normal, made myself a coffee and checked my pigeon hole for mail. Normally it is empty but this morning there was an official looking envelope with just my name on it. Sitting down on a nearby chair I tore open the envelope to see a note from Liam asking me to see him immediately at the beginning of my next shift.

Having spoken to George and asked him to go on the morning prison rounds without me (showing him the note as I did so) I made my way up to the Governor's office and knocked on the door wondering what he wanted to see me about.

"Come in!" called the familiar voice of Liam.

As I walked in and smiled in his direction he gestured for me to sit down at the desk in front of him, I was a little surprised to find that there was only the two of us in the room with no sign of Max or Adrian. When I made a comment to this effect I was told that this was a confidential meeting and was to be kept secret until a definite outcome had been reached. I was intrigued by this statement and asked him to elaborate.

"Okay Sam, I will explain. Do you remember the post-punishment meeting we had with Tyler? You do? Good. Well I've been doing a lot of thinking since then and the report you submitted to Max yesterday crystallised the matter for me and I've decided to put my plans into action but I wanted to run them past you for your input. I have decided to create the role of 'Volunteer Punisher', one for each wing, they will be responsible for the implementation of inmate punishment under the new rules introduced in March under the close supervision of the Volunteer Co-ordinator. It will serve two purposes, firstly it will free up our own officers and secondly it will lock our tougher prisoners into a role which should restrain their more unruly tendencies."

"Right Sir, but where do I fit in your plans and why do you need my input?" I asked, still none the wiser.

"Well, I am seriously considering making you the Volunteer Co-ordinator. If you are interested in this role I will elaborate further, there's no pressure but I am very impressed with your attitude and popularity with the inmates. I believe you are an ideal candidate."

"Thank you, it's fair to say that I am interested but what is involved and will it affect my normal duties?" I replied deep in thought.

"Once I have assessed your training needs and brought you up to speed, then you will be responsible for the selection, training and supervision of the volunteer punishers. You will also be responsible for their punishment should they break the rules of their roles. As you are no doubt aware the prison philosophy is to lead by example, so we will expect you to do so too. Your behaviour must be exemplary while on duty and be able to perform all the tasks you expect the inmates to do. I have drawn up for your reference a manual outlining the volunteer role and the sexual activities they will have to be adept at. As to it affecting your normal routines it is impossible to say at this stage as we have no idea about the amount of time the role will require. This is something we can assess as we go but there's no need to worry, we have no intention of overloading you!"

"Sounds good to me, I'd love the opportunity to increase my experience and value to the prison service so please count me in. Is there any chance of seeing the training manual?"

Beaming broadly Liam reached behind him and pushed a posh looking presentation black folder with my name on it, I guess they had every intention of me taking on the role. I guess my ambition must be a little predictable?! Opening the front cover I scanned the introduction and turned to the volunteer role section and started reading avidly. From the corner of my eye I could see Liam watching me with a slight smile on his face, ignoring it I carried on reading. I was intrigued to read that the volunteer's uniform was to be simply a red beret and a leather belt worn around the waist to which attaches two small tubes, one of KY and the other Crisco. No other items of clothing are permitted.

Looking up I asked "Will I be expected to wear this uniform and what about the inmates who are not permanently naked?"

"Absolutely not, your uniform is that of a prison officer, that doesn't change in any way. As to the inmates, if they want to be volunteers then they have to wear the uniform, there will be no exceptions on this point. The uniform is designed to set them apart from the other inmates, be distinctive but at the same time not give them too much authority. After all compared to prison officers and the majority of inmates they will still be virtually naked."

I nodded my understanding and carried on reading through the manual, I was just getting to the section about sexual activities when the phone rang breaking my concentration. Liam spoke on the phone for a couple of minutes, hung up and announced that events had overtaken us

"Please feel free to take the manual and read it at your leisure when you get home, but please keep it to yourself as the contents are confidential. I have scheduled your assessment for first thing tomorrow morning, I will get Max to reschedule your morning timetable to accommodate the assessment. Okay then? I'll see you tomorrow morning in Richard's consultation room"

With that the meeting was clearly over so I stood up, shook Liam's hand and made my exit with my folder under my arm. I discreetly put the folder into the boot of my car for reading when I get home and went back to work.

This evening I made myself comfortable and read the manual from cover to cover. It was very well written and covered all the areas I could think of when it came to the volunteers and the role. However when it came to the sexual activities expected to be carried out I couldn't believe what I was reading, it was very graphic and left nothing to the imagination! I must admit I was sporting a hard on until I remembered that Liam had told me that I would be expected to be an expert in all areas of the manual both on the giving and receiving as I would be training the volunteers.

Ho hum! I could always back out but that would be the coward's way, after all I have been happy to undertake some of the activities listed in the manual so why not go with the flow and see how far I can stretch my boundaries? Not only that, my standing in the eyes of Liam and his team would be diminished and possibly jeopardise my shining new career. I went to bed wondering what tomorrow would bring.

THURSDAY 8TH APRIL

Oh diary, where do I begin? It has been one hell of a long and exhausting day. Starting at the beginning would be the best place I guess, here goes.

Got up early, showered and shaved in preparation for my assessment with Liam, had breakfast and got to work twenty minutes early. I clocked on, checked my pigeon hole and then made my way over to Richard's (the prison doctor) consultation room in the medical centre. Knocking on the door I waited for an answer as I could hear muted voices on the other side. Finally I heard a "come in" and I opened the door and went in to be greeted by Liam and Richard who were sitting round Richard's desk discussing what looked like a medical form much like we had completed for the inmates during the post punishment sessions.

"Ah do come in Sam, sit on the couch for a moment please while I explain what this morning's assessment is going to consist of" Liam said looking up from the paperwork.

I did as I was told without comment.

"Did you read the manual I gave you yesterday?" Liam asked.

"Yes Sir, from beginning to end. It certainly made for interesting reading and quite an eye opener!" I replied smiling.

"Indeed! I'm glad you liked it. Richard is going to do the usual medical checkups on you, we will then assess your body's capabilities so we can determine what exercises you will need to undertake in the following days. Okay so far? Good. As before all we ask is for you to trust us, follow instructions and know that whatever you are asked to do is for your own benefit. Right let's make a start. Firstly, would you please remove all of your clothing; you can place them on the chair in the corner and then stand facing us by the couch." Liam said with a deadpan face.

I remembered what he had been like during the interview process and how he could change from being affable one moment to very hard and stern in the blink of an eye. He wasn't the Governor of the prison for nothing! So without hesitation I disrobed as quickly and efficiently as possible, neatly placing my uniform and underwear where indicated. In less than two minutes I was standing in front of the couch, naked as the day that I was born with my hands behind my back (well I wanted to appear as relaxed as possible).

Richard then spent the next ten minutes going over my body with a fine tooth comb (I don't mean literally) noting down every statistic, measuring my heart rate, blood pressure, peak flow etc. You name it he checked it with great care and fed the results back to Liam who faithfully wrote them down on the form. When he was satisfied he left the room for a moment before returning with a familiar contraption. I gulped quietly to myself, it was the portable colonic irrigator and I had seen this device in operation only nine days ago on (or rather in) Jarek so I knew what was coming next!

"Sam" Richard said "please turn to face the couch and bend over resting your elbows on it, then spread your legs apart as far as is comfortable."

I did as I was told without saying anything, what was there to say?

Before long I felt greasy fingers feel between my cheeks and explore the length of my crack before finding their target, my anus. Then with one deft movement I felt a glob of grease being pushed inside and a couple of fingers massage my ring before they too were pushed up my rectum. I groaned in spite myself and was told by Liam to relax as much as possible, it would make it a lot easier for me if I did.

I was just getting used to the intrusion when I felt the fingers being removed to be replaced by the cold metal douching tube making my hole twitch in response. I looked over my shoulder out of curiosity; the tubing looked a lot smaller than it felt! Richard looked up at me and winked before returning his concentration to the task at hand. He switched the motor on and the irrigator started humming and vibrating, within seconds I felt warm water flow up into my rectum. Just when I started to feel full, the flow reversed and the water/faeces mixture left my body before the tube was pushed further up inside me, from the feel of it my inner ring had been breached and the tube travelled up into my bowels. It felt strange, not exactly painful but not comfortable either. I can only estimate that this went on for about fifteen minutes before Richard announced that the whole of the tubing had been inserted and no more faeces was coming out. He then slowly withdrew the tubing, I was relieved when it finally left and my hole was once more free to close up.

"Well done Sam, that went very smoothly" Liam announced, stepping over to me as Richard removed the machine from the room. "Now I would like you to climb up on the couch, lay on your back, bring your knees up to your chest and hold them in position using your arms."

"Yes Sir." I said and did as I was told.

"How are you feeling so far?" Liam asked as he snapped on a pair of latex gloves and started to grease them up.

"Okay, a little exposed. It's not the first time I've been in this position Sir, Richard can vouch for that." I said trying to sound as confident as possible and grinned in Richard's direction.

"He's right" Richard confirmed. "I had him like this just about a month ago in fact."

"Good. I am now going to assess your anal ring's tightness. You are of course familiar with the process because I know you have carried out those tests yourself on the inmates during the post-punishment assessments. I won't waste breath explaining them to you, I am going to get straight down to business, so nice steady breaths Sam, try to relax and enjoy the experience!" Liam said chuckling as he smoothly slid one finger up my exposed rectum.

I didn't actually find one finger uncomfortable; I guess being fucked by Sayeed put paid to being tight in a virginal way. I closed my eyes and practised relaxation methods in head which helped enormously when Liam inserted two fingers, there was distinctly less room available for them. He is skilled at his art I thought because I expected him to immediately try for three fingers but no, the two fingers slowly rotated and pushed in and out of my hole relaxing my ring remarkably quickly. As I felt three fingers attempt an entrance all thoughts of mantras and relaxation methods flew out of the window, I was now getting curious about the action going on at my backdoor. Lifting my head I looked between my knees to find that I couldn't see very much as my cock and balls were neatly blocking my view so I let my head fall back onto the couch. All the while those three fingers were rotating and pushing inwards but my ring was now at full stretch and I was groaning loudly in protest.

"How much have you got in there because I don't think I can take any more Sir" I asked with a slight trace of worry in my voice.

"I have currently got three fingers fully inserted but don't be alarmed I am stopping there, for today at least. We have a lot of work to do on your hole to get it in shape for the task ahead. There's just no way you can train the volunteers at present, this because you cannot demonstrate all of the techniques and you will risk serious injury if you attempt to. Starting from tomorrow morning, you are to come straight here at the beginning of each shift and we will start your training in earnest. Do you have any questions?" Liam asked as he withdrew his fingers, removed his gloves and wiped his hands on some tissue.

"No I don't think so." I replied quite truthfully.

"In that case, you're free to wipe yourself clean, get dressed and return to normal duties for the rest of the day. Don't forget Sam, none of this is to leak out yet." Liam announced all smiles now.

"Thank you, I won't forget." I replied rolling of the couch and walked rather stiffly over to the box of tissues to wipe my bum clean of all the grease before getting dressed as instructed.

Back of the prison wing George tried fishing to find out what I had been doing but despite his best attempts I managed to avoid any slip ups and evaded his traps. Eventually he gave up and the day carried on as normal. At long last my shift was over and all I wanted to do was to have a long hot shower and vegetate in front of the TV with a beer or two or maybe surf the internet for an hour or two.

It wasn't until I was halfway home that I remembered that I was supposed to be going jogging with Aaron and Jason, damn! Perhaps they might cancel and I will still get to have my evening on the couch after all. No such luck! At 7.00pm on the dot there was a ring on the bell and I opened the door to be greeted by two grinning young men telling me I must be getting past it as I took so long to answer the door. Past it indeed! I'll show them I thought to myself. While they sat in the living room watching the TV I quickly got changed into my running gear, then we were off for a deliberately brisk jog twice round the park. Mission accomplished, I had two exhausted young men panting like there was no tomorrow by the end of the jog, while I had hardly broken into sweat.

"Never mind boys" I said with just a very slight smug tone in my voice "I'll get you as fit as an old man like me before much longer."

"Ha ha ha" was all they could manage between gasps for breath. Walking back to my flat we had to stop a couple of times due to cramps and stitches but eventually we got there and their mood lifted a little. As I turned the key in my door they were back to being their joking selves.

I let them shower first like I did on Monday, this time Aaron went first as he had to get home early to baby sit. By the time Jason returned from his shower with as usual a towel wrapped round his waist, Aaron was dressed and flying out the door with a "See you guys on Sunday at the Leisure Centre, bye!"

I decided it was time for my shower and invited Jason to make himself comfortable while I took my shower, he accepted my invitation with a nod and sat down on the sofa with the TV remote control. Five minutes later I was in the shower soaped up and just about to rinse off when there was a knock on the bathroom door and before I could call out I heard the door open.

"Sorry Sam, I know you're having a shower and I really hate to invade your privacy but I'm bursting for a pee and I can't hold on any longer. Do you mind if I quickly use the loo? I won't be a minute." Jason said with a pleading tone in his voice.

What could I say? He was already in the room.

"Sure go ahead Jason. Just be careful where you look, you might see more than you want to!" I said trying to be as jovial as possible as I rinsed the soap out of my hair and eyes.

"Don't worry about me, I've seen loads of naked men, don't forget I've always played loads of team sports and you get to see plenty in the changing rooms afterwards."

I carried on rinsing off, I kept my eyes closed because I have this hatred of getting soap in my eyes (have had ever since I was a kid). By the time I turned the shower off I had expected the bathroom to be empty again, but no Jason was still very much present and was even offering me my towel! At a little loss for words I simply took the offered towel with a smile and started to dry myself off. There was little point in pretending modesty when he had just about seen everything there was to see. I couldn't help but have the feeling that he was enjoying seeing me naked so I asked him outright.

"Jason, do you always hang around in the bathroom when someone is having a shower?"

"Guilty your honour!" he said without hesitating. "Unlike Aaron's old man, mine is very liberal. Ever since a kid we, that is my dad and brothers, have always been very relaxed about our bodies, none of us think twice about walking into the bathroom when another is having a shower or using the loo. Okay with my mum it's a bit different but then she has her own en suite bathroom which makes things a lot easier. She's even used to us walking around the house naked, okay that's normally after a night on the tiles or during hot weather admittedly. I guess that is why I feel so comfortable here; you and dad are very similar in some ways. I hope I haven't made you feel uncomfortable by acting like this and please don't say anything about this to Aaron because he wouldn't understand and he'd only get the wrong end of the stick."

"Fair enough, I hear what you're saying, however I would prefer that you be upfront about things like this, people can get the wrong idea you know."

"Okay Sam, I hope I haven't offended you at all." Jason said contritely.

"Offended? No not at all. Surprised? Well, yes I guess so." I replied as casually as I could manage.

Well, I suppose I must be a bit of an exhibitionist (as if you hadn't guessed by now) and decided that I would play a game with Jason to see if my feelings were correct or if he was being totally genuine and innocent in his actions. Having towelled myself dry I sprayed some deodorant on and then walked out of the bathroom, still starkers heading towards the kitchen. Behind me I could hear Jason's footsteps following me not too far behind. Judging him to be visual range I opened the fridge door and reached in for a couple of cans of beer which were on the bottom shelf at the rear. In order to do this without crouching I had to spread my legs a little and bend at the waist, unfortunately this action exposed my hole and my tackle dangled nicely in the space between my thighs. I heard a stifled murmur so having hold on the cans I quickly stood upright and turned round in one smooth movement, catching Jason by surprise. There he stood, leaning against a work counter, feet crossed at the ankles, towel around his waist and just the beginnings of a tent pole!

"Would you like a beer? Can I offer you anything else?" I asked as innocently as possible.

"Anything else?" Jason replied, voice raised just a little. Something must have been lodged in it because he had to clear his throat before continuing "What do you have in mind?"

"Dunno really, I've got some chips in the freezer, or I can do us a salad. Actually, if you want to have a look in the cupboards and let me know if there's anything you fancy. Personally I'm going to have a salad as I have to watch my weight these days, I don't want to get belly or fat bum!" I patted both as I said this.

I sensed a deflation in him as he realised I wasn't suggesting what he thought I had. His towel still had a slight tent pole but he ignored it as he stood up straight and said "If a salad is good enough for you then it's good enough for me, after all it's me who needs to lose the weight. Look at you, there's not an ounce of fat on you anywhere!"

Smiling in acknowledgement I set about preparing a ham salad, not giving my nakedness another thought but making sure that I struck suggestive poses wherever possible. Jason didn't say anything untoward but his tent pole never went down one little bit. Once we had eaten we moved into the living room and watched the 10 O'clock news on ITV. I sprawled out on the sofa, making sure that my tackle was nicely displayed and Jason sat in the armchair, for some reason he seemed to have trouble concentrating because out of the corner of my eye I noticed he kept glancing in my direction. After the news he decided that he needed to be getting home and so retrieved his clothes and got dressed before bidding me good night. Poor boy he just couldn't help but look at my body one more time as he shut the door behind him, on the other side of the door I was grinning to myself knowing that my intuition had been right all along.

FRIDAY 9TH APRIL

Last day of the week thank God! My poor hole will be getting a rest for a couple of days, from prying fingers at least.

Richard and Liam were waiting for me in the consultation room as I arrived, and it was straight down to business. I was told to strip and assume the position for being cleaned out. I won't bore you with the details but it was exactly the same process as yesterday, although a little easier as I knew what to expect. The I was told to hop onto the couch but this time stay on all fours with my head on my hands (actually this position was identical to the one I got Jarek to assume last Tuesday).

It wasn't long before I felt latex covered fingers tickling my anus, making me wriggle a little before I felt the familiar sensation of cold Crisco being pushed into my hole and smeared all round it. First one finger went in, then two, all the time they were rotating and massaging the anal ring. Their movement was hypnotic and I was almost in a trance when I felt a third finger join them. I shifted my weight a little and was asked if I was okay, all I could do was respond with an affirmative grunt. The three fingers massaged their way for what seemed an eternity, my hole was getting looser and I was just beginning to feel restless when they were withdrawn and I was told to climb off the couch and stretch my body for a minute while Richard fetched the next piece of equipment. Did I say piece of equipment, more like a cross between an item of clothing and an instrument of torture!

As I was limbering up, touching my toes and then the ceiling etc, Richard walked back into the room carrying what looked for all the world like a leather thong. I said as much to him and he nodded in agreement.

"You are right Sam. That is exactly what it is, although not one you are able to buy in Marks & Spencer! I just have to connect the attachment and we're ready for your first fitting."

Fitting for what? I asked myself. I didn't have long to wait before I found out. Richard reached into a drawer and pulled out a box of what looked like black rubber objects, light bulb in shape with a metal screw thread at the neck end. There followed a brief discussion between Liam and Richard before an agreement was reached and the required object selected. Richard then picked up the throng and appeared to screw the "light bulb" onto the narrow part of the thong. Sometimes I can be so thick because I still didn't have a clue about what was coming next! When he was satisfied that all was in order he knelt down on the floor and asked me to stand in front of him facing away, which I did. He then asked me to step into the outstretched thong, which I did, only then did it occur to me what the bulb was for.

"Please pull the thong up to your waist and maintain that position." Richard instructed.

I did as I was told, then I felt a hand reach between my legs and take hold of the bulb before placing it against my anus and gently pushed it upwards. It felt bigger than it looked and was certainly bigger than the three fingers I had just accommodated.

"Spread your legs a little and push out as if you're about to drop a log." I heard Richard advise from behind me.

Well that paints and interesting picture I thought, but again did as I was told. All I can say is it worked, by spreading my legs I ended up squatting slightly and as I pushed out I felt Richard apply more pressure. In less than a minute the head of the bulb made its abrupt entrance into my rectum and my ring clamped shut tight around the neck.

"Aaaaaargh! That hurt!" I groaned.

"It's okay, your ring will calm down in a minute or two, it's just not used to stretching that extra bit" Liam assured me. "What we want you to do is to wear this thong when you go to bed each night, leave it in place all night and then remove it in the morning, okay?"

"Um, yes, okay I guess. Can I take it out now?"

"Is your anus still aching?" Richard asked.

"It is a little, I also feel very full like I need a crap badly." I admitted quite frankly.

"In that case you need to keep it in a little longer to allow your body to adjust to the intrusion. Please climb up on to the couch and lay down on your front as if you're going to have a massage, then RELAX." Liam instructed.

As I lay there relaxing doing my best to ignore the object within, I felt fingers slip underneath the thong and explore the boundary between the neck of the bulb and my ring. For a couple of minutes they massaged all the way round several times before withdrawing and grasping the neck. I then felt the bulb being gently tugged, then pushed in further, wiggled around and then the cycle started again.

"How does it feel now?" Liam asked as Richard continued his ministrations.

"Okay actually thanks, I no longer feel any discomfort at all which I am surprised about" I replied.

"Good, that is progress indeed. We're now going to take it out now so just relax and as before push out gently." Liam said.

It came out with a plop, slightly uncomfortable but certainly not painful like it had been going in. I was then told the training session was over, I could clean myself up and get dressed. As I was dressing Liam reminded me that I was to wear the thong & insert the bulb each night until the next training session on Monday. Then it was back to work, this time George didn't bother asking where I'd been as he knew I wouldn't say.

This evening just before bed time in the privacy of my own bathroom I tried to insert the bulb again. Although I was using the same grease that Richard had given me, this time it just seemed so much harder! No matter how I tried it just wouldn't pass my golden gates. I was getting very frustrated. Then I recalled the trick about squatting and pushing out at the same time, I am so glad no one was there to watch, it was all rather undignified. There I was squatting over the toilet with rubber bulb in one hand, the rest of the thong in the other hand to prevent it trailing in the water and me pretending to have a dump! Mind you, once again the trick worked, in it popped as quick as you like, but boy did I break out in a sweat and groan. It wasn't so much painful more like a throbbing toothache which slowly faded away. With the bulb inserted I stood up and pulled the thong on and made my way to bed. What I do in the name of duty.......

SATURDAY 10TH APRIL

Dear diary, if I am honest I thought today was going to be one of those unremarkable days but actually it ended on a high note so I guess I can't complain.

Woke up this morning after a good night's sleep, I had totally forgotten about the thong and bulb so was a little confused by the feeling as I normally sleep in bed with just a T-shirt on.

Went to the bathroom to remove it using the same trick as last night, I was surprised to find that my ring really didn't want to let go of it but after a bit of huffing and puffing it shot out along with a load of shit behind it – major yuk! Not the best sight or smell first thing in the morning; I retrieved it from the pan and gave it a very thorough washing along with my arse which felt strangely loose. It was, I could easily stick two fingers up inside with no problem or lube!

Having recovered from that shock I got dressed, shaved, had breakfast and went shopping for the mundane things in life like food and groceries. Then home to more mundane things like housework, washing and ironing.

By late afternoon I was totally bored so I called Tom to see what he was up to. He said he was glad that I had called because he and Chrissie were entertaining Mike, Aaron and his wife Sally, Jason and his girlfriend Kirsty this evening and if I could join them it would make the numbers even. I leapt at the chance to have dinner with my two best mates, they're always good for a laugh and Chrissie is lovely as is Sally. Kirsty I don't know but knowing Jason she is bound to be pretty and educated. We chit chatted for a while before Chrissie came on the line and begged me to come as we hadn't seen each other since the wedding, that was settled then!

Eight O'clock on the dot finds me knocking on the front door, which opens to reveal a laughing Chrissie (already half cut) holding a glass of red wine. She squeals in delight (that's Chrissie for you) and gives me a hearty one-handed hug before dragging me inside and shutting the door behind me. By the sound of it I'm the last to arrive as the house is buzzing and rather noisy. I tell Chrissie that she is one swell looking lady in that little black dress, which only causes her to giggle all the more and informs me that my smooth tongue and an eye for the ladies hasn't changed one little bit over the years (if only she knew the half of it!).

The sound of our voices in the hallway attracts attention and Tom sticks his head round the living room door, shouts hello and tells me to join the crew in the living room while the ladies finish preparing dinner. I do as instructed and as I walk into the room I am greeted by a united "hello" from Mike, Aaron and Jason all trying to offer me a can of beer or glass of wine. Holding my hands up in mock surrender I take a can of beer and proceed to make small talk with them until dinner is announced.

Dinner (or rather a three course banquet) was truly scrumptious, for starters it was homemade potato and leek soup with croutons. Main course was roast duck breast served with a medley of green vegetables, rosti potato cakes and a rich port sauce. For dessert homemade vanilla ice cream marbled with dark chocolate and a raspberry sauce followed by the obligatory coffee and mints.

It was during the coffee round that attention turned towards me and I received a good natured grilling over my current job as a prison officer. I talked about my role and the inmates I came into contact with (without revealing their real names) and some of the incidents that I had encountered. I successfully managed to avoid mentioning the sexual nature of some of my encounters and the new prison rules etc. I also managed to avoid any reference to the fact that I was no longer 100% heterosexual in my thoughts or activities. After what seemed like ages the attention turned to physical fitness and finally Kirsty came out of her shell. She thanked me for taking Jason under my wing, although he has only just started his training with me she has already noticed a difference. He has started to eat more healthy food, drink less alcohol (this night being an exception) and has been religiously doing all of the exercises I had given him. She thinks in the right light she can make out muscles underneath his belly! This brings resounding laughter from all except Jason who pulls a hurt expression before throwing me a sly wink. Then Sally nudges Aaron and makes it clear that he has no room to laugh as his middle is beginning to spread! Tom regains control of the situation by expressing the fact that really all the guys in the room (except me, of course) could do with a little more exercise and less girth round their middle, perhaps Mike and he could join the rest of us on Sunday at the swimming pool and see how they get on. I thought this was a splendid idea, but what about the ladies though? By the end of the conversation we were going to be a group of eight in the pool on Sunday, I wonder if we can get a group discount?

I finally staggered in through my front door at about 1.30am (technically Sunday I know but I don't count it being the next day until I've been to bed and woken up again) and was all set to collapse into bed when I saw the rubber bulb waiting on the side for me. I ummed and aahed over it, thought sod it one day won't make any difference, then changed my mind and picked it up on the way to the bathroom.

I sat on the toilet and emptied out as best I could then greased my arse up and also the bulb. Perhaps it was the alcohol in my system or my deadened sense of time but it (the bulb) seemed to disappear up inside me more easily and quickly than I expected. It did have one unexpected side effect, it gave me a raging hard on as it gently rubbed and banged against my prostate from the inside. There was no way I could go to bed like this, so with one hand feeling the neck of the bulb and my ring clamping hard round it, and the other wrapped round my cock I jacked myself of to a pretty earth shattering orgasm over the bathroom basin. Deciding now enough was enough I really needed to get to bed I washed myself off (and the basin), pulled up the thong and made my way to the bedroom where I quickly succumbed to oblivion.

SUNDAY 11TH APRIL

If I'm honest diary, today didn't actually start until about 11.45am when I woke with a jolt to the sound of my phone ringing about six inches from my ear – not a good way to start the day if you've got a little bit of a hangover....

I was just a little groggy when I picked up the phone and mumbled a hello down the line only to be greeted by the chirpy tones of Chrissie.

"Morning Sam! I just thought I'd give you a quick call to make sure you got home safely & that we're still on for the swimming session this afternoon. How's the head this morning?"

"Urrr morning Chrissie, I think, what time is it? Yeah got home okay and yes I'll be there at the leisure centre at 2pm as agreed! My head is still on my shoulders but feeling distinctly tender, I guess that will teach me to finish up that last bottle of red with you... how's your head by the way?" I asked as I came to, slowly.

"I'm just fine, thanks" Chrissie assured me "must get on, still got some clearing up to do before we meet up. As to the time, it's nearly mid-day. See you shortly, byeee!"

And then she was gone. Just as well she woke me up as I didn't have all that much time to get spruced up etc. First things first, into the bathroom to shower and remove a certain object. Crikey, my arse must be getting like a bucket because it's getting easier to take the bulb out, I didn't have to squat over the toilet and strain, I simply started to squat down and as I did so it popped right out with little discomfort. Curiosity got the better of me, I just had to assess the damage to my hole, not only did two finger slide right on up inside with no trouble but so did three! Progress indeed, I'm sure that Liam will be pleased. However I had no time to dwell, I quickly showered and shaved before getting dressed and packed my bag with my swimming gear.

I got to the leisure centre just before 2pm to find Jason and Kirsty waiting outside for me and the others; we made small talk and recounted the events and conversations from the previous evening. Throughout our conversation I monitored discreetly Jason's behaviour towards me, but he acted impeccably and not once did he act in anyway other than being Kirsty's partner, to my relief. Ten minutes later the others had arrived and we made our way into the changing rooms.

With the five of us (Tom, Mike, Aaron, Jason and myself) getting changed it was a very relaxed affair, even Tom seemed at ease and managed to joke around as we undressed and got into our swimming trunks. Privately I had to agree with Tom, both he and Mike were carrying a decent sized spare tyre round their middles. They will definitely need to go on a diet and exercise regime before they can join Aaron, Jason and myself jogging round the park on a Tuesday and Thursday. An hour later after a mixture of hard swimming and relaxed messing around in the water the eight of us are sitting round a table in the cafe overlooking the swimming pool. I was lost in thought when I felt a sharp nudge in my ribs bringing me back to the present.

"Well Sam, what do you say? Are you up for it?" Aaron asked with a slightly exasperated tone to his voice.

"Up for what?" I asked in all innocence.

"Having a last lad's night out this Friday before we cut out all the booze and grub as part of our diet and fitness regime" Tom explained.

"Yes, sounds good to me. Is it down the Kings Head shall we make it a special night and go into town?" I asked the group in general.

"Oh it's got to be town if it's going to be our last night out for a long time!" Jason cried out all enthusiastic like a big kid.

"That's decided then" Chrissie announced "girls we're going to paint the town red too! Kirsty and Sally, get your thinking caps on, we have four days to plan our night out."

Shortly afterwards the conversation naturally dried up and we went our separate ways.

MONDAY 12TH APRIL

Back to work already, oh how the weekends pass so quickly. The alarm clock went off and I swung into action on autopilot, even removing the rubber bulb from its night time lodging in my rectum had become part of my routine. I hate to admit it but I could insert and remove it with ease....

At the prison I made my way directly to Richard's consultation room and knocked on the door before walking in to find that Richard was alone. He greeted me with a warm smile and explained that it would just be the two of us to start off with as Liam had been called away at the last minute but he hoped to join us later. With the preamble over we got straight down to business, I stripped naked and Richard cleaned me out thoroughly using the portable colonic irrigator. Then having climbed onto the couch, kneeling on all fours in the usual position Richard examined my anus to assess my progress with the rubber bulb. I felt him smear the Crisco round my hole and then fingers moving around the outside and inside of it. The movement was constant and I had difficulty keeping a track on how many there were and what they were doing, it all became a pleasurable blur.

"Well Sam, I can see that you have followed our instructions and the result is very pleasing indeed. You should be proud of your achievement, your progress is excellent." Richard announced as he withdrew his fingers from me.

"Thank you Richard, I must admit it was not easy at first but by this morning I really become accustomed to it and I was even finding its presence pleasurable in a weird kind of way. When you say I have progressed, by how much and what is the target you have in mind?"

"I'm glad you are finding the insertions pleasurable, that is one of our objectives, you will then be able to pass this knowledge on and be able to demonstrate it to the trainee volunteers at the appropriate time. As to progress, on Friday morning you were just able to take three of Liam's fingers, however this morning you were able to easily accommodate three of my fingers and so I am moving on to the next step of your training. By the end of this morning I expect to be able to insert at the minimum four fingers, but hopefully depending on your ability and willingness to stretch I will be able to insert the whole of my hand into your rectum. Then for the next couple of mornings we will be working on depth before moving onto width. How does that sound? I bet you're glad you asked that question now aren't you?" Richard said with a hearty chuckle.

"Mmm I think I will reserve judgement on that for now, if you don't mind. To be honest, I'm not in a position to protest; after all I've had my fist up Jarek a couple of times now. He's survived the experience intact and even seems to enjoy it despite being straight." I replied looking over my shoulder at him as I spoke.

"Okay, shall we carry on then? Before we do, are you comfortable or do you need to stretch your legs because it may be some time before we can stop again." Richard asked.

It was a good idea so I climbed down off the couch and did a number of stretching exercises under the watchful gaze of the doctor. After five minutes I climbed back onto the couch and assumed the customary position.

"Sam, I'm going to start stretching your anal ring further than it's ever been to date, so relax as much as you possibly can. If at any time you feel pain you must let me know immediately. Discomfort is to be expected but pain is a big no no, do you understand?"

"Gotcha, I will do." I mumbled with my face half buried in my hands.

Almost immediately I felt more Crisco being packed into my rectum and then pushed further inside by a couple of fingers, I could feel the grease softening and melting because it's presence seemed to diminish gradually until I could no longer sense it. Unlike the fingers! There were definitely three fully inside me constantly twirling around, pushing in and then pulling out and repeating the whole cycle. I gave up counting after the fifth cycle and my mind began to wander all over the place. I was broken out of my trance with the sound of the door opening and Liam's voice greeting us both.

"So guys, how is the patient doing?" Liam asked laughing at his own joke

Richard, without slowing or stopping his hand movements in any way, proceeded to discuss his findings and plans at great length. It was all very technical and made me feel like an object or piece of stock, as a result I quickly lost interest and started drifting away again. That is until I felt a hand reach beneath me and take hold of my bollocks, giving them a quick massage before moving onto my erect cock. I didn't even realise I had an erection.

"So Sam, I see you're not adverse to the treatment the good doctor has been administering, this is excellent news and I hope you are as proud of your progress as we are. You will make a very good Volunteer Co-ordinator, as you have a prison officer, your can do attitude has not gone unnoticed I can assure you. Just out of interest, do you know how many fingers are currently in your hole at the moment?" Liam asked.

I tried to count Richard's fingers which were still moving round in their usual cycle but my anus had become so desensitised that I had no option but to guess so I said "Three?"

"No, Richard actually has four fingers fully buried inside and from where I'm standing I don't think it will be much longer before his thumb will be joining the other fingers."

"That's good" was all I could think of to say.

After what seemed an eternity I began to feel a new sensation in my rectum, it was one of fullness and my ring felt tight like it hadn't felt since the day I was fucked by Sayeed. Richard's hand had stopped its motion and was stationery, no, that's not quite true, it was moving very slowly if at all in the direction of my rectum. My ring was finally putting up some resistance and so he applied a little more force to his pushing resulting in me moving a little up the couch.

"Sam" Liam said with a serious tone to his voice. "I want you to breathe deeply and do your best to relax as much as possible, we're almost there."

"Yes Sir." I said through gritted teeth as it was getting distinctly uncomfortable now.

Then all of a sudden as I was doing as I was told, it hit me like a tidal wave, drawing an "aaaghh!" from my lips, my ring gave up its resistance and allowed Richard's coned hand to slide inside, as it did so his hand balled into a fist and my ring clamped shut around his wrist.

"Jeez! Is that really your fist inside me?" I growled.

"Oh yes, it certainly is." Richard confirmed "I'm going to hold it still so that you can get accustomed to its presence then I'm going to move it around and I want you to tell me how and what you feel okay?"

"Okay" I said panting heavily "For a start it felt like my ring was on fire, then I felt I desperately needed to go to the loo. Both of these sensations are fading now leaving me feeling very full down there but not unpleasantly so. As you move your hand around I can feel it both from the inside and also the outside which seems very strange indeed. Ah, now you've just brushed my prostate because I've felt a surge of blood to my cock which had started to go soft again."

"Excellent feedback Sam, you're really in the zone now. Keep those memories secure because you're going to need them when training the volunteers so that you can tell them what to expect." Liam said before continuing "In a few moments Richard will start to withdraw his fist, there may again be some discomfort at the point of exit, but as with the rubber bulb the more you do it the more you get accustomed to it and the less discomfort there will be."

Richard then added "Start breathing deeply, relax and imagine you are going for a dump, push a little but not too much. Ready? One, two, three here we go."

"Eeeeeeyooow!" I cried as Richard's hand was released from my hole, leaving it gaping wide before it slowly closed up again. I collapsed slowly onto the couch in exhaustion, sweat pouring from every pore in my body. I laid there motionless, my mind was all over the place as if I'd had too many pints on a Friday night, however my peace was abruptly disturbed a couple of minutes later by a pair of hands pushing my thighs apart and then exploring the crack between them. Before long once more I felt fingers exploring my hole and then smoothly glided on inside; my poor ring was too exhausted to put up much resistance. At the same time Richard lifted my hips and slid a pillow underneath me to raise my bum slightly into the air and provide Liam with easier access to my hole.

"Well done Sam, that's it, push out a little, welcome my fingers. Great! That's now four fingers inside, let's tuck that thumb in behind them and see if you can take my hand too." Liam encouraged me.

I backed onto the invading fingers as best I could while pretending I wanted to evacuate my bowels, the technique seemed to be working because before very long I felt the cone of his fingers getting wider than ever and then came that sticking point when the widest part is reached. That moment seemed to last forever but then with a momentary burning sensation his fist slid inside me with my ring closing slowly around his wrist. I reared up in response but this time was able to keep the desire to growl almost within, just a little bit crept out between my gritted teeth.

"Excellent work!" was all Liam said in response before saying "Right then, I'm going to pull out now and then that's today's training session over with. I know I've said it several times already, but very well done Sam, I'm proud of you."

"Thanks Liam, it would be great if we could call it a day, my arse is getting a little sore now!" I said quite sincerely.

Five minutes later after a bit of pulling and puffing (on my part) Liam's fist vacated my rectum to my relief and I was provided with several wads of paper towelling to wipe myself clean of all the grease which had been smeared over my nether regions. As I did so Liam asked me to take some time out of the normal routine today and draw up a plan and schedule to select the six Volunteer Punishers out of the prison community ready for presentation to him in the morning. No pressure then! As I got dressed back into my prison uniform Liam reminded me that this is still highly confidential so no talking about it, he didn't want the inmates to get wind of it before the prison is ready to roll it out. I agreed that I would keep it strictly to myself.

Back on the prison wing George asked me if I was okay as I seemed a little quiet, I grimaced and said that I had a stomach ache (which was true). He was genuinely concerned and said that I should take a break after the rounds had been completed this morning. I took him up on his offer as this would be an ideal way to somehow draw up a "beauty contest" come competition to select the six "lucky" volunteers. By the time I returned to work I had at least half an idea about what I was going to suggest, the rest of it I would think about tonight, which I did over a large pot of coffee and all distractions excluded i.e. no TV, the answer phone twitched on, my mobile switched off and the door bell disconnected. There was no way I was going to be disturbed!

TUESDAY 13TH APRIL

It was a late night last; I was up until 1am putting the finishing touches to my presentation until it was polished to my satisfaction, so when the morning alarm went off I wasn't really ready to get up and face the ordeal waiting for me at work. But like the trooper that I am I got up and was actually a little early for work, down to the traffic I'm afraid not my superhuman speed.

I will cut out the repetitive bits diary, after all you know that each day this week I will be going straight to the consultation room where I will be cleaned out and fisted by either Richard or Liam or both in order to 'educate' me. Actually this morning it was only by Richard and his sole mission was to get my anal ring totally used to being stretched wide by a fist, so for thirty minutes he methodically pistoned his fist in and out of my hole until it no longer caused me any discomfort and in fact I was actually beginning to enjoy it despite myself and the situation I was in. All too soon it was over and after withdrawing his fist for the last time Richard showed me techniques for closing my hole up again as if nothing had ever happened. I was impressed and my regard for Richard has increased immensely as a result.

Dressed once more I made my up to the Governor's Office and knocked on the door, decidedly nervous and holding my presentation folder under one arm.

"Come in!" Liam called out.

As I opened the door and strode in trying to appear confident I was in for a shock, I was expecting to be making my presentation to Liam. Instead I was greeting by the smiling faces of Liam, Max, Adrian, Archie (the prison officer who had greeted me when I arrived for my interview) and George.

My face must have been a picture as I stopped in my tracks and stammered out a "Hello guys, I wasn't expecting to see you all here this morning."

After he had stopped chuckling Liam said "Sorry Sam, sorry about the lack of warning about your audience. I decided that you were nervous enough about doing the presentation without having the added pressure of knowing that you would have an audience too. You are no doubt wondering why the others are here."

"Yes Sir, I am more than a little curious after all that you have told me." I said quite frankly.

"As you know Max and Adrian are my deputies and business partners so are always included on major decisions like this volunteer business. Archie is here because he is an ex-union representative and his experience will be invaluable in ensuring that all we do is legal and above board i.e. make sure that the relevant rules and regulations are adhered to. Finally George is here as a witness and will be taking minutes for the meeting, he has also been part of your assessment to see if you kept your vow of silence. I am glad to learn that not one drop of information has George received from you and so you have passed that test with flying colours. Right then if everyone would like to make themselves comfortable Sam will start his presentation."

Gulp here goes I thought!

"Okay, please bear with me for this is the first presentation I have done in a long while so I apologise if I appear a little nervous." I said after clearing my throat a couple of times. I looked down at my notes to give myself breathing space and time to gather my thoughts before continuing.

"My assignment has been to establish a method to find six Volunteer Punishers, one for each prison wing. It will allow us to identify which inmates have the drive, desire, ability and the right attitude to carry out this important function. After a lot of consideration I realised that it will need to be a combination of management selection and peer selection, you know a bit like the TV show 'X-Factor' except the voting public will be fellow inmates. This is how I envisage it will run.

Week 1:	We announce the competition and make it clear that it is open to all willing applicants with the auditions being held in the Chapel. The method of selection will be by answering questions, those that get the answer wrong will be eliminated; inmates who answer correctly go on to the next round of questions. By the end of the evening the number of applicants will be whittled down to twenty four applicants.
Week 2:	This week each contestant will be given a task to complete which lasts all week. At the end of the week the inmates will vote on who carried out the tasks most successfully. Twelve inmates will be eliminated by the voting to leaving twelve remaining contestants.
Week 3:	This week it steps up a gear. Each contestant now has to don the uniform of a Volunteer Punisher and start training in all aspects of the role. During the day they will learn the theoretical aspect of the role; then in the evening the contestants will receive training in the practical aspects in the Chapel's punishment room. The whole session will be watched by the inmates in the auditorium area and at the end of the training session the inmates will vote off the least favourite or capable contestant. This will be repeated each day until there are seven contestants left.
Week 4:	The final week sees the volunteers carrying out their duties for real, each day they will be moved to another wing so that all inmates can assess them in action before the final vote at the end of the week.

That gentleman is the outline of my selection process. Do you have any questions or concerns?" I asked.

"Thank you Sam" Liam spoke up "that was well presented and I like your idea very much. However I do have a question, you mention management selection but I can't see where in the weekly elimination schedule our influence can be exerted."

"That's a good question Liam" I replied smiling. "My intention would be that ahead of the competition we will select a number of inmates who we consider suitable, meet with them in private and feed them the right answers so that they will make it through to the final twenty four. It is then down to them if they make it to the final."

"I like it!" Max announced "A cunning way to get our favourites into the final, yet we will appear to be totally open in allowing the inmates to democratically choose their punishers."

"Well said Max, I think we should run with this one" Adrian said thoughtfully "What does everyone else think?"

There was a unanimous decision to accept my proposal so it was signed off by Liam there and then. Next came the nitty gritty stuff, sitting round the meeting table we thrashed out the timetable, the design and wording of the competition, the questions to be asked at the audition round and what the tasks the contestants would need to complete. Last on the agenda were the inmates we would like to see included in the final twenty four contestants.

After much discussion and at times heated debate, the twelve inmates we agreed that should be included were Tyler, Flick, Eduardo, Dinesh, Jarek, Tony, Bert, Darren, Carl, Martin, Gus and Sayeed. The timing for the individual briefings would be within a couple of days of the posters going up. It would be done discretely so that no one, least of all the inmates would suspect that anything untoward was going on. The posters will be put up on Friday 16th April   so that the inmates have the weekend to discuss and think about entering the competition. With that agreed the meeting was over and it was back to work for us, however with most of the morning gone it was a just short stint for me before my shift finished.

I got home and the first thing I did was to step into the shower with a cold can of beer, I wanted to wash the last traces of the grease from my body that tissues just simply couldn't do along with the accumulated sweat from my pre-meeting nerves. With the beer warming my insides and the hot water pounding my body all my cares and thoughts about today's events slipped away down the shower's plug hole.

Towelling myself dry I turned my attention to this evening and the impending arrival of Jason and Aaron for our jog around the park. The two lads arrived a little later, dropping off their change of clothing and we made our way to the park. I decided to be kind to them tonight and started the jog off gently only starting to pick up the pace in the latter half of the lap. Just to add a little pressure to the exercise I engaged them in conversation while jogging, they quickly sussed my tactics but I wouldn't allow them to let the conversation drop. At the end of the first lap I let them catch their breath while jogging on the spot before we carried on with the second lap, as it happened they led the way and I let them dictate the pace which I didn't mind in the least. Who would? I had two pairs of pert buttocks straining beneath running shorts, muscular thighs and arms pistoning back and forth in unison. They were a sight for sore eyes indeed! By the end of second lap I came to the conclusion that their level of fitness had increased perceptibly. I kept this thought to myself as I didn't want to boost their egos too much! To extend the exercise I insisted they jog back to my flat much to their moaning.

As they staggered up the steps to my front door I was chuckling inside, the sight of their sweat soaked clothes and bedraggled appearance was a far cry from their normal cock sure attitude that comes with guys in their prime. I unlocked the front door and held it open for them, as they passed by all I could smell was very sweaty bodies – Yuk with a capital Y!

"Right you two, no lounging around on my nice clean furniture with your sweaty, dirty clothes until you have showered and changed. I mean it. Run along while I sort out some refreshments." I said before walking off and headed for the kitchen to raid the fridge for fruit juice and whatever I could find to eat.

A minute later I heard the shower running and the familiar sound of Aaron whistling floated in from the bathroom, it was such a trivial domestic sound that it caught me by surprise when I started to wonder what it would have been like if I had had children with my ex-wife. I was still thinking about it when I heard footsteps behind me and a "can I do anything to help?" brought me back to the here and now with a jolt.

Looking in the direction of the sound, the sight that greeted me made me lick my lips in reaction, I caught that action in mid motion and discreetly pulled my tongue back in. There stood Jason as cocky as ever, smirking, stark bullock naked, framed by the doorway using the lint to hold onto. I took a moment to take in his physique, his hairy muscular legs and finally his cock which was standing at half mast and bobbing to erection under my gaze.

"Jason, what on earth are you doing?" I asked in mock exasperation.

"I'm only doing what you told me to do." He replied, walking into the kitchen and standing rather close to me. "After all you did say that you didn't want us touching your nice clean furniture with our dirty clothes. I thought I'd prevent that from happening by making sure they were out of harm's way from the start. Did I do wrong then?"

"Noooo, I suppose not" I replied.

"And you did say that you run a relaxed joint here, did you not?" he continued.

"Yes, this is true. Okay okay, now that you're here why don't you help yourself to a drink while we wait for Aaron" I suggested trying to keep my voice on an even keel and resist running my hands over his pert buttocks.

Thankfully Aaron joined us within a couple of minutes with his towel firmly wrapped round his waist, he did a double take at Jason's nudity before shaking his head and wryly commenting "have you no shame boy?"

Laughing Jason said "None at all, now that you've finished hogging the shower I can perhaps use it myself!"

As Jason disappeared into the bathroom Aaron turned to me and asked "Doesn't his antics bother you at all?"

"No, not really" I replied "If anything, he makes me laugh and he reminds me of myself when I was his age. Why? Does it bother you?"

Aaron was thoughtful for a moment then said "Yes, I guess it does. He is so brazen in the way he flaunts his body, okay he's not bad looking but why does he have to do it so much?"

"Well, if you got it flaunt it I guess is the rule that he's working by. To be honest you both have great bodies and are decent looking so I am a little surprised that you are not more like Jason." I said sitting down at the kitchen table with a glass of orange juice in one hand.

"I've got Dad to thank for that, he's instilled in me a conservative view of exposing my body and it's very hard to overcome."

"I find that if you want to overcome a mental block then the best way to do this is to face it and do the very thing you find hard to do." I said in the most fatherly tone possible.

"So in my situation if I want to be more like Jason what should I do?" Aaron asked seemingly puzzled by my latest statement.

"Simple" I replied "remove your towel and let it drop to the floor. Remain naked until Jason returns and it's time for you to go on your way. I will ignore your nakedness like I did with Jason, I am sure that you will find that before long you will feel more relaxed. The more you practise being naked, the more comfortable you will become with your body."

"Are you serious? What just drop my towel? Okay, if you say so, but don't tell dad will you. I don't want him to think I'm queer or anything." Aaron said with just a touch of edginess to his voice.

"Yes, yes and of course I won't. You don't have to do anything you don't want to but I just thought it would help. After all at your stag do you stripped off in public happily enough." I said shrugging my shoulders and took a sip of my juice.

"That was different, I was drunk and I got swept up in the moment. Right now I'm stone cold sober but I hear what you're saying. I guess, we're in private and no one's going to see or say anything, so here goes."

Taking a deep breath Aaron unfastened his towel and let it drop to the kitchen floor but kept his crown jewels covered with his hands. Standing there a little self-consciously he looked at me for approval.

"That's all very well but my towel is getting dirty on the floor so please pick it up, fold it neatly and put it on the side over there please, then why not come and sit down at the table and have a juice with me. That way you will still be naked, getting accustomed to being so but not feeling like you're on display all the time." I said, deciding that I would not let him get off the hook so easily.

Sighing, Aaron did as he was instructed, picking up the towel and folding it necessitated him uncovering himself and as he walked back to the table I got a good view of him and his tackle. Although his hair was a blonde (dark straw if we're being accurate) his body hair and pubes were several shades darker, made all the more striking by his naturally fair skin. Whereas Jason was a very big boy (10 inches by my reckoning at the stag do), Aaron was more your average guy which I wonder is perhaps part of his modesty problem. He made a good attempt of appearing relaxed but it was clear that he was relieved to be sitting down covering his modesty.

I let him be and we made small talk, I was good as my word and made no reference to his nakedness. Jason sauntered into the room, still naked and flushed red all over from the hot shower. He looked a little startled at the sight of Aaron sitting at the table without a stitch of clothing on and started to smirk.

"Less of that young man, it's all very well for you to flash your tackle around without a care in the world but not everyone is as confident as you. Aaron is trying to overcome his shyness and you laughing at him isn't going to help. We're taking it one step at a time and the first goal is to get him accustomed to being naked." I admonished him and then smiled encouragingly at Aaron.

"Thanks Sam, I appreciate your support. Jason, as my best mate, I would also appreciate your support, this is not easy for me as you well know." Aaron piped up.

Putting his hands up in the air in mock surrender Jason said "Okay guys, I get the message and I am sorry for not being more supportive. A thought has just occurred to me, this is a safe place for us to be naked without judgement as we've already discussed previously. Why don't we make it a rule that whenever we come over clothes are not permitted and we all have to be naked, that way Aaron will get all the practice he needs and won't feel the odd one out. What do you reckon?"

"Sounds like a good idea to me" I nodded in agreement. "What about you Aaron?"

"Yeah, sounds cool to me, it will make things easier for me.... I guess. But no word of this is to leak out right?"

Both Jason and I nodded in agreement before I said "Well that's sorted then, perhaps I can go for my shower now then."

"Aren't you forgetting something Sam?" Jason asked; then added in response to my quizzical expression, "You are still wearing your running gear, if this is a clothes free zone; they need to come off NOW!"

Chuckling at his impudence I nodded in agreement, stood up from the table and proceeded to remove my trainers placing them under the table where I normally keep them. Then I peeled off my muscle vest, pushed down my running shorts, leaving just my jock strap to go. Then in one smooth movement I pushed them down too, stepping out of them I put all my dirty washing into the washing machine before turning round with a smile on my face and arms spread wide and saying

"Are you happy now? I think this is enough for one day, I could do with a shower and you guys have got women to get home to, so get dressed and vamoosh. I will see you on Thursday."

A little while later I had my flat back to myself and enjoying my second shower of the day. As the soap suds rinsed away I slowly stroked my cock thinking about Jason's hot body and all the ways I would like to ravish his body given half the chance. Just as my imagination had me on my knees, with my hands wrapped round his waist and my face buried between his cheeks licking his tight little heiny hole, my balls decided it was time to unleash their load sending several jets of creamy spunk arching across the shower to hit the glass shower door and slowly slide their way down.

Recovering from my intense orgasm I looked down at the slug trails with disgust and quickly showered the congealing cum down the drain. And that diary brings the end to a very tiring day indeed.

WEDNESDAY 14TH APRIL

Compared to yesterday, today was average really. Well average that is if you call having your boss stick his fist and half his forearm up your arse! No word of a lie, I kid you not, by 10am this morning I had been cleaned out and prepped by Richard. Okay Richard had been loosening up my hole ready for Liam who then using his experience pushed his fist further up my rectum than I thought humanly possible. Apparently he had found breaking the resistance of my inner rectal ring a challenge, but one that he was up for, and eventually succeeded in doing. Unable to stifle the groan I growled like a grizzly bear, face flushed red and sweat pouring down my face my inner ring opened up and his fist slid on by up into my bowels. Only the width of his muscular forearm prevented him from going in all the way to his elbow. I looked down between my legs (I was laying on my back with my arms wrapped round my knees) with an expression mixed with awe and horror at the sight of his arm half buried inside me, while Liam had a look of pure angelic rapture.

"Sam, you are a star do you know that? I have never worked with a guy who is so willing to explore his boundaries and push far beyond them. I have seen you in action as a fisting top, now I have seen you in action as a fisting bottom and I am very impressed indeed, you are so versatile. There is absolutely no way that I will consider any one else for the role of Volunteer Co-ordinator." Liam said with a great deal of pride in his voice.

"Thank you Sir, I guess I have the army to thank for being able to push personal boundaries but I'm really not sure what the benefit of having your forearm buried in my butt will be in my role as Volunteer Co-ordinator." I asked as politely as I could.

"It's not so much the actual act you understand, although it must be said you have a very fine arse, but it is more of a test of your willingness to put your trust in me. Your level of trust is commendable, I couldn't ask for more" Liam responded and at the same time started to slowly withdraw his arm and fist.

As my inner ring was breached by his hand I arched my back in response, groaning as I did so. Some part of me must have enjoyed it as my previously flaccid cock slowly engorged with blood until as his fist finally slipped out of my anus my cock was fully erect and bursting to erupt. My ring must have been slow to close because I could feel cool air flowing into my rectum before being expelled as my rectum closed up along with my ring. I lay there relaxing with my eyes closed for a moment, I was about to get up when I felt something warm and wet enclose my cock's head.

Startled I looked up to see Liam's head slowly descending on my cock until he had swallowed the whole of my shaft in one smooth move, then slowly and lovingly his head started to bob up and down. Jeez it felt good! I let my head slink slowly back on to the couch, closed my eyes and gave myself up to the sensations of the gorgeous blow job I was being given. Finally with my hips bucking wildly I could hold back no longer and I gave into the impending orgasm. Load after load of jism shot out of me and straight down Liam's throat, not one drop did he let slip out and he didn't stop sucking until my cock had run dry and receded to its flaccid state once more. I looked up at Liam in askance.

"Sam, it's the least I can do considering how you have accepted without question all that I have asked you to do. I wanted to show you that as far as I am concerned this is a two way street and I have an inkling that it was an acceptable payback for you." Liam said with just a trace of a smile on his face.

"Yes Sir, it was an unexpected bonus that's for sure!"

"Right then, before we get back to normal duties is there anything you want to talk to me about?" Liam asked quite casually.

"Actually, there was as it happens. I know we agreed that we would speak to our preferred candidates once the posters have gone up but I'm concerned about timescales and I just can't see us getting through all the candidates in time without suspicions being aroused. I am hoping that you will allow me to start talking to them today" I said as I cleaned myself up and started to put my uniform back on.

"Sam, you're in charge of this venture now, if you think that's the right thing to do, then go for it. All I ask is that you keep me posted on events or if you encounter any problems. Okay?"

With that the training session was over and I headed over to the prison wings and pay the first candidate a visit, namely Flick on A-Wing. Since the 48 hour removal of personal possessions punishment Flick had been true to his word, he had behaved himself and not got into any more trouble, thereby keeping his possessions and clothing in the process. However he had lost none of his cockiness and as I walked into his cell closing the door behind me it was very much on show in his mannerism and posture.

After he bantered with me about why I was paying him an unannounced visit I got straight down to business and explained about the purpose of my visit. I outlined the role of the volunteer punisher, broadly what would be involved and that we actively wanted him on board. Once Flick made it clear he was interested I gave him a run down on the questions that would be asked so that he would have the correct answers to get through the qualifying round. As he never asked about the uniform I kept quiet on it remembering his reaction to being stripped naked for his punishment. I decided that he could cross that bridge when he got to it. My final comment was for him to keep his mouth shut about our little meeting and to remember to register his application when the posters were put up on Friday. Flick's mind was racing with the possibilities as I walked out of his cell.

On to B-Wing where I met just the person I was looking for playing snooker with a fellow inmate, who was just about to pot a red ball. Taking the opportunity while Tyler was waiting to play his turn, I walked up to him and whispered in his ear.

"Tyler, I know you're playing snooker but I need to have a private chat with you right now in your cell, alone. It will be only for a few minutes and then you can continue with your game."

Tyler frowned for a second, glanced at me but seeing that I was being serious nodded once in agreement and told his play mate that he would be back in a minute to continue the game. As Tyler was a force to be reckoned with there was no argument from the other guy.

As I followed him up the metal staircase to his cell I could not help but admire his muscular frame and jet black skin which had the optical effect of making him look like a moving obsidian statue. On entering his cell I closed the door behind me, turning round I was faced with the vision of Tyler sprawled out on his bed, hands behind his head, legs spread and his python of a dick snaking across one thigh. His balls hung loosely down between his legs. Despite my best intentions I could not help but look at them remembering the day that I had managed to accommodate the whole of his mammoth cock down my throat. Tyler chuckled loudly before inviting me to do the same thing again for him.

"Thanks for the offer" I replied "and as flattering as the invitation may be, I am here on official business not for personal pleasure. How have you been getting on since you voluntarily surrendered your clothing?"

"Oh man, I've been having a ball!" Tyler laughed again. "At first I was quite self-conscious, I know that might sound strange coming from me but it's true I really was. It's one thing when you are stripped as a punishment, you have no choice in the matter, but after the post-punishment meeting I voluntarily gave my clothing away in the hopes of becoming a volunteer punisher. I had to come up with a plausible story as to why you've kept my clothing and I'm not kicking up over it as the other inmates expected me to do. After a few days it was old news and the guys stopped asking me questions and simply accepted that I was going to remain naked from now on. It was made easier after Jarek's antics because suddenly I was no longer the only inmate to be permanently naked. Now no one takes any notice except those that are either gay or trying to usurp my position as top dog on this wing."

"Go on" I urged "I feel a story waiting in the wings just waiting to be told!"

"Do you remember how I told you when you first raided my cell that I had trouble getting any form of relief in this place?" he asked.

"Uh huh, I sure do"

"Well that isn't a problem anymore. There's a young lad on this wing, I'm sure you know him because he's received the 48 hour no clothing punishment too, by the name of Gus. He's very self-confident and easy going." Tyler said.

"I think I know the guy, he looks very similar to Jarek but his hair is paler." I asked pretending to be uncertain.

"That's the guy!" Tyler agreed nodding with a smile before continuing "It must have been the day he got stripped as punishment I first really got acquainted with him properly so to speak. I was sitting in the canteen during our lunch break, chatting as normal to a couple of old timers when Gus walks over with his lunch on a tray and sits at our table opposite me. I don't take much notice because up till now we've moved in different circles, however mid-way through his lunch he makes out that he's dropped his fork and crawls underneath to retrieve it, or so I think."

"What happens next?" I ask, genuinely curious.

"The next thing I know is a pair of hands pushing my knees apart and a pair of warm wet lips kissing my knob end. I don't know who was shocked the most; me, my knob or the guy I was talking to! I looked under the table in surprise while my cock rapidly stood to attention under Gus's expert administrations. No word of a lie he had swallowed the whole of my cock down to my balls within thirty seconds, and oh boy the feeling was out of this world! His head was bobbing, my body was sawing and I couldn't help by groan with pleasure. All too soon I could hold off no longer and with a shudder my balls exploded jism down his willing throat. He only came up for air when my cock ran dry and was back to its normal size, then he resumed his position at the table without looking at me, with fork in hand and continued eating his meal cool as a cucumber."

"Now that's what I call a lunchtime treat!" I laughed.

"From that day on any time that I've wanted to dump a load I've only had to nod in his direction and I get to plunge my cock either down his throat or up his arse. Tell you what though, he's a dirty bugger, he's even got me to shove my fist up his arse right in up to my elbow! My eyes nearly popped out of their sockets he got me to do it. I didn't think it was humanly possible, but he's shown me otherwise on several occasions since then. So I've got myself a regular little bitch now and I couldn't be happier. Well that's not strictly true, I wonder when I'm going to hear about this volunteering business otherwise I'm going to think someone's having a laugh at my expense and I won't be very happy if that's the case" he said throwing me a menacing frown.

"Actually that's what I came to talk to you about...." I said and then spent the next twenty minutes going through the details of the selection process, the auditions, questions, tasks etc. I got him to repeat the questions and answers so that there would be no mistakes made preventing him from being a finalist. I left him lying on his bed looking like the cat that got the cream.

My final visit of the morning was to C-Wing where I bumped into Eduardo enjoying a cigarette by the main door. This made things easier for me because I invited him to join me for a short stroll round the exercise yard where I made small talk before doing the whole sales pitch on the volunteering, after only a minute or two's thought he decided he was definitely up for the challenge so I gave him all the other necessary information before leaving him to finish his second cigarette while I went off for lunch.

After lunch I headed off to D-Wing in search of Dinesh, where I found him in the general lounge area reading "The Times" newspaper under the finance section.

Laughing I said "Planning your next big scam Dinesh? You do realise that you're going to be inside for several years yet don't you?"

"Oh yes Sir, but I can always dream and a man has to have plans for when he is released you know." He said looking up at me and smiling.

"Indeed, you're right. Do you have five minutes to spare, I have a proposition for you which you might find interesting."

"Well, I'm not going anywhere as you've pointed out and this paper can wait, so fire away you have my attention" Dinesh said with a deadpan face.

I was getting polished in my presentation and in no time at all I had another volunteer in the bag and so it was off onto my next target, Jarek in E-Wing.

Jarek was also eager to be a volunteer, the only question he really had on the subject was the matter of a uniform. He had been hoping that he would get some form of clothing back but as previously explained to him; that simply wasn't going to happen. The closest thing he will get to clothing is either the boiler suit for visiting times or the red beret and leather belt. Other than that he was up for the competition and hopefully become the one doing the giving rather than receiving for a change.

My final target for the day was Tony from F-Wing, I found him in his cell busy writing a letter which he quickly turned over on my entrance to the room. As I shut the door behind me he began to look concerned and asked

"Is there anything wrong Sir? I don't recall being warned about an impending visit from management."

"There isn't and there wasn't, but relax, I've come about a matter which might be of interest to you." I said in my best conspiratorial tone.

"I'm all ears Sir, carry on then".

Tony is a very astute guy, he grasped all the things I said instantly including the things I hadn't said, such as the uniform. When I explained it to him he asked if he could wear the beret and belt as well as the usual jeans and T-shirt. I explained it was all or nothing and that he would have to forgo the pleasure of wearing clothes if he wanted the prestige of being a volunteer punisher. After much umming and aahing he finally decided that he would give it a shot, he had nothing to lose (other than his clothes) and it might be a laugh.

Once that visit was over I rejoined George to do the final round of the day before making my way home feeling mentally exhausted. I was pleased to get home and veg out for the evening without having to do anything or say anything to anyone.

THURSDAY 15TH APRIL

No rest for the wicked as they say, back to work early the next morning and straight into Richard's consultation room to be cleaned out and stretched to within an inch of my life. Today instead of depth Richard and Liam were going for width, by the end of the session they managed to squeeze two hands into my butt at the same time. Now this was going some and was not at all enjoyable for me compared to the other exercises. I was distinctly sore by the end of the marathon session and my anus took quite some time to close up again. But at least I would be able to take on the biggest hands, such as Tyler's, should the need arise Liam and Richard assured me. Thanks, I think! All morning my bum throbbed, only easing off as it got to lunch time.

In an attempt to take my mind of the aching I threw myself into speaking to the other six candidates left on my list to talk to. Deciding to get the hardest sell over with first I made my way to A-Wing looking for Sayeed, I really wasn't looking forward to this one because he's a tricky devil and with him you really have to read the small print, as I have found out to my cost!

As the prison rounds had just been completed and breakfast a distant memory, most inmates were in their cells getting prepared for their daily jobs, whatever they may be. Sayeed was no exception, as I walked into his cell he was donning his outdoor overalls ready for his shift on the prison farm. He looked mildly irritated to see me but I chose to ignore it. I shut the cell door behind me and asked him to sit down.

"Is this absolutely necessary Sir? I'm going to be late for my shift and don't want to get into trouble with the farm manager because of an unexpected interruption to my schedule." Sayeed had definitely got out of his bed on the wrong side this morning.

"There is no need to take that tone with me Sayeed, what I want to talk to you about won't take long and it is in your best interest to think about seriously. If the farm manager asks where you've been you can say that I called you into a meeting on behalf of the Prison Governor; that should keep him off your back. Now shall we start again with a little less attitude?" I asked in a very reasonable tone.

"Ok fair enough, sorry Sir, what was it you wanted to speak to me about?" Sayeed asked in a more conciliatory tone.

I outlined the volunteer punisher's role, placing more emphasis on the mentoring and fatherly roles than the sexual activities as I knew it would appeal to his sense of morality and social consciousness. I deliberately left out any mention of a uniform, at this stage he knew nothing about it and it would only scare him off. He sat there silently deep in thought, occasionally throwing a guarded look before finally speaking.

"I will certainly give this idea a lot of thought but I have some questions which I would like answers to before I make up my mind either way. Firstly why have you asked me, what is in it for you? Secondly, why must I keep it secret? Thirdly, giving me the answers ahead of the audition is cheating; doesn't it make the competition unfair?"

"Good questions" I replied "clearly there's no pulling the wool over your eyes! Firstly, we, the management selected you for your social standing with the wing. We want someone that the other inmates can look up to. Secondly, you must keep it a secret because the posters don't go up until tomorrow and we don't want news to leak out ahead of time. Thirdly, yes technically you could call it cheating but it won't make the competition unfair. The only advantage you will have is in the first round auditions where it is questions and answers. It will be whittled down to twenty four contestants, including yourself, after that if you become a volunteer punisher then it will be down to your hard work and merit. It's entirely up to you, personally I think you will make a great volunteer but it is your decision."

Sayeed was silent again for a couple minutes before finally agreeing with my reasoning and confirmed that he would be willing to participate in the competition and would abide by our rules. Thanking him for his time I left without delay to allow him to get to the farm without being too late.

Next port of call was B-Wing and a far easier customer, Gus, the guy who was now Tyler's fuck buddy amongst other things. He was a push over, I appealed to the tart in him making sure I highlighted all the sexual perks that came with the role, I didn't even have to mention the uniform for him to be sold on the idea. The only difficulty I had was to get him to understand that he had to keep our meeting secret from everyone, especially Tyler of all people!

After leaving Gus I made my way over to C-Wing and met up with Bert, an old timer in his fifties with just three years to go before his release. Despite his years he kept himself fit and was considered by management as being a very stable character generally popular with the inmates on the wing. Personally I get on well with him as we have a similar sense of humour and outlook on life. I was straight with him about the volunteer role, the pros and cons and why I was asking him to consider the position. Like Sayeed he considered it for several minutes before giving a "tentative maybe" then changing his mind to a "yes, okay".

From Bert it was on to Darren, Carl and Martin on D, E and F-Wings respectively. Although all three men were physically very different; temperament-wise they were generally level headed, laid back with good sense of humours but didn't take fools gladly and wouldn't take shit from anyone. In fact perfect candidates for the roles! With a little bit of sales patter I had them all in the bag and my mission was complete. Twelve candidates of the management's choosing which will give us a fifty fifty chance of getting the right guys into the volunteer roles.

I was behind time when I got home, I had barely half an hour before Jason and Aaron were due to arrive so it was a dash into the bathroom, quick strip wash and change into my running gear before they rang on the door bell raring to go. If I'm honest my mind was elsewhere throughout the two lap jog round the park and before I knew it I had two guys beefing at me that I hadn't let up in the pace or giving them a half way breather like

I normally did. I was a little unsympathetic in my response pointing out that they were here to get fit and lose some weight, no pain no gain! It did however bring my attention back to the task at hand and I was more focused from there on.

As I walked up to my front door and put the key in the lock Jason reminded us of our agreement made on Tuesday evening about clothing being banned within my flat. We all nodded that we remembered and promptly stripped off our running clothes once the front door was safely shut. As I wore the least clothing I was the first one naked, I picked up my sweaty clothing and put them into the washing machine. On my return Jason had by then stripped naked and was busy trying to cajole Aaron into removing his final piece of clothing, his pants.

"I hear what you're saying Jason and yes I know I agreed to do it but I just don't feel comfortable stripping completely when I am all hot and sweaty." Aaron said with a slight whine to his voice.

Taking control of the situation I said "That's fine Aaron, keep your pants on until you have your shower, then once you've had your shower come back to us with your towel on. Then if you feel comfortable you can take it off or leave it on whichever is good for you. At the end of the day you need to take it at a pace that is right for you."

"I would prefer to do that if you don't mind, I won't feel so pressurised so may be more relaxed about it." Aaron said smiling in my direction before walking towards the bathroom, as he passed Jason he stuck his tongue out in an exaggerated manner.

Both Jason and I laughed in response, shook our heads and made our way into the kitchen where we waited in our customary fashion making small talk until Aaron returned with towel wrapped firmly around his waist. I went next for a shower, during which I hatched a plan to give Aaron a goal to aim for regarding his acceptance of his naked body. So while Jason had his shower I discussed my idea with Aaron about building his self-confidence, to my surprise he was actually receptive to it. To cut a long story short we agreed that in the summer we will as a group (Tom, Mike, Jason, Aaron, Chrissie, Sally, Kirsty and myself) take a trip down to Brighton and do some sun bathing on the beach, more specifically the nudist beach! Something to look forward to, not sure how we're going to broach the subject with the others though.......

FRIDAY 16TH APRIL

D-Day for me at work, the day my project starts for real. Thankfully I no longer had to attend Liam's training sessions so my arse got a rest at last! This morning the posters went up all round the prison advertising the auditions that were going to be held on Monday 19th April in the Chapel and I think it's fair to say that there was a great deal of interest judging by the reaction of the inmates and the conversations that could be heard all over the wings. Some guys were serious others were in it for a laugh, but none had a clue about what really lay ahead. Apart from twelve inmates who had at least some idea about it. During the morning and afternoon prison rounds I was fielding questions left, right and centre. In the end George gave up on me leaving me to answer the questions while he carried on doing the cell inspections.

It was exciting thinking that my project was about to be launched but I was more than a little nervous because I need to pull it off big time otherwise my reputation will be in tatters. Not that my colleagues have any doubt about my abilities or ambition, so I can at least take comfort from that.

By knocking off time I was glad for the peace and quiet of my car whilst driving home and then my beloved flat, which has always been a sanctuary for me when the world comes crowding in like it did today. Not that I'm going to be in for long as tonight I'm out with the lads for that final food and drink binge before Mike and Tom do some serious dieting and exercising care of yours truly.

So diary, that's all from me for one day as I have to get ready, put some smart clothes on spruce myself up before meeting the others in town. I don't think I will be in the mood for writing when I get home later.

SUNDAY 18TH APRIL

Oh my God! Oh my God! I can't believe how this weekend has panned out.... if someone had told me what was going to happen I would never have believed them, in fact I still have to pinch myself to believe it.

Friday night in town went pretty much as expected, lots of food and far too much beer and spirits were drunk but we did have a brilliant time. Everyone was in good spirits but by the end of the night Jason was by far the drunkest in the group, so much so that Aaron and Tom both said that Kirsty would go mental when she sees the state of him.

"No shee woooon't, she lovesh me sho mush" Jason protested.

"Not in that state she won't!" Tom chided

"Well what are we going to do with him until he can sober up?" Aaron asked, suddenly concerned about his best mate.

"I can shleep at Shams flat, he'sh got a shpare room" Jason announced and then proceeded to hic up loudly.

"Um, I guess he can do. I mean I do have a spare room so he could kip down in there. Once he's slept the alcohol off he can go home and do some making up with Kirsty" I said appearing to think things over.

"That's settled then" Tom agreed. "Thanks for taking the burden on, I really don't think Chrissie would have appreciated me bringing a drunken Jason home. We had too much of that when they were younger!"

"No problem, glad to be of service." I smiled all the while hoping that Jason wasn't going to throw up everywhere.

Waving the other guys off I steered Jason through my front door and half pushed, half guided him into my spare bedroom/office and plonked him onto the bed. I removed his shoes and made sure that he was comfortable before closing the door behind me.

By now I had the munchies again, alcohol has that effect don't you find? I made myself a coffee and was standing in front of the fridge peering inside trying to decide what I fancied eating when I nearly jumped out of my skin. A pair of hands had snaked their way round my waist and met in the middle, at the same time a lager laden mouth breathed on the back of my neck before planting a firm kiss on it. I stood there rigid before exclaiming

"Jason, what the hell do you think you're doing?!" and pulled away at the same time, turning to face him.

"Something I've wanted to do for a very long time!" Jason replied in a husky voice, he didn't seem to be drunk anymore.

Before I could react he stepped up to me, with one hand he pulled me towards him and with the other he held the back of my head so that I couldn't pull away. I opened my mouth to speak and found it instantly covered by his hungry mouth. His tongue darted out and thrust its way past my lips (which had started to close in reaction) and proceeded to ravage my mouth mercilessly. I was so taken aback I did nothing to resist, it felt so strange having a masculine mouth kissing me, I have only been kissed in this way by women in the past. Desire inside me ignited and my hands left my side to explore the body pressing into me, I pulled him closer to me, I could feel his erection through his jeans pressing into my equally erect cock which was straining to be released. I started to kiss him back, pushing his tongue into retreat before thrusting my tongue into his mouth. I don't know for how long we kissed but my lips and chin were starting to get stubble burn – a first for me. Our hands became more desperate in their exploration and if my cock got any harder I was going to explode!

Jason must have read my mind because without saying a word he stepped away from me, his eyes were full of lust and his chest was heaving. Then he took my hand and still not saying anything pulled me out of the kitchen and effectively dragged me into my own bedroom. Once inside he pushed me backwards onto the bed where I lay sprawled out wondering as to what would happen next. I didn't have long to wait to find out because he dived onto the bed landing between my outspread legs and expertly undid my jeans before yanking them down around my knees along with my boxer shorts. Standing up for a moment he pulled them off me entirely before jumping onto the bed again and taking my throbbing cock in his hand.

Looking along my body and into my eyes he whispered "You don't know how many times I have dreamed of being in this situation. I'm going to savour every minute of this"

Not knowing quite how to respond I smiled encouragingly and dropped my head back onto the bed. Delaying no further Jason started to lick the shaft of my cock as if it were a lollipop coating it liberally with saliva before moving onto my cock head. I raised myself up onto my elbows to watch him; his eyes were closed as he slowly and smoothly swallowed the whole of me right down to the base. I had to concentrate so hard on not cumming there and then, I thought of mundane things until I was under control before I could relax and enjoy the expert blow job I was receiving. The sight of his handsome face bobbing up and down, lips wrapped round my shaft was a sight to behold and I'm sorry to say that it wasn't long before I couldn't restrain myself any longer. My hips began to buck and my head dropped back down again on to the bed just as my cock exploded sending jet after jet of jism down his willing throat. I was panting heavily from the orgasm but he was totally unfazed as he carried on sucking my cock until it had gone soft, only then did he reluctantly let it drop from his mouth. I thought he had finished with me but no, not by a long chalk. Without missing a beat he started licking and mouthing my balls, at the same time his hands reached out for my legs, once he had hold of them he pushed them up and back towards me. Understanding what he wanted I wrapped my arms around my knees to hold them in place. His tongue then travelled down from my balls along my crack until its goal was reached, my hole. He licked and lapped at my ring, in and out it darted round and round until even I could feel it relaxing and welcoming the intrusion.

While he was occupied down below I managed to gather enough thoughts to think about lubrication and remembered that I still had some of the Crisco Liam had given me, in my bedside drawer. Reaching across the bed I managed to open the drawer and retrieve it without Jason losing a stroke.

"Jason mate, you might want to use some of this" I said offering him the opened tub.

"Sure thing Sam, I have just the thing for that" Jason replied with a chuckle and immediately took a glob of it and greased up his cock.

Then throwing me a wink he placed his cock at my entrance and slowly pushed. Bearing in mind my recent training at work he had no problem getting past my ring and his cock, despite being a whopping ten inches in length, quickly disappeared inside. When he was in as far as he could go he took hold of my knees, pushed them aside and leant forward intent on kissing me. I reached out and pulled him towards me at the same time wrapping my legs around his waist to keep him buried inside me. We kissed passionately for the longest of times, finally coming up for air he gave me one last kiss before he nuzzled and bit my neck and shoulders as he started to slowly fuck me. He might be young but he was certainly experienced and/or talented in the art of fucking! He had the knack of hitting my prostate with every stroke and boy did he have stamina. On and on he fucked me gradually gaining in pace and force, I was loving every single moment of it. My head was rolling on the pillow with groans escaping from my lips in time to his thrusts and my legs tried to pull him ever closer to me until his balls were at risk of being swallowed too!

As they say, all good things must come to an end and with a grunting cry Jason's body went rigid, spasmed several times before he collapsed exhausted onto me panting heavily. I kissed him tenderly on the cheek and held him in my arms while he got his breath back. My legs released their grip and I stretched them out straight again which caused Jason's now subsiding cock to slip out of me dribbling a little bit of after-cum across my thighs. We laid there motionless for several minutes without saying anything, however his body pressing into mine aroused my cock from its slumber and I decided it was my time to show this youngster that an old man can still have a few tricks up his sleeve.

So I reached across him to where the Crisco tub sat abandoned and took a generous handful before rolling a sleepy Jason on to his front and spreading his legs. He made protesting noises but I played deaf and started to smear the Crisco along his crack and pushed some inside his anus. Now I understood his concerns for his ring was tight and he knew the size of my cock. He must be an anal virgin; I smiled to myself and thought 'I'm going to have one tight hole to fuck tonight!' In view of this fact I took extra care and attention to warming up his hole. First I inserted one finger and stroked his prostate which persuaded him that this wasn't such a bad idea after all. Then when he was relaxed with one finger I introduced a second finger and so on until I could get three in. By this time he was raring to go so I climbed on top of him, supporting myself with my elbows and slipped my cockhead just inside his ring. He reared up in reaction and his ring clamped down tight. I remained stationary until he released his grip and then gently applied pressure pushing my cock inside inch by inch. Finally I was fully inside, what a gorgeous feeling to be inside a tight hole, not only that the view before my eyes was hot too. Jason was lying with his head on his hands which accentuated the musculature of his back, further highlighted by the shadows cast by the hallway light. I was having difficulty remembering how I ever found a woman sexually attractive, but then again it's like comparing day with night. Both are very different but each beautiful in its own way. Back to the task at hand and I quickly became consumed by the passion of the moment and was fucking Jason's arse like there was no tomorrow. Again all too soon I climaxed and shot my load deep inside him before rolling him onto his side, lying spooned together with me still up him. I never lost my erection and five minutes later I was ready to go again, this time I took it more leisurely and as I slowly fucked him I reached over and stroked his cock until he had another erection. Somehow by coincidence or good luck we climaxed at the same time, my sheets definitely needed to be changed now! Finally our lust was spent for now and we drifted off into sleep.

It was early the next morning when I next woke up, the sun had just risen and was streaming in through the windows; I never had the sense last night to close the curtains. Jason was still asleep looking positively angelic, oh how deceptive that man can be I thought to myself. I guess this is the sight Kirsty must see most mornings, the thought of her brought up pangs of guilt and it took the edge of the post-sex glow I still had about me. Mentally I shrugged my shoulders, it takes two to tango and he was the one who had initiated the action, I certainly had no intention of spilling the beans to Kirsty or anyone else. Jason is a big boy (literally) and can choose his own path, who am I to judge?

Anyway, where was I? Oh yes lying in bed watching the man I had shagged the night before. Deciding I was hungry and definitely needed a shower as a certain present deposited the night before was about to make an exit, sooner rather than later. I crawled out of bed as quietly as possible so as not to disturb sleeping beauty and tiptoed to the bathroom. First port of call the toilet, then into the shower to wash off the smell of sex, and finally have a shave.

Twenty minutes later I was in the kitchen brewing a pot of coffee and grilling some bacon for a sandwich when I heard the shower running so I set the table for two and put some more bacon under the grill. By the time I was buttering the bread and pouring out the coffees Jason sauntered into the room, towel wrapped round his waist and hair all tousled.

"Did you sleep well?" I asked brightly.

"Yeah, like the dead thanks. Is that bacon I can smell? I'm starving!" Jason replied casually as he sat down at the table and poured himself a cup of coffee.

This whole situation was so surreal, in my kitchen sat a man young enough to be my son, who I had known virtually all of his life, and had a girlfriend of his own yet sat here as if this was the most natural thing in the world. It then occurred to me that this can't have been the first time he had been in this type of situation. Sitting down opposite him I passed him his round of bacon sandwiches and as I ate mine I planned what I was going to say to him.

However Jason beat me to it by thanking me for breakfast and for taking care of him so well last night. Taking care of him had more than one meaning I smiled inwardly. He asked if I had any objections to him calling Kirsty to let her know that he was fine and would be home later. I shrugged my shoulders and said "Be my guest". He stood up and wandered into the living room to retrieve his mobile before returning and sitting back down at the table once more. With his cup of coffee in one hand and his mobile in the other he quick dialled Kirsty and chatted away to her for about ten minutes. Oh boy was he a smooth operator, he had her eating out of his palm in no time and I'm not even convinced that he actually apologised for not going home last night. At the end of the conversation he swore that he loved her and would be home by lunchtime.

"You've done this before haven't you?" I casually asked taking a sip of my coffee.

"Done what? Had sex with a man or been unfaithful to Kirsty?" he asked with raised eyebrows.

"Both. Does she know that you bat for both sides? Or that you have been unfaithful."

"No one knows that I do on either counts and that's how exactly how I want it to stay" he responded giving me a hard stare.

I held my hands up in mock surrender before bursting out laughing stating "I'm not judging you Jason it's just that last night came as a bit of a surprise, a very pleasant one granted, but a surprise none the less but this morning you seem totally relaxed and gave a very polished performance which led me to suspect that you've done this before."

"You caught me fair and square Guvner" Jason replied with a sly smile.

"So tell me what made you pull that stunt last night? You weren't as drunk as you were making out were you? Why pick me, I'm old enough to be your father and there are plenty of young guys out there who'd be more than willing to take your cock whichever way you want it." I said in all seriousness.

"Like I said last night, and I meant it, I have wanted to get you into bed for so long I have forgotten a time when I didn't want to. Ever since I was about fourteen years old I have fancied you like crazy. I used to hang onto every bit of information I could get when you were in the army and I was so jealous of your wife thinking she was in bed with you each night. You have no idea how many times I have just wanted to touch your body or have you hold me in your arms. I can remember listening to the conversations Aaron had in school and if there was any suggestion that you would be going to his house I would find a way to gatecrash the barbecue or party." Jason admitted quite candidly.

I was silent for a moment before responding. "I don't know what to say, I never had a clue that you felt like that and if I had known I probably wouldn't have been very receptive in those days. I was too busy being a man's man at the time and no one was going to say that I was anything other than a real 100% heterosexual alpha male. It's only since I have worked as a Prison Officer that I have even contemplated that there could be another side to me that hadn't been explored. Thinking about it I do seem to remember you being on the scene a lot when you were a teenager, we simply put it down to you and Aaron being inseparable buddies."

"Yeah" Jason replied, deep in thought remembering the past "we were and still are I guess. It has been very hard sometimes keeping these feelings hidden from view and a couple of times it has nearly slipped out but as far as I am aware no one suspects my bisexuality. I love Kirsty very much and I want to be with her, but there is this other side of me which needs to be satisfied at the same time. Up until now I have been having one night stands when I get the opportunity but I have grown tired of these casual and sporadic sessions which somehow no longer feel as satisfying as they once did. I guess if I was honest I would like to find a guy who loves to have sex with no strings attached."

Again I thought for a moment before replying "So let me get this straight in my head, you are looking for a guy who is prepared to have sex with you on an ongoing basis but is happy to keep it secret and isn't looking for a relationship with you? I guess it would help if you liked the guy too?"

"Got it in one! Any ideas on where I should look for this guy?" Jason asked raising one eyebrow.

"Well....... I suppose if you are having trouble finding someone I guess I could help you out in the meantime. I love sex, am not looking for a significant other; we get on okay and can keep my gob shut. What do you reckon? The other bonus is that you have an excuse for coming round here as I'm now your fitness trainer." I said trying to sound matter of fact as if this was the most normal thing in the world.

"Great minds think alike! If you're up for it I definitely am but I've just realised the time, if I'm not careful I'm going to be late and that is something Kirsty does NOT like." Jason said closing the discussion on the subject by jumping up and heading for the bedroom to get dressed. Within ten minutes he was flying out of the door with a promise that we will have to this again real soon. Yeah yeah I thought, where have I heard that before?

The rest of Saturday was spent flitting between surfing the internet, watching the Sports Channel and reluctantly doing mundane chores round the flat.

Sunday was pretty mediocre if I'm honest, went to the leisure centre for the weekly swimming session with the guys which was very surreal as Jason acted perfectly in character as if Friday night had never happened. I don't honestly know if I was relieved or disappointed, either way tomorrow (Monday) has been looming large in my mind.

MONDAY 19TH APRIL

The atmosphere in the prison today has been electric; it only found a release in the evening when it was time for the auditions in the chapel. Standing on the podium with Liam, Max and Adrian at my side I looked out over a sea of expectant faces and began my speech welcoming each and every contender for the six positions of Volunteer Punishers. There must have been nearly six hundred men in the room as it was standing room only (all the chairs had been removed earlier in the day). Having explained the rules of the audition tonight I asked the men to hold their competition passes in the air for without a valid pass they will be excluded from the competition and escorted from the chapel immediately

"Right folks!" I called out loudly "let's get the competition under way. Okay, listen up. For starters it's a simple yes or no for the answer. Question one, do you think that by being a volunteer punisher this will give you authority over other inmates? You have five minutes to make your mind up."

For a minute or two there was silence then slowly a whisper was heard and then more as inmates decided to discuss the whispering got louder and louder until I had to shout for silence in the room.

"Okay guys, times up. Put your hand up in the air with your pass clearly showing if you think the answer is yes." I announced. Around two thirds of the room put their hands up.

"All the yes's are to move to the left side of the room where Liam is standing and all the no's are to the right where Max is standing. Please do so as quickly as possible so we can keep to the timetable."

For a couple of moments there was a swirling mass of bodies as the inmates divided into two groups. George and a couple of other officers patrolled the divide to ensure that there were no sneaky jumpers after the results were announced. As the inmates quietened I announced the correct answer.

"The correct answer to this question is – YES – you will have authority over other inmates. You will follow directions from the prison staff and be given certain powers which will be confirmed later in the competition. All those that have answered incorrectly are now to leave the chapel by the main door and surrender your passes to Liam as you go."

There were groans of disappointment from the 'No' group but they followed the instructions and slowly filed out of the room leaving four hundred inmates in the competition.

"Question number two." I called out "Do you have the right to humiliate in public an inmate who has broken the prison rules? Again this is a yes or no question and as before all the yes's to left and no's to the right."

This time the room was split fifty fifty, the correct answer was 'no', after the yes's had left the room two hundred inmates remained and the questions continued.

"Question number three. If an inmate approaches you for advice or assistance regarding anything providing it's legal are you obliged to help?"

Again the room was evenly split, the correct answer was 'yes', once the no's had left the room one hundred inmates remained.

"Question number four. Once an inmate has broken the rules and the punishment initiated, do you have the right to engage in any sexual activity of your choosing and whenever you want? Same as before this is a yes or no question with all the yes's to left and no's to the right."

The room was deadly silent, the inmates looked stunned and then a few started to grin wickedly at the thought of the question's implications. This didn't stop them from being indecisive and it took longer for the dividing up to finalise. In the end it was split with sixty saying yes and forty saying no. Yes was the correct answer so we were left with sixty inmates, the chapel was now feeling decidedly emptier.

"Question number five. If we told you that the uniform of a volunteer punisher consists solely of a red beret and leather belt with no other clothing being permitted, would you be prepared to comply with this requirement?"

This time the reaction from the inmates was more animated and I heard a few gasps, whistles of astonishment and a couple of "no ways!" but surprisingly at the end of the dividing there were thirty five yes's and twenty five no's. I had been expecting a lot fewer yes's considering what had been asked, but I was relieved to see that the twelve inmates I had primed were still in the running.

"Right guys, we're now down to thirty five and there are only twenty four can go through to the next round. This is going to be your first challenge. Scattered around the prison in the public areas are twenty four white envelopes, inside will be a red ticket with 'VP' embossed in silver. The twenty four men who successfully find the envelopes will be the ones going through. After I say go, you are free to search for them. On your marks, get set, go!" I cried out.

In one surge the thirty five men raced out of the room determined to be the ones to find the tickets. Once the chapel was empty Liam came over to me and congratulated on how well it had gone so far. I smiled an acknowledgement, inside praying that the rest of the competition would run just as smoothly. It took about five minutes for the first contender to come back in the room and about half an hour for the twenty fourth to stumble back into the chapel clearly exhausted having scoured the prison for the last remaining ticket. On his entry the chapel door was locked behind him, with a note outside advising the other eleven men that they were out of the competition.

"Okay guys; the first selection round is now over and this is where the hard work begins! Starting from tomorrow and continuing until Sunday you will be split up into six teams of four. Each day you will be on a different wing carrying out specified duties. Then on Sunday the rest of the prison inmates will vote for who they feel undertook the duties most willingly and most successfully. The twelve with the most votes will go through to the next round. Any questions so far? No? Okay, then I'll explain a couple of rules. You are free to reject the tasks set you but by doing so it will immediately disqualify you from the competition, equally if you decide that this competition isn't for you then you are free to leave at any time. That's all for now, you are free to leave and return to your cells, get a good night's sleep because the next six days are going to be hectic for you. In the morning you are to report to the main reception where your instructions will be published. Good night gentlemen."

There as a small round of applause from the inmates and prison staff, to whom I bowed before we all left the chapel and went our separate ways.

Back at home, I flopped onto my sofa mentally exhausted from today's events and took my time enjoying a cold beer letting my mind go blank. I was only roused from this state by the sound of my mobile phone bleeping to let me know a text message had arrived.

Sod it! I thought to myself but couldn't resist seeing who it was. It was Jason, just asking how my day had been – if only you knew – and shall we have another session after swimming on Sunday 25th April as Kirsty is off to visit her best friend in Manchester that day and will be staying overnight. I text back saying that sounded a great idea and to make sure he had a good night's sleep because he was going to need it....

TUESDAY 20TH APRIL

I was in even earlier at work than usual, I simply had to make sure that the instruction leaflets had been printed correctly, that I was in position and prepared for when the twenty four contestants arrived at the main reception. I was idly chatting to Andy, the security guard on reception when they started turning up en masse. It was like being hit by a tidal wave! They were full of enthusiasm and couldn't wait to see what tasks they were to be set, I wasn't sure if they would be so happy when they saw what was required though.

I spent the next ten minutes explaining that they will be given a number of tasks which everyone will have to participate in and complete to the best of their ability. The other inmates will be watching their every move and at the end of the six days will be voting for the contestant who has most impressed them. I then read out the daily tasks to them:

1.   Assist with the cleaning & maintenance of the prison facilities.
2.   Assist the prison officers during the daily cell inspections.
3.   Befriend new arrivals, help them settle in & offer assistance where required.
4.   Befriend inmates who are having difficulty socialising, help them network & offer assistance where required.

They were quiet for a few minutes while it sank in before Sayeed put his hand up and asked politely what the purpose of these tasks was.

"As ever Sayeed, you ask a very pertinent question" I said smiling broadly to him and the others in turn "and I am happy to answer it. Task one involves you doing chores which others normally refuse to do or do so unwillingly, thereby proving your ego and pride is not going to be a barrier to your progress. Task two requires you to distance yourself from fellow inmates sufficiently to help the prison officer search the cells, sometimes against the inmate's wishes. Do you have the integrity to do this? Task three, this is a demonstration of your social skills and ability to relate to others who may be feeling vulnerable. Finally, task four. This will involve you dealing with inmates who will already be known to you, so you will have to overcome any personal prejudices you may have about that person as well as using the same skills as for task three. Any questions?"

No one answered so I split them up into the six teams making sure that any guys from the same wing were split into different groups. I then sent them on their way having explained in greater detail what they need to do but that a large part of it will be down to their own initiative and reminded them that their every move will be watched by the inmates. Then to add just a little bit of pressure I said that I would be round doing spot checks at random times of the day which brought a collective groan from them all.

I spent most of the day doing exactly that and catching up with the other officers making sure that the contestants were doing what they were supposed to be doing (which I was pleasantly surprised to find that they were doing, but it is only their first day).

This evening I actually enjoyed going for a run with Aaron and Jason, it was great to be doing something that didn't require a great deal of thought (apart from making sure that I wasn't going too fast for them). After our cooling down exercises and walking back home I commented on the fact that I could see improvements in their fitness levels and perhaps we ought to up the ante a little by doing two and a half circuits. Surprise, surprise this brought groans of protest from them but as their coach my word goes so as from Thursday we will be jogging further. I also dropped in the fact that I will be doing a physique check after the showers to ascertain if they have been doing all of the exercises I set for them.

After we had all had showers it was time for the physique inspection. As was now customary Jason and I were naked but Aaron was still hiding within his towel, not for long though. With Aaron watching while sitting on the sofa I got Jason to stand up straight in the middle of the lounge with his hands down by his sides looking forward. I then took my time examining him from head to toe making positive comments whenever I found an improvement in his muscle tones and reduction in his fat layers. I then focused on areas requiring attention. Giving Jason a sharp but playful slap on the bum I told him to make himself comfortable as it was now Aaron's turn.

With a sigh of resignation Aaron stood up and assumed the same pose Jason had and I repeated the procedures that I had done with Jason. In all fairness both of them had made good progress and said so, this brought smiles and thanks from them. While Aaron was momentarily distracted by the compliments I until his towel and whipped it away before he could protest. I continued with my inspection pointing out that the towel had impeded my progress and simply had to go! Jason decided to go one better and retrieved the towel before putting it into the washing machine so Aaron had no choice but to join us in nakedness – he's a little devil, that Jason! Aaron was rather petulant for a few minutes following this stunt but eventually got over it and by the time they dressed to leave he was relaxed enough to take his hands away from his crutch and behave more normally.

WEDNESDAY 21ST APRIL

Work has been a little surreal today, the contestants have moved on to another wing as instructed getting on with their tasks with little supervision, so there has been little training for me to do. The feedback I have been getting has so far been positive, although it is too early to say if it will have lasting effects on the prison system. I could almost believe that it was business as usual except that we had some volunteers in helping us out.

THURSDAY 22ND APRIL

Dear diary, nothing much to say. Today was much the same as yesterday, the only difference is that Liam called me in to his office for me to give feedback which I did in as balanced a way as possible. Even running tonight with Aaron and Jason was par for the course. Aaron summonsed up the courage to drop his towel part way into the evening which I acknowledged with a smile and nod. Jason thoughtfully made no issue of the matter.

SUNDAY 25TH APRIL

Sorry for not having written for the last couple of days, with nothing going on there doesn't seem much point in writing anything. Today has been different, in fact a first for me, I have been to a Sauna for the first time! Me at forty five, going to a gay sauna of all places..... but I am getting ahead of myself (as usual).

As I read the Sunday paper over breakfast a text came through on my mobile, it was Jason, cancelling our session no doubt I humphed to myself. But I was wrong, the message actually read:

"There's been a change of plan. Kirsty wants me to wave her off from Euston Station so I can't go swimming. Meet me outside Euston Station at 3.30pm and we can go into town. Please say you can make it. Jase xx"

Mmm I thought to myself, sounds interesting so I text him back agreeing to meet him as arranged. In the meantime I had a swimming session to attend. Due to time constraints I would have after the swimming session I took a change of clothing with me to the leisure centre. I paid to hire a locker overnight acting as casually as possible so as not to attract attention to my plans. Afterwards I quickly donned my clean change of clothing and made a discreet exit heading for the tube station. I was running five minutes late when I arrived at Euston to find that Jason was already waiting for me. I went to apologise for being late but from the expression on his face it was clear that he was simply relieved that I had turned up at all. I asked him what the plan of action was for this afternoon and evening. He refused to divulge any information saying it was all taken care of and that I should just relax and enjoy the experience. Fair enough so I let him have his way.

Our first port of call was Leicester Square, more specifically the cinema where we watched the recently released "Alice in Wonderland" which was very well made but a little on the weird side. I kept this last thought to myself as Jason clearly loved every moment of it (perhaps it's an age thing). From there we walked over to China Town and enjoyed a sumptuous three course meal in an expensive looking restaurant, all paid for by Jason despite my protests to pay my half. Finally stuffed with food beyond comfort levels we sought refuge in a coffee house in Soho and watched the world go by chatting about anything that came to mind. Finally when I thought we were going to call it a day the final surprise was revealed, well, only as we walked up to the front door actually. In bright rainbow neon lettering were the words 'Manzone Sauna" – there was no way you could mistake what this establishment was! I looked at Jason in surprise and asked him if this was where we were headed, indeed it was and without further delay we went inside.

Not knowing what to expect I looked around me studying every detail, at first glance it looked very much like a hotel main reception with a butch looking guy in his early sixties manning the desk. As Jason paid our entrance fees he gave me a curious glance up and down, stopping momentarily at crutch level before smiling briefly at me and handing us a couple of white towels and locker keys. He asked if we had been before and offered us a tour of the facilities, but Jason politely declined as he had been here several times already. He headed straight to the only door available and indicated that I should follow him, as we got to the door the receptionist pressed a button and a buzzer sounded releasing the lock on the door. On the other side of the door was a small changing room with lockers along one wall, on the opposite wall stood three doors, one with a sign saying 'rest room', one with 'showers' and the other 'amenities'. Wasting no time we stripped off our clothes and wrapped the rather small white towels around our waists before locking our clothes away and walking through the amenities door and into the corridor beyond which had several doors on either side.

"So Sam what do you fancy trying first?" Jason asked with a smile "They've got a steam room which is hot and wet, a sauna which is hot and dry, a Jacuzzi, a massage parlour and exercise room."

"Well I don't fancy the exercise room" I replied "we get enough of that already, nor the massage parlour. I think I will try the sauna first."

The heat hit me as I opened the door, it was like walking into a furnace and I could feel sweat bursting out of every pore as I stepped inside. The lighting was dim inside, provided by one solitary red light bulb, but it was enough to make out the two tiered slatted wooden benches running along each of the walls. There were already five men in the sauna, ranging in age from late teens up to early seventies and all were wearing the obligatory white towels. In one corner stood the heater with what looked like hot pumice stones, adjacent to it was a metal bucket of water and a ladle for putting water onto the stones. As I walked down the aisle between the benches I tried to make visual contact with the guys but most had their eyes closed or were staring down at the floor, avoiding eye contact. The only one who did look up was a young lad who appeared to be in his late teens who smiled shyly at me, if you ignored the spots he was cute in a goofy sort of way. I felt a tap on my shoulder and with a very pointed look on his face Jason indicated where we should sit. Strangely the seat I was offered was out of eye line of the youth, I mentally shrugged my shoulders, if Jason wanted to be jealous over a smile let him.

Jason and I chit chatted for a few minutes but it was just too hot to talk so the conversation died out and we sat in silence soaking in the heat and feeling the sweat trickle down our bodies. After what seemed an eternity Jason admitted defeat and we escaped into the relatively chilly corridor to cool down. I decided that I needed to wash off the grime and sweat from my body before I did anything else so I headed back to the changing room and straight through the door marked 'showers'. It was just as I expected, a communal shower area much like the leisure centre except for the fact that here they provided soap and shampoo! Hanging my towel up on a convenient clothes hook I stepped over to the nearest shower head and turned the tap on. Eeeek! The water was cold but quickly warmed up and I lathered myself up, as I did so I heard the shower head next to me start to run, glancing over I saw Jason doing the same thing. Boy was he a sight to behold and the sight of him washing was somehow erotic, so I asked him if there was anywhere more private that we could go and you know.....

"Easy tiger!" Jason laughed "There's plenty of time for that later, just chill out, we've still got the steam room and Jacuzzi to go yet. It's my turn to choose, so I think the Jacuzzi is next followed by the steam room. Come on old man."

With that he turned off the shower, picked up his towel slinging it over his shoulder, not bothering to dry himself and opened the door to the changing room. Only then did he look to see if I was following, which I was just a couple of steps behind. The Jacuzzi room was actually quite busy with about four other guys already sitting in the bubbling water and another couple standing around talking while idly watching the others. Luckily there was enough room for us to squeeze in although it was a bit cosy (okay, sardines might be a better description!) I sat down gingerly not wanting to slip and make a fool of myself and I noticed that Jason did much the same. He quickly settled back and closed his eyes enjoying the sensations the bubbles were causing. I however was more curious about the fellow occupants of the Jacuzzi and casually looked round the pool. Just regular guys really I thought to myself, as I did so I felt a hand slide it's way slowly up my thigh to my groin and then over to my crotch. Startled by this development I glanced over the owner of the hand, who looked at me with a tentative smile and pleading expression. I would have put him in his early sixties, not bad looking for a man of his age and then seeing that I wasn't about to punch him his smile broadened before he looked down and concentrated on exploring my body. I spread my legs a little to allow him easier access, his fingers by now had hold of my balls and were gently rolling them, my cock was rapidly rising to attention and the head was just poking up above the frothing water. I expected the hand to stroke my cock but instead the hand went lower and I felt a finger trace the outline of my anus before very gently pushing the tip just inside my hole drawing a satisfied sigh from my lips.

"Do you like that? I can give you something better if you would like" the owner of the finger whispered trying to be discreet as possible.

"Yeah I guess I might. How do you fancy a little company? I'm with this gorgeous guy so we come as a pair." I replied, sounding out his sincerity.

By now Jason had focused in on the conversation and seeing the state of my cock put two and two together instantly. Raising one eye brow he looked at me with a grin and said "you don't waste time do you?"

"Nope" was all I said in response before turning back to the guy and asking "Well?"

The guy must have thought he'd died and gone to heaven because he had a big grin on his face and said he knew just the place to go. Five minutes later we were in one of the 'rest rooms'; designed apparently just for this type of activity. There was a single bed sized couch covered in black plastic along with two armchairs covered in the same material. Beside the bed was a coffee table with a lamp and a big bowl containing condoms and sachets of lubricants. We didn't waste time with pleasantries like closing the door behind us or asking names but got straight down to business.

Having seen the size of our cocks the guy decided that he wanted to be bottom after all so Jason pulled on a condom, then bent the guy over the couch before lubricating his hole and shoving his cock up him, sparing him no mercy. The poor guy cried out and wriggled trying to escape his ordeal without success. As Jason hammered away I climbed up on the couch and kneeled before the willing victim, taking hold of his head I impaled him on my own throbbing erection. I stopped for a moment to allow him to adjust to it before I started to fuck his face. Jason told me not to come and as soon as we felt like we would then we were to stop and swap places. Before long this is exactly what we had to do! I could feel pressure building up in my balls so I called time and we swapped positions. As I slipped on a condom I asked the guy if he was okay, with a slut happy grin on his face he said that he was indeed.

This time Jason sat in one of the chairs while the guy was on all fours with his head between Jason's legs, slurping with great gusto on the naked cock in front of him. I knelt down and slid my cock easily into the guy's sloppy hole and started to steadily fuck him. Behind me I heard the creak of the door opening and saw the young guy I had previously seen in the sauna peering through the doorway unable to believe his eyes. I motioned for him to join us and do whatever feels right for him. Needing no second telling the youth stepped inside and quickly lost his towel, his cock was resembled him, long and slender with a nicely shaped head. He stood in front of me with his cock half mast, with one free hand I guided it into my mouth and sucked it into life. It grew before my eyes but although it was nice and long it wasn't as hefty as Jason's, just as I was getting into the rhythm of sucking it he pulled away and walked over to the bowl picking up a condom and sachet of lubricant. He quickly donned the condom and knelt down behind me, pushing me forward a little before applying the lubricant to my hole. Just from the way his fingers moved I could tell he was no novice and sure enough before I could think of saying no he had gently and smoothly slid his cock deep inside me and was slowly beginning to fuck me as I fucked the guy in front of me. I guess this is what they call a meat sandwich; it was certainly a novel experience feeling my cock buried deep inside an arse while a cock was stuffed up mine. I looked over to Jason, told him it was such a great feeling that he might like to try it too. So there was a brief interruption while we rearranged ourselves. Jason stood up put another condom on, then willing guy crawled half onto the chair while Jason reinserted his cock up his hole, I then shuffled forward and pushed my cock up Jason's hole, finally I felt the youth's cock slide back inside me. For the next five to ten minutes this human daisy chain groaned and grunted before one by one we shot our loads and collapsed on top of the person in front. This impromptu orgy came to a natural end when youthful guy and willing guy made it clear that they were going to have their own private party and wandered off to another rest room for some privacy.

I smiled at Jason and then said "I don't know about you sunshine, I have had a great time here and it's been a real eye opener but I am bush whacked and would like to call it a day."

Jason's smile wavered momentarily before being fixed back in place "Sure thing old man, there's always another time? Shall we go for a shower and then head back to yours?"

"Come on don't be like that Jason, I've got work in the morning and I don't want to be too late in getting to bed. Of course we can do this again, I've really enjoyed myself. Would you like to stay overnight?" I asked.

Jason laughed and raised his hands in mock surrender "Okay okay! You win and how could I refuse when you've made such a tempting offer?"

Taking charge of the situation I took him by the hand and forcibly led him back to the showers where we thoroughly washed off the stale smells of sex and the sauna in general. As we stepped back out into the street I was reminded of the children's story 'The Lion, the Witch & the Wardrobe', this is how they must have felt stepping through the wardrobe having left Narnia behind.

Two hours later I was laying in bed with Jason snuggled up against me, head on my shoulders with one arm draped across my chest sighing in contentment. I don't like to admit it but I was feeling pretty pleased with myself, for I had shown Jason that between the sheets not only can I be a rampant beast but I can also be a considerate lover. We had fucked each other in just about every position possible and swapping roles several times, I don't think I have one drop of spunk left in my balls! I simply held him tight against me enjoying the moment, not wanting to break the spell. Somewhere along the line we must have drifted off to sleep because the next thing I knew was the alarm going off and the morning rush was underway..........

MONDAY 26TH APRIL

First task this morning was to collect up the votes submitted by the inmates via the ballot boxes on each wing, then take them to the Governor's office for counting and verification by Liam.

By mid-morning the twelve contestants through to the next round were: Tyler, Flick, Eduardo, Dinesh, Jarek, Tony, Bert, Darren, Carl, Martin, Gus and Sayeed. Okay folks I guess the cynical reader might say that it was all a fix but I swear to you the voting was absolutely free and the counting was not fixed in any way. I just like to think that the management got it right first time round.....

I quickly printed out the list of remaining contestants and put up the notices on each wing stating that training will begin in the chapel this evening after dinner and the twelve contestants will be given their new uniforms. The whole prison was quickly buzzing with the news and it continued throughout the afternoon right up until the time I began my welcoming speech, only then did it go quiet.

The contestants sat in the front row of the auditorium waiting to be called up one by one. Tyler and Jarek were the easiest as they were already naked and in fact they ended up wearing more than they started with! But the others were a different story. After those two Flick was next, I called him up on to the stage congratulating him on making it through to the next round and presented him with his red beret and leather belt. Shaking my hand and thanking me he made to walk off the stage as had Tyler and Jarek before him. I called him back and explained that as a volunteer punisher his uniform was the beret and belt, nothing else was considered appropriate and he would have to surrender his clothing immediately or forfeit his place in the competition. He narrowed his eyes at me momentarily, said nothing before grinning mischievously and started to undress handing to me each item of clothing until he stood there naked in front of me. Only then did I give him permission to don his uniform and return to his seat in the audience. Looking down into the audience everyone was enjoying the spectacle except for the remaining nine contestants who were less than happy with what lay ahead but knowing they had no escape route without forfeiting their place in the competition. One by one they collected their new uniform and surrendered their clothing, surprisingly once on stage they acted with good grace and didn't show any of their real feelings. When all twelve were dealt with I called them back up on stage and lined them up in a row facing the audience.

I then made my final speech of the evening "Gentleman, before you stand the final twelve contestants all vying for the six positions of volunteer punisher. For the next five evenings we will ask you to sit in this auditorium and watch the practical training sessions taking place next door. At the end of the evening we will ask you to vote for the contestant who you consider to be the least capable or willing. The training will be filmed totally live and you will be able to see and hear everything as it happens, there will be no faking or trick photography, what you see is what is happening."

Then turning to the contestants I said "Let's get the show on the road, we will now make our way next door and start the training."

There was a short round of applause which subsided into whispering conversations as I led the twelve guys off the stage, down the aisle and through to the training room. Inside waiting for us were James, Max and George positioned behind the video cameras along with Richard who was preparing the shower area. I pointed to a spare couch and told them to remove their berets and belts and place them on the couch as they won't be needed. Briefly glancing at the cameras they did as they were told before joining me in the shower area.

"Okay guys, tonight we are going to focus on personal hygiene both externally and internally. During the course of this evening Richard and I will be demonstrating the cleaning methods that are to be used on a daily basis when you are carrying out your role a volunteer punisher. Then following the demonstration ALL of you will undertake the cleaning methods, I don't need to remind you that every move you make is being recorded and scrutinised by the audience next door and any reluctance may cost you dearly in this competition." I told the men who were standing in a semi circle round me.

As I allowed this information to sink in I started to remove my prison uniform, folding it neatly and passing it to Richard who stood ready to take it from me. Finally I stood in just my boxer shorts, then smiling at the others I pulled them down and handed them to Richard too. I was now as naked as the rest of them.

"Firstly, and I'm sure you all know how to do this, I am going to show you how to wash thoroughly. There is nothing more important than personal hygiene especially as you will be virtually naked twenty four seven. Then afterwards I am going to show you how to clean yourself out internally too." As I announced this I walked over to the shower unit and turned the shower on, adjusting the flow until it was an ambient temperature.

"Come closer because you all need to see this."

The guys shuffled forward positioning themselves so that they could all see me properly. I then spent the next ten minutes showing how to soap up every part of my body including my crack, balls and under the foreskin. Then I demonstrated how to rinse the soap off again afterwards. By now Richard had joined the group with a small pot of Crisco in one hand and when I nodded in his direction he turned the shower off and prepared the douching tube for me.

"Right guys, now comes the fun part! I am going to wash all the shit and detritus out of my rectum so that should a cock need to find its way up my arse it won't come out covered in the brown stuff. You can laugh if you want but I expect this to become part of your daily routine and I will be doing routine inspections of your rectums to make sure you are doing this a matter of course. Richard will explain what he is doing and what you need to remember when it comes round to your turn because you will be practising the method on each other."

I glanced round the group to gauge their reaction to my announcement but with the cameras in close proximity they were careful to keep straight faces and merely nodded in the right places.

Having connected the douching tube to the shower Richard explained to the contestants that the water flowing through it must be just above a trickle and be around body temperature, too cold and it will cause cramping and too hot will burn. Then the tube needs to be greased up and so does the anus. With that he indicated that I was to join him facing away from the contestants, then, I was to bend over at the waist with my hands pulling my cheeks apart.

Out of the corner of one eye I could see a camera moving in for a close up and out of the other eye I could see the guys also moving in for a close up. Then with that I felt the familiar touch of Richard's fingers greasing up my hole and gently inserting the douching tube. It was at that point I heard several gasps from the guys as they realised that this would be happening to them very shortly. In a strange way I was enjoying all this attention until I felt the pangs of a bloated rectum full of water and faeces. I was told to hold it as long as possible by Richard before being given permission to evacuate the contents down the nearby toilet. This process was repeated three times, after which Richard was satisfied I was fully cleaned out.

Standing up straight I thanked Richard for his assistance and asked who wanted to go first. As no one volunteered straight away I randomly selected Eduardo and asked him to take my place in the shower area and assume the same position that I had a few minutes ago. I knelt down behind him and savoured the view of his glowing white cheeks in contrast to his brown back and legs, as he pulled his cheeks apart his ring glistened pinkly and opened very slightly. I took the tub of Crisco from Richard, placed it on the floor before smearing a glob of it around his ring and just inside, when I was satisfied he was greased up sufficiently I took the douching tube, greased that up and inserted it into Eduardo's rectum drawing a quiet groan from his lips. As water flowed into him I gently massaged his ever increasingly bloated stomach, explaining what I was doing all the while, then when he could take no more I pulled the tube out and let him sit down on the toilet to release the water. The force in which it flew out made us all laugh releasing some of the tension in the room. Then it was time for Eduardo to assume the position again and the process was repeated for another two times before the effluent ran clear from his backside.

Deciding it was best to take charge I didn't ask for a volunteer, instead I selected Dinesh, Jarek and Gus in that order because I knew that they had to be familiar with the process as they could all accommodate fists and there was no way to be able to do this without being cleaned out first. Sure enough they took the cleaning out in their stride and were comfortable enough with it to crack a couple of jokes with the other guys while it was going on. Then it was Tony's turn and he was the last of the easy ones, all the remaining guys had only ever had a finger up their bums!

That was about to change, starting with Sayeed, I had a score to settle with him and he was going to be a tough one to crack. But crack he did, having seen five guys before him being cleaned out with no difficulty pride would not let him back away from this challenge. So after I crooked a finger at him as Tony rejoined the crowd he assumed the required position and obediently spread his cheeks wide. Once again I was given the treat of seeing his tight pink anus nestling amongst the black hairs of his crack. Not giving him time to react I started to grease up his hole with a generous amount of Crisco, I took my time in doing so savouring the chance to get my fingers up his arse. Slowly but surely his resistance broke down and I was just able to insert two fingers into his virgin hole, after some more warming up and words of encouragement he was sufficiently relaxed to be able to comfortably accommodate the two fingers. Deciding he was loose enough I inserted the douching tube, I made sure that there was enough of the tube up there that he knew what it felt like to have a cock inside him. He was panting from the exertion and I could see that his face was flushed as well as his neck and shoulders. Reaching underneath him, I accidentally brushed against his genitals and was surprised to find that he was erect, considering his attitude during his post punishment meeting this was not the reaction I had been expecting. However I kept my thoughts to myself and concentrated on the task at hand which was to massage his expanding stomach. All too soon he was fully loaded with water and I allowed him to empty himself out into the toilet under the watchful gaze of the other guys and the cameras. As with the preceding guys I cleaned him out a further couple of times before releasing him for his ordeal.

Flick and Tyler were next and just like Sayeed were anal virgins so they took some breaking into! With Tyler he was definitely a crowd puller (possibly because of his reputation) and when the douching tube was pushed inside more than one guy clapped and whistled. Flick was a different matter, he was more concerned with image and once he realised that he wasn't about to lose face he readily submitted to the anal intrusion. Of the four remaining guys Bert, Darren, Carl and Martin only Bert seemed to show any reluctance in being cleaned out and he deliberately hung back until last. From my point of view it was game up for him, he had been the only one of the twelve guys to show any hesitation or reluctance, but that would be for the audience outside to decide not me, management no longer had a say in the matter.

Finally some two hours after entering the training room all twelve contestants had been cleaned out, allowed to don their uniforms again and were standing up on stage waiting for the results of the voting. I had to give the contestants credit, they all walked back up the aisle with heads held high and when other inmates called out to them they waved back in response with grins on their faces. They gave no sign of any tension as they waited for the votes to be counted. After five minutes of waiting with baited breath Liam handed me an envelope, I opened it with great ceremony and read out the one word written on the paper within the envelope – Bert. There was deliberately no indication of the number of votes he had got, it was sufficient for him to know that he was no longer in the competition. After a short thank you speech by Bert he removed the beret and leather belt and handed it to me as he was required to do. He stood there expectantly waiting for his clothes to be returned. I informed him that all the contestants clothing had been confiscated as soon as the training session had commenced and was locked away within the Governor's office for safekeeping. Unfortunately this meant he would not be able to gain access to his clothes until tomorrow morning when the offices were open again. In the meantime he would have to remain naked until then. Consider it a booby prize for being voted off I suggested with just a trace of a smile. There was nothing he could do except shrug his shoulders and leave the stage with as much dignity as he could muster to the applause of the audience. As he left the room I closed the meeting by confirming once again that the next round would take place at the same time tomorrow here in the chapel where things will be taken to the next level.

I didn't get home until late that evening and as I sat eating my supper I realised that I would not have time this week to join Aaron and Jason for their Tuesday and Thursday runs. I sent them both a text message from my mobile informing them that for this week only due to work commitments I would not be able to join them in their runs but they were not to use that as an excuse to avoid doing it! Aaron replied within minutes saying that it wasn't a problem and that he'll see me at the leisure centre as normal at the weekend. Jason however didn't respond until much later, in fact I was just about to turn my phone off when his message arrived. He said that it was okay with him but hoped that I wasn't getting cold feet with him after the weekend. Stupid boy! I thought to myself, I was a little more tactful in my reply however. I assured him that there was no way I was getting cold feet and it was simply down to being on late shifts all this week. He then came back asking if he could stay over tomorrow night as Kirsty was still away? Not having the energy to argue I agreed to his request, if I'm honest I was just a little bit pleased with his eagerness to sleep with me again.

TUESDAY 27TH APRIL

Dear diary, I'm going to skip the boring bits of today and jump straight to this evening's training session in the chapel. It was slightly different tonight in the fact that Adrian was acting as compere in the auditorium whilst I and the contestants went straight to the training room next door and as before they removed their uniforms putting them to one side. As with last night James, Max and George were the camera men and Richard acted as shower assistant.

Standing in front of the eleven contestants I explained to them that the first task of the evening was to clean themselves inside and out. They were expected to do it without assistance as they had been shown how to do it the previous evening. No one made a move until they heard the creak of a video camera moving, this seemed to jolt them into action and this time Tyler took the lead and stepped up to the shower and made a great show of soaping himself up and then rinsing himself off. It was hard not to stand and gawp at him, as I've mentioned before he is pure beefcake, black as coal and hung like a horse. Then, not bothering to dry himself he bent over spreading his legs a little and greased up his little puckered hole. Next he took the douching tube, adjusted the flow of water through it and the temperature before carefully sliding the tube deep inside him. He remained in that position until he felt enough water had flowed inside before removing the tube and squatting over the toilet. On my instruction he hovered over the seat so that I (and the cameras) could see the colour of the effluent. Naturally on the first clear out it came out brown but by the third clearout it was clear.

Not wanting to be out done Flick announced that he would go next. As he showered I could not help but watch his dragon tattoos move as his washed himself, they were quality tattoo s and seemed to have a life of their own. Before long he was cleaned out and it was then the turn of Gus, then Carl and so on until all eleven guys were done.

While the last few guys were busy cleaning themselves out I went to the metal cabinet and retrieved eleven dildos of average cock size along with five tubs of Crisco and placed them all on a nearby couch ready for the next stage of their training. Calling them over I told them that as adult males we knew that they had experience in the art of fucking in an active capacity, however in the role of volunteer punisher they may be required to participate in man to man sex in a passive capacity. The purpose of the next exercise is to introduce their anus and rectum to having an object i.e. a cock up inside them, and as a responsible organisation it is safer to do it this way than to allow them to be fucked by another inmate without having any prior experience. As I was talking I looked round the group I could see a couple of faces looking worried, one was Sayeed (no surprise there!) and the other was Martin. I mentally made a note of this to ensure they got special attention from me.

I then went on to say that I recognised that some guys had already got experience of having cocks up them and if they didn't mind they would take the bottom role to start off with so the others could be taught the correct technique for inserting the dildos. There were no objections and I didn't expect any given the nature of the competition so I asked Eduardo, Dinesh, Jarek, Tony and Gus to get down on all fours on the floor facing away from us with their heads on their hands. This had the effect of raising their bums in the air and exposing their holes to us, what a sight indeed, five puckered holes waiting to be stuffed. Next I instructed Flick, Tyler, Darren, Carl and Martin to collect a dildo each and a tub of Crisco and then kneel down behind a hole of their choosing. Sayeed asked me why he had not been included, I explained that I already knew that he was experienced in stuffing holes and that I wouldn't insult his intelligence by getting him to do this exercise. His pride was intact with this assurance and he nodded his understanding. Walking over to the group I told them to liberally grease up the holes in front of them all round the outside of the ring and then to take another glob of grease and push it inside the anus with two fingers and smear it all around as much as possible. Next they were to grease up the dildo and place the head of it at the entrance, tell the recipient to breathe deeply and relax before very slowly and gently pushing the dildo inside. Keep pushing until the dildo is fully inserted up to the silicone balls, place your hand on the base of the dildo to keep it in position and let it sit there for a couple of minutes before slowly pulling it back out. I told them to leave just the head inside and then push it back in again, then, with the other hand they were to reach between the recipients legs and take hold of the cock. Next while they slowly fuck the bottom they are to stroke the cock and wank off the recipient until he cums, only then can the dildo be removed. I asked them if they understood the instructions, I simply got nods of agreement as the five guys were concentrating on the tasks at hand. It was reminiscent of a porn film watching the five guys in a row being fucked with the dildos and wanked off. After about five minutes I heard Tony grunting and then the distinctive splat of jism hitting the tiled floor, I told Darren to remove the dildo and clean Tony's hole up using the tissue I handed to him. Watching Darren do so I noted that Tony's hole closed up quite quickly indicating that he obviously doesn't get that much bottom action inside! A couple of minutes later Eduardo came, followed by Gus, Dinesh and finally Jarek. However their holes were slower to close up (as I expected) because they saw more action and were capable of taking larger objects. Whilst their holes remained open I pointed out to the "tops" that this was a good sign and indicated that the bottoms were completely relaxed. Now that they were all cleaned up I announced that it was time to swap!

The "tops" were a little hesitant in kneeling on the floor but after words of encouragement from the "bottoms" they did indeed swap positions. Eduardo now knelt behind Tyler, Dinesh behind Carl, Jarek behind Flick, Gus behind Martin and Tony behind Darren. I told Sayeed it was now time for him to join the other "bottoms" and that I would be taking care of him today. He threw me a quirky smile in response before assuming the same position as the others. I asked the new "tops" if they had any questions and reminded them to take extra care with their "bottoms" as they were relatively virginal, all shook their heads before starting to grease up the waiting holes. Confident that they knew what they were doing I focused on Sayeed's hole before me. Following my own instructions I greased up his hole and pushed two fingers inside, he reflexively gripped my fingers before relaxing again. I then replaced my fingers with the dildo and as the head pushed up inside him I am sure that I heard him sigh. I let him get adjusted to the intrusion before sliding the rest of the dildo up his rectum. As I started to fuck him with the dildo I reached between his legs to find that he was already erect and his cock was throbbing. It didn't take many strokes of the dildo to bring him to a growling climax and a large puddle of jism lay on the floor beneath him. I removed the dildo, wiped him clean and congratulated him on doing so well. He looked over his shoulder and smiled weakly.

Once everyone had finished the exercise and donned their uniform again it was time to tidy the room up and make our way back to the auditorium for the results of the voting. This time I had no idea of who would be voted off as they all seemed to have performed okay, if pushed I would guess it would be either Darren or Martin as they had seemed slightly shy and quieter than the others. We stood on the stage in a row, with me at one side, like last night the contestants stood up straight with pride and their hands clasped behind their backs in a show of confidence while we waited for the results. Finally Liam came over and handed me the envelope, with slightly shaking hands I tore it open and read out the name on the paper – Martin. As I read out his name his face showed his disappointment but he gave me a nice smile as I shook his hand in commiseration before asking him to surrender his uniform to me. With good grace he handed me his red beret and leather belt before bowing to the audience and walking out of the auditorium to remain naked until the following morning. I congratulated the remaining ten contestants and once again closed the proceedings by inviting everyone back for the next session tomorrow evening.

Back at home I quickly ate and had a shower before texting Jason to let him know that I was ready for him to come round. Twenty minutes later there was a ring on the door bell and I let him in with a casual hello, his response was more energetic. He shut the door behind him then grabbed me in a bear hug before pushing me against the wall and kissing me forcefully on the lips.

Coming up for air, he took a step backwards grinning and said "Boy have I missed you! I've wanted to do that ever since I last saw you....."

"But that was less than forty eight hours ago." I pointed out laughing, his cheerfulness was very contagious.

"Can we go to bed now?" Jason asked taking my hand and pulling me in the direction of my bedroom.

"In a hurry or something? I thought you were planning to stay the night."

"I am but the time for talking is later, I need you NOW!" he said hoarsely as we reached the bedroom.

He pushed me onto the bed and started ripping my clothes off. He was in a hurry but didn't fumble once (I take this to be an indication on his experience) as my T-shirt, socks, jeans and boxers left me and flew across the room landing in a pile – quickly followed by his own clothes. By the time he joined me on the bed we both were sporting erections, there's nothing like raw passion to get a guy turned on! He lay on top of me, supporting himself on his elbows and started to kiss me on the mouth before moving onto nibbling my neck and shoulders. Deciding to turn the tables on him I reached up and pushed his head down my body. He took the hint and kissed his way down my body and tracing my hairline with his tongue until he reached my intended target, my pulsing erection. Taking his time he repeatedly licked the shaft applying copious amounts of saliva as he did so before placing the cockhead between his lips and looking up at me with lust filled eyes. Before I could say anything he went down on me and swallowed my entire cock in one smooth movement. Aah! The feeling of his warm moist mouth and throat was heaven! I could not help but flex my hip pushing myself further (if that was possible) down his throat. He gagged a little but quickly recovered and then started to give me a fabulous blow job. Not wanting to be selfish I tapped him on his shoulder to get his attention and then told him to scoot round so we could sixty-nine.

Giving me a thumbs up he carefully manoeuvred his hefty frame round so that his crotch was immediately above my head without releasing my cock from his mouth and barely missing a beat in his blow job. I looked up to be greeted by the sight of his ten inch erection less than an inch from my face, I stuck my tongue out just managed to lick his piss slit. Reaching up with my hands I gently pulled his hips do towards me giving me easier access to him. I abandoned all restraint and energetically sucked on his cock. I don't know how long we carried on like this because we didn't stop after the first orgasm. The first warning I had was when Jason's hips shuddered slightly and his cock expanded a little then suddenly my mouth was full of his salty jism. I struggled for a moment to swallow it all but manage I did and I continued to suck him until he started to soften. I thought he might pull off me but no, he lowered himself slightly so I couldn't pull away and concentrated on my needs. By the time I was ready to shoot he was hard again and actively fucking my mouth. This cycle was repeated several times before we admitted that we were spent and exhausted by our efforts. As he crawled his way back up the bed and into my arms a thought wheedled its way into my brain and it was one that I couldn't ignore. I looked at his handsome face and all I could think was that no matter how wrong it was or how much trouble it may cause, I was not going to let him get away from me. I'm not sure if I can at this stage call it love but the thought of letting him go is very painful to me.

WEDNESDAY 28TH APRIL

Day three of the training and tonight we got the contestants, after the now customary cleaning out, to give each other blow jobs and swallow the jism before getting them to fuck one another to orgasm. Now that we were really getting down to serious action it was intensely erotic, I am sure that we could do a side line in gay porn films! Yet despite this I found I was going through the motions of being the trainer rather than being really into the scene as I had been the previous two evenings. In fact I was glad when it was all over and we were once more standing before the audience waiting for the vote. The result did not come as a shock to me, Darren's number was up when he spat out Flick's jism in disgust and walked over to the shower without permission to wash his mouth out. He seemed relieved to be handing in his uniform and marched off stage with barely an acknowledgement to the audience.

Back home I reflected on my distracted state of mind and I quickly realised that Jason was the cause. I just couldn't him out of my mind nor decide what do to resolve the problems I could foresee surrounding our relationship if it were to continue. For tonight at least there is nothing to be gained by torturing myself, I will just have to have a candid talk to him at the weekend after swimming.

THURSDAY 29TH APRIL

After a good night's sleep and giving myself a stern mental dressing down I was more able to focus of today's activities. Which is just as well as tonight's session in the training room was a lot more intense and even more erotic (for me at least) than yesterday. We were now down to nine guys – Flick, Tyler, Eduardo, Dinesh, Jarek, Tony, Gus, Sayeed and Carl. The competition was heating up and they were clearly determined to outdo each other to ensure their place on the next round.

By now I didn't need to supervise their cleaning out as they were now doing automatically and actually helping each other, possibly to gain favour with the audience I imagine. That left me free to help Richard get the toys ready for action as tonight's aim was anal stretching. Each guy would have four butt plugs, ranging in size from small cock size up to large fist size, which by the end of the evening they had to be able to fully insert into their rectums with ease. I liberally greased each one with Crisco and arranged them in size order, smallest at the front and largest at the back, on the floor in a circle. This was so that the contestants could monitor each other's progress and act as an incentive to do better themselves.

I explained what was required from them this evening, saying that each time they successfully inserted a plug they were to stand up and bend over displaying the buried plug for the group to see and for my inspection. It wasn't a race but to pass this round each guy needed to have inserted all four plugs, failure to do so would mean instant disqualification without the need for the audience voting. The nine men looked at one another with expressions that ranged from confident to apprehensive but none had time to dwell on the matter as I clapped my hands and told them to get started.

In no time at all Dinesh, Jarek and Gus had inserted all four plugs (not surprising as they can all accommodate fists up their back sides) and were free to act as encouraging mentors for the remaining six guys who were still trying to expand their horizons if you follow my drift. Eduardo and Tony were quickly onto the third plug whilst the others were having a hard time on the second plug. It was time to lend a helping hand, so I instructed Flick, Tyler, Sayeed, Carl, Tony and Eduardo to get down on all fours with their bums in the air, as they had done on Tuesday. Then Richard and I each took the biggest plug and started to slowly and gently fuck Eduardo and Tony with them until with groans from each man the huge butt plugs sank inside and their rings clamped firmly down on the plug's neck. We left them to get accustomed to the massive intrusion before starting to slowly pull them out and reinsert them. After about ten minutes their holes were totally stretched out and they could swallow the plugs with ease. Their ordeal was now over and were allowed to shower themselves thoroughly clean. Whilst we were doing this Dinesh, Jarek and Gus had taken the third plugs and mirrored our actions on Flick, Tyler and Carl. Sayeed was left waiting until I was free to assist. Progress was a little slower with these four as they were less anally stretched than the rest but after a lot of encouragement and words of advice they all managed to take in the third plugs. As with Tony and Eduardo we left them for a minute before starting the fucking actions. Finally they were ready for the largest plug and half an hour later even Flick was now proudly impaled on the fist sized plug. The highlight of the evening for me was when Sayeed spontaneously shot his load all over the floor as the widest part of the plug slipped past his protesting anal ring.

Tonight the audience voted off Carl, the only reason I can assume is that he perhaps showed the least enthusiasm with the butt plugs or perhaps was the least photogenic.

FRIDAY 30TH APRIL

Dear diary, I can't believe another month has flown past, how time flies when you're having fun! Or should that be when you're working like mad and only getting a little bit of fun on the side......

Thankfully for my sanity at least, tonight was the last evening of the training sessions and the contestants have been whittled down to seven with Tony being voted off. Again as with Carl I think it was more down to the way he came across with the cameras rather than anything he did wrong.

Last night was relatively easy as far as pushing anal boundaries go, well I think so at least, tonight was going to be the final boundary to be crossed. After being cleaned out I told them that they were going to stand in a ring facing the back of the guy in front. Then having liberally greased up one hand and the arse in front with Crisco they were going to fist each other until the recipient had cum with or without manual assistance of the fister.

Standing back I observed the daisy chain fisting with a rock hard erection, the only thing holding me back from whacking off was the fact that the three cameras were all over the place trying to record in close up detail each fist as it slid in and out of the hole it was impaling and I needed to maintain a professional stance throughout. By the end of the fistathon eight guys lay collapsed on the floor in a sweaty, dirty heap totally exhausted and spaced out for their experiences.......

Having cleaned themselves inside and out again under a hot shower, I handed them their uniforms again before we strode back into the auditorium for the final vote off. After Carl was voted off Liam and I thanked everyone involved in the competition for all the hard work that went into making it a success. Then we thanked the competitors for participating in every task set before them and pushing their boundaries so willingly, and finally we thanked the audience for their votes and we hoped they enjoyed the spectacle. We also pointed out that they had selected the volunteer punishers themselves so they had no room to complain should they not like the results further down the road! The final speech I had to make was tell the remaining seven contestants that from tomorrow onwards they will be assuming the role of a Volunteer Punisher twenty four seven and would be expected to act accordingly at all times. Next week will be their final assessment when one last contestant will be voted off leaving the six permanent punishers.

After that they were free to go and enjoy their last night of relative freedom, talking of which I was now free myself to go back to my normal shift patterns and get back to having a social life again. Okay, that can be read as seeing more of Jason........ Mmm, now that's a problem waiting to be solved.

DIARY OF A PRISON OFFICER - PART 3

SATURDAY 1ST MAY

Dear diary, why are good ideas so much harder to put into practice than they seem when dreamt up? Over the last couple of days I'd resolved to speak to Jason about our relationship, such that it is, and admit to him that I just can't get him out of my mind. But every time I think about 'us' all I can see is a nightmare in the making. Let's face it there's nothing simple about the situation.

I'm old enough to be his father for I'm in my mid-forties and Jason in his early twenties. That alone is a concern to me plus the fact that that he's the best mate of the son of my best mate, Mike. He's got a girlfriend, Kirsty, who he's been with for ages and I've met. So that's a little awkward. A lovely girl but a little needy for my liking and seems to have Jason wrapped around her little finger. On top of that all of my friends consider me straight and I have no idea how they would react if they found out that I enjoy sex with men let alone with someone half my age and known to them!

I spent a long time this morning in bed churning the issues over in my head trying to find a solution that didn't involve emotional carnage in the end. Thirst and hunger drove me out of bed long before a solution came to mind, giving up on the subject I pulled on a pair of boxers and padded out of the bedroom. As I ate my breakfast I checked my mobile phone for messages. It bleeped several times, one text from James at work and two from Jason. I dealt with James's text first for he just wanted to know if I was still paying him and Lucas a visit tomorrow, I confirmed that I was and looking forward to it. Reading Jason's texts made me laugh, he is such a tart. The first message read 'I want.....' and the second read 'YOU'. Still chuckling, I replied 'You can....' before sending another 'LATER'.

He didn't reply so I got on with my day until I met up with the gang at the leisure centre for our normal Saturday swimming session. They were all there and even Chrissie and Kirsty joined us in the pool to swim twenty or so lengths. It was only afterwards and in the relative privacy of the changing room that Jason acted other than his normal 'straight' self. I had removed my wet swimming trunks and was towelling myself dry when having looked around to make sure we weren't being watched he cupped my arse cheeks with his hands and gave them a quick squeeze.

"God you're horny" he whispered in my ear before stepping away quickly as Tom turned in our direction.

"Sam are you joining us for dinner tomorrow?" Tom asked as he pulled his trousers up.

"Sorry I can't. I'm out all day tomorrow, perhaps next weekend?" I replied as Jason gave me a questioning look.

"Sure no worries" Tom reassured me with a smile "it was a last minute idea, that's all."

"Where are you going tomorrow?" Jason asked from underneath his towel as he dried his hair.

"Into town, why?"

"I was hoping to call round for an hour or so tomorrow afternoon for a little bit of....." he trailed off as he dropped the towel on the floor and grabbed his tackle to emphasise his point.

"You're out of luck I'm afraid, prior engagement and all that. What about later today?"

Our conversation was abruptly interrupted as Aaron and Mike joined us and the topic changed to Aaron's experiences as a new dad. Nothing else was said between Jason and me until later that evening when he text me simply stating 'meet me outside Arkwrights at 9pm'. My interest was piqued and so I did. The shop in question is an open all hours store five minute's walk away from my flat. I arrived a couple of minutes early but Jason was already there parked opposite the shop. Spotting me he waved me over with a grin and as I crossed the road towards him he started the car's engine. He waited for me to fasten my seat belt before he leant over and gave me a quick kiss on the cheek.

"Thanks for coming" he said as he steered the car into the flow of traffic.

"This is all very mysterious, so where are we headed?"

"I know a secluded spot just perfect for what I have in mind."

I made no reply instead I watched the passing scenery and stroked his thigh at the same time. I smiled to myself as I watched him squirm trying to concentrate on driving while my hands reached higher up his leg. In the end he begged me to stop unless I wanted him to have an accident. What type of accident I didn't know, I could think of a couple but I withdrew my hand as a trip to hospital wasn't my idea of an exciting evening!

We drove through areas I wasn't familiar with until we parked up in an unlit back street adjacent to a canal. A little nervous of our surroundings I looked at him in askance. He laughed at my expression and told me not to worry as this was a favourite spot for him.

"Favourite?" I asked "Do you come here often?"

"A few times. The police don't know about it as far as I know, anyway less talking more action!"

With that he got out of the car and waited for me to join him before locking the car and disappearing into the darkness. I ran to catch up with him, I didn't have far to go, just round the corner was a bridge over the canal and there he stood. I could just make him out in the deep shadows and as I stood in front of him I could see that he already had his trousers around his ankles and stroking his cock to erection. The size of it still took my breath away for it was over ten inches long, not as big as Tyler's but far bigger than anyone else I knew.

I didn't say a word as I sank down to me knees and held his rock hard cock in my hand. Slowly I brought my mouth closer to it and kissed the head lovingly. I could taste the faint trace of soap mixed with a slight saltiness as I licked all around the flange and his piss slit. I heard him whisper words of encouragement and then felt his hands on the top of my head slowly pushing me downwards. Willingly I opened my mouth and impaled myself on him, as he hit the back of my throat I gagged a little before adjusting my position so that I could swallow the rest of him down my throat. At the same time I wrapped my hands around his hairy muscular legs to support myself as my head bobbed up and down on his pole. I was in heaven! How I love to suck this young man's cock! From his groans it was clear that he was enjoying it as much as I was.

I was totally oblivious to our surroundings, so focused on the cock in my mouth that I didn't hear the echoing footsteps approaching us until their owners started giggling. I hesitated in my head bobbing but resumed once I realised that Jason was totally relaxed, clearly we weren't at risk for his hands continued to guide my head. The adolescent giggling receded until at a safe distance they cried "fucking poofs!" Neither of us responded for we were too far gone in our passion to care and shortly afterwards I felt Jason's body tense before he erupted sending jets of jism shooting down my throat. Enthusiastically I swallowed each load and it was only with reluctance that I let his now flaccid cock slip from my mouth.

He surprised me by pulling me up into his arms, as he gave me a bear hug he kissed me hard on the lips before driving his tongue into my mouth. I was so pent up that I thought was about to explode there and then! My hands slipped down to my jeans and without conscious thought undid the waistband and flies to release my aching cock and balls. I started to stroke myself but my hand was knocked away and replaced by his mouth. It didn't take me long to cum and as I shuddered from the orgasm I felt him hold me steady as he swallowed my seemingly endless amount of jism.

Wiping his mouth with the back of his hand he walked back to the car, seeming to be a hurry to get going. As we each sucked on an extra strong mint I asked him why he was in such a rush. Scowling in response he concentrated on driving before almost reluctantly he told me that Kirsty was under the impression that he'd only gone to buy some petrol. Ah, I thought to myself, that explains the 'wham bam thank you ma'm attitude. Clearly now was not the right time to discuss my feelings for him, it would just have to wait for another day.

SUNDAY 2ND MAY

As much as I enjoyed the al fresco session last night today, in hindsight, I feel a little down if I'm being honest. I had planned to open up to Jason but it was clear that he only had one thing on his mind and emotional talk wasn't it. I should have known better, he's a player and he's happily doing it behind Kirsty's back. Why would he be interested in how I feel? He had said he wanted no-strings fun and I had agreed thinking that would be enough for me. But it wasn't enough now that I was falling in love with him. Did I just say 'love'? Silly old fool, so whose problem was it? Mine all mine.

Enough moping for one day, I had other things to do like getting my arse over to Southwark where James and Lucas live. An hour later I was sitting on the half-empty southbound tube train taking me from Angel to London Bridge. With no one sitting opposite me I caught sight of my reflection in the window. The darkness of tunnel walls only seemed to accentuate the white hairs in my beard and hair but at least it hid the wrinkles. I studied myself turning my head from one side to another until I noticed that I was being watched by a disapproving old lady. I smiled at her slightly embarrassed before turning my attention to the adverts lining the carriage walls.

At London Bridge I changed trains for Southwark, this time the carriage was packed and on a warm late spring morning the temperature was uncomfortable. Thankfully it was only one stop and I was glad to get out of the underground and into the welcoming sunshine. My destination was just a short walk from the tube station and before I knew it I was buzzing their intercom in the entrance way of the 1930's block of flats.

It was the first time that I'd seen James outside of work so when he opened his front door I was surprised to see him dressed in what I would call hippy clothes. For some reason with him being a sports coach I had imagined that he would wear sporting gear all the time. My expression must have broadcast my thoughts for he looked down at himself and with a rueful smile explained that this was his preferred style, much more comfortable than the tight fitting Lycra he wore at work. I held my hands up in mock surrender and assured him that I was caught off guard that was all. In fact I thought the flowing clothes suited him. From the kitchen I heard sounds of movement and as I made myself comfortable Lucas appeared carrying a tray of coffee and biscuits.

With introductions over (this was the first time I'd met Lucas) we got down to the purpose of my visit. Sad as it may sound but it was work related, for James and I never get the chance to talk about anything other than immediate needs of the inmates. Over the last month we have tried unsuccessfully to discuss the health and fitness levels of the inmates but due to work demands the meetings always get cancelled or postponed. So we decided to meet outside of work, hence today.

The lack of fitness and obesity levels has been made more obvious since the introduction of the new regime and inmates being more closely monitored. Over the next hour we talked through our concerns and ideas to solve the problem. By the end of the conversation James had decided that sports should become a mandatory part of prison life and be included within the punishment regime if inmates refused to exercise. To give them goals and make it less of a chore I contributed the idea of having team sports like football or rugby and have a league for teams to compete, we could even have a charity event or something like that.

Lucas, bless him, must have been bored stupid but he sat there patiently until the work talk had dried up. Only then did he join in the conversation by asking me about my views on environmental issues in London. James just looked at him with raised eyebrows but fair enough I thought we'd talked shop for long enough. Now it was his turn to talk about a subject that interested him and boy was he enthusiastic about it! By the end of the afternoon I knew about all the pollution and traffic problems Londoners face daily along with the dangers James and he encounter as cyclists every day from motorists. Somehow during the conversation I had given him the impression that I was totally with him on the subject, which now made me his best buddy. So much so that he asked me if I would join James in supporting him with his latest venture, I would be doing him a massive favour. James looked at me in alarm but I didn't catch his look until I had readily agreed to his request.

It was only after I had said yes that I found out that he was going to be taking part in the London   Naked Cycle Ride in just over a week's time. As it was on a Wednesday I would have to take a day off but sounded like a laugh, at least we would only be watching and Lucas needed the moral support to take part. While Lucas was out of the room James moaned that he'd been trying to put him off this venture for ages but with my helpfulness there was no way out. I smiled apologetically but I couldn't see what the problem was and Lucas seemed genuinely pleased with the outcome.

MONDAY 3RD MAY

Oh diary, why do I do it to myself? Bank holiday Monday, the sun shone all day and what had I done, only volunteer to do overtime, typical. I could have spent the day sunning myself in the park watching the world go past. But there again work was enjoyable and I did earn double pay at the same time.

It was day one of the final week for the Volunteer Punisher contestants and they were to be put through their paces from the start. At 9am prompt they walked into the Governor's Office where Liam, James and I were seated in a row behind his long table. I was reminded of my interview in this office just a few months ago. They were a handsome sight, seven men in a row standing to attention wearing nothing but red berets and a leather belt around their waists. From Tyler, the huge black man with an equally huge cock to the short but fiery Flick they stood motionless, with hands by their sides like little soldiers, staring at the wall behind us.

Quite deliberately we said nothing for several minutes, partly to unnerve them and partly to enjoy the view before with Liam leading the way we inspected them. Liam focused on their uniform, straightening a beret here and tightening a belt there. James assessed their bodies for muscle tone and excess fat, he felt just about every inch of their bodies from head to toe writing up his findings on a clip board as he went. My role in this inspection was medically based. I had to establish if they had maintained their receptivity and a willingness to obey our instructions.

So as Liam and James walked slowly down the line of men I started my own inspections. First to be assessed was Tyler, one of my favourite inmates for both his physical attributes and his personality. Having donned a pair of latex gloves I stood in front of him and cupped his hefty balls in my hand. Gently rolling them around I judged their fullness or in this case lightness. As his cock rose to attention he moaned under his breath, I think they were words of encouragement but either way I had to focus on the task ahead and not be distracted by the enormous black pole of his. I asked him if he had unloaded recently and my suspicions were confirmed when his nodded in response.

I then moved on to the next man in line, Jarek and did the same assessment before going onto Gus, then Sayeed, Flick, Eduardo and Dinesh. James and Liam waited patiently for me to finish but I noted that they had prepared themselves for the next assessment by donning gloves too and opening a fresh can of Crisco. I stood with them discussing my findings before asking the seven men to turn around, bend over and pull their cheeks apart.

Without hesitation and in unison they did as they were told presenting us with a view of seven backsides and seven anuses showing signs of recent stretching. An excellent sign in my opinion but only the final test would determine if their rings had remained sufficiently loose to comply with our requirements. Leading the way Liam greased up Tyler's arse and quite casually pushed his fist past his anus bringing a grunt from the big guy. Wasting no time he withdrew before moving on to Jarek and repeated the same manoeuvre. James then slipped his fist up Tyler for a second opinion. Again I brought up the rear, so to speak, as each contestant was fisted by the three of us in turn. I have to admit I loved the feeling of my hand slipping past their stretched ring and being enveloped by their silky smooth hot rectums.

I could have cum there and then but was too professional to do so. I just hoped the damp patch wouldn't seep through my shorts and into my trousers! Having been handed paper towelling to wipe themselves off Liam told them to stand to attention again before informing them that they had passed what would be a weekly inspection all the time they remained Volunteer Punishers. James followed up by telling them that they weren't in as good a shape as he would like and so their next destination was the gymnasium.

I watched them file out of the office following James as instructed admiring their virtually naked bodies, the uniform just seemed to emphasise their state of undress.

"They're fine specimens aren't they?" Liam asked jolting me out of my reverie.

"Yes, I think that's fair to say" I nodded sagely "their attitude and willingness to obey is good too."

"Almost as good as yours" Liam winked before returning to his desk and looking towards his in tray.

I cleared with Liam that I could take the 12th May off as annual leave before returning to my normal duties on the prison wing. Late morning Eduardo joined me on the wing looking exhausted from his time in the gym. Personally looking at his slim body I didn't think he needed much improving but that decision wasn't mine to make. The rest day was spent mentoring Eduardo showing him what's involved in cell searches, how to relate to the inmates and what to do when they needed help.

This evening I went for the usual run with Aaron and Jason, I wondered what it would be like considering Saturday night's events. But I needn't have worried for the atmosphere between us was fine, Aaron clearly didn't know anything about our meet up and Jason acted as if I hadn't seen him since the swimming session. Their fitness levels had improved and we ended up running twice around the park before they showed any signs of tiring. So for good measure I told them to do press ups, squats and sit ups in the park. They just looked at me as if I had been kidding but I led by example and got on with the exercises myself. By the end of the last set of sit ups they'd had enough and panting breathlessly we headed back for my flat.

I held the door open for them and they filed past me wordlessly in the hallway. I closed the door behind them and waited for them to continue into the lounge but Jason blocked the way with his hands on his hips grinning.

"Come on guys, you know the house rules. Get your kit off!"

"Okay okay" I said with a mock frown but did as I was told. Within seconds I was standing there starkers with a pile of sweaty clothing on the floor.

As was Jason but Aaron was still reluctant to strip off like he had been before but to my surprise he did remove his shorts too revealing his smooth muscular backside to me. Satisfied Jason gave his friend a clap on the back and winked in my direction. He hung back allowing me to squeeze past him and as I did so he gave my bum a pinch enough me to jump a little. He mouthed me a silent 'later' before following me into the lounge. With what had become our normal routine I let them shower first while I rustled up some food and drink in the kitchen.

I heard a mobile ring from the lounge and heard an exasperated Aaron speaking into his phone, concentrating on the conversation he walked into the kitchen pulling faces at me before with a sigh terminated the call. He had a cross expression on his face and his chest was flushed red emphasising his anger. Quite arousing really for his cock was half erect where he'd been idly playing with it as he spoke.

"I'm sorry Sam but I've got to go right now, domestic emergency naturally. Anybody would think that I can't have time to myself now I've got a kid!"

"Hey no problem, you get going. I'm sure that Jason will help me eat this food without too much encouragement."

He quickly dressed into his normal clothes and with yet another apology he disappeared into the night leaving Jason and me alone again. Shame really for I had enjoyed discretely watching his hot little body but if I'm honest Jason was hotter and we would at least have some private time together. Wasting no time I sauntered into the bathroom where Jason was just stepping out of the shower and looking gorgeous as ever. He looked up in surprise at my entrance but it quickly changed into a grin.

"Where's Aaron?" he asked.

"Domestic crisis had to leave in a hurry."

"Aw that's a shame, now what are we going to do?"

"Oh I can think of a few things" I replied as I stepped into the shower and soaped myself up.

He leant against the wash basin with arms crossed and watched me through the glass shower walls. Without touching himself once I noticed his cock rising to full mast until it stood upright pointing to his belly button, clearly he liked what he saw! By the time I had finished in the shower he must have got impatient waiting for he'd disappeared. Curious to know where he'd gone I grabbed a towel and drying myself I went looking for him. I found him in my bedroom, having pulled the duvet back he'd retrieved the KY and Crisco from my bedside drawer and was lying face down with his legs spread wide. From where I stood I could see his hairy crack and balls spread out on the sheets.

Without saying a word I climbed onto the bed and knelt down between his outspread legs. With my hands I spread his cheeks and pressed my face into his crack. I breathed in deeply savouring the mix of soap and his natural musky smell. My tongue had a life of its own and before I knew it I was licking and lapping all around his puckered anus making it quiver in response. I heard sighs of contentment as he pushed his bum back against my face driving my tongue inside his rectum. This was a first for me and wasn't sure if I wanted to do this, but in for a penny in for a pound as they say. With my tongue I explored the fleshy creases just inside his anus smoothing them as I went but naturally they reformed as soon as my tongue moved on. Either way Jason loved every second of it growing ever more vocal and animated in his hip movements.

I only ceased my energetic rimming when my own needs became so urgent I thought I was going to explode without touching myself. Lifting my face away from his crack I asked him to pass me the KY. I watched him with his head still buried in the pillow grope blindly with one hand over the top of my bedside drawer until he found the lube. I took it from his outstretched hand and squeezed a generous amount into my hand before smearing it along the length of my shaft and cockhead. I didn't need to lube his hole for I'd left plenty of spittle there from the rimming. A little clumsy in my impatience I climbed on top of him positioning my cockhead at his entrance as I did so. He must have been as keen as I was for as I did this he pushed back impaling himself on me in the process.

He reared up in response to the sudden intrusion and looked over his shoulder at me. I rested my weight on his hips and drove myself fully into him, then kissed him on the side of his stubbly face. I buried my face into his still damp hair and breathed in deeply savouring his smell. Slowly I thrust my hips in and out of him enjoying the way he clenched as I pulled out and then relaxed as I pushed back inside. My sense of urgency seemed to have disappeared as I focused on the beauty of our union until that is nature took its course and I could hold back no longer. With a final thrust I climaxed sending my jism into his rectum in pulse after pulse.

I lay there for a long time, longer than I needed to, just enjoying our closeness and the feeling of his naked skin against mine. Eventually Jason became restless and twisted his body underneath until he lay on his back looking up at me with a lustful look on his face. With his erection pressing into my stomach there was no doubt what he wanted from me so kneeling I reached for the KY and quickly lubed up his cock and my hole. With a teasing slowness I aimed his cock and sat down on it in one smooth move. I felt like a rodeo star on my bucking bronco as he tried to thrust more of himself into my willing arse. In this position it was harder for him to cum so I got to enjoy the ride for longer, my arse was so loose by the end of it I felt like I had been fisted again. I did think about introducing that into the game but decided against it, I just wanted to keep it simple - for now.

Afterwards as we lay exhausted from the lovemaking I stroked his chest and casually mentioned about how much I enjoyed having him in my life and my bed. He kissed me before admitting that he too enjoyed our time together, which wasn't quite the same thing as I'd said. So I pushed the subject a little further by asking if he could imagine us ever living together. He froze for a moment seeming to hesitate as if trying to find the right words to say. What he said was disappointing for he wanted to keep things as they were, just a bit of fun, no strings because he loved Kirsty too. I shrugged my shoulders and let the subject drop.

The conversation became a little awkward after that and it wasn't long before he made his exit to my relief. I'm not sure that I want to play this game much longer, was never into head games and there's only one person I can see going to get hurt and that's me. I'm going to have to think long and hard about what I want to do.

TUESDAY 4TH MAY

Dear Diary, nothing much to say really apart from the fact that I can't get Jason out of my head nor can I decide just what to do about him.

WEDNESDAY 5TH MAY

The volunteer punishers have really settled into the routine and although it is still a contest the other inmates are acting towards them as if they're already doing the job for real. Today I had Sayeed with me and we worked well together. He seems to have got over the issues he had previously and is more relaxed about the nudity and gay sex bit. As much as I would like to get him into bed I have to remain professional at all times so I kept my hands and thoughts to myself, I just casually watched him as he interacted with the other inmates and went about his duties.

It was late morning when the warning siren went off which meant something was kicking off. Even though it was on another wing we ran out of our wing and over to B-wing where we could hear sounds of fighting. On entering the wing I saw that George, Mick, Jarek and Dinesh were trying to break up a fight between Vince and three other inmates whilst the fight was being watched by the rest of the wing. Several of the inmates were egging them on, it wasn't often they got to see such a large fight especially after the new regime rules had been introduced.

I glanced around the wing establishing what needed to be done first. Sayeed beat me to it by yelling at the top of his voice

"Back into your cells, NOW! Any more encouraging this violence and I'll have you dragged before the Governor before you can count up to ten!"

To back up his command he strode menacingly towards the first inmate, who took one look at Sayeed's frowning face and disappeared into his cell slamming the door behind him. I was impressed and nodded in encouragement, not that he needed any because he was on a mission. Within a couple of minutes all the inmates except for the still fighting foursome were back in their cells even if it was with more than a little grumbling and swearing at us. Sayeed rejoined me with a big grin on his face and a swagger which I found more of a turn on than irritating.

All that needed to be down was to break up the scrappy fight which my colleagues were having trouble stopping. I indicated to Sayeed that we should take Vince down first as he appeared to be the main protagonist, nodding his agreement we strode over to our target who was more intent on punching the inmate closest to him. Catching him by surprise I rugby tackled him bringing to the floor with a thud and before he could react Sayeed sat on him pinning him to the floor. I grabbed my handcuffs and scrambled to secure Vince's arms behind his back preventing him from lashing out. Climbing to his feet Sayeed dragged Vince roughly by his collar into a sitting position while I cautioned him about making things worse for himself.

With him out of the way we quickly overpowered the other inmates, who in all fairness had calmed down considerably once Vince had been neutralised. Perhaps they'd realised the shit they'd just landed themselves in by acting like brawling thugs. Once we had all four handcuffed we frog marched them into solitary confinement where they would be held until they had been interviewed separately to establish what had happened and why. But that wouldn't be down to us as we had to get back to our wing and resume our normal duties.

THURSDAY 6TH MAY

Well diary, it didn't take long for the investigation over yesterday's fight to be concluded. Max had interviewed each in turn and come to the conclusion that Vince had been the instigator having taunted the other three inmates almost constantly over the previous couple of days. Eventually they'd lost their temper and argued back, this gave Vince an excuse to throw the first punch and it quickly turned into an unstoppable brawl. Thankfully none of the inmates needed medical attention and this morning were released from solitary confinement.

Oh I nearly forgot the best bit, being the volunteer punisher co-ordinator I was released from my normal duties so that I could oversee the release and punishment of the four offenders. The first to be processed was Keith, an unassuming man in his late thirties doing time for commercial burglaries. He'd been the least involved and so had the lightest punishment. I unlocked the door of his holding cell and followed Jarek into the cell where Keith sat looking distinctly nervous at our sudden appearance.

He was right to be nervous for Jarek was determined to prove he should be a punisher and so stood directly in front of the seated man with arms crossed and a frown on his face. In a quiet but menacing voice he told Keith to stand up, remove his clothing and hand it to me. Keith looked as if he was about to argue but changed his mind when he saw that Jarek meant it. He stood up with difficulty as Jarek was standing deliberately close to him and had to squeeze past him before he had room to undress. Avoiding our gaze he looked at the floor while he unbuttoned his shirt, removed it before handing it to me. I dropped it into the plastic bag I was holding and indicated to him continue undressing. Sighing he removed his shoes and socks before dropping his trousers. He handed those to me before standing there in his just his pants.

"Do I have to remove these too?" he asked in a whining tone.

"Yes" Jarek replied.

Sighing again Keith pushed his pants down, stepped out of them and reluctantly placed them into the bag I held out towards him. Naked and with his hands covering his genitals he look very uncomfortable as he followed us back up onto his wing. As he walked back to his cell the other inmates whistled and catcalled, which he did his best to ignore but what he couldn't ignore was his belongings in a clear carry box standing outside his cell door. He looked shocked and hurried into his cell, forgetting to cover himself up in the process. Sure enough his cell was bare of all personal belongings. Jarek with just a slight smirk told him they would be returned to him in 48 hours providing he behaved himself.

I left Jarek on the wing while I returned to the isolation wing to oversee the others being released. Hanif was the next one to be processed and he was more difficult to deal with. Sayeed however spoke to him in Arabic and after some cajoling removed his clothing until he was standing in just his pants but refused to take them off. Despite his best efforts Sayeed could not persuade him to remove them so I signalled to him that it was time to use a little force. Hanif looked at me in panic and then at Sayeed when he was grabbed by the shoulders. I quickly stepped forward, knelt down and in one smooth tug pulled his pants down around his ankles. Like Keith he tried to cover himself with his hands but Sayeed grabbed them and pinned them behind his back allowing me full access to his genitals.

They were worth studying for his balls were decently sized and so was his circumcised cock. Gently I massaged his balls and stroked his cock to see how big it would grow. He pleaded in Arabic, presumably for me to stop but Sayeed shut him up again in Arabic. Blushing a deep red he didn't say another word just stood there looking everywhere except in my direction. Despite his protests he grew hard quite rapidly and I soon had a seven inch cock in front of my face. Oh how I was tempted to put it in my mouth! Before I gave into my urges I released my grip and quickly gathered up his clothes into a plastic bag and strode out of the room. The poor guy was forced to walk back onto the wing sporting an erection which simply wouldn't go down. He too received a welcome onto the wing which grew more vocal when the inmates saw his cock. Unlike Keith he didn't seem surprised to see that his possessions had been consigned to the box outside his cell.

I didn't wait to see how he got on, that was left to Sayeed as I marched back to the isolation unit. I arrived just in time to see Flick unlocking the door to Ned's cell, the guy who received the brunt of Vince's insults. He lay relaxed on his bed with hands behind his head and a sly smile on his face.

"Come to get me have you?"

"That's right Ned. You're going back to your cell" Flick replied matching his tone.

"Right you are then" Ned said as he rolled off the bed and strode towards the door in one smooth move.

"Not so fast" I said blocking the door with my body.

"Now what?" he asked feigning innocence.

"Under the new regime rules you have forfeited your clothing and possessions for the next 48 hours, as you well know" Flick answered taking a step towards him.

"No fucking way! I'm not going to strip for you or any other fucker!"

"Take them off yourself or we will do it for you" I said in a neutral tone.

"Up yours" Ned growled as he tried to push past me.

Clearly it was time to exert my authority so with one hand I held him back and with the other I retrieved the tazer from my jacket pocket. He caught sight of the tazer as I hit the power button before pressing it against his body, the look of horror changed to a grimace as his muscles spasmed uncontrollably. Jerking like a marionette he fell to the floor groaning from the pain.

Wasting no time Flick and I set about removing his clothes, working together we quickly parted him from his trainers, socks and trousers. But he was a tough guy for already he was recovering from the effects of the tazer and fought against us as we made to remove his sweatshirt and shorts. I had no choice but to use the tazer on him again, this time for longer which rendered him virtually unconscious. Now he was compliant so off came his shorts and sweatshirt leaving him naked as the day that he had been born.

"Why do they have to do it the hard way?" Flick asked me as he stuffed the inmate's clothes into a bag.

"Dunno" I replied with a shrug "but that's not our problem. Cuff his hands behind his back for it's time to give him something to think about. He'll think twice next time he wants to rebel against the system."

Flick raised his eyebrows but did as instructed without comment. Once Ned was restrained I spread his legs with my feet and knelt down between them. Gesturing for Flick to join me on the floor I spread Ned's arse cheeks exposing his tiny puckered anus. I then told him to squeeze a generous amount of the lube onto Ned's hole and test his tightness. Grinning he did so and pushed against the hole with his index finger but the grin soon disappeared as Ned clenched against the intrusion and growled a protest to his treatment. However we had the advantage for he would eventually tire and when he did Flick's finger slid fully up inside his rectum bringing another cry of protest from Ned.

With his finger firmly in place and stroking Ned's prostate Flick leant down and whispered in the man's ear

"If you think this is bad wait until you get a cock up you."

Ned panicked and thrashed around only serving to fuck himself on Flick's finger. Eventually he calmed down when he realised that we hadn't made move on him. Once he was still again I told him that if he agreed to comply with our instructions then Flick would pull his finger out and he would be free to return to his cell, minus his possessions. He still had a rebellious air about him so with his spare hand Flick started to stroke himself hard. That was enough to make Ned's mind up for him and he quickly agreed to our terms. Minutes later he was back on the wing but only once he was in his cell were his handcuffs removed.

Vince was the last inmate to be dealt with but Tyler and I had a different punishment in store for him. As we unlocked the cell door he was waiting for us, having heard the commotion with Ned he looked worried. He was confused when we just stood at the cell door and invited him to come out, his hands had been on his belt ready to unbuckle it but they fell to his side as he realised we weren't telling him to strip. Walking past us the worried expression disappeared to be replaced by a slightly smug look as he thought he was being let off.

The smugness didn't last long for confusion returned as we led Vince out of the prison building and towards the prison deliveries yard. As we entered the yard we were greeted by a sea of faces arranged around the yard four rows deep. Standing in the centre of the yard were Liam and Jarek both wearing prison regulation aprons to protect Liam's suit and Jarek's bare skin. The need for protection was obvious in front of them was a lit brazier half full with burning logs. In the bright sunlight it was hard to see the flames leaping up from the wood but the heat generated was obvious as we drew closer.

With Tyler and me acting as guards we steered Vince over until he was standing next to Jarek. Only then did I notice the two plastic boxes stacked high with clothes and personal possessions which I knew belonged to Vince. I'm not sure if at this stage Vince had realised what was about to happen, if he had he didn't show it. Once we were in position the guards closed the gates sealing everyone into the yard and at the same time no escape for Vince. Liam made a brief speech thanking everyone for taking time out of their busy schedules to witness Vince's punishment. At the mention of his name and the word punishment it finally dawned on Vince that his ordeal had only just begun.

Speech over Liam stepped back to become part of the audience leaving Jarek in control as a form of payback for all the trouble Vince had caused him in the past. Jarek wasted no time in telling Vince that he had broken the rules for a second time and due to the seriousness of the latest incident, the only suitable penalty was for the permanent loss of all his clothing and possessions. Any further punishment would be decided by his co-operation with instructions given to him in the next half an hour. Vince audibly gulped and looked nervously around at the audience watching him intently. Jarek asked him if he understood, Vince nodded but said nothing before looking over at the plastic boxes. I think that was the moment when he recognised the contents as being his possessions.

Jarek told him to fetch the two boxes over to the brazier, once he had done so he was told to place each item one at a time into the flames. Vince hesitated as if to say something but then thought better of it. Slowly he reached down and retrieved a handful of magazines, glanced at them before throwing them into the brazier. Slowly the pages curled before bursting into flames with a plume of smoke. Vince didn't notice as he selected the next items to go and then the next and so on until the first box was empty. As he turned his attention to the second box which contained clothing I was sure that I saw tears in his eyes. A little bit of me felt sorry for him, it must be hard to see all your prized possessions go up in smoke so publicly but he had brought it on himself at the end of the day.

Finally the last of the clothes in the box surrendered to the flames, unable to watch them Vince carried the empty boxes to one side avoiding everyone's gaze. He rejoined us and asked if that was it now. Laughing Jarek told him that the punishment was that all of his possessions were being confiscated and he still owned some. Confused Vince just looked at him until Jarek pointed out that he was wearing them. Vince shook his head a couple of times before he remembered the threat about not co-operating. With a sigh he pulled his sweatshirt off over his head and threw it onto the fire followed by his T-shirt. Then he sat down on the ground and unlaced his trainers before handing them to Jarek followed by his socks. Jarek waited patiently as Vince stood up before wordlessly returning the trainers and socks back to him. It had to be Vince who put his stuff into the fire. As they smouldered and caught alight Vince unbuckled his belt and undid his trousers letting them fall to the ground. He stepped out of them, balled them up and threw them into the brazier. He now stood in just his pants, taking a deep breath he quickly pushed them down and dropped them into the fire before he could change his mind.

Now he stood before us totally naked and without a single possession to his name. He would now have to rely on other inmates generosity from now on and which is part of the rehabilitation process. Vince covered his tackle with his hands and looked in our direction.

"Come on guys. Tell me that I've been punished enough now" he pleaded.

"Well you have obeyed instructions if a little reluctantly" Jarek replied with a thoughtful expression "what do you think Sam?"

"Mmm I agree with you Jarek but there's just one suggestion I would like to make as we all have busy schedules."

"What's that?"

"We carry out the medical assessment here and now. That way we won't have to take time out tomorrow to do it."

"Excellent idea, I like your thinking!" Liam called out from the sidelines.

"Let's get on with it then" Vince sighed.

There was a slight delay as we waited for Richard to fetch the necessary paperwork from his office and then with me carrying out the physical checks Richard wrote my findings down. I asked him about his sexuality, he replied straight but that meant little in prison. As I weighed his balls in my hand I guessed that he hadn't come in a while which might explain his aggressive tendencies if he was frustrated. His cock responded well to my touch and despite his 'straightness' he appeared to enjoy my hand stroking his shaft. He wasn't so keen though when I told him to turn around, bend over and pull his cheeks apart. But he did it.

Lubing up my index finger I stepped up close behind him and pushed my finger firmly up his rectum. He cried out and would have pulled away if it hadn't been for Tyler's quick reactions. In a second he had Vince firmly in a headlock, that guy wasn't going anywhere! Having checked him out internally I withdrew my finger and announced that in my opinion he was a virgin, anally at least.

"That needs to be corrected" Jarek declared "he'll be no use to anyone if he can't take a cock up his arse."

This brought a round of applause from the audience and a verbal protest from Vince, which of course was totally ignored by everyone especially Jarek who was clearly turned on by the situation. He was already rock hard and within a minute had lubed up his cock and pressed it against Vince's clenched anus. Jarek slapped Vince's arse hard bringing a cry from him, as a distraction method it worked well, he forgot to clench allowing Jarek's cock to force its way past his tight ring. Jarek buried his cock in one firm thrust and then stopped to allow Vince to grow accustomed to the intrusion. That didn't stop Vince from crying out at the top of his voice that he was being raped.

A nearby inmate shouted at Vince that he should shut up and take it like a man. Then to emphasise the point he removed a shoe and then a sock before striding over with the balled up sock and shoved it into Vince's mouth silencing him instantly. Jarek in the meantime had started to thrust in and out with force and grunted enthusiastically with each stroke. The inmates clapped in time to the strokes which only urged Jarek on to ever more energetic thrusts. It seemed like ages but in reality was probably only five minutes if that, suddenly he started to buck and spasm before collapsing on top of Vince. Breathing heavily he pulled out and wiped his still leaking cock on Vince's cheeks.

Only then was Vince released from Tyler's grip and the yard's doors unlocked. Half an hour later the prison was back to normal as if nothing had happened. All except Vince who had slunk back to his cell to find that it was bare except for his mattress and blanket. Apparently he didn't show his face for the rest of the day, only appearing for the evening meal which he ate quickly sitting alone and away from everyone.

FRIDAY 7TH MAY

Sorry diary I was so caught up with the events at work yesterday that I forgot to mention last night's activities with Aaron and Jason. It's weird for while Jason was distant and distracted Aaron was closer and more focused on me. I tried to get Jason to tell me what was going on but he just shrugged and changed the subject. While he was in the shower I quizzed Aaron, all he could think was that perhaps he was having problems with Kirsty as they'd been arguing a lot recently. Mmm I thought to myself, perhaps it's time to back off and let them sort things out. When I suggested that we call it an early night after both had showered Jason seemed relieved while Aaron disappointed to be going home early. I smiled apologetically and promised a slap up meal on Saturday after swimming if they fancied it.

As for work nothing special really, business as usual with no disruptions to speak of perhaps Vince's punishment had reminded the inmates what could happen to them if they copied his antics. Oh nearly forgot, James asked me to call round his place tomorrow, apparently they have a surprise for me. I was both touched by the invitation and curious about what this surprise might be so arranged to drop by early the next morning.

SATURDAY 8TH MAY

My surprise turned out to be a bicycle of all things! James and Lucas are keen cyclists, in fact that is how they met in the first place, both being members of the London Out & Proud Cycle Club. I was led out into their back garden and made to close my eyes as Lucas unlocked their garden shed and did whatever he needed to do. I could hear rustling of plastic sheets and then with a pretend fanfare I was allowed to open them. Propped against the shed was what to me looked like a brand new bicycle painted a dark metallic blue. I guessed it was an off road bike because it had chunky tyres and didn't have the racing bike handles.

"Do you like it?" Lucas asked enthusiastically.

"I love it!" I admitted "But you shouldn't have, it must have cost a fortune."

They both burst out laughing at my presumption. Once they'd regained their composure Lucas explained that strictly speaking it wasn't a gift for me but I could use it any time I liked i.e. this coming Wednesday in fact. It was a new bike but was going to be a spare one for anyone who wanted to join them but didn't have a bike. I blushed with embarrassment which caused them to laugh again before James apologised for their rudeness. I gave them both a hug before trying out the bike for size. After making a few adjustments to the bike I rode it around the garden for a couple of laps, it felt strange for I hadn't ridden one for many years. The novelty soon wore off and I handed the bike back to Lucas before I made fool of myself with it. Over a coffee we discussed the plans for Wednesday, as this was Lucas's adventure and they had the bikes I suggested that I come over to them and then we could all cycle to Hyde Park.

The rest of the day I spent mooching around at home until it was time for the swim session at the Leisure Centre, which went as normal. I had begun to notice that everyone's fitness was improving because more laps were being swum and there was less messing around. I have to admit the one who's made the biggest improvement is Jason and is now giving me a run for my money. He's lost virtually all of his tummy fat and looks more muscular than before. He was a sight to behold even with his swimming trunks on for they just emphasised the size of his packet. Whatever had been wrong with him on Thursday must have been sorted out because he was back to his usual self, full of banter and showmanship.

My offer of a slap up meal had been accepted, the only fly in the ointment was that Tom and Mike invited themselves round for a boy's night out, so to speak. So thinking quickly on my feet I decided not to cook but instead telephoned my local Chinese restaurant and ordered a virtual banquet for my guests. Expensive but so much easier than cooking for five at short notice! I really enjoyed the evening in fact, sitting around (fully clothed) eating and drinking while watching Sky Sports on TV.

Unfortunately it meant that there was no chance for Jason to stay behind without arousing suspicions. But that didn't stop his from flirting with me whenever the opportunity arose. Somehow the risks he took turned me on and it was all I could do not to just say 'fuck it' and drag him into the bedroom. At one point we came very close to being discovered. I was getting more cans of beer out of the fridge in the kitchen while the others were in the lounge watching the TV. All except Jason, he'd casually followed me and pushed the door behind him, hard enough for it to be almost closed but not quite. I jumped when he placed his hands around my waist and pressed his crutch into my backside.

I spun round and whispered "What the hell are you doing? The others are only in the next room!"

With an impish grin he just shrugged his shoulders before leaning forward and kissing me on the lips while his hands explored my back. I returned his kiss and was about to explore his mouth with my tongue when out of the corner of my eye I spotted the kitchen door opening. Quickly I pushed Jason away, grabbed a couple of cans and thrust them into his hands before saying in a loud voice.

"I've only got enough cans left for one each so if you want any more you'll have to go down to the off licence."

"Typical!" Aaron said with a touch of annoyance in his voice "Jason, why do you always have to do it?"

"Do what?" Jason asked a little warily.

"Abuse Sam's hospitality of course. Is it not enough that he's paid for dinner tonight without you drinking him dry and expecting more?"

"Oh right. Yes, now you put it like that I guess I'm out of order. Sorry Sam I didn't mean to take you for granted."

It was my turn to shrug. I couldn't have been cross with him even if the accusation had been true. Wordlessly I shared out the remaining cans between Aaron and Jason before shutting the fridge door and running myself a glass of cold water. Jason allowed Aaron to lead the way and as he walked past me he winked and blew me a kiss. I grinned back thinking 'you horny fucker' as I followed them back into the lounge. I was exhausted by the time they left just before midnight. I was tempted to leave clearing up until the morning but I knew that I had work in the morning and I hate waking up to a mess.

SUNDAY 9TH MAY

Dear Diary, another long day at the office but at least it was all on overtime and paid at double rates. The reason for me going in was that today was the finals of the Volunteer Punisher competition when the seven contestants would become six and take up their permanent positions within the prison system.

First things first the chapel had to be set up ready for the final round of voting and initiation ceremony. It was a hive of activity as the inmates who'd volunteered to help set out the chairs in row after row all facing the stage. Out the back in the punishment area another team of inmates cleaned and sanitised every piece of equipment and the whole of the shower area. Half way through the setting up in walked seven inmates from the maintenance department carrying what looked like metal office chairs. On closer inspection however I realised that they had been modified, the cushions had been removed leaving just the metal frame before what looked like a moulded plastic seat had been attached to it. When I say moulded I mean there were hollows where your bum and legs would be if you sat down on it, but what really caught my attention was the smooth fist sized dildo come butt plug sitting in the centre of the seat where your arsehole would be. I couldn't see any seams where it joined the seat so I presume it was one continuous piece of plastic. I could only assume that they had been designed for the contestants tonight, boy was I glad I wouldn't have to sit on those seats!

It was around 7pm that the finals started but it seemed like I had been there for most of the day with only short breaks taken to eat and get a change of scenery. As the chapel doors were unlocked the expectant inmates filed in and jostled for the best seats at the front. It took over half an hour to get them all seated and quiet so that Liam could start his introductory speech and then call the contestants to the join him on the stage. One by one Tyler, Jarek, Flick, Sayeed, Dinesh, Gus and Eduardo climbed onto the stage and stood proudly in a line with hands behind their backs wearing just their red berets and leather belts. Liam took his time to thank them for all their hard work over the last week and for their willingness to undertake everything asked of them. This brought a round of cheers and handclaps from the audience and embarrassed smiles from the contestants.

Eventually he got down to business and opening an envelope he announced that the voting had been counted and double counted before being verified by Adrian and Max as correct. The first contestant voted through was Eduardo, Liam congratulated him who then bowed to the audience with a big grin on his face and went to walk off. He didn't quite make it for Liam called him back and told him his first duty as permanent Volunteer Punisher was to demonstrate to the inmates his willingness to obey prison officers and that he could do whatever he might tell the inmates to do. Eduardo looked confused until he was told to sit down on the first chair. He just looked at Liam a little startled but clearly understood what was being asked of him because he took the can of Crisco offered to him by myself with just a trace of a smile.

We stepped to one side to allow the audience a clear view of Eduardo and his chair. He must have known that his every move was being watched for he made his actions slower and just a little theatrical. He stood beside the chair so he didn't obscure the view as he smeared the white grease all over the fist sized plug before using the excess to grease himself up. Then in a move which surprised me he turned away from the audience and climbed onto the chair backwards. Using the back of the chair for support he positioned himself over the plug and lowered himself until the tip of it disappeared between his cheeks. Now I understood what he had done, by facing away from us we were allowed a perfect view of both his bum and the plug as it slowly disappeared inside him. Using gravity and his body weight do all the work he took deep breaths as the widest part of the plug overcame his anus's resistance and slid up into his rectum. With his bum now resting on the seat he looked over his shoulder at us and raised his fist in the air in triumph.

After the applause subsided Liam announced the next successful contestant and that was Flick. Knowing what was expected of him he thanked the inmates for their votes before scooping up a handful of the grease and copied Eduardo's performance to the letter. I stood there mesmerised by the sight of his slim white bum impaling itself on the black plug. It didn't seem possible that he would be able to swallow such a large object but swallow it he did and in less time than Eduardo had taken. If I didn't know better I'd have said that it had been deliberate judging by the satisfied grin he had on his face.

The other successful contestants were Tyler, Sayeed, Dinesh and Jarek. Within what seemed only a few minutes we had the six winners all lined up in a row each with a plug stretching their rings wide open. I have to admit I didn't understand why there was a spare chair left over when Gus had already been told that he'd come last in the voting and therefore had to return his uniform immediately. He now sat in the front row of the audience, naked and downcast for he had told me on several occasions during the last week that he was confident that he would get through to the final six. Now he would have to wait until tomorrow to get his clothes back again and return to being a regular inmate.

Just when I thought the evening was about to end Liam had one final surprise for us. Addressing the audience but looking directly at me he announced that there was one person missing from the line up on stage. He paused in his speech as he was handed a flat box by Max, with a flourish he opened it and revealed a black beret with six gold stars on the front of it and a black leather belt. My heart leapt into my throat as I put two and two together, now I knew why there was a spare chair and for who those items were intended. Me.

I didn't have time to think beyond that because Liam with a congratulatory smile announced that Prison Officer Sam Telby (me) had tonight been promoted to the new role of Volunteer Punisher Coordinator. Apparently I had been honoured by having a brand new uniform designed for me which I would be wearing from here on. This was news to me and I wasn't sure that I was ready for such a radical change. Let's face it I'm used to wearing the regular prison uniform of trousers, shirt, jacket etc. But like a lot of things that had happened since I'd started working here the decision had been made for me.

Liam asked me to join him up on stage to collect my new uniform which I did to loud cheers and wolf whistles from the inmates. I felt nervous standing next to him looking over the sea of expectant faces. Up to now I'd been in control of the competition but suddenly the situation had been reversed thanks to my boss. I stood shifting my weight from one foot to another while I waited to see what would happen next, I didn't have long to wait. Liam held the box out to me and asked me to try it on for size, although his mouth was smiling his eyes weren't. I was under no illusion that he was serious about this and expected me to comply without argument.

With a smile plastered on my face I took the box from his outstretched arms and in a loud voice thanked him for both the new uniform and promotion to the new position of VPC. I made a show of inspecting the beret and belt before placing them back in the box and onto the floor in front of me. Liam gestured with his hands for me to hurry up so with the smile only slightly faltering I removed my jacket and folded it up before passing it to Liam. Out of the corner of my vision I could see the VP's watching me over their shoulder and more than one had a grin on their faces, they must be loving this turn of events.

With quick efficiency I pulled my shirt from out of my trousers and unbuttoned the front and cuffs. As I shrugged it off my shoulders I felt the cool chapel air waft around my naked chest making me shiver slightly as I folded the shirt up. Liam took it with a grin and nodded towards my shoes. Okay okay I thought to myself, I'm going as fast as I can! Kneeling down I removed both shoes and socks, stuffing them into the shoes before passing them to Liam. Standing up again I undid my trousers and let them fall to the floor revealing my pale blue boxer shorts. Casually I stepped out of them and rolled them up to prevent them from creasing. I looked out across the room feeling the sense of anticipation coming from the inmates. For a moment I considered backing down but that would be professional suicide so before I could reconsider I grabbed the waistband of the shorts and pushed them down to my ankles and quickly stepped out of them.

Now completely naked I stood as straight and proud as I could while Liam placed the black beret on my head and fastened the belt around my waist. The room was abruptly filled with the sound of hand clapping and whistling from the inmates. I nodded towards them in acknowledgement and raised my hands in a gesture of victory before thanking Liam once more for the honour of wearing this uniform. He smiled back at me and asked me to join the VPs on the seats. In a quiet voice I told him that I wasn't able to do that as I hadn't cleaned out prior to this evening as I hadn't foreseen the requirement to perform.

He frowned and reminded me that he expected better preparation in future for I had to lead by example at all times as per the agreement that I had signed before taking up the role. I apologised and promised that it wouldn't happen again, in the meantime I would use the douching facilities in the chapel. Liam had other ideas and with only a few minutes delay I saw the mobile douching machine (previously used with Jarek prior to his punishment in the stocks) being wheeled onto the stage by George and Mick.

Under Liam's directions I turned my back to the audience, bent over at the waist and pulled my cheeks apart. I was reminded of the first test on the day of my interview but my thoughts quickly returned to the here and now as I felt fingers smear grease all around my anus. Then the cold metal of the douching tube pressed against my ring before being pushed inside. Immediately I felt the tepid water flow into me and then flow back out again taking the faeces with it. This cycle must have been repeated at least a dozen times until George in a loud voice confirmed that the effluent was now running clean. Only then was the tube removed from my arse and I could stand upright again.

While the cleaning out had been going on my chair had been prepared for my use, there was so much Crisco on the fist plug that it was almost white in colour. There was no point in delaying the inevitable so without further ado I stood astride the chair and lowered my backside until the tip of the plug was just inside my ring. I raised my clenched hands into the air above my head and let my body sink down driving the plug up into my rectum. As it got to the widest point I paused, took several deep breaths and relaxed my body trying to welcome the intrusion as I had in the past. Moments later my ring gave way and I was now sitting on the chair feeling very full from the impalement and exposed knowing that the audience had just witnessed everything. There was no going back for me nor anyway for me to hide behind the prison uniform.

The initiation ceremony was now over and the show was brought to a close. As the inmates filed out they shook their heads in wonder as we climbed off the chairs revealing gaping arse holes which were slow to close up (certainly it was in my case at least). The six VPs and me were the last to leave the chapel which gave us time to talk freely and share thoughts on this evening's proceedings. The first thing I did was to congratulate the six on successfully becoming VPs and to say how smart I thought they looked in their uniforms which they would now wear by right and not just on loan. This compliment was returned by Tyler who also expressed the surprise we all felt about the uniform I had been given. Perhaps in hindsight knowing Liam as I do I should have expected this outcome but I hadn't and it made my reaction to it all that much more genuine. I'd like to think I had just gone up in their estimation.

MONDAY 10TH MAY

Today was the first day of me wearing my new uniform for real and it was nerve wracking for me to start with. Just before my shift was about to start I stood in the male staff room gazing into my locker at the beret and belt wondering if this had all been a management joke. But no, it hadn't, this was for real and there was no going back for me not if I wanted to keep my job that is. Sighing to myself I stripped off my day clothes until I was naked and then donned the beret and belt. After stuffing my clothes into the locker I attached the prison keys and all my usual paraphernalia to the belt. Unlike the VPs I wasn't obliged to engage in sexual punishment of the prisoners (unless I chose to of course) so didn't need to have tubes of KY or Crisco attached to my belt. I studied myself in the full length mirror and had to admit that if I ignored my nakedness I still looked like a prison officer.

I don't think all of the prison staff had been made aware of my new position or uniform. Certainly not the office staff for most did a double take at the sight of my nakedness and some of the younger members appeared uncomfortable with it. I smiled in response but carried on regardless with my duties, they'd just have to get used to it as I was too. I was surprised by how little the other prison officers made of it, they took it in their stride, perhaps because of the new regime rules the sight of naked men was no longer a novelty. The only comment George made was that I was a braver man than him because there was no way that he would or could do what I had done last night or doing now. I took that as a compliment and thanked him as we started our prison rounds.

As for the inmates a few tried it on making suggestive comments or behaving as if I was now one of them, a big mistake on their part as they found to their cost, but most just took it in their stride probably for the same reasons as the prison officers. The shift passed without incident and by the end of it I had grown more accustomed to my virtual nakedness but I was still glad to get my day clothes on again before going home.

This evening after our twice round the park and post run exercises Jason and Aaron stayed at my flat for longer. It was nice for me to have the company because in recent weeks I'd begun to feel lonelier at home. Perhaps my feelings for Jason have only served to emphasise that I am single and have been since my divorce a couple of years ago. I don't mind sleeping alone but lying next to the warm body of somebody you have feelings for is so much better, especially if that person is a hot young guy like Jason.

After our showers Jason and I continued with our no clothes policy although once again Aaron chickened out and insisted on keeping his towel wrapped around his waist. Neither Jason nor I pushed the issue, we just let him do what he wanted, how could we do otherwise when he no longer had an issue with our state of undress? At the beginning he'd been uncomfortable with the whole subject and I'd thought that he'd spill the beans to his dad but now he was more relaxed and sometimes joined in.

Having ate a healthy chicken salad in the kitchen we sprawled out in the lounge drinking not so healthy beer and channel hopped in the search for something interesting to watch. By chance we stumbled upon a re-run of an old Bad Lads Army episode where the 1950's style recruits were put through the ordeal of square bashing and keeping their accommodation clean and tidy. Aaron and Jason kept laughing at the poor lads being verbally abused by their Sergeant and the punishment meted out whenever they screwed up. By the end of the programme they were certain that it was all a fix and didn't reflect reality.

That was when I let slip that I knew better and immediately wished that I'd kept my mouth shut. In unison they looked at me in surprise before they remembered that I had served in the army for twenty years. No matter how much I tried to change the subject they would not let the matter drop until I had told them about some of my experiences which I had kept secret all these years. To give myself some time to think I fetched some more beer from the fridge before turning off the TV and handing each a can. Making myself comfortable in my armchair I described the first few months of being a new recruit in the army as a naive eighteen year old. In that short space of time I and the other recruits endured several hazings organised not only by our sergeants but also by regular soldiers.

The first hazing happened just a couple of days after I'd arrived at the training camp. In the early hours of the morning I was abruptly woken as the door to our dormitory was flung open and the shouting began. I sat bolt upright in shock as five or six dark figures strode down the centre of the room upturning our beds and spilling us onto the floor as they went. I was too slow in my reactions and before I knew it I was laying on the floor half covered by my mattress and a tangle of sheets. As I scrambled from beneath the bedding I felt a hand grab hold of my arm and drag me to my feet. No sooner had I steadied myself than my arms were pulled behind my back and my wrists were bound tightly together. I cried out in protest and received a hard slap across the back of my head before everything went black. I froze in panic thinking for a moment that I had gone blind before realising that something had been put over my head. I found out afterwards that it was simply a pillowcase but at the time I didn't know what it was. A hand on my shoulder steered me out of the dormitory and into the cold night air. I could hear the sound of feet scraping on the floor behind me so I presumed that the other recruits were receiving the same treatment. We didn't walk far before being told to stand still and not move again until we were told otherwise. Too scared to disobey I stood there for what seemed like eternity and slowly froze from the cold night air. The worst was yet to come. At some point I heard footsteps approaching and a familiar voice was shouting obscenities loudly in our direction. It was our Sergeant. Within a few minutes our wrists had been unbound and the pillow cases removed from our heads. He then spent the next twenty minutes berating us for not only being caught unawares in the dormitory but also for letting our beds be trashed. It wasn't until after our passing out parade that I learnt this was a favourite trick our Sergeant liked to play on his new recruits.

If that hazing had been frightening it wasn't anywhere near as embarrassing as the second one I experienced early one morning two weeks later. After breakfast our section underwent two hours of square bashing with the threat of a five mile cross country run if we didn't do it to the satisfaction of the Staff Sergeant. Everything seemed okay as we were dismissed from the parade ground and told to head for the shower block to wash the sweat off our bodies. Nothing unusual in that order, we'd done it countless times before. So off we headed and hung up our uniforms in the locker area before hitting the showers en masse. Within minutes the room was full of steam as the hot water bounced off twenty naked bodies as we washed, laughed and joked around under the showers.

Without warning the water ran cold and laughter turned to yelping with the sudden temperature change. We were making too much noise to hear the footsteps in the room next door or of our locker doors being opened and closed. It was only when we ran out of the shower room that we discovered that we had had visitors. Every locker had been opened and emptied of their contents, there was nothing left in the room not even a solitary towel for us to dry ourselves. We stood there dumbstruck as we absorbed what had happened in what could only have been a few minutes.

Shock turned to anger over the theft but we didn't have time to plan our next move because the Staff Sergeant appeared unannounced with our Sergeant close on his heels. Automatically we stood to attention and saluted our superiors. Both men seemed oblivious to our nakedness as the Staff Sergeant stood in front of us and told us that our performance on the square had been dismal. He was so disgusted that he was doubling the run to ten miles and that we were going to do it now under his direct supervision. One brave lad, I think his name if I remember correctly was Stu O'Hanagon held up his hand and pointed out that our clothes had been stolen. Our Sergeant marched over to him and with his face only inches away from Stu's yelled in his face that if he and the rest of the section were so careless as to lose their clothes whose fault was it? Stu realised his mistake and admitted that it was ours. Satisfied the Sergeant stepped back as the Staff Sergeant continued berating our lack of skill during the square bashing. We stood motionless like statues under his barrage of abuse until he ordered us back to our dormitory to collect our running shoes but nothing else.

Ten minutes later we stood to attention in two rows of ten, naked except for a pair of running shoes, feeling very exposed and foolish. It was made even more embarrassing because the other sections had been lined up to form a human corridor out of the training camp and up to the sentry posts at the main entrance. On the blast of his whistle we set off jogging past the Staff Sergeant and along the corridor of jeering recruits and serving soldiers. At first I tried to cover my assets but it was impossible to run properly so I gave up and let everything swing freely if you get my drift. We were given a very loud send off by the sentry guards in the form of a thirty second blast of the warning siren, nothing like drawing attention to us. Although the heath land surrounding the camp was owned by the military direct access to it was limited to only a couple of entry points neither of which were close to us. We were therefore obliged to jog along a public road running parallel to the perimeter fence for over half a mile before we reached the nearest entry point. Unfortunately for us the road we had to run along was also a short cut for locals between the nearby town of Belford and the A303. This meant that we were further humiliated as some of the passing motorists stopped their cars to watch us run past them.

I was relieved to get onto the heath and begin the cross country for real. By the seven mile mark I was exhausted and I wasn't alone, there were several of us at the back of the group dragging our feet. But we weren't allowed to rest, not for one minute, we had to keep going no matter how much pain we were in. It was hell and I was so exhausted by the time we had completed the ten miles and looped back to the entry point that I didn't have the energy to run along the road. I was just grateful to have stopped running and I didn't care who stared at my mud splattered body as I walked back to camp with the other guys. Back at in the shower block we found that our possessions had mysteriously been returned, strange that.

I thought long and hard before telling Jason and Aaron about the third and final hazing incident. It was something I had felt a lot of shame and anger about at the time, I had suppressed the memory of it for so long but now in view of recent events it seems quite tame. It was the night before our passing out parade and the whole camp was celebrating on site. Naturally we drank too much and got very rowdy, in the end the Staff Sergeant intervened to calm things down. Well that was his excuse anyway. He selected six of the most drunk recruits, which included me, and got us to play army 'party' games. The common theme was that the one that came last had to strip naked and run round the parade ground before being out of the games. This brought out the competitive streak in me and there was no way I was going to run around naked, not again.

Little did I know that the worst humiliation that I had ever endured was about to befall me. It was now just me and one other guy left, the final round was a general knowledge quiz, best out of three and I lost. The Staff Sergeant made me strip naked (no surprise there) but what happened caught me by surprise. My sergeant approached me from behind grabbed my wrists and quickly tied them together behind my back. Then he pushed on my shoulders forcing me to bend over at the waist and kicked my legs apart. He kept his hand on the small of my back to keep me in position before whispering in my ear that if I knew what was good for me I would take whatever happened next without complaint, to show that I was a real man. I nodded my understanding of his implied threat so did my best to relax not thinking about what was to follow. I didn't have long to wait for the Staff Sergeant told the winning recruit to stand in front of me and drop his pants and trousers. Grinning the recruit did as instructed and moments later I had a rapidly growing cock and a pair of hairy balls just inches from my face. The Staff Sergeant then grabbed my head and moved it until my mouth was at the right height. Needing no encouragement the recruit stepped closer to me and fed his erect cock into my mouth until I was gagging on it. I heard the Staff Sergeant tell him to ignore my gagging and just fuck my mouth like he would a woman's pussy, so he did. Thankfully the rough face fucking didn't last long as the lad was so excited that he shot his salty jism into my unwilling mouth after only a dozen thrusts.

This wasn't enough humiliation apparently for me because I was then roughly pushed to the ground with my face on the cold floor and my arse sticking up in the air for all to see. After only a slight pause I felt something cold and wet being smeared around my anus before a finger was rammed deep inside me. I cried out both from the shock of the entry and the pain that it had caused me. The Sergeant squatted down beside me and stuffed my own pants into my mouth to serve as a gag, yuk! I heard laughter all around me and I had never felt so ashamed in all my life. But what happened next was even worse. The finger withdrew and was replaced by something much larger and initially it hurt a lot more. As it forced its way up into my virgin arse my Sergeant informed me that I was being honoured, with tears in my eyes I just looked at him before he announced that I was being fucked by the Staff Sergeant! I just closed my eyes and tried to ignore what was happening to me. In the end and to my surprise the pain subsided and it even began to feel okay, not that I ever admitted it to anyone. The fucking seemed to go on forever until eventually with a groan he came and shot his load of jism into me.

My ordeal still wasn't over even after he pulled out of me and stood up. They rolled me over onto my back and pushed my legs up and back until they rested on my chest. Between the gap between my thighs I could see the Staff Sergeant tucking his semi-erect cock back into his trousers. I found it hard to believe that anything that big had just been up my arse. He turned to the audience and told them that I was hungry and needed feeding, did anyone have anything to eat? I watched them as they shook their heads, of course they didn't, everything was provided by the army. Then my Sergeant piped up that he had a couple of bananas in his room, like an idiot that I said that I liked bananas. They laughed at my naivety but the order was sent to fetch the two large bananas. I got to eat them all right but not in the way that I had been expecting. Kneeling down before my exposed backside my Sergeant slowly peeled the banana so that everyone could see what he was doing. I opened my mouth in anticipation only to feel like a fool as he started to push the banana into my arse. This brought a round of laughter from the recruits and I blushed bright red from embarrassment as more of the banana slipped into my rectum. It felt just like a cock but bigger and softer. As the last bit of it disappeared from sight he started to peel the second one and aimed it at my hole. This time he had more difficulty getting it inside me because of the first one already there so it tended to break up into pieces. But it all went inside, that man was not going to be defeated by my arse hole. I felt so full and desperate for a dump that when I was finally released I just ran to the toilet block and let the shitty mushed up bananas fall into the toilet pan.

That was as much as I was going to tell Aaron and Jason, it was already more than I had intended. I looked at them with raised eyebrows but they were silent for a moment as they absorbed the information I'd given them. I knew that they'd enjoyed the tales because Jason was sporting an erection and Aaron's towel had a tent pole. I threw caution to the wind and walked over to Aaron and undid his towel exposing his hard on to the room. Kneeling down I caressed it with one hand while with the other I fondled his balls.

He opened his mouth to protest, clearly my move had come as a shock to him (as it did me in hindsight), but he closed it again as my own mouth slowly swallowed his cock head. Now an experienced cock sucker I swallowed the whole of his modest sized cock in one smooth action bringing a sigh of pleasure from him. I focussed on giving him a blow job that he would remember for a long time. While I concentrated on Aaron, Jason must have decided to join in the action for I heard my bedroom door open and close before he knelt down behind me. Anticipating what was coming next I spread my legs a little to give him easier access. Sure enough within the blink of an eye he was pressing his cock against my anus, due to my earlier stretching he was able to slide his massive cock up me with ease. I heard Aaron gasp in surprise, I'm not sure if that was because Jason was fucking me or that he slid in so easily.

Either way I didn't care, I was being spit roasted by two handsome young men half my age and I loved it from beginning to the inevitable climax. After we'd cleaned ourselves up Aaron began to have a guilt trip, he fretted about what we'd done and did this make him gay? I assured both of them that a little man on man action didn't make you gay after all I'd been in the army for twenty years, been married and now worked in the prison. Did he think I was gay? Forcefully he shook his head but I don't think he was entirely convinced. I also assured him that whatever happened within my flat would stay a secret and I wouldn't be telling anyone. That did at least make him feel a bit better being a married man and all that.

Having got his way with me Jason wasn't worried about staying behind and left at the same time as Aaron, so that was another missed opportunity to share my feelings with him. Was I disappointed? Yes if I'm being honest.

WEDNESDAY 12TH MAY

Dear diary, sorry about the lack of entry for yesterday but I had nothing to say. My mind was full of Monday night and the anticipation (or perhaps uncertainty) of what was going to happen today. I waited for the rush hour commute to calm down before I caught the tube over to James and Lucas' home in Southwark. Unfortunately due to over running engineering works I arrived some twenty minutes later than anticipated. As I raised my hand to press the intercom the main door was flung open and a very relieved Lucas greeted me theatrically fanning his face with his hand.

"Thank god you're here!" he cried "I thought you'd changed your mind or something."

"Of course not! Sorry I'm late but the underground was dreadful, it would have been quicker for me to walk...." I replied with an apologetic smile.

"Well you're here and I'm so excited! Are you looking forward to it?" Lucas asked as I followed him up the communal stairs to their flat.

"Mmm I'm not sure really, I've never been to a protest rally before so I don't know what to expect."

"Neither do I! But I know I have to do something to raise public awareness about the dangers we face every day in this city."

I was about to reply when James called out a greeting to me from the kitchen and asked if I would like a drink before we left. I never got to reply to him either for Lucas shouted back that there was no time as we had to get ready now otherwise we'd be late. By now James had joined us in the living room grinning mischievously, I suspected that he knew we were on a time limit and was simply winding Lucas up. As before both were dressed in loose fitting 'hippy' style shirts and trousers, not in my opinion suitable for cycling. I expressed my reservations and immediately wished I hadn't for they both laughed and gave me a slightly patronising smile. James disappeared for a moment before returning with two sets of cycling outfits.

"So what will you be wearing today Daddy?" Lucas asked with a twinkle in his eye.

"Touché" I replied with a wry smile knowing that I'd been totally wrong footed.

"Would you like to borrow some of our gear?" James asked as he headed into their bedroom.

"Please, if you've got anything that will fit me that is" I replied as I followed him.

"Should have as we're pretty much the same size" he said over his shoulder as he rummaged through his wardrobe.

With a satisfied grunt he turned round holding aloft two small pieces of material which he unfolded before my eyes, one was a T-shirt and the other a pair of shorts. I raised an eyebrow because to me they looked more suitable for a child than a fully grown adult like me. James assured me that the material was very stretchy and would fit me just fine. I took the clothes from him still feeling dubious but willing to try them on for size, certainly my jeans and jumper would not be suitable clothing later on. I asked him where I could change my clothes, he shrugged his shoulders and said here was just fine.

Fair enough, it was no problem for me considering that James had seen me naked on more than one occasion so I wasted no time in pulling my jumper and T-shirt off over my head. I folded them up before trying on the cycling shirt, as I pulled it down over my chest I realised that he was right for the material was incredibly stretchy and fitted me like a glove. Satisfied I quickly removed my trainers and socks before pushing my jeans and boxers down to my ankles and stepped out of them in one smooth action. A quiet wolf whistle startled me and reflexively I turned in the direction of the sound. There stood Lucas with arms folded across his chest, leaning against the door frame intently staring at my backside, or rather my cock as I was now facing him.

I smiled to myself for it wasn't the first admiring glance I'd ever received so I let him get an eyeful as I pulled the cycling shorts up until they met the shirt. Only then did I look in the mirror to see how I looked in the outfit. I think the word striking rather than smart sprang to mind, the main body colour was an intense royal blue with flashes of electric blue and golden yellow running down either side on both the top and shorts. The material fitted so snugly that it left nothing to the imagination. I did a twirl for the two guys and asked them what they thought, both said very nice but wouldn't elaborate further.

James then found me a pair of cycling shoes before he and Lucas changed into their own outfits. I left them to it as I headed off to the toilet to have a pee as I knew we were due to leave soon. Half an hour later we set off on our bikes, using the cycle lanes we headed for Waterloo Bridge, over the Thames and along the Strand and the Mall before reaching Hyde Park. By the time we arrived at our destination I'd already had two close encounters with cars and for the first time I really understood Lucas's passion over the environmental and safety issues for cyclists in London.

James and I let Lucas lead the way after all this was his adventure and we were only there for moral support. The assembly point for the cyclists was obvious, apart from all the bikes that is. In one corner of the park they'd gathered for the pre-cycle meeting and to undress, however they were completely surrounded by onlookers and photographers recording every moment. We looked at one another as we dismounted our bikes a little shocked by the throng of on lookers. Lucas with a determined expression reconfirmed that he still wanted to go through with this he wasn't going to give in to nerves.

I for one applauded his attitude and told him to go for it. However once he'd registered his attendance with the group leader his confidence faltered as a female reporter walked over to him and wanted to interview him. He looked at us helplessly and my instincts told me he was about to back out, so I did the only thing I could do and that was to join him and offer support during the interview. James just looked on shaking his head in disbelief. Unfortunately for me the reporter somehow got the idea that I too was taking part in the cycle ride. Perhaps it was because I came across as being more confident than Lucas I don't know. Anyway to cut a long story short having asked us a long list of questions she asked if we minded being videoed. Before we had a chance to refuse her cameraman joined us and started recording every move we made.

It was almost time for the cycle ride to begin. If Lucas was to take part he was going to have to be quick. He looked at me and asked if I would cycle with him, he really didn't want to do this on his own. Inwardly I cursed him but outwardly I smiled and told him that I would before looking to James and asking him to join us. He shook his head vigorously and said that there was no way he was going to strip off before the cameras etc. In that case I informed him he could look after our clothes as we had nowhere to store them. That suited him just fine and he happily took charge of our shorts and shirts as we peeled them off leaving us naked except for our cycling shoes. The cameraman and reporter appeared to enjoy the show we put on for them as we continued talking to them totally naked.

The starting klaxon sounded so the three of us quickly mounted our bikes and followed the rest of the cyclists. We had to push our way through the throng of photographers to get out of Hyde Park and into the Mall. It all felt very surreal to me, firstly to be cycling at all because I hadn't done this for years and secondly because I wasn't used to the stares we received from the public as we sped past them. I had seen protest rallies on TV in the past but this was different, I guess perhaps because it was a more casual non-vocal protest and also because it was fun being naked in a very public place where everyone else was dressed. Lucas rode beside me not wanting to be left behind as the cyclists naturally thinned out as we rode off down the Mall towards central London. James being fully clothed was more relaxed and slowly fell behind, to such an extent that by the time we reached the houses of parliament he was nowhere to be seen. I just hoped that nothing had happened to him as he had our clothing. I made a point of waving to the cameras and bystanders as we passed them, I figured that as we were being watched and recorded I might as well appear happy about it.

The seven mile ride terminated at London Bridge and the cyclists quickly got dressed again, all except for me and Lucas. We had to wait nearly ten minutes before James showed up very apologetic for he'd taken a wrong turning. Wrong turning? How could he when he was following a cycle rally? Mmm I suspected he'd stopped off at some point and hadn't been able to catch up in time. I was just glad to get dressed as I was increasingly conscious of the officials watching us suspiciously.

Back at their flat I stayed for a late lunch before returning home. I wanted to see if I'd be on the news tonight.....

THURSDAY 13TH MAY

Fame eluded me last night, none of the main terrestrial channels made any comments about the cycle ride. I didn't know if to be relieved or disappointed by the lack of news coverage but at least no one at work (other than James of course) knew about my escapades yesterday.

The same can't be said for Aaron. As soon as I answered the front door to him and Jason this evening he started asking what I had been up to yesterday all innocent like. I smelt a rat with his sudden interest in my activities so I played it cool and matched his innocence with my own not giving too much away in the process. The more he pried the more I evaded, it became a game for me as I was certain that he knew something. After the second lap around the park Jason had become suspicious about our conversation and wanted to know what was going on between us. I shrugged my shoulders and told him to ask Aaron as he seemed to be so interested in my personal life. Aaron just smiled and said he would find out soon enough. In response Jason just sighed, shook his head and turned his attention to increasing the pace of our run.

Back at the flat and after our showers we sat round the kitchen table eating the pizzas I'd ordered while waiting for my own shower. It was only after he'd finished his pizza did Aaron start to drop hints that he knew about my day off yesterday. First he mentioned seeing me on TV last night. That got Jason's attention and mine too. I raised my eyebrows and asked him if he was sure it was me he'd seen. Like a cat about to pounce he sat up straight in his chair and with a wicked grin said that he was and that Sky News had aired a very interesting feature about the   London Naked Cycle Ride. Out of the corner of my eye I saw Jason looking from me to Aaron and back to me again. I didn't dare look in his direction otherwise I would have burst out laughing so instead I asked Aaron what that had to do with me. With a smug expression he told me that I had been interviewed by a female reporter for Sky News and I had been videoed removing my blue cycling gear along with another guy I was standing next to. He asked me if I wanted him to continue. Now I did laugh and shook my head before admitting that yes that had been me.

I spent the rest of the evening telling them all about yesterday and my experiences. I found it curious that the two guys had very different reactions for Aaron had thought it a great laugh while Jason didn't in the least. Odd really considering what a joker and exhibitionist he can be. I found out why later that evening. Aaron left about 10pm saying that he really had to get home to wife and baby while Jason seemed content to stay. He was on his mobile when I returned to the lounge having waved Aaron off, he was talking animatedly into it almost angry in fact but as soon as he saw me the tone changed and he terminated the call. I looked at his with raised eyebrows, he raised his own and exclaimed that women can be a pain in the arse. He'd told her that he wouldn't be home tonight as he was too drunk to drive and would be sleeping in my spare room.

That was his cover story of course, he had no such intention, getting into my bed was his aim and he succeeded in record time. Our love making was far from gentle, he was like a man possessed and fucked me in just about every position he could think of, not stopping until his balls must have run dry from the number of times he'd shot his load up my arse. Don't get me wrong I thoroughly enjoyed the rutting, almost as much as I enjoyed gently fucking him afterwards when his energy was spent. We must have drifted off to sleep for I woke with a jolt as I felt him climb out of bed. I asked him if he was okay, not really came his reply. Then he sat down on the edge of the bed and looked at me over his shoulder. I asked him to share what was troubling him, so he did. I now know that he's finding this situation with the two of us harder than I am. He's torn between the two of us and doesn't know which he wants the most. He loves Kirsty with all his heart and feels guilty about her but when he's near me he can't control his lust (he won't use the word 'love') and when he's away from me he can't stop thinking about our times together.

I pulled him back into bed and held him tightly while he cried from all the pent up emotion he felt inside. I didn't know what to say other than that he knew where I was and could see me any time he liked, I wasn't going to pressurize him one way or another. This definitely shows all the signs of a disaster waiting to happen.

FRIDAY 14TH MAY

Nothing much to say today, in fact I feel a bit subdued and don't feel like talking. Jason left early this morning, we didn't speak much he was in a hurry to get home and change for work. I let him get on with it. Work was okay I guess nothing out of the ordinary. Oh I tell a lie, yes there was something that happened. We, the prison officers that is, had a meeting with Max and Liam who informed us that next week we have five inmates arriving having been transferred due to bad behaviour. Word has got round about our success with reducing violence on the wings and we had been recommended to sort them out. Liam saw this as an opportunity but we weren't so convinced. We shall see.

SUNDAY 16TH MAY

Dear diary, I'm totally pissed off. Nothing has gone right this weekend. My washing machine broke down yesterday morning so now I'm reduced to using the launderette until I can save up for a new one. Then in the afternoon on the way home from the launderette with my hands full carrying the large holdall bag of clean washing I tripped up the stairs badly bashing my knees. I've been resting them today and so haven't been able to go swimming with the gang. Has anyone been round to see if I'm okay (read that as Jason)? Have they fuck! That's why I'm so pissed off. I seem to be doing all the caring and receiving nothing in return. Things have to change I've decided.

MONDAY 17TH MAY

My knees were a little better today, enough for me to walk around without too much of a hobble but just enough to get teased at work. I can live with that, at least they care!

The five transferees arrived today. They're going to be trouble with a capital T I just have that feeling about them. Mid morning the message came down, they'd passed the induction and screening process so now could be shown to their cells. For staff safety they were brought on to the wing in either pairs or singly.

The first to arrive was Faisal, Egyptian by birth but had lived in London since he was twelve. Now twenty one he was the tallest and heaviest of the gang, striking rather than handsome with an easy smile. But that smile was deceptive for he had a vicious temper and had assaulted more than one officer since starting his sentence. I escorted him from the reception area to the wing and his cell. His reaction to my virtual nakedness was not quite what I expected for he did a double take before giving me the once over. Then with a crooked smile he said that the rumours about this prison were true and that we were into weird shit. I just raised my eyebrows before replying that the new regime worked well regardless of how it appears from the outside. He just shrugged his shoulders and entered his cell without looking back.

The next two guys, Bruno and Serge were both French and looked so similar that they could have been brothers. Nineteen years old and it showed for their behaviour was a mix of youthful arrogance and lack of confidence now that they were away from their other gang members. They appeared shocked by the fact that I wore just the black beret and belt with my gear hanging from it. They spoke with a heavy accent and asked why I was dressed like that. I told them it was a long story and once they'd been here a while and learnt the regime rules they'd understand better. They didn't appear convinced and kept asking if they'd be forced to wear similar clothing. I laughed and told them not if they behaved themselves. By the time they arrived at their cell (they were lucky to have been assigned one together) they had recovered from the shock and the underlying cockiness had returned.

The last two Yalvac and Erdem really were brothers and came originally from Turkey. Erdem was twenty and Yalvac twenty six and the gang leader but unlike the two French lads weren't similar in appearance. Erdem being tall and painfully thin and Yalvac virtually the same height as me but a lot heavier built. I could see why he was the gang leader for he oozed the self-assured confidence that alpha males have. Unlike the other three men their reaction unsettled me, yes they appeared surprised but as they spoke to each other rapidly in Arabic they appeared to be appraising my body, every bit of it. Yalvac stepped closer to me and went to stroke my naked chest but was stopped in his tracks when I warned him that if he did I would have him up for assault. He wasn't to touch me unless invited to by myself. He glowered at me and muttered under his breath but did at least drop his hand back down to his side, they walked silently behind me to their cell but each step of the way I could feel their eyes burning into my back.

The rest of the day passed without incident and I got home only too glad to rest my aching knees, there was no way I could go running so I text the two lads to cancel the run. All I got was an okay from Aaron and nothing from Jason which pissed me off no end after the lack of concern over the weekend. Diary, I am edging ever closer to calling the whole thing off unless he changes his attitude towards me.

WEDNESDAY 19TH MAY

I knew those new guys were going to be trouble, it has already started. Yalvac had a visitor today, a family member who had close ties with the gang's criminal activities. The visitor was his cousin and being aware of the connections we watched both closely during the visiting period. Mick who'd been supervising had a feeling that something had been passed to Yalvac but didn't actually see what it was. We made the decision to let Yalvac return to his cell before carrying out a cell search and that is exactly what we did except that it wasn't quite that easy!

Mick and I walked into his cell about five minutes after his return and told Erdem to leave which he did after exchanging glances with his brother. Yalvac didn't appear pleased to see us and he was even less pleased when we told him that we were doing a cell and strip search for prohibited items. When he asked why we informed him of our suspicions to which he laughed and assured us that we wouldn't find anything but we could search if we wanted.

For the next half hour we thoroughly searched every inch of that cell without success which meant that we now had to do a strip search of him. He had been calm and confident up until that point but now his demeanour changed towards us becoming aggressive. We told him to calm down otherwise it would only make things worse for him but he didn't listen and launched himself at Mick. I had no choice but to tazer him which I did twice before he succumbed to its power writhing around on the floor in agony. Seizing the opportunity we pounced on him and quickly removed his trainers, socks, trousers and sweatshirt checking each for concealed items. Nothing. He now lay there in just his underpants groaning to himself. I nodded to Mick before I knelt down, grabbed the waistband and pulled them off him. Naked now there was only one place that he could hide anything. I rolled him on to his side and manoeuvred him into the foetal position allowing me easier access to his backside.

Mick passed me a pair of latex gloves and once they were on a small tube of KY. With my index finger lubed up I pushed my way into his tight arse bringing a cry of protest from Yalvac. I ignored him as my finger explored inside his rectum and almost straight away I found what I'd been looking for, a foreign object not supposed to be there. By the feel of it a small bag, carefully so as not to damage the bag I manoeuvred it until it was close to the anus and then inserted a second finger to grip hold of the bag. As I pulled it out Yalvac complained loudly that I had assaulted him as he hadn't given me permission to do the body search. I just told him to shut up and sit on the bed while we confiscate his possessions.

While this was going on Mick called Dinesh and asked him to fetch one of the plastic boxes used to contain confiscated items. Five minutes later Dinesh arrived with the box and helped us to remove Yalvac's possessions and clothing. By the time that we'd finished he sat on his bed naked with just a blanket to call his own. He was furious with us and given the chance he would have attacked again, but three against one is not good odds especially when he's had a tazer used on him already. As we walked along the landing with Dinesh pushing the box (has got wheels) he commented on the Yalvac's horniness. I agreed that he was a horny guy but definitely trouble and one to be watched carefully.

THURSDAY 20TH MAY

The main story at work today has yet again been Yalvac. Just before lunchtime he decided to kick off big time in the games area and out of the blue attacked another inmate by the name of Will. His excuse under interview was that Will had given him the eye up and made a suggestive comment about his backside. However this version wasn't supported by witnesses or Will's statement. The truth was that Will and another inmate had been playing pool, looked up as Yalvac approached and then carried on playing. The next thing they knew was that Yalvac jumped on Will and started thumping him on his body and chest. Will fought back and another inmate raised the alarm. Yalvac was placed in solitary confinement to cool off while Will was sent to the medical unit for assessment. Thankfully he only sustained bruising and was released shortly afterwards.

From time to time I checked on Yalvac in his cell, each time I did so he just glowered at me and told me to piss off. I just shook my head glad that I wasn't him for to be so angry all the time must be horrible. He was still in solitary confinement when I finished my shift.

This evening I managed a lap of the park with the two lads but my knees started hurting again so I left them to it while I sat on a bench near the park entrance. I hated my exercise being restricted by my injury but I had to let it heal properly otherwise it's recovery would be delayed. Back at my flat neither guys seemed comfortable, for once both kept their clothes on which made me wonder if something had been said between them since our little threesome. I made no comment about this nor did I when Jason made excuses to leave when Aaron did. It was only much later as I was getting ready for bed did Jason text me apologising for earlier on, I'd been right for Aaron had been giving him a hard time about it. He wanted to know if he could come around tomorrow evening, just him as Kirsty would be out and we could spend some time together. Without thinking I text back agreeing to see him tomorrow, I guess I was thinking with my dick when I sent that text.

FRIDAY 21ST MAY

Dear diary, sometimes I enjoy my work so much that I just wouldn't want to work anywhere else! After the usual tour of the wing and cell inspections it was time for Yalvac's post punishment assessment which I would be carrying out with Flick's assistance. George escorted the inmate from the solitary confinement area to the medical room where Flick and I were based for this session. After a loud knock on the door Yalvac entered looking calmer than he did yesterday and less hung up about his nakedness judging by the way he didn't attempt to cover himself up. He stood there patiently with his hands hanging by his sides as I familiarised myself with the paperwork that needed completing. I then did the speech about what would be involved and how he needed to comply with the procedures if he was to have his possessions returned to him today.

He nodded his understanding and seemed to take it all in his stride as I donned my latex gloves and asked him questions which Flick then noted down. He was straight on the outside but out of necessity would have sex with men in prison but only as a top. I walked over to him and examined his body closely for any signs of injury from his fight not previously noted but there wasn't. That was my excuse anyway! I then inspected his balls weighing them in my hands. Judging by their heaviness I'd say that he hadn't had sex in a long time no wonder he was so aggressive. I told him to bend over and grab his knees he frowned but did as he was told. I knelt down with my face inches away from his bum and with one hand spread his cheeks. For the second time this week I inserted my finger up his arse, it was so tight and such a turn on. As I stroked his prostate I reached underneath him and felt his cock rapidly expanding. He protested loudly but he didn't try to pull away from my finger or remove my hand that was stroking his now throbbing erection. I asked Flick to join us and give Yalvac a blow job which he did without hesitation until Yalvac shot his pent up load into Flick's willing mouth. During all this activity I had been finger fucking him working up from one finger to two. My intention had been to fuck him before the end of the session but he was simply too tight, it would have to wait for another day.

With the assessment over I peeled off my gloves and sat down behind the desk again. I took my time to write up my notes for out of the corner of my eye I could see him idly playing with himself as he stood there waiting for his possessions to be returned to him. Before it became obvious that I was stalling for time I filed the paperwork away and asked Flick to unlock the box containing Yalvac's clothes and possessions. He quickly got dressed muttering in Arabic to himself before picking up the rest of his possessions and left without looking back.

The prison grapevine reported back to us that Yalvac was very unhappy with the treatment he'd received during his punishment using the words 'assault' and 'victimisation' over and over like a mantra to any inmate willing to listen. I ignored the prison gossip, as far as I was concerned he'd been justly punished and the matter was now closed.

Besides I had other things on my mind or rather a person on my mind, Jason naturally. Once at home I raced around tidying up and making sure that I had enough food and drink in the fridge. I didn't, so quickly popped down to Arkwrights to replenish the beers and groceries. I hadn't been back long when there was a knock on the door, Jason had arrived. I opened the door and stepped back to let him pass.

As I closed the door behind him I felt his hands grab hold of my waist, turn me around and pull me towards him. I looked up into his smiling face and felt my heart skip a beat for that man in my eyes is just so handsome and horny as hell. I reached up and stroked his short cropped beard for it was a new addition to his face and in my opinion only added to his sexiness.

"Do you like it?" he asked with a twinkle in his eyes.

"Very much" I replied as I stroked his beard again before pulling his head down for a kiss.

When we came up for air he admitted that even though Kirsty hated it he had grown it because he liked my beard and somehow made him feel closer to me when we were apart. A beard could do that? I wondered to myself but I wasn't going to argue whatever the motive behind it was, not when it suited him so well. I followed him into the kitchen admiring the way his bleached jeans and muscle vest accentuated his physique, they left little to the imagination. Making himself at home he headed straight to the fridge and retrieved two cans of beer, opened them and handed one to me as he drank from his own. I drank mine more slowly and turned my attention to cooking spaghetti bolognaise. All the time he was so tactile rarely leaving my side and keen to hold me whenever an opportunity arose.

This was such a contrast to our recent interactions that the cynic in me became suspicious wondering what was to follow. But at the same time the romantic in me just wanted to enjoy the moment and hope that this was a positive sign for our relationship. Over dinner we casually chatted about anything and everything going on in our lives, it was so nice to have this time to ourselves. It just felt right like we were a regular couple doing normal things.

The relaxed mood continued all evening as we chilled out on the sofa until that is I started yawning. Jason correctly took this to be a sign I wanted to go to bed but sleep was the last thing he had in mind for me, not that I was complaining. While I tidied up in the kitchen he headed for the bathroom, it wasn't long before I heard the shower running and him singing. I smiled to myself before quickly finishing what I was doing and headed for the bathroom. Opening the door I was greeted by the vision of Jason covered in soap suds washing his tackle and in the process arousing himself for his cock was already at half mast. I stood there for a moment just enjoying the display before he realised that I was there and smiled a little sheepishly at me. I gestured for him to continue as I stripped leaving my clothes in a pile by the door and joined him in the shower.

I helped rinse him off before I let him wash and do the same for me, it was so touching the way he acted towards me and arousing at the same time. Again I felt that we were real lovers and I forgave him the times when he had been thoughtless and let me down. If it had been my decision I would have had sex there and then in the shower but each time I made a sexual approach he chuckled before batting my hand away. After the shower he towelled me dry kissing me all over my body as he went and then led me into the bedroom. I learnt tonight what it truly meant to be passive for Jason took total control of me and the session. I loved the feeling of letting go and being the centre of attention. Over the next hour he rimmed me almost to orgasm, then sucked my cock until I thought I'd explode if he didn't stop! Finally he fucked me in just about every position I could imagine, by the end of it I was so loose I thought he'd complain but if he noticed he didn't say anything. Once he was spent and couldn't cum anymore he gave me one last blow job and managed to swallow every drop of my pent up jism. Heaven was where I was right then and as I drifted off to sleep held in his arms I prayed that it would stay like this forever.

SATURDAY 22ND MAY

Today was the day that my heart broke for the first time since I divorced my cheating wife. It started well, I woke up still held in Jason's arms and as I stirred he pulled me closer and kissed the back of my neck. But the call of nature was insistent so I just had to get out of bed and head for the bathroom. As I shaved he joined me and watched me from the doorway with that 'just got out of bed' look about him.

Over breakfast we made small talk before I steered the conversation towards our plans for the rest of the weekend. I should have noticed the change in atmosphere then but I was still feeling so loved up from the night before that I was oblivious to it. In hindsight he had become a little cagey and gave vague answers to my questions and that should have rung alarm bells but it didn't. This proved to be fatal and like a blind man I stumbled on edging closer to the moment when there was no going back for either of us.

It started when I was washing the breakfast crockery. I casually mentioned the fact that I had enjoyed the last twelve hours so much that I wished we could live like this always. I heard a sigh behind me and turning round I saw him shaking his head with a frown on his face. He told me that it wasn't going to happen not now or ever. I was stunned for it felt like someone had punched me in the stomach and then kicked me in the balls for good measure. Like an idiot I asked him why, hadn't he enjoyed last night too? Silently he nodded and then with tears in his eyes he proceeded to tell me that this was going to be the last time that he could do this with me for Kirsty had become suspicious of us and thought it sick that someone old enough to be his father should be so close to him. So last night had been a farewell send off, that at least explained his romantic intensity towards me. From somewhere deep inside me an all consuming rage coursed through my veins and poured out of my mouth venting its fire on him. I told him how hurt I was by his deceit, that I was fed up with the games he played with my head and heart.

And then I made him choose between her and me, even though I knew what the outcome would be. Of course he chose Kirsty, after all he said that he loved her and it was clear that she was the easier option. I was a thrill and a guilty pleasure for him as and when he wanted me. Well no more, it was all or nothing and I ended up with nothing. Red faced from temper and with tears streaming down his cheeks he stood up and stormed out of the kitchen, he left a few minutes later having got dressed and slammed the door behind him.

I spent the rest of the day reeling from the emotional fallout of our 'breakup'. The anger inside burned for many hours before cooling to numbness and then by this evening I felt down. I regretted my outburst but knew that in my heart this day would have happened sooner or later, better to get it over with and move on I told myself. If I said it enough times and forcefully enough I might just believe it too. It was late evening when a text message arrived on my mobile phone. It was from Jason, all it said was 'sorry'. I deleted it without replying and turned my phone off, I didn't want to speak to him, not today.

SUNDAY 23RD MAY

Very hard to put pen to paper, I don't want to relive today for it's still raw in my mind and the hurting hasn't gone away. The nightmare for me was I had to carry on with life as if nothing had happened otherwise suspicions would have been raised and I didn't want that to happen, no way. Every a Sunday I go swimming at the leisure centre with the gang, which meant that not only would I have to see Jason but I would have to speak to him and Kirsty exactly as I normally would.

Every bone in my body screamed at me not to do it but like a man facing his own execution I did it anyway. With a fake smile on my face I greeted everyone in the main lobby before heading for the changing rooms with Mike and Tom. I kept my distance from Aaron and Jason, I didn't ignore them I simply focused on my friends which made it easier for me. Out of the corner of my eye I could see him discreetly watching me but I wasn't going to go down that road. I'd made up my mind and there was no going back, not now. Tom must have sensed something was wrong because he asked me if I was okay, I smiled half heartedly and said that I thought I was coming down with a cold or something.

Satisfied with my explanation he nodded before stuffing his gear into the locker and headed for the pool, quickly followed by me. I couldn't avoid Jason forever and eventually he cornered me in the pool and he too asked me if I was okay. I shrugged my shoulders and told him that I'd get over it and didn't he have a girlfriend he should be with? As soon as I said it I regretted that bitchy comment because he flinched and with a hurt look on his face he swam away. Thankfully he didn't approach me again. In the centre's cafe I fended off invitations from Chrissie to join them for a meal pleading that I really wasn't feeling well and just wanted to get home and rest. Both her and Tom appeared concerned but said that was perhaps the best thing for me. It wasn't a total lie because watching Kirsty making a show of kissing and cuddling Jason was turning my stomach.

MONDAY 24TH MAY

Nothing special to impart to you diary, not really, work's been okay. James did mention that he's sitting down with Adrian to work out the finer details about his fitness plans and will let me know how he gets on. At home I called off the run with Aaron and Jason because it would look odd if yesterday I said that I was coming down with a cold but today there was no sign of it. Aaron text back wishing me a speedy recovery and Jason just text 'ok', I didn't reply to either.

THURSDAY 27TH MAY

Apologies diary for the lack of entries over the last few days, the reason is simple, this is the first chance I've had to sit down and write. It's hard to know quite where to start, I know the obvious answer is at the beginning but I'm not sure I want to relive the experience if I'm being honest. I'm hurting both physically and mentally but as usual I'm jumping ahead of myself so at the beginning it will have to be.

Tuesday morning started off perfectly normal, there'd been no reports of trouble overnight and so Jarek and I carried out our wing round in the usual fashion. The round went smoothly enough if a little slow because the inmates were in a good mood and wanted to chat which was fine with me. Even Yalvac was sociable, he appeared to have got over his punishment episode and asked me if I would do him a favour once the round was over by checking a letter he wanted to send home. Touched by this request I agreed to drop by later that morning and so I did.

I realised that I had made a mistake as soon as I walked into his cell. The door had been open and I could see him sitting on his bed reading a book, nothing out of the ordinary so I just said hello as I stepped over the threshold. What I hadn't realised and only saw out of the corner of my eye when it was too late were the other two men hiding behind the open door. In what seemed like slow motion I stopped in my tracks and turned my head towards them instantly recognising Faisal and Erdem. At the same time Erdem slammed the door shut with a loud bang. The trap had been sprung! Instinctively I hit the panic button on my belt activating it at the same time Faisal punched me in the stomach. The force of the punch was hard enough to knock me backwards onto Yalvac's bed where I collapsed clutching my stomach in pain totally winded. I tried to get up to attempt an escape but they were too quick for me.

Erdem wedged a chair under the door handle preventing it from being opened from the outside while the other two pounced on me. While Faisal held me down Yalvac picked up my fallen beret, examined it briefly before throwing it to one side and then turned his attention to my belt. This was of more interest to him. He unbuckled it and roughly pulled it from underneath me not caring that he scratched me in the process. Shock turned to anger and so I fought harder and more vocally against the two men. Another mistake for it only gave them an excuse to use yet more violence towards me. Yalvac ignored me but told the other two to silence me, which they did very effectively. Erdem repeatedly punched me around the head and face before stuffing a dirty pair of Yalvac's pants into my mouth as I cried out in pain. At the same time Faisal grabbed my balls and squeezed them hard.

I don't know what sickened me more, the waves of pain emanating from my face and balls or the smell and taste of the dirty pants shoved in my mouth and held in place by Erdem's hand. As the pain subsided I became aware of a siren wailing in the background. I just hoped that it was because of my panic button as it would mean I would soon be rescued. They had heard it too and Fasial swore at me before grabbing my balls again. I just looked at him in panic, my fear must have been clear to see for he just laughed before massaging them roughly and then letting them go again. If I could I would breathed a sigh of relief but that would have been premature because Yalvac had other plans for me.

With him sitting on the other bed he directed his accomplices like a king would his subjects and they did his bidding quite happily. Roughly I was rolled over onto my front and my hands tied together using my own belt, I took the opportunity to spit the pants out and breathe clean air not smelling of sweat and piss. Erdem stared at me perhaps wishing me to say something to give him an excuse to rough me up again. No chance. I kept my mouth shut and closed my eyes as I laid my head on the bed facing away from him. Nothing happened for a few minutes as they chatted animatedly in Arabic, presumably about me but it also might have been about the sounds of footsteps approaching along the corridor. The siren was still wailing when I heard the cell door being repeatedly banged and George shouting for them to open the door.

Yalvac shouted back that they'd open the door when they were ready and not before, he warned George not to try anything stupid otherwise I'd get sliced and my death would be his responsibility. Shit! I was in serious trouble. I hadn't faced this sort of danger since my time in Belfast serving in the army. I turned my head to face the enemy in time to see Yalvac retrieving a handmade blade from beneath his mattress. I'd heard about this type weapon being made by inmates and used to deadly effect. The body was made from a toothbrush with the single razor blade melted into the brush head. He saw me watching him and with a malicious smile waved it towards me with a slicing action, his meaning was clear, he'd have no problems about using it on me.

My hopes for a quick rescue were dashed as I heard George call out to me to hang on in there before he walked away judging by the sound of receding footsteps. Faisal chuckled and told me that I'd better pray that they would be kind and let me see the end of the day. I remained silent unsure what response they expected from me, it must have been acceptable because I didn't get a backlash from them. Again there was a rapid exchange between them in Arabic before Faisal climbed onto the bed and pulled my legs wide apart.

In his thick accent he told me that my virgin white arse was about to be broken in by a real man as a lesson not to fuck with their gang. Virgin arse? I don't think so but at least I had warning of their intentions. Erdem knelt down beside my head and whispered into my ear about how much he was looking forward to hearing me beg for mercy and not let Faisal shove his big cock up my arse. I closed my eyes and blocked his voice out as I focused on the finger exploring the crack between my cheeks until it found my hole. There it stopped and pushed gently against my ring. I heard what sounded like something landing on the bed beside me then Faisal shifted his weight as he picked up the object. From the feel of the cold gel being applied to my hole I assumed it had to be KY or something similar. The blunt head of his cock pressed against ring and then with one brutal thrust he shoved is cock straight up me.

Despite my sexual capabilities the sudden intrusion hurt big time, I yelled out in pain and struggled to escape the impalement. It was of course futile for Faisal had immobilised me by resting his hips on my bum as he used his body weight to drive more of his cock into me. Without any consideration for me he started to thrust in and out just as forcefully as when he'd first entered me. The pain seemed to last forever and I began to wonder if he had injured me internally but then the pain began to subside and even felt good. I couldn't help but respond by pushing back to meet his thrusts. This didn't go unnoticed by Faisal and in between thrusts he told the other two that I was a willing fuck hole. Erdem muttered something under his breath which I couldn't quite hear but Yalvac must have for he laughed and told him to go for it.

The next thing I knew was that Erdem had removed his jogging bottoms and climbed onto the bed in front of me. He knelt down with his outspread thighs either side of my head with his cock dangling just millimetres from my face. I could smell an unpleasant mixture of stale piss and sweat, my stomach churned at the thought of his poor personal hygiene. He either didn't see my reaction or didn't care because he lifted my head up and told me to suck him off as enthusiastically as I was pushing back against Faisal. I knew I had no choice so ignoring the smell and taste of his ripe cock I opened my mouth and started sucking on it to get him aroused and clean it at the same time.

Thankfully the taste quickly disappeared and my technique soon had him rock hard. He came very quickly catching me by surprise as his jism hit the back of my throat making me gag in the process. I struggled to swallow his load without choking or biting his cock but I managed it and as a reward he slapped me across the back of my head a couple of times telling me that I was a good cock sucker and should be their bitch. I remained silent on that one instead I focussed on Faisal who was still energetically fucking my increasingly sloppy hole.

He took so long that I thought he would give up but no, doggedly he went on until finally he climaxed and collapsed on me exhausted from his exertions. I grunted as the wind was driven out of me by his body weight landing on top and was only able to breathe properly again when he climbed off me and the bed. Again they spoke quickly in Arabic which was frustrating for me because I couldn't understand what they were saying. It had to be about me, or the rest of the prison or both because occasionally they'd gesture towards me and the cell door.

When their little discussion had finished Yalvac looked down at me and with a sneer on his face told me that he was going to break my hole open so that I'd never be able to shit again properly. I stared back at him trying to work out what he meant but gave up and decided my time was better spent praying for my rescue. The prison had gone strangely quiet, the sirens wailing had stopped and I couldn't hear any noise from the wing. I wondered if the other inmates were on lock down. My thoughts were abruptly interrupted as I felt hands grab hold of me and I was manoeuvred into a kneeling position with my arse stuck up in the air facing Yalvac. I was held firmly in position by Erdem's hand on my head and Faisal pushing down on my shoulders.

The next thing I felt were fingers exploring my hole and Yalvac commenting that Faisal had already half-ruined my hole making the job easier for him. He applied more of the lubricant before pushing his fingers into me until I think he must have had three or four inside. The other two egged him on telling Yalvac to stop wasting time and just shove his fist up me to teach the white piece of trash a lesson. White trash eh? I'd show them I fumed to myself. Once this was over I was going to show them who was boss on this prison wing. But for now I just had to bite my tongue and concentrate on relaxing my ring if I didn't want him to injure me. Thankfully his hands were quite small, it only took a little bit of effort for me to be able to swallow the whole of his fist.

By the tone in his voice I gathered that Yalvac was disappointed that I had been able to take his fist without screaming the place down or begging for mercy. I smiled to myself for that at least was a small victory but one that wouldn't last for long. He thrust his fist in and out of my hole a few times before becoming bored. After washing his hands he decided that the fun was over and announced that it was time for me to meet my God. Oh shit shit shit, he's really going to do it I thought to myself wondering how much it would hurt and if it would be quick. All these thoughts flashed through my brain in the time that it took them to roll me over on to my back and wave the blade in front of my face.

I felt real fear and my lips quivered as I tried to stop myself from crying. It was as I sniffed back the tears that I smelt it, faint at first but getting stronger by the second. The others hadn't noticed it yet and I wondered where it was coming from. From the draught I could feel on my body I guessed the only source could be the air conditioning unit in the ceiling. The smell was familiar, floral but clinical at the same time, similar in fact to anaesthetic. By now the others could smell it too and were alarmed by what it meant. I didn't know or care for it had begun to have an effect on me, I was drifting off to sleep feeling very drunk. The last thing I recall before passing out was the sound of a body collapsing onto the bed next to me.

How long I'd been unconscious for I don't know but when I came round I realised that I was no longer in that cell thank god! My next realisation was that I had a pounding headache and hurt all over, enough to make me cry out as I tried to move. I looked around what appeared to be a small hospital ward, then it clicked, it was and that I was still in the prison. Then a familiar face walked up to me, Richard the prison doctor, with concern written across his face he asked me how I felt while he checked my blood pressure and vital signs. I told him that I felt like I'd been in a boxing match on the losing side but more importantly thankful to have been rescued. He filled me in on what had happened and how they'd got me out. Management (Liam and Max) had watched the whole episode using the CCTV camera that is installed in every cell. They had initially hoped that Yalvac would soon tire of his escapade and release me but when it became clear that he was intent on doing me harm they took immediate action. Using the air conditioning system they pumped a general anaesthetic into the cell, just enough to render us unconscious before the riot trained officers forced their way in. The three offenders were now safely in solitary confinement awaiting their fate.

He asked if I remembered what had happened during my captivity, I nodded causing pain to fill my head again and gingerly I felt my face and head wincing as I did so. I was sure I was going to have bruises all over my face before long. Several hours later and only when Richard was satisfied I was fit enough to walk around unaided I was released from the ward and sent home in a taxi paid for by the prison.

Yesterday (Wednesday) I spent at home on company orders to recover from the day before. I felt like a fake because I didn't feel ill I just felt I'd been beaten up, which I suppose is exactly what had happened. Whenever I saw my reflection in a mirror I swore that the bruises had got bigger and darker, they were all over my face! Bored I watched daytime TV until I could bear it no longer and then went for a walk, only to return home when I grew tired of people staring at me.

I had a surprise visitor this evening. The doorbell rang, worried that it might be Jason I ignored it and let it ring. But whoever was on the other side of the door was insistent and kept pressing the buzzer. Sighing I gave in and opened it to find Liam standing there with a card and bottle of wine still dressed in his work suit. I stammered a hello from the surprise and let him in apologising for the state of the place as I did so. He waved the apology away telling me that he'd come to see me not to inspect my home. He must have stayed for at least an hour chatting over a drink in the kitchen about all sorts of things not just my experience yesterday, although that was his purpose for visiting. It was nice to have a decent conversation after being on my own all day and he seemed genuinely concerned about me. I was sorry to see him go. Alone again I decided that I was going back to work no matter how much I ached.

So today I returned to work, still aching and tender to the touch but at least it was good to have the company of my colleagues and even the inmates. I felt self-conscious walking around with just my beret and belt on for there was no disguising the bruises which had now fully developed in all their multicoloured glory. I needn't have worried though for the bruises seemed to have become a badge of honour if you like. My colleagues admired me for returning to work and normal duties so quickly and without a fuss. As for the inmates I'd been quite popular before due to the way that I had interacted with them, now they were on my side more than ever. Several of them promised revenge on Yalvac, Erdem and Faisal as soon as they were released from solitary confinement. It took a lot to persuade them that revenge was unnecessary for the three men would be severely punished under the regime rules. It was now in the Governor's hands to decide the extent of their punishment.

They reluctantly accepted my assurances that punishment would be meted out fairly in public for all to see but they still offered their services if required. It gave me a boost knowing that even though I was the 'enemy' they held me in such high esteem.

Just before the end of my shift Liam called me into his office to let me know that the three men had been interviewed and were due to be publicly punished in the Chapel on Tuesday 1st June at 7pm. He asked if I would like to participate in administering the punishment. Too damned right I would! Not surprised by my acceptance Liam promised that I would be in charge of the evening's entertainment. With that topic concluded he toyed with his pen for a couple of moments before giving me a searching look. Hesitating he asked me if I had any plans for the coming bank holiday weekend. Puzzled I shook my head for in truth I didn't apart from swimming and perhaps a run with Aaron and Jason if I felt up to it.

He caught me by surprise when he asked if I would like to go for a drink with him on Monday night, no pressure. He just thought it might take my mind off recent events. I didn't know what to say for at that precise moment in time a night out on the tiles was the last thing I fancied doing but neither did I want to offend him. He had shown me more care and attention than he needed to plus he was my boss, so saying no was going to be a tricky thing to do.

He smiled at me encouragingly and raised his eyebrows as he waited for my response. Throwing caution to the wind I decided to accept his invitation as I had no other plans and it would be more fun than sitting alone in an empty flat. His smile became a grin and he clapped me on the shoulder promising that he'd take good care of me and that he'd pick me up at 9pm on Monday evening. With the arrangements sorted out I left still feeling a little stunned by the turn of events. Dear diary, I'm still not sure what Liam's true intentions are for the invitation but as the saying goes time will tell.

FRIDAY 28TH MAY

I think everyone's on a mission to look after me! George and Mick both asked me if I would like to go for a drink with them after work, which I politely refused because they're nice guys but I don't really want to see them outside of work. Then at lunchtime James invited me to join him and Lucas at a Eurovision party that a friend is holding tomorrow. I went to say no but then at the last moment changed my mind, after all I do like the two lads and I haven't got anything else planned.

SUNDAY 30TH MAY

Dear diary, what a hangover I've got today. My head's pounding and my whole body feels poisoned by quantity of alcohol I consumed. Yes I know it's my fault, I'm an adult after all, nobody forced me and poured the drink down my throat. Well that's not strictly true, I did get held down but not for drinking purposes!

The party started innocent enough. Their friend's house is less than half a mile from where they live so it was just a short walk for the three of us. We each presented a bottle of wine as we stepped over the threshold to the party host (Sally) and in return received a kiss on the cheek and quick hug to welcome us. The party was already in full swing and the house full of talking and laughter, it was a pleasant contrast to my silent and empty flat. I took to Sally straight away, she looked about the same age as me but youthful in her sense of humour and how she interacted with the other guests. I got the feeling that she enjoyed a houseful and being surrounded by young people (excluding me of course). While Lucas chatted with Sally James led me into the lounge and introduced me to the crowd of guys and girls sitting around on anything that would serve as a seat including the floor.

At first I felt a little awkward what with me being the only one over thirty and I was so conscious of their stares at the bruises covering my face. Seeing my discomfort James explained that I worked with him at the prison and had been held hostage and beaten up by three inmates before being rescued. This must have changed the way in how they viewed me for their looks of suspicion changed to a mixture of admiration and pity in varying amounts. For what seemed like ages they asked questions about being a prison officer and what it had been like being held hostage. I answered as truthfully as possible leaving out the sexual and nudity aspects, that was strictly top secret and I wasn't going to break that golden rule with people I hadn't met before.

By then Sally had returned to the room carrying a tray laden with glasses full of wine, both red and white. That was the start of the alcoholic consumption. By the time the wall mounted TV was turned on for the beginning of the Eurovision Song Contest I had drunk two glasses of white wine and about to start the third. We each picked out of a hat the name of a country taking part in the contest, whoever picked the winning ticket would win a prize. It was only a small prize, if I remember correctly it was a £10 M&S voucher, but that was besides the point for it added a bit of excitement to what for me was a very long programme. I drew Spain while James had Denmark and Lucas Ireland.

I kept my fingers crossed about winning but I wasn't really into the competition for I was having too much fun laughing with and at the youngsters. As they (and me) became more and more drunk the conversations became more convoluted until they were almost nonsensical. Yet they understood what they were talking about, it's been a long time since I've had those sorts of conversations.

Germany won the contest with Turkey second and Denmark third which pleased Lucas although he didn't get a prize he did at least get a placing unlike James and me. The party wound up just after midnight. We helped Sally tidy up before staggering out the front door with an equally drunk Sally inviting me round anytime I fancied. I appeared to have made a new friend although James seemed to think that it wasn't only friendship she had on her mind. I shrugged off that suggestion, I had only just got used to enjoying man to man sex and wasn't sure if I wanted to go down the bisexual road. Anyway one party and a drunken invite does not constitute a relationship.

Back at their place the drinking carried on for those two were fired up and wanted to continue with the party. I should have gone home at that point, but I didn't. At stupid o'clock I finally passed out from too much alcohol, my last memory was of sitting in their arm chair with a glass in hand watching them dancing (well swaying really) to Lady Gaga's 'Bad Romance'.

I surfaced sometime later totally disorientated. I was no longer sitting in the arm chair instead I was lying horizontal with my head on a pillow. How did I get home? I wondered to myself. I just lay there with my head pounding vowing never to drink again and then I realised that I wasn't alone in my bed. I had shifted my weight and brushed against two other warm naked bodies. With an effort I prized my eyelids open to see the back of James's head only inches from my face and when I looked behind me I saw the smiling face of Lucas. He had woken up when I had stirred. He mouthed a 'morning' before snuggling closer to me and wrapping an around my waist. I returned his smile before looking around the room and discovered that I never had made it back to my home for this was their bedroom. I closed my eyes against the pain caused by the bright morning sun streaming in through a chink in the curtains and wondered what had happened in the missing hours.

I had a good idea because before long I felt Lucas's hard cock sliding along the crease between my cheeks and by the feel of it my crack was slippery. Unable to help myself I pushed back against him signalling my acceptance of his advances and then felt his cock head press against my anus and slip easily inside. What followed was a long lazy fuck for Lucas didn't appear to be in a hurry to climax. I loved how he held me close while nibbling on the back of my neck as his cock slid slowly in and out of me. Our movements woke James who still half asleep rolled over and sat up before pulling the duvet back exposing our naked bodies joined at the hips. He reached over and fondled my balls and semi-erect cock before giving me a lingering kiss on the lips. I made to return the kiss but he pulled away laughing and climbed out of bed with more energy than I thought possible.

He announced that he was off to prepare some breakfast while we two finished our shag. After Lucas had climaxed I stumbled into their bathroom and enjoyed a reviving hot shower along with a much needed sit on the toilet. Feeling fresher but still hung over I got dressed having found my clothes in a pile on the floor in the lounge. I waited while the two lads did the same. Later we enjoyed several cups of strong coffee and warm croissants while discussing the party last night at Sally's before moving onto our own party afterwards.

Like I said I have no recollection of what happened between being in the arm chair and waking up in their bed this morning. But between the two of them they filled in the missing gaps for me. They had continued dancing long after I'd passed out before deciding it was time for bed, they woke me up so that I could sleep in their spare room. Apparently I kept calling them my two boys and insisted that I wasn't sleeping in the spare room for we had always shared my bed when they were over. I blushed bright red because although I didn't remember saying that, in my own mind it was clear to whom I was referring. Of course neither James nor Lucas did and they assumed that it was just the drink talking (I let them keep that assumption) so they took it as an invitation for a threesome.

And that so I'm told is exactly what followed. Despite being very drunk I managed to fuck both of them and be fucked by them in turn. I was also double fucked towards the end which was a massive turn on for Lucas and a first for him. James knew my anal capabilities and he said he was tempted to go further but I passed out again after the double fuck neatly bringing the session to an end.

Oh my god was all I could say by the end of breakfast and apologised for my drunken behaviour. They both waved the apology away saying that we'd all had a good time, no one got hurt so why be sorry about it? I liked their logic. It wasn't until early afternoon that I felt able to make it home and so after much hugging and an invite for a repeat session echoing in my ears I caught the tube home again. I should have walked for the noise and bumpy ride did nothing to help my headache or nauseous stomach.

MONDAY 31ST MAY

Do you know something diary? That Liam is a nice guy, I'm surprised that I've never really noticed it until now. Okay that may have something to do with the fact up that I've only ever seen him in the working environment and as a boss. Tonight was different though. He text me to say that he was on his way and almost dead on nine o'clock he rung on my door bell. A little nervous I opened the door to find him standing there dressed quite casually in jeans and a collared shirt, both expensive by the look of them and matched by highly polished shoes. I felt a little inadequate dressed in my black combat trousers, white muscle vest and short sleeved shirt open to the waist.

I welcomed him in before telling him I'd better change my outfit for something more suitable. He laughed and told me not to be so daft, it wasn't a fashion show and besides I looked good as I was. I smiled and did a mock bow in acknowledgement of the compliment. Five minutes later I was sitting in his silver BMW with the top down feeling awestruck as he drove across town to our destination. I'd never been in such an expensive car and luxuriated in the feel of the leather seats, I did however have the sense to keep my thoughts to myself.

We made small talk as he concentrated on driving out of London. He wouldn't tell me where we were going only that he thought I would enjoy it and that tonight was his treat. I went to protest and say that the least I could do was buy the drinks but he gave me that look of his that said he had spoken and that was that.

Our destination proved to be an upmarket gastro pub on the edge of Richmond Park. As it was a warm evening we sat outside in the pub's garden and ate our meal there. The waitress gave me a funny look as she took our order, I guess the bruising on my face had caught her attention, but she never said anything and hurried away. I made light of it by joking that I should take up boxing as a career. Liam caught me off guard by saying that would be a bad idea for it would spoil my handsome face.

My fork laden with mashed potato froze mid way to my mouth as I glanced up in astonishment at the compliment before it continued its journey. As I swallowed the food I just raised my eyebrows because I couldn't think of anything witty to say in response. He gave me a quirky smile before continuing to eat his own food. Nothing more was said until we'd finished the main course and waited for the deserts to arrive, only then did Liam elaborate further.

He admitted that for a long time he'd been attracted to me but had done nothing about it for professional reasons, until now that is. It was only after the hostage incident and my beating that he realised how strong his feelings were for me. I didn't know what to say in response so I just let him talk while making encouraging noises in the right places. He'd made discreet enquiries to establish if I was single or not before making his move, finding that I was he'd plucked up the courage to ask me out. For the first time I really studied him. He was taller than me by about four inches, slim build with just a little bit of a paunch, in his fifties and quite attractive with his blonde hair nearly silver at the temples. His blue eyes twinkled with good humour but I had seen them turn glacial when angered. He was clean shaven and for me it was some consolation that his face showed the same signs of aging as mine did whenever I saw myself in the mirror.

He had caught me off guard for I had expected this dinner out to be a sort of compensation for last week or to talk about business. I had guessed that he liked me from the way we interacted at work and from the fact that he'd employed me in the first place but I hadn't suspected that he felt this way towards me. In between mouthfuls of Tiramisu he told me snippets about his life outside of work, like me he'd been married but differed in that he had two grown up children who he never saw these days. Not since his wife found out about his sexuality and returned to Australia taking them with her. Over the years he tried to maintain contact with them but she had made it difficult for him and once they were adults they too made it clear that they didn't want to see him.

There were tears in his eyes as he divulged this fact and his pain was clear to see. Without thinking I reached out and held his hand giving it a reassuring squeeze. He looked down at our hands before glancing up at me and apologising for being so emotional on our first date. Date? Yes I guess that is what it was, a date. He placed his spare hand over mine and thanked me for being such a nice guy and all that. I laughed before warning him that I'm only human and have my off moments too (thinking what a bitch I'd been to Jason in the swimming pool).

He only let go of my hand when the waitress brought the coffees over and he paid the extortionate bill. By now it was getting too dark to see properly and the midges were beginning to find us so we moved inside and spent another hour chatting by the bar. This time over safe subjects like sport and our shared enjoyment of fitness, although I suspected from his paunch that his 'enjoyment' was more for my benefit than reality. As we drove back into London the conversation became a little awkward when he asked me if I would like to stay the night and I had replied a little too quickly that I would prefer to take things slower and enjoy getting to know one another better before taking that next step. He went silent on me as he drove ever closer to my home. The truth is I don't really know how I feel about him at this stage, yes he's a nice guy and a good boss but do I fancy him? Mmm the jury's out at present. Pulling up outside my flat he looked directly into my eyes and asked me if I had enjoyed myself and would I be prepared to go on another date with him? I got the timing right this time when I answered yes to both questions, for that was the truth. Satisfied he gave me a goofy smile before driving off. I lay in bed for ages thinking about the implications that tonight might bring for me, in the end I gave up deciding to go with the flow and enjoy what comes my way.

TUESDAY 1ST JUNE

Back at work I played things cool giving only vague answers when questioned about my weekend. I didn't see either James or Liam until the evening when it was time for the three men to be punished in the chapel. As with previous sessions in there the inmates had been keen to get good seats, this time even more so because of who was involved and the reason for their punishment.

Liam along with his two brothers compered the evening's entertainment while Tyler, Flick and me carried out the actual punishment. I was determined that I was going to enjoy myself and exert my authority over them so that no one was in any doubt about who was in charge.

The first task was to bring the prisoners over from solitary confinement and this was done by Jarek, George and Sayeed. From what I was told afterwards Faisal and Erdem had come quietly enough but Yalvac still simmered with anger over his treatment and the lack of clothing. That was his problem and he was reminded of that fact several times during the evening. They were led onto the stage naked with hands tied behind their backs and dog collars around their necks. Apt in my mind for they'd acted like a pack of dogs, Tyler winked at me as if he'd read my mind. They were made to stand facing the audience while Liam read out the offences they'd committed that now demanded punishment. Give them their due they stood there defiant looking out over the sea of faces, but the only person they wouldn't look at was me.

After the opening speech we led them into the punishment room and straight over to the shower area. Watching Richard and James set up the douching equipment seemed to be a punishment in itself for them because it was then that they realised what was about to happen. Yalvac was the first to be cleaned out, having fastened him to the metal rings in the floor and walls to prevent his escape I took pleasure in greasing up his hole and pushing the douching tube up into his tight rectum. Boy did he bitch about it, he shouted out that he was being abused hoping that someone would come to his rescue and at the same time clenched his cheeks together. Both tactics were useless. No one was going to help him for they were too busy watching the big screen showing all the action being videoed by Max and his muscles soon tired allowing the smooth metal tube to slide past his protesting sphincter.

I held the tube in position with one hand and with the other massaged his stomach as the water flowed deeper into him. James stood next to me waiting with a bucket ready for my signal. Once Yalvac's stomach was sufficiently distended I pulled the metal tube out of his arse and told him to hold the water in until I told him otherwise. He groaned in protest but did as instructed. Quickly I placed the bucket on the floor between his legs just in time to catch the brown foul smelling effluent cascade out of him. As it slowed to a trickle I reinserted the metal tube and asked James to empty the bucket. Three times this process was repeated until I was satisfied that the water was running sufficiently clear and he could be released from his shackles.

Faisal was next to be cleaned out and Tyler had that pleasure which he did with relish. Whilst that was going on I told Yalvac to climb into the examination chair and used the leather restraining straps to tie him down and prevent his escape. He was pretty calm although he glowered at me when he thought I wasn't looking but this soon changed when he saw me wheel over a butt fucking machine and attached a life size dildo to the shaft. Calmly I greased up the dildo and then his exposed anus before positioning the head of the dildo so that it just touched his hole. He looked at me through his outspread thighs and pleaded with me to spare him this indignity but it was in vain for his fate had been sealed by his actions in that cell. I wasn't about to show him mercy when he hadn't shown me any.

With a smile I pushed the machine forward until the head of the dildo disappeared into his hole. Ignoring his yelp of pain I turned the machine on and set it to slow to start off with then stood back and watched the dildo slide forwards until it had virtually disappeared all the way into his arse before it slid back again leaving just the head inside. Satisfied that the machine was working correctly I turned my attention to Faisal who had just been released from the shower area. I led him over to the St Andrews Cross and made him stand in front of it facing towards it and then secured each of his limbs to the cross. From over his shoulder he watched me as I went to the metal cabinet and retrieved a set of weights which I then attached to his bollocks. He cried out from the pain as the weights pulled his balls down until they were swinging gently between his legs. I leant forward and whispered in his ear that he now knew how I had felt when he had grabbed and pulled my balls.

He hung his head in shame and sniffed a couple of times to suppress the tears welling up in his eyes. Tough mate I thought to myself, I've only just started on you. Without saying another word I returned to the cabinet picked up a wooden paddle and set about smacking Faisal's arse with it. Thwack, thwack, thwack the paddle sounded loudly as each smack landed leaving a red mark behind. It served two purposes for the paddling stung in itself but also as the pain built up Faisal started to wriggle in an attempt to avoid the paddle, in doing so it made the weights swing around bringing more pain to his balls. I loved it, so much so that I had sprung a boner and decided to fuck him there and then. But before I could do that I had to sort out Erdem who by now had been cleaned out and stood patiently to one side with a look of fear on his face.

I told Tyler to take him over to the massage couch, strap him in face down and to loosen him up with a rectal massage. Erdem broke out in a sweat as he looked at me and then at Tyler with his massive hands but he was helpless as Tyrone escorted him to the couch and quickly secured him. I watched long enough to see the first of Tyrone's fingers slide up Erdem's greased hole. Before I returned my attention to Faisal I asked Flick to change Yalvac's dildo for a bigger one, it was time to start his stretching for real. Again I supervised the changing of the life sized dildo for one that was about the size of Tyler's cock (huge in other words) and reinserted bringing another round of protest from Yalvac. I loved the way the machine continuously slid the dildo in and out of his hole without a pause or break in the rhythm. Despite his protests I noted that his cock was semi-erect so he must be enjoying the experience to some degree, not that it mattered if he didn't. His hole was going to be stretched whatever happened.

Now I could return my attention to Faisal and without further delay I greased up my cock and positioned myself behind him with my cock pressing against his clenched anus. Despite everything he was still trying to resist, I had other ideas and so without warning using a knee I sent his ball weights swinging bringing a cry of pain from him. It distracted him from what I was doing and as his anus relaxed I shoved my cock up him with one thrust until I could go no further. This brought another howl of pain from him but I ignored him as I set about giving him a fuck that he wouldn't forget in a while. Unfortunately it didn't take long for me to cum as I had been aroused for so long this evening. Never mind there was a long way to go yet and besides Tyler deserved a break from the massage he was giving Erdem.

So pulling out of Faisal with my cock still dripping jism I wandered over to Tyler and invited him to break Faisal in a little bit more. With a happy grin on his face he left me with Erdem and set about stuffing his massive cock up the unlucky guy's backside. Faisal did his best to avoid the impalement but with Tyler holding him firmly in place there was little he could do as the jet black shaft inch by inch disappeared into his rectum stretching him wide as he went.

Turning my attention to Erdem I carried on where Tyler had left off. Quickly I greased up my hands and assessed how far Tyler had got with the anal stretching. I was impressed, with my hands being smaller than his I was easily able to insert three fingers and set about introducing the fourth. Over the next hour the three inmates were stretched wider and wider until with a round of applause from the other guys in the punishment room and cheers from the audience in the chapel each took a fist up their backsides.

My fist was firmly buried in Erdem while Flick had his up Yalvac and wanked the lucky guy at the same time. The one who had it the hardest was Faisal for he had to accommodate the largest fist in the prison, Tyler's. I have to say he did look fucking horny spread out on the cross with the ball weights swinging gently and his back arched as his arse was stretched wide around Tyler's ebony wrist. I nearly shot another load there and then!

They had one final humiliation to undergo before their punishment was complete. Released from their restraints they were led out into the chapel's auditorium and with the sound of catcalls and whistles filling the air they stood in a row on the stage. Liam did his customary closing speech before announcing one last treat for the audience and that was if anyone needed a piss before returning to their cells they should form an orderly queue by the stage. I watched with interest to see what he had planned, I didn't have long to wait once about a quarter of the inmates had queued up as instructed. Liam then told the three men to kneel down facing the audience with mouths open and eyes closed. They looked horrified having guessed what was about to happen but seeing Liam's stern expression they did as they were told.

Personally I've never been into water sports but there was something arousing about watching three naked guys reluctantly swallowing stream after stream of golden piss from the patiently waiting inmates. What didn't go in their mouth sprayed all over their faces, hair and trickled down their bodies. Strangely once the other inmates realised what was happening they too needed to take a piss. In the end nearly every inmate had pissed in or over Erdem, Faisal or Yalvac. Their humiliation and punishment was now complete. I just hope for their sake they've learnt their lesson and will behave themselves from now on.

WEDNESDAY 2ND JUNE

Totally knackered today after yesterday's long shift, didn't get home until very late and then had an early shift which meant little sleep for me. Thankfully it was quiet work-wise, the inmates were in good spirits and the three punished ones kept their heads down recovering from their ordeal. Erdem and Faisal had had their clothing and possessions returned but Yalvac had permanently forfeited his much to his annoyance. But he was under no illusion that should he try to wear or use either his brother's or anyone else's clothing then he would be punished again. This was something he was keen to avoid.

Late into my shift I was called into Liam's office for a debriefing on last night's performance and feedback from the prison wings. With the business issues finished he hesitated for a moment before looking at me with a serious expression and told me again how much he had enjoyed our date together on Monday night. I agreed with him that I had too which brought a smile of relief to his face. Then he asked if I would like to go on another date this coming Friday. His smile got even bigger when I agreed without hesitation.

THURSDAY 3RD JUNE

Tonight was the first time that I had seen Aaron and Jason in ten days (not that I'm counting I hasten to add) but it feels like a life time. No, in fact, it feels more like a watershed moment has happened during the intervening time. A veil has been lifted from my eyes and I can see them as the young, slightly immature men they really are. Why was I prepared to risk everything for Jason? Admittedly he is handsome has a hot body and a big dick but doesn't know what he wants from life. While Aaron, well he's Aaron, easily led and lacks the confidence to be himself. Neither can think beyond their own immediate needs.

It was during our run that I came to the decision that this was going to be our last session together, to be honest their fitness levels were pretty much as good as they were going to get and no longer needed my mentorship. That was the reason I gave them as we walked home back to my flat. It was hard to ignore the hurt puppy dog looks Jason kept giving me but if I gave in to them I'd be back to square one again and I was not prepared to do that. As soon as they'd finished showering I ushered them out of my flat as quickly as possible before I gave into temptation.

Alone again I consoled myself to the fact that my life had moved on, Jason was in the past and my future lay elsewhere. I have my career to focus on and perhaps the beginnings of a new relationship?

FRIDAY 4TH JUNE

James caught up with me today at work. He wanted to let me know that he'd thrashed out a plan of action with Adrian regarding the fitness regime that he hoped would be introduced shortly, providing Liam and Max agreed to the proposals of course. I was genuinely pleased to hear this because having just closed off one avenue of exercise I was keen to establish another one before I start getting out of shape.

He also invited me to join him, Lucas and Sally for a take away at her place tonight. I had to apologise and say that I would love to join them but I had other plans, perhaps another night? Disappointed he said 'sure' and I'm certain he was about to ask what my plans were when I was rescued by the arrival of George wondering if I was going to do any work today? Cheeky beggar but at least it got me out of a potentially tricky situation. There was no way I was going to tell James I was dating the prison governor. Mmm does that sound a bit premature considering at that point I'd only been on one date? Anyway I digress. I must remember to arrange something with James so that he doesn't think I'm going cold on him and Lucas.

Anyway diary, I'm cutting my entry short because I just have time to shower before Liam is due to arrive and we head off into town. I will catch up with you tomorrow because I suspect that I won't get home until late tonight.

SUNDAY 6TH JUNE

My feelings about it being a late night were correct, the one thing I got wrong was that I would be home yesterday, in fact I only got back early this evening. I don't know quite what to say, other than I've had one hell of a great time with a man I like more and more the better I get to know him. I am talking about Liam of course.

Friday night he picked me up and we went to a lovely little restaurant in Covent Garden, again he paid, no expenses spared. We just seemed to click if you know what I mean, there was none of those uncomfortable silences when you don't know what to say next and through our conversation I realised we had so much in common. By the end of the meal we were flirting outrageously with one another and so it was no surprise to me when Liam called an early end to our night in town and suggested we go back to his place.

There was no way that he could be that tired for the night was still young so there could only be one thing on his mind. Being the perfect gentleman I agreed with his suggestion and let him make the first move when we got back to his house. I didn't have long to wait before he did but what surprised me was that our time in bed actually felt like we were making love not just having rampant sex like it had been with Jason. He was caring, attentive and took his time with everything he did. As a result our eventual climaxes were heightened enormously. That night we made love a couple of times before drifting off to sleep.

It must have been mid morning yesterday before we finally got up and pottered around doing nothing much in particular. I had expected to be dropped off home soon after breakfast but he made it quite clear that he was enjoying my company and that I could stay as long as I wanted. So I did. Last night we went to a nightclub aimed at, shall we say, the more senior end of the market somewhere near Vauxhall. I'd never heard of the place but apparently Liam had gone there several times when he was in the mood for company and I could see why. The club played a wide range of music and was packed with club goers, none of whom were under thirty years of age. It was relaxed but still very much a meat market all the same.

Without bragging about it I reckon I could have pulled at least three guys that night but I wasn't interested for I was having too much fun with Liam. We danced, drank and danced some more until we were tired, heading towards the lounge area we bumped into a couple of guys Liam knew. He introduced me to them as his boyfriend. That made me feel good inside and I held his hand in a public gesture of affection, he didn't let go of my hand for a long time.

I stayed at his place again, it really was very late by the time we got back and I just wanted to crash out. No love making tonight, just a simple cuddle was enough for me I was that tired. In the morning it was a different matter and it was early afternoon by the time that we had sated our appetites for each other. He made me feel special that's all I can say. It was with reluctance that I had to return home to my flat and prepare for the week ahead. As soon as I closed my front door I missed him and hated the emptiness of the place.

MONDAY 7TH JUNE

Back to work and back to reality, well sort of. On opening my locker to stash my day clothes I found a note taped to the inside of the door. There were just five words written on it in bold 'In my office at Noon" and just in case I didn't know who it was from there were two letters in the bottom right hand corner, L and H. I chuckled as I quickly folded up the note and hid it in my clothing before donning my beret and belt.

It was hard to concentrate on work and time dragged as all I could think about was Liam and what he wanted, apart from the obvious that is. Eventually it was time. I knocked on the Governor's door and patiently waited outside until I heard him call out 'enter'. Closing the door behind me I looked towards his desk and stopped in my tracks by what I saw before me. Laid out on his desk was an impromptu picnic complete with basket, thermos flask and blanket. He laughed at my surprised expression and quickly explained that he had really wanted to go for a picnic over the weekend but we'd not got round to it. So decided to throw caution to the wind and have one at work, well it wasn't very nice outside so why not have it inside?

With a rueful smile I agreed with him and helped unpack the basket. Despite the unusual backdrop our picnic was fun and in a screwy kind of way romantic. After we had eaten our fill Liam gestured for me to join him and so having removed my beret and belt I sat on his lap. Encircled by his arms I leant into his shoulders and savoured our moment of closeness.

Unfortunately we had left the door unlocked and so got caught out when the door opened without warning. In strode Adrian and Max holding papers in their hands engrossed in their conversation. We froze in surprise and waited for the inevitable as their conversation ground to a halt as did their feet once they realised the office was occupied. I shifted my weight as I prepared to climb off his lap but he held me firm and told me to stay where I was.

Max looked confused for a moment before he smirked raised his eyebrows and asked Liam to explain both the picnic and our compromising position. Now I did extract myself from his arms and retrieved my beret and belt, donning them quickly I gave him a kiss on the lips and thanked him for the lunch. He returned my kiss, winked and told me that he'd call me after work. I felt the three brothers' eyes following me as I left the room and closed the door behind me. As I strode back to my wing I couldn't help but wonder what Liam was saying to his brothers.

He never did call me. Instead he dropped by my flat with a bag full of fish and chips, yummy and they went down a treat. As we ate the food, in between mouthfuls, he explained that he'd told Adrian and Max the truth about us. They have never kept secrets from each other. Bracing myself I asked what their reactions had been, he shrugged his shoulders and said they were cool with it providing it didn't compromise either our work at the prison or cause jealousy problems with the staff. He'd agreed with them to keep our relationship under wraps for the time being. I nodded but made no comment as I ate another mouthful of fish. He stayed the night.

TUESDAY 8TH JUNE

The gossip on the wing is the love affair between Tyler and of all people, Faisal. I'm not sure it's on the same emotional level as mine and Liam's but it is certainly a whole lot more public. Ever since his punishment a week ago Faisal has followed Tyler around like a lost puppy. He no longer has anything to do with Yalvac or his gang. Instead he's chosen to move into Tyler's cell and live under his rules. By his own admission Faisal has become Tyler's bitch and is happy to drop his shorts or get down on his knees whenever and wherever Tyler tells him to regardless of who is present.

I have to admit they make a handsome and imposing couple. Both are large in stature with Tyler being jet black wearing just a red beret and black leather belt. Faisal is classically Arabic in appearance with his dusky skin and thick black beard. He now only ever wears a muscle vest and shorts to display his physique, Tyler won't let him wear anything else. Not that Faisal minds, he'll do anything now to please his man. As far as I'm concerned it means that there's one less inmate on the prison wing to cause trouble for us.

On a personal front, Liam's due round any moment so dear diary I'm going to love you and leave you. I'll spill the beans tomorrow.

I can't believe the pace at which our relationship is developing. It's only been ten days since we started dating but already Liam and I are talking about our future together and what our hopes are for it. I suppose it feels longer because we see each other every day at work and now we spend the nights together too. Liam has already mentioned the 'L' word but I'm still not sure I feel the same way just yet. Don't get me wrong I like him very much and the time we spend together but it seems a bit premature to be in love already. Perhaps I'm just kidding myself about needing time or I'm putting hurdles in the way so that I don't repeat the Jason mess again.

THURSDAY 10TH JUNE

Over dinner tonight Liam casually mentioned that he's going to be away from tomorrow until Sunday, he and Max will be visiting a failing prison in South Wales. I asked why and was told that the Ministry of Justice had been in contact with him for they were impressed by the successful turnaround of HMP Ollerton and were keen to explore the possibility of them running this particular prison. Curious I asked which prison would that be only to be told that at this stage it was secret in case the deal didn't come off, too commercially sensitive and all that. He was enthusiastic about the visit but was less happy that we would not be seeing each other until Monday.

Our lovemaking that had a greater sense of urgency tonight, as if he wanted to have as much of me as possible to see him over our period of separation. I did point out to him that it was for only three days and then we would be together again and yes, I would miss him as much as he missed me (which I have no doubt will be true). On reflection it is perhaps a good thing that he will be away for I have to go to Mike's 50th birthday party on Saturday and will no doubt spend much of Sunday with a hangover!

FRIDAY 11TH JUNE

Finally caught up with James and apologised for turning down his invitation last week. He acted a little distant towards me but after sweet talking him and confessing that I had arranged to go on a date that night he was soon back to his normal self again. He pestered me about who I had seen and was I still seeing him. Laughing I told him it was top secret I couldn't tell him who but yes I was still seeing him and things were going very well indeed. He wasn't happy about me keeping my man's identity a secret but did admit that I appeared a whole lot happier these days.

Casually I asked him if he and Lucas were free tonight, which he was and so I got to have that take away round their home after all. This time though there was no bedroom games for a start I didn't get drunk and it didn't seem right to shag around knowing how I felt about Liam. After all we were only apart because of his work commitments. Lucas seemed disappointed when he broached the subject only to have James close it by telling him that I was in love with a mystery man. For some reason I blushed, it made it all that more real when someone else said it. Not trusting myself to speak I simply nodded and grinned in response to Lucas's raised eyebrows.

I didn't stay late because I need an early night in preparation for tomorrow for it's going to be a long day.

SATURDAY 12TH JUNE

Today's entry won't be long because I've just got time to shower, have a bite to eat and get dressed up before heading over to the Sundown Nightclub where Mike's party is being held. You may remember this is where Aaron had his stag do and where he publicly swore revenge on his dad for the stage games they played. I wonder if he will remember his promise? I hope not because in the past Mike has not always been receptive to tricks played on him.

I'll catch up with you tomorrow, wish me luck and that I don't get too drunk.

SUNDAY 13TH JUNE

Oh my god, last night was a night that won't be forgotten in a hurry that's for sure! Yes I did get drunk but not so bad that I can't remember what happened. The party was again held on the top floor in the room with the large dance floor, own bar and stage. The only difference was that this time the wives and girlfriends had been invited so I was sure that any party games would be tamer. I was wrong.

Everything was going as it should be. Tom, Mike and me were having a relatively quiet drink and chat by the bar occasionally joined by their wives while the younger ones were dancing and larking around as expected. Until that is a female voice interrupted the music announcing that the games were about to begin. Games? Mike mouthed at me, I shrugged my shoulders for I knew nothing about this and tried to think where I'd heard that voice before. Then it dawned on me, the voice belonged to Zara the Russian hostess from the stag do. Tom and Mike must have recognised her voice too judging by their expressions.

We didn't have time to discuss the implications of this latest development for with a fanfare of music Zara and Ingrid dressed in black leather strode onto the stage and asked the audience if they'd like to play a game? The party goers had by now migrated to the front of the stage and being quite drunk reacted enthusiastically to the question. I was a little concerned by the fact that Aaron and his group of friends had responded the most vocally. This time the girls called out for three volunteers for a simple game of 'higher or lower'. It was of course a set up because everyone in the room including the women turned and looked at us. Aaron was going to get his revenge after all.

Mike looked at Tom and me before asking "How bad can it be? They wouldn't dare do the games they did at the stag do, not with the women present, surely?"

Again I shrugged my shoulders because I simply didn't have a clue and Tom just laughed nervously taking another swig of his drink.

All attention was on us by now and with a triumphant cry Zara announced that she had found her volunteers as she pointed directly at us. We had no choice but to join them, so with a round of applause we climbed up on the stage and stood next to Zara as Ingrid set up the easel and shuffled an oversized pack of playing cards. She asked us our names and then went on to explain the rules of the game. We had to guess whether the next card to be drawn by Ingrid would be higher or lower than the previous one. Simple? Yes we all nodded. She then went on to add that for every correct answer we would win a £5 voucher for the nightclub but if we got it wrong then we would lose an item of clothing. Mike scowled at his son who just grinned back and gave him a double thumbs up. I looked down at Chrissie and silently mouthed 'help me' but she just laughed and shook her head, she was enjoying this as much as the guys were.

We would take it in turns to guess the cards, Mike went first. The eight of clubs was drawn first, he guessed lower and Ingrid drew the next card which was the three of hearts. He wiped his brow in exaggerated relief and was told he'd won a £5 voucher. Tom went next and said higher, the Jack of hearts was drawn and he too won a voucher. I was confident with my guess so I said lower but was stunned when the Queen of Diamonds was drawn. 'Off! Off! Off!" came cries from the audience. With a sigh I removed the suit jacket that I'd been wearing and threw it into the audience before the game continued. I've never been very good with games of chance. So it wasn't a big surprise to me that by the time I was standing in just my boxer shorts, I had only won £15 of vouchers. Mike had only lost his jacket, shirt and tie. Tom done a little worse and had also lost his shoes and one sock.

The inevitable happened and I lost my final guess, I had no choice but to remove my shorts and throw them into the cheering audience. By the end of the game I had only won £20 while Tom did better with £40 and Mike best of all with £55. If we had thought being made to stand naked on stage before everyone we knew was the end of the matter we were mistaken. As we made to walk off stage with our tackle covered by our hands we were called back for the final game of the evening.

It was going to be a game of dare with the winner of the last game going first. If you did the dare you got your clothes back but if you refused or failed then you had to pay a forfeit. Mike went first. He was blindfolded and then following Aaron's verbal instructions had to find his way to the bar. It was fairly straight forward for him once he had climbed safely off the stage, the only things he had to be guided around were the tables and chairs. A few minutes later to his relief, the blindfold was removed and handed back his clothes.

Tom went next, having been blindfolded he was verbally guided by Simon to the entrance door and back again before being allowed to remove the blindfold and get dressed again. With the two men giving me encouraging waves Zara told me that my dare was to walk blindfolded all the way down to the main entrance of the nightclub and back again guided by Jason. Despite having had too much to drink there was no way I was going to do that dare, being naked in public wasn't the problem, after all I'm virtually naked every day at work. Rather it was the idea of placing all my trust into Jason when so vulnerable filled me with horror. Hesitating only for a moment I announced that I was refusing the dare and would do the forfeit instead.

Zara just looked at me and asked if I was sure, I smiled and confirmed that I was. Without further ado I was blindfolded and made to kneel down. I heard footsteps approaching and then the rustling of material with the chink of metal hitting the floor. To my ears it sounded like somebody or rather several bodies undressing but how did that involve me and how would it be a forfeit? I didn't have a clue but soon found out when in a loud voice Zara announced that my forfeit was to correctly identify from memory the four guys who had been on stage during the stag do. That part was easy I thought to myself for I could remember quite clearly who the four guys had been Aaron, Jason, Simon and Lee. Without thinking I asked how was I supposed to identify them when I was blindfolded?

In hindsight I guess this was a mistake on my part because with a wicked chuckle she said that I was to identify them using my hands but the only part of their body I could touch was their genitals. There was a gasp from the audience and a chuckle from the four guys standing nearby. If I got the name of the guy wrong my forfeit would be to give that person a blow job, so no pressure then! Again there was a gasp from the audience but me I merely smiled to myself in anticipation for the treat I was about to receive.

Somehow and I really don't understand why but I managed to guess the wrong guy each and every time, blame it on the drink I say. By the end of my forfeit I'd given each guy a blow job and swallowed four loads of jism down my throat. Oh my god I was as happy as a pig in shit and so turned on knowing the real identity of each guy but having the perfect excuse to get my lips around their cocks and sucking every one of them dry. As I got into the swing of the blow jobs I could hear that there had been a mixed reaction from the audience at first but then they got more enthusiastic as time went on.

As my blindfold was removed I looked up and saw the four young men looking very pleased with themselves as they pulled their trousers back up again. Finally I was given back my own clothes and allowed to get dressed again. Back at the bar having rejoined my two best mates and in between mouthfuls of my drink I asked them what they had thought of my performance. Tom was so close to the mark when he said with a dead pan expression that he would never have guessed that that had been the first time I'd given another guy a blow job. I just raised my eyebrows and kept my mouth shut for fear of confirming his suspicions. As for Mike he looked less than happy and admitted that he wasn't comfortable with the idea of me giving his son a blow job. I hate to think what his reaction would be if he knew half of what I had got up to with his son and Jason!

I guess I stayed perhaps another half an hour before slipping away and catching a taxi home. I was getting drunker and my tongue was loosening with each mouthful. I realised that this could be a problem because Jason had begun hanging around us and trying to get my attention none too discretely. I waited for him to go for a pee break before bidding good night to my two best mates.

When I finally woke up it was early afternoon. At some point I remembered to check my mobile phone and found that I'd had several text messages from Liam and one from Jason. I deleted Jason's without opening it and read Liam's which were of far more interest to me. He'd sent one to say they were leaving the hotel where they'd been staying, another when they'd made a convenience stop and a final one to say that he was now home and missing me. That made me smile because in truth I was missing him too so I text back admitting to it and that I was looking forward to seeing him at work tomorrow.

MONDAY 14TH JUNE

There's only one thing I can think about writing today diary for it's blown me away and if it happens will be life changing to say the least.

On arrival at work this morning I found another note from Liam in my locker asking me to see him at lunchtime. I wondered if it had anything to do with his recent trip or if it was just to see me after our long separation. It turned out to be a bit of both.

While I ate my packed lunch he briefly outlined his visit to HMP Wenvyre, as soon as he mentioned the name it rang a bell for it had been in the national press recently over management issues and poor inmate facilities. They'd toured the prison and then been in a prolonged meeting with the prison governor and the HM Prison Service representative. The outcome of which was very positive as far as Liam was concerned. It looks very much like he and his brothers will shortly be adding another prison to their portfolio. By the time that he'd finished telling me about their plans including all the facts and figures my head was spinning from all the information.

I had just one question, why was he telling me all this and what was it to do with me? With a triumphant smile as if he'd been waiting for me to ask this question he announced that he would be in charge of the new venture. My face dropped for I knew it would mean that he would no longer be working here at HMP Ollerton and I couldn't see him commuting to Wales every day. It would kill our relationship just when it was beginning to grow.

Seeing my change in attitude Liam asked me what was wrong so I told him about my fears for our future. He held up his hands and apologised explaining that his intention was for me to move with him to Wales and for me to become his second in command, like Max is here. My mouth fell open in surprise and all I could say was 'oh' for I had not been expecting that at all.

He's given me to the end of this week to get my head round the idea and to decide if I want to accept his offer. Even now after twelve hours my head is still whirling with the implications of his offer. Do I accept his offer? If I do it means leaving behind everything and everyone I've known for years. Admittedly I'm falling in love with him but it's daunting to think about starting from scratch with a man I have only really known for a very short time. Okay, it's a huge leap up the career ladder and I can't see me getting a similar offer elsewhere. But am I ready for such a big change? But what happens if I reject his offer? He will go anyway and our relationship will end. We'll have a new governor, Max, will it be the same here? No. How long will I be happy doing the same job and how long will it take me, if ever, for me to get to the same position Liam is offering me?

So much to think about and so little time......

TUESDAY 15TH JUNE

Still mulling on my options and no closer to a decision, I feel like a pendulum swinging from one opinion to another depending on whom I with at the time. When I'm with Liam I can't bear the idea of being left behind, especially when he's holding me close and twinkling his blue eyes at me. But when I'm alone at home or at work I'm not so sure about leaving the familiar behind. Is that sufficient reason to let him go?

I've also been getting texts from Jason. I'd have thought he'd have got the message by now because I've simply deleted them with opening them. I don't know why he's pestering me but I wasn't prepared to talk to him to find out, it's simpler to ignore them while I have more important issues to worry about.

WEDNESDAY 16TH JUNE

Why is it diary that just when I have made my mind up fate goes and throws a spanner in the works? Last night I stayed over at Liam's and talked through my concerns with him until the early hours, I was exhausted but at least I knew what my decision would be. What I want right now is an early night in bed alone so that I can get some sleep. After a long shift on top of little sleep I felt like a bear with a sore head growling at everyone and everything. Liam made the wise decision to give me some space at least for one night. All I have planned right now is to have something to eat, shower and bed.

But my plans were thrown off course right from the start. As I trudged up the communal stairs to my flat I got the feeling that I wasn't alone in the stairwell. Spooked I glanced behind me to see if I was being followed but I was looking in the wrong direction.

"Hello Sam"

I spun round at the sound of the masculine voice. There sat Jason cross legged leaning against my front door.

"What the hell are you doing here?" I asked frowning to mask my surprise.

"You won't answer my texts. So how else am I going to get to talk to you?"

"What's there to say that hasn't already been said?"

"Can I come in?" he asked as I stepped round him and unlocked the door.

"You've got five minutes, I'm knackered and need my bed" I growled.

"Okay, I just want to talk."

I headed for the lounge without offering him a drink, I felt a little mean but I didn't want to make him feel so welcome that he stayed longer than absolutely necessary. Despite my tiredness my cock had begun to twitch just looking at his handsome face.

"So what have you got to say to me?"

"I've missed you. At Dad's birthday party I realised just how much."

"What you mean is, me giving you a blow job reminded you of what you'd been missing, right?" I asked with irritation colouring my tone.

"Don't be like that but yeah I guess so" he admitted with a shrug of his shoulders.

"Well you've had your chance, I was there for the taking but you made your choice clear and now you've got to stick with it."

"Can't we be like before?"

Oh my god he's using those puppy dog eyes on me I groaned inside, just for a second my resolve wavered before I got it back under control and in a firm tone replied.

"No. A lot has happened since we split up. I've moved on and have started a new relationship. Anyway I won't be around much longer."

"Oh I see" he said crestfallen "but I love you Sam. I don't want you to leave."

"You're not listening to me Jason" I sighed in exasperation "I'm in love with another man, it's too late. You should have told me that you loved me weeks ago then things might have been different."

"But I didn't realise that I loved you until our argument and you stopped wanting to see me. Can we remain friends at least? Where are you going?"

"I'll be moving to Wales to work at another prison, I've had a promotion you see. I guess we can remain friends as long as you don't pull this stunt again."

"I won't if you promise not to ignore my texts in future. Can I have a hug please?"

That was a mistake because as I held him in my arms the suppressed emotions and desires reignited, before I could stop myself I kissed him. He kissed me back and started to undress me. I did nothing to resist.

Later as we lay in bed exhausted from our union I wrestled with my emotions. Why had I allowed myself to be seduced by this young man again when I had made it clear that I had moved on? Did I still have feelings for Jason? The answer I guess is yes. Do I really love Liam? Again the answer to that question is yes. I'm still that pendulum, this time swinging between two men. Dear diary, I've got to make up my mind once and for all about what I really want in life.

EPILOGUE

SATURDAY 14TH APRIL

The big day has at last arrived, one that I have been both dreading and anticipating in equal measure. I wait nervously dressed in my best suit and readjust my tie for the umpteenth time. The man I love more than life itself stands beside me smiling indulgently and tells me to relax for it will be okay and over soon. I smile anxiously and squeeze his hand in response, I can't believe I'm behaving like this but then I never have liked churches.

I look around taking in the sea of happy faces and the ancient church interior. I wonder how many guys through the centuries have felt as nervous as me, standing on this very spot before a vicar. He too tells me to relax, easy for him to say he's done this ceremony countless times before but this is the first time for me.

Then I see them, Jason and Kirsty walking down the aisle with their new born daughter in Jason's arms. Spotting Liam and me they smile and Kirsty does a little wave. I return it aware that everyone is watching us. The four of us stand around the font while the vicar does his speech before saying "I baptise you Samantha Jane....."

Outside in the bright spring sunshine there are endless photos taken of the baby in various combinations of friends and family. It was during this time that Kirsty approached me as I stood to one side seeking a little peace from the chaotic milling around.

"Sam! There you are" she said stating the obvious.

"Here I am indeed" I replied smiling warmly "it's been a lovely Christening."

"Yes it has" she agreed "that's what I wanted to thank you about."

"Oh? I haven't done anything to warrant a thank you."

"But you have. Thank you for agreeing to be Samantha's god parent and thank you for not taking Jason from me."